Alaskan Dawn

Edie Claire

first of the Pacific Horizons novels

Dedication

For my husband of twenty-six years.
Here's to at least twenty-six more.

Acknowledgments

Many thanks go to author Lauren Royal, for her insights into California living; to Teresa Stewart, for her insights into the legal mind; and to Alaska Saltwater Tours, for the best boat trip ever.

ALASKA

Chapter 1

"I've decided to go to Alaska," Haley announced.

There, she had said it. Her tone had been just right, too. Gentle, but firm enough to show that the topic wasn't open to debate.

Her sister's eyes widened with alarm. "Now? But you *can't!*"

Micah's screeching plea made Haley wince, even though it was exactly what she expected. As were the brimming tears and trembling lower lip that followed. Micah wasn't ordinarily this irrational. She had always had a tendency for emotional outbursts, true, but Haley hadn't seen her sister this unraveled since they were teenagers. The strain of the last month had taken its toll on her.

On both of them.

"I can, and I am," Haley answered, gentling her voice further. If she didn't handle this right, Micah would go into a full-blown meltdown, which was the last thing either of them needed. "There is absolutely no medical reason I can't get on a plane and spend a few days somewhere else besides here. My staying in Newport Beach won't make the results come back any faster."

"No, but—" Micah bit her lip, no doubt struggling to come up with a rebuttal that would hold some sway with her logical-minded sister. Haley knew exactly what Micah was thinking. She always knew. They were twins, after all, even if they couldn't be more different.

"But what?" Haley prompted. "Don't you think one of us should at least take a look at Uncle Randy's property before we decide to sell it?"

"I don't see why," Micah retorted. "Of course we're going to sell it. What would we do with some shack in the middle of Alaska?"

"Who said it was a shack?" Haley replied. "We don't know what shape it's in. That's my point. Maybe the place would make a nice summer getaway."

Micah frowned. "You know perfectly well that neither one of us has ever had the slightest desire to even *go* to Alaska." Her lower lip started to tremble again. "You're just looking for an excuse to leave town!"

Haley held her sister's gaze. Micah's clear blue eyes, wavy blond hair, and curvy figure had always rated her "the pretty one." Haley, in contrast, was tall and lean, with straight, chocolate-brown hair and penetrating green eyes that, while not unattractive, had earned her the dubious compliment of being dubbed "the responsible one."

"Maybe you're right," Haley replied calmly. "Everything you just said is true. I *do* want to get away for a few days. Is that so wrong?"

Micah's eyes flashed with panic. She had no real reason to demand that her sister stay put, and they both knew it. They also both knew that, if reasoning failed, emotional manipulation would be next.

Micah's eyes welled up with tears again. "This is because of last night, isn't it? I told you I was sorry! I know I shouldn't have pulled you and Mom into it, but I was just so upset with Tim. When he—"

"It's not just about last night," Haley broke in. Witnessing the horrendous argument between Micah and her husband the previous evening had been painful enough at the time. She had no stomach for hearing it rehashed this afternoon, which her sister would certainly do if given the slightest encouragement. "It's the entire situation."

"I know that all this testing has been difficult for you, Haley," Micah pleaded. "It's certainly been more than you signed on for, and I appreciate everything you've done more than I can say. But running away now won't help anything, and I *need* you here while we wait. I'll go crazy worrying otherwise!"

I need you, Haley. Please? Pretty please?

No other expression encapsulated more perfectly the current of Haley's life — the insidious undertow that, more and more now, she was certain would eventually drown her. They were twenty-nine years old. When they were little, Micah was shy and had needed her. When they were fourteen and their father died of a heart attack and their mother fell apart, it was Haley who had been Micah's rock. When they were in college and Micah struggled with anxiety, Haley had been by her side. Only when Micah had gotten married did Haley allow herself to believe that her sister would finally be all right without her. Then came the miscarriages. More anxiety. The depression. Now, they were *here*.

Was she running away?

Hell yes, she was.

Haley leaned forward and laid her hands on her sister's arms. She would not be manipulated. Not this time. "Micah," she said heavily.

"You will worry no matter where I am. But I need to get away. I need a change of scenery. Some fresh air. Something to take my mind off those test results and reduce my general stress level. How many times have the doctors told us that stress is our worst enemy?"

Micah clenched her jaws a moment. "I know you're right," she admitted. "But I still don't want you to go. Surely we can figure out something to take the stress off without your having to go so far away!"

"I need this," Haley dared. "I need it for me."

"But you can't leave without taking *my* baby!" Micah fired back.

A flash of heat rose in Haley's cheeks. She would not lose her temper with her sister. They had played that scene out many times before, and it never ended well, for either of them. She had agreed to serve as her sister's surrogate, and she would see that commitment through to the end, come what may. "That is true," she replied, working hard to keep her voice level, even as she wanted to scream. "But I promise to take good care of both of us. You know I will."

Micah looked away. A tear coursed down one cheek. "How long?" she squeaked.

Haley released a breath with relief. "A week. I'm leaving the day after tomorrow."

Micah whirled back around with another panicked look. "They have OBs in Alaska, don't they?"

"Of course they do. I've already looked one up, so I'll have a number just in case. But I won't need it. I'm not due for another visit for nearly three weeks." Haley searched her sister's eyes. She was certain that the real, relatively mature Micah was still in there somewhere. But all Haley's efforts to help her sister regroup and refocus had failed, and she was losing her own sanity in the process. "I'll be fine. The baby will be fine. We'll be back before you know it. Okay?"

Micah swiped the tear off her cheek and nodded. "I know you wouldn't do anything to put the baby at risk, Haley. I'm sorry if I snapped at you. If you really think a change of scenery would do you good, then go. But just for a few days. And stay in touch, okay?"

Haley started to nod, but stopped herself. She and Micah didn't lie to each other. Her survival plan might not be fully formed yet, but she knew it would not include answering texts every three and a half seconds. How she would block out the constant barrage of angst streaming from the cell phones of both her sister and her mother, she wasn't sure. But that shoe would have to drop later. Preferably after she was on a plane.

Haley ignored her sister's question and smiled. Right now, she had Micah's blessing for the journey. It was more than she had hoped for. Certainly more than she'd be likely to get from their mother.

"Have you told mom?" Micah asked, seemingly reading her twin's mind.

Haley shook her head. "Not yet."

"She won't like it," Micah predicted. "She'll tell you pregnant women shouldn't fly or something."

Haley allowed herself a sigh. "I'm sure she will. But I'm going anyway. I'll call her tonight. I want to know what she remembers about Uncle Randy."

"All I remember is his having a beard and talking on and on about nothing interesting," Micah said glumly. Neither of the girls had known their uncle, aside from one brief visit he had made to California when they were eight. Haley's father had only rarely mentioned his brother's existence, and Haley remembered no more about him than Micah did. But she would be forever grateful that the man had remembered his nieces in his will. With luck, the rural property he had left them would have no cellular service.

"Where will you stay?" Micah asked anxiously.

Not for the first time, Haley cursed the mind-reading thing. "I don't know yet. If I can get the keys to Uncle Randy's place and it's decent enough, I may stay there. If not, I'm sure I can find a hotel. The property's only a couple hours from Anchorage, and the nearest town looks like it's a tourist destination, so I shouldn't have any problem. It's not like I'm going to the wilderness, Micah."

Although...

Haley stopped herself. The fact that the word "wilderness" held such unexpected appeal was telling. She was hardly the outdoorsy type. The closest she'd ever gotten to camping was summer Girl Scout retreats at Camp Scherman where she and Micah had slept on bunks in lighted cabins and "roughed it" by walking outside to the restrooms. Living in a beach town, her mother's idea of vacation had always been a week in Las Vegas or Reno. Haley herself had not ventured from the West Coast in years, with the exception of brief trips to Chicago and Houston on business for the firm, which didn't count. Her own dreams of a getaway extended no further than visions of fluffy white bedding in a five-star hotel where she checked in with an alias and drowned her cell phone in the toilet.

This sudden, fierce craving for the solace of a spider-filled cabin in the middle of nowhere had to mean something. God knew she hated spiders. Most likely, it was a warning sign.

She planned to heed it.

Impulsively, she reached forward and gave her sister a hug. "Thanks for understanding." She stepped back and headed to the door of her sister's apartment to let herself out.

"Haley?" Micah called after her. "Just..." Her voice cracked, then broke off. Her eyes filled with tears again.

Just come back okay, please? Both of you.

Haley smiled back at her sister through eyes that were equally moist. "I promise," she replied.

Chapter 2

Will there be a drug store nearby? Haley wondered to herself as she packed a sample of virtually every over-the-counter medication she was allowed to take into her travel bag. Insect repellent, itch cream, antacids, that stuff for cold sores... She didn't use any of it often, but the thought of being without it disturbed her. Aside from her cursory research online into car rentals, road directions, and decent hotels, she knew nothing whatsoever about Alaska. Either the state in general or the portion of it to which she was headed.

She had spoken with Ed Miller, her uncle's business partner and the executor of his estate, only briefly on the phone. Randy and Ed had co-owned a boat dealership in Anchorage for the last twenty years. Randy had lived in a small apartment over the store, and he had never married or had any children. Two years before his death, he had purchased an "investment" property over a hundred miles away near the smaller port town of Seward. He spent his free days there during the summer, living in a house that sat deep within the parcel's fifteen acres of woods, while renting out the two small cabins closer to the road. A month ago he had died unexpectedly of a heart attack, just like his brother and father before him. His will had left his share of the business to his partner and the remainder of his assets to his nieces.

Such was the sum total of Haley's knowledge. Her specific questions about the house and cabins had gone unanswered, as Ed admitted that he had never seen them. Had all this happened at any other time in her life, Haley almost certainly would have authorized the property's sale sight unseen. She would have just sat back and waited for the check.

She threw a can of sunscreen into her suitcase. Did people get sunburned so far north? It was July, so they must. And weren't the days really long during the summer?

Her cell phone rang, and she looked at it with a sinking feeling. She had meant to call her mother last night but hadn't gotten around to it, and she'd had no time today. She had been insanely busy at the office trying to tie things up, a feat at which she had not even come close to succeeding. For associates at Merriweather, Falstaff, and Tynes, vacation was a theoretical concept. Ambitious young lawyers were expected to pretend they didn't want time off, much less need it. Announcing that she would be taking a full week off on forty-eight hours' notice was tantamount to resigning.

She had been surprised to realize she didn't give a damn.

Her phone rang for the third time, and she continued to frown as she picked it up. If Micah had reached their mother first...

"Hey, Mom. What's up?"

"Shouldn't I be asking you that?" a terse voice replied.

Micah had definitely reached their mother first.

"I'm sorry, Mom," Haley apologized preemptively. "I've been meaning to call all day, it's just been crazy. I guess Micah told you?"

"That you're going off on some spur of the moment trip halfway around the world? Yes, she told me. Do you really think that's a good idea, in your condition?"

"I think it's one of the best ideas I've ever had," Haley replied, steeling herself for another battle. Micah's irrationality might be a temporary aberration, but for Michelle Olson, the condition was permanent. As long as the girls could remember, their mother had unpredictably alternated between overinvolved hovering and abject neglect, depending on her mood. As children, they would have appreciated more of the former. But the surrogacy situation had elevated Michelle's smothering to a whole new level, and Haley's patience with her mother's drama was running short. "My flight leaves tomorrow morning, and frankly, Mom, I can't wait."

"Oh. Well. If you're sure."

Haley tried to let the quavering, fretful tone of her mother's voice wash over her without effect. The actual words Michelle used were never important. The woman communicated entirely via tone.

"I am sure," Haley responded. "I really need to get away, Mom. There's no medical reason I shouldn't, and Micah's okay with it."

"Is that what she told you?"

Haley closed her eyes and took a breath. It was an old, old game among the three of them. Michelle had never been an authoritarian parent, leaving any unpleasantness of discipline to her husband. After Mike died, she had suspended all pretense of parenting and strived only to be the girls' best friend. The result was a form of guidance in which she never actually disapproved of anything the girls did, but instead would try to steer their actions through not-so-subtle injections of guilt.

Michelle would never tell Haley, for instance, that staying in

Newport Beach until after the baby was born was the right thing to do. Instead, she would make the case that Micah didn't want her sister to leave. And historically Micah would then do the same, insisting that although she herself was fine with whatever sin Haley was contemplating, their mother would be horribly upset.

Haley couldn't remember a time when she hadn't been aware of exactly how that game was played. More difficult to explain was why it almost always worked.

"I don't know what Micah told you, Mom," Haley said firmly, tossing an extra blister pack of Gax-X in with her meds. "But she gave me her blessing. I'm sure she'd rather I not leave. But it really isn't up to her." She zipped up the bag, tossed it in her suitcase, and began to count socks. According to her weather app, daytime highs in July should be in the upper sixties in Seward, but the nights could be colder. She wasn't used to colder. Nor was she used to rain.

Both sounded heavenly.

"You're not still sore from the amnio?" Michelle persisted, artfully posing her objections in question form. "The doctors don't think that traveling so soon afterwards will increase your chances of a miscarriage?"

Haley decided that eight pairs of no-show socks would be enough. Then she threw in a few pairs of fuzzy long socks as well. She might be out at night, and her feet always got cold on airplanes. "No, and no," she answered.

"What about motion sickness on the plane?"

Haley cracked a grin. Her mother was really reaching now. "I've never gotten airsick in my life, and if I didn't have trouble with nausea in the first trimester, why would I have it now?" She began to sort her underwear.

Michelle made a low grumbling noise. Then she tried another angle. "Is the firm okay with your taking so much time off right now? I mean, what with your maternity leave coming up so soon?"

"Well, they haven't fired me yet," Haley replied with intentional flippancy. With luck, her mother would think she was joking.

There was a long pause on the line's other end. When Michelle spoke again, her voice was awash with misery. "So when do you leave? And how can we reach you?"

Haley felt her heart begin to lighten. Her mother had accepted defeat, and relatively quickly. "I leave tomorrow," she replied. "And I'll let you know."

She tossed her entire supply of newly purchased preggo undergarments into her suitcase and turned to her closet. She had no cold-weather clothes, aside from the three business suits she'd bought for winter trips to Chicago and a few ancient ski garments. She threw in her one and only pair of long underwear and hoped the waistband would stretch. She had no prayer of getting into her high-school ski pants, which had always been tight. The parka was probably overkill, but she threw it in anyway.

She answered a few more of her mother's questions mechanically, packing clothes into her suitcase as she talked. But one question stopped her.

"I just don't know what we're going to do about Tim," Michelle lamented. "Do you have any ideas?"

Visions of last night's insanity rushed back into Haley's head. "Mom, there is nothing we can do. There is nothing we should do. Tim is a good guy. They'll work it out themselves."

"How can you be so sure?" Michelle asked. "I have to wonder how well any of us really know him. After what he said about... Well, you know. How can Micah ever forgive something like that?"

Haley rubbed her face in her hands. The inappropriateness of the situation wasn't entirely her mother's fault. When it came to personal matters, Micah had always been overeager to share. It was Micah, after all, who demanded that both Haley and their mother gather in the couple's apartment while they awaited the early results from the amniocentesis. The tension between Micah and Tim had been unbearable, both before and after the results came in. The drama that unfolded was so bitter that, despite what she'd just told her mother, Haley had indeed begun to question whether the couple's marriage could survive the strain.

"He's hard on her, you know," Michelle commented.

"She's hard on him, Mom," Haley countered, regretting the words even as she said them. She could not allow herself to be sucked any further into her sister's woes. The mere thought of it brought up images of drowning in quicksand.

"Haley!" her mother chastised. "You're not seriously taking his side? How could you?"

"Of course I'm not taking his side," Haley said quickly, knowing every word she said would be transmitted back to Micah within the hour. "I'm not taking sides, period. I'm just saying that I think we should stay out of it. Okay?"

"I'm only trying to be supportive of your sister," Michelle responded with a sulk. "Is that so wrong?"

Haley shut her suitcase. She picked up the phone. "I know you love Micah, Mom. So do I. But I have to go, now. I'll let you know when I get to Anchorage, all right?"

There was a pause. "So, how are you getting to the airport?"

"Tim offered to drop me off."

"He's in favor of your taking this trip?"

"He doesn't seem to object, no."

Michelle harrumphed. "Well, he wouldn't, would he?"

Haley stifled another urge to scream. "I really have to go now, Mom. Love you. Bye!"

She waited long enough to hear an answering farewell, then shut off her phone altogether.

Just one more day, she told herself, fighting back the dark feelings that had been clawing at the edges of her psyche for weeks now. She had done it. She was going to escape.

She was going to feel better soon.

She had to.

"You want me to help you with that?" Tim asked uncertainly as Haley reached into his trunk to pull out her bag. She stopped, then straightened and looked at him. Her brother-in-law was an inch shorter than she was and weighed about the same. Ordinarily, she would not think twice about hefting her own suitcase around, even if it did weigh close to fifty pounds. But she wasn't supposed to be doing that sort of thing anymore, was she? Not when she was four months' pregnant.

"Sure," she replied awkwardly.

Tim smiled at her and pulled out the suitcase. Then he dragged it up over the curb and extended its handle toward her. The sound of a jet taking off blasted over their heads.

"Thanks for the ride," Haley said once the noise quieted. "And thanks for... well, you know."

Tim's lips twisted with chagrin. When Micah had freaked out about Haley's leaving once again just this morning, Tim had immediately come to his sister-in-law's defense — a selfless act he would undoubtedly pay for later. "You deserve some time away, Haley," he said softly. "Micah knows that. She just can't help the worrying. In her finer moments, she really does want you to relax and have a good time.

We both do."

"Thank you," Haley said sincerely. She liked her brother-in-law. He was sweet, unassuming, and on the timid side, which set him in sharp contrast to the sea of aggressive lawyers and business moguls she generally associated with. More important, he was hopelessly, desperately in love with her sister.

God help him.

"We owe you more than we could ever say," Tim continued earnestly. "I know Micah expects you back in a week, but as far as I'm concerned, you should stay as long as you need to. I know that—" he broke off with a guilty look. "I know that she hasn't been making this easy for you. And lately, neither have I." His face bore a tortured expression. "I'm sorry, Haley. About everything."

Haley felt a twist in her gut. He and her sister should be in a good place right now. They were expecting a baby. Finally. After so many years of trying. When Haley had conceived, they'd been over the moon. Then came the prenatal testing.

"It's not your fault," Haley assured, meaning it. She might disagree with some of her brother-in-law's opinions, but she didn't fault him for being human. The results of the chorionic villus sampling they had received the month before had been devastating. The unexpected news had scared the hell out of Tim, and he had reacted accordingly. If her sister had only given him the time and space he needed to work through his emotions, things might have turned out differently. But there was no explaining that to Micah. Micah was inconsolable.

"Thanks for saying that," he replied uncomfortably. He looked at his watch. "Is there anything else I can do for you?"

"No," Haley answered. "I'm good."

"If you think of anything later, call me," he insisted. "I mean it, Haley. Anything you need."

He opened the door of his car and began to get in, but turned to say one more thing. The sound of another jet taking off drowned out his words, but she could read his lips. And his eyes. *Enjoy yourself.*

She smiled back. "I intend to."

Chapter 3

The view out the plane window took Haley's breath away. She had flown over the dry, endlessly brown peaks and valleys of the West many times, and some of them had been capped with snow. But never had she seen mountains like these. Glistening white peaks reached high into the clouds, snow-covered from tip to foot, with ribbons of white flowing from their bases and curling down into the icy sea. No signs of human habitation, past or present, marred the forbidding landscape. Every aspect of the mountains' cold white beauty declared a simple message: This is no place for humans.

Move along, and let us be.

Haley smiled. She was only too glad to heed that warning. She felt privileged even to see such splendor. She had no desire to conquer it.

She continued to gaze out the window as the plane began its descent toward Anchorage. Misty clouds rose up to shroud her view, and she realized her heart was thudding loudly. This was real. She was *here.*

What *here* looked like, however, she could only guess. Increasingly heavy clouds hugged the windows all the way to the tarmac, and as the plane taxied to its gate, large droplets of water streaked the Plexiglas and bounced off the wings and pavement below.

The woman beside Haley groaned and pulled on a jacket. "Well, I guess we can say goodbye to the sun for a while." She shook her head and made an announcement to no one in particular. "Why anybody would live anywhere but California is a mystery to me!"

Haley smiled noncommittally and turned back to the window. *Rain.* She might not like it all the time, but right now, it looked pretty damn beautiful.

She took her time collecting her bag and moving through the terminal to the car rental desks, admiring the decor along the way. The airport was themed with native art and life-sized figures of wildlife, including bears and giant red fish she assumed must be salmon. Within an hour she was sitting behind the wheel of a rental car with the city of Anchorage spread out before her.

At least, she assumed the city was out there. The rain was coming down so hard she could barely see beyond the next stoplight, and the mountains she had longed to glimpse seemed to have disappeared entirely. Nevertheless, her spirits remained high as she plodded through the traffic with her carefully marked-up printout lying across her knees. Her first stop, as planned, would be her uncle's boat dealership. Beyond that, she had no plans. She might make her way on to Seward tonight. She might not. For the first time in as long as she could remember, no one else was counting on her to do anything in particular.

Sweet.

She found her uncle's boat shop in an industrial-looking area a block away from a small lake. Taku Lake Boat Sales, Inc. consisted of an older-looking square brick building fronting the street and a newer warehouse-type structure behind it. Both were attached by tall chain-link fences to a sprawling lot filled with various-sized boats, boat parts, and trailers. Haley pulled into the gravel area in front of the brick building, got out of her car, and ran to the door.

Heavy rain pelted her as she moved, quickly soaking through the lightweight jacket she now realized was useless as a raincoat. By the time she pulled open the door and hustled inside, her hair was plastered to her face and she could already feel the moisture soaking through her shirt.

"Coming down good out there, isn't it?" a male voice boomed from behind the service desk.

Haley looked up to see a man in his late fifties step out and come toward her, smiling with amusement. He was tall and heavy-set, with a full head of bushy white hair and an impressive beer belly neatly enclosed in an oversized polo shirt.

"You could say that," Haley responded, studying him. His voice sounded familiar. "Are you Ed Miller?"

His eyes lost a bit of their twinkle. "I am. You're Randy's niece?"

She nodded and extended a hand. "Haley Olson. It's nice to meet you."

Ed shook her hand, all signs of his previous jocularity now absent. "I'm sorry about your uncle."

"I should tell you that I'm sorry," Haley replied, feeling awkward. "I only met my uncle once that I can remember, and that was a lifetime ago."

Ed gave a solemn nod. He gestured for her to follow, then led her back behind the service counter to a cluttered office area, where he motioned her to a chair. He opened a locked desk drawer and pulled out a ring of keys. "It's going to take a while for everything to get through probate, like I said on the phone," he explained solemnly. "But the sooner you and your sister decide whether you want to sell his place, the sooner I can get things moving. As for whatever personal property he has out there, if you don't want to auction it off, you'll have to decide how to split things between the two of you. I had an estate company look at what he left in the apartment upstairs, but they said there wasn't enough value to cover an auction, so unless there's something you want, I'll be donating it to charity. I don't really know what he's got out at Seward. He used to have a four-wheeler, but last I heard, it was busted. His truck and his boats he didn't own outright. They belong to the business."

"I understand," Haley replied.

Ed sat back in his chair and exhaled heavily. "I feel bad I haven't gotten out there yet. I need to go, at least to pick up the truck. It's just... well, I'll be honest with you. The way he died..." he shuddered slightly. "I just haven't been up to facing it."

Haley sat up. "The way he died?" she repeated. As next of kin, she and her sister had been notified of their uncle's death by the medical examiner's office. But she hadn't thought about where or how his heart attack might have occurred.

Ed lowered his eyes and squirmed. "Oh, I'm sorry. I thought they would have told you."

"Told me what?" Haley insisted. "He died of a heart attack, didn't he?"

Ed's eyebrows lifted. "Really? A heart attack? Well, I... I guess that makes sense."

Haley cheeks flushed with heat. What wasn't he telling her? "The only information we received was the official cause of death. We were told the date it happened and we were given your name as the executor, and that's it. Is there more we should know?"

Ed's expression clouded. His body tensed. "Well... all I know is what the state troopers told me that night. Randy had driven up there planning to stay just two days, and when he didn't come back to work on the third, I figured something must have happened. His phone was going straight to voice mail, but that didn't mean anything. The reception up there's next to worthless. I knew he had landlines in the cabins, though, so I looked in his desk and got the number for the one he's got rented, and I called the tenant. That guy said he hadn't seen him since the day before, but he'd go take a look. Next thing I know, the state patrol's calling to tell me Randy's dead."

Ed's voice didn't waver, but the mistiness in his eyes made Haley sure that he'd been genuinely fond of his business partner. "When I asked what happened," he continued, "the trooper said they didn't know for sure. They found his body out by the back door of the house, lying on the ground. He'd been dead for a while. There was—"

His voice cracked.

Haley remained silent.

"They said the body had been mauled by something," he continued after a moment, his voice grim. "So they called Fish and Game, and Fish and Game told them that Randy had just called them the day before complaining about a nuisance bear."

Haley's blood ran cold. The man could not be serious.

"Fish and Game was supposed to go check it out," Ed said softly. "But I never heard what they found. I never heard any more about it. When I called the state patrol back they told me they didn't know anything conclusive and that it was up to the medical examiner's office to rule on cause of death."

Haley sat still for a moment, stunned. "They told me it was a heart attack," she repeated.

Ed nodded stiffly. "Well. That's a comfort, then. Maybe it wasn't–" He broke off and shook his head. "Just be careful out there, all right? Maybe give Fish and Game a call. If they think a particular bear's a risk, you know, they'll shoot it." He stood up and extended the ring of keys toward Haley. As she rose with him and reached out to accept it, she realized her hand was shaking. She steadied it.

"Everything you need should be on there," Ed continued. "That's the ring he had on him at the house. The police brought it to me and I took off the boat keys and the ones to the business. I'm not sure what all else is on there. I'm assuming the house and the cabins. There's one for the four-wheeler, and looks like a couple padlock keys."

A bell dinged in the front room.

"When can I expect you back?" he asked.

Haley struggled to keep the current conversation in focus. "I'll be in Alaska a week," she managed. "I don't know when I'll be back in Anchorage. Can I call and let you know?"

He nodded and took a step toward the door. "That's fine. You have my number. I need to check on this customer now, if you don't mind."

"Of course," she agreed, moving with him back out into the front room. "I'll be in touch."

They exchanged a final thank you and goodbye, and Ed turned his attention to the two older men waiting for him at the service counter. Haley opened the door and stepped outside into the pouring rain.

Mauled.

She ran to her car, jumped in, and started the ignition.

"He died of a heart attack," she told herself firmly, slipping out of her drenched jacket and cranking up the heat. Her uncle had *not* been mauled to death by a bear. If he had, why wouldn't the medical examiner's office have told her that? And wouldn't such a story have been on the local news, where Ed would have heard it? It was nonsense. Her uncle had been found right behind his own house, after all, not hiking off in the bush somewhere.

She looked at her watch. She still had plenty of time to get to Seward.

If she wanted to.

Her phone vibrated. She pulled it out of her bag with a growing dread.

Two more texts from Micah. Four from her mother.

I'm so glad you have reception! Micah chirped. *Tell me everything!*

Should we set up a schedule for when you're going to check in? Her mother inquired. *Maybe every couple hours? I just talked to a woman whose daughter went into labor at 22 weeks and the baby died! Did you remember to pack your vitamins?*

Haley closed her eyes and breathed slowly for a minute. Then she stuffed her phone back into her bag and pulled out her maps of the Seward Highway.

Ed had said that her uncle's house had no reception.

She would take her chances with the bear.

Chapter 4

The rain continued steadily as Haley made her way out of Anchorage and onto the Seward Highway. The wide, shallow waters of Cook Inlet spread out to her right, while to her left, steep rocky bluffs towered above the road. Snow-capped mountains almost certainly lurked in the distance behind the clouds, but she could catch only glimpses of them as she concentrated on driving safely down the snaking two-lane road.

An hour later the highway left the water and began to slope gently up into a green valley labeled as the Chugach Mountains. Haley's mood lightened as the rain slowed to a trickle, permitting her first breathtaking views of lush forests, green peaks, and soaring white mountains beyond. The traffic thinned considerably as she drove, and for long moments she enjoyed a rare sensation of being the only human in sight. Almost too soon, she neared the outskirts of Seward.

She reached for the directions to her uncle's cabin, then checked her watch. Blinking a double-take, she turned to stare out at the sky. Despite the clouds, it was still light out. She would have guessed it was late in the afternoon. But it was actually well into the evening.

No matter. Haley's spirits were so buoyed by the natural beauty surrounding her that she wasn't nearly as tired as she thought she would be. She would have a quick look at her uncle's place, then drive on to a hotel in Seward.

She found the crossroad she was looking for without difficulty, but as she turned onto it, her muscles began to tense. The road wasn't paved. It was little more than a gravel lane, and as she followed its twists and turns deep into a dense woods, the rain began to pick up again.

Bad idea, Haley.

She considered turning around, but the narrow road offered no convenient place to do so, and the next crossroad on the map was less than a mile from her uncle's place anyway. She steeled herself and kept going. In a few minutes, the road opened up again, and she breathed a sigh of relief as several other houses came into view. Her uncle wouldn't live in *complete* wilderness, after all.

As she drove up level with the houses, her enthusiasm dimmed again. One of them was all right — a standard A-frame with cedar siding. But the other two looked like they'd been thrown together by grade-school boys using gleanings from the local dump. Dented metal roofs, bare plywood, exposed blue fiberboard, random fluffs of insulation... and seriously, was that an *outhouse?*

Haley's hands gripped the steering wheel tighter. The road surface had become more and more pitted, and every pit was filled with rainwater. She flinched as her front tire dropped sharply into a hidden hole.

Oh, please. The last thing she needed was a flat.

She made her last turn. The new gravel road was no better than the last one, but at least it wasn't any worse. Haley followed its winding turns uphill and deeper into the woods, weaving constantly to avoid suspicious-looking puddles. Just when she was about to bag the whole idea and try a three-point turn, she spied another building ahead, right where her uncle's rentals were supposed to be. She relaxed a bit as two picturesque log cabins came into view, standing on either side of a wide gravel driveway. The cabins were small, but solidly built, and their chink-and-daub construction, stone chimneys, and inviting porches made them every bit as cozy-looking as Haley had hoped. Furthermore, if the multiple wires connecting them to the poles on the road were any indication — and they certainly should be — the cabins were fully equipped with power and phone service.

Haley smiled to herself as she drove on past them and down the drive. Her uncle's own house must be quite nice, indeed.

She followed the drive about a quarter of a mile before the larger structure came into view, and she craned her neck forward anxiously to see it. The rain was getting worse again, and to her dismay, her uncle's driveway had only deteriorated the farther she drove from the cabins. The thickly graveled parking area by the road had turned to a mere smattering of gravel over dirt, and here, at journey's end, she saw nothing on the ground but old tire tracks in the mud.

She lifted her eyes with trepidation.

Her uncle's house was a friggin' nightmare. Balanced on short, clumsy looking stilts, the L-shaped monstrosity was a hodgepodge of weather-treated decking, warped plywood, tacked on tar paper, exposed drywall, corrugated sheet metal, and small, dirt-covered windows. A square roof covered the open part of the L, forming a dark and uninviting porch littered with plastic bins, lawn chairs, paint cans, bottles, two rusted grills, and a giant stack of rotting firewood.

Haley put her foot on the brake and shifted into park.

Are you kidding me?

Who in their right mind would live in such a dilapidated mess while renting out such attractive cabins? Thoroughly baffled, she pulled her keys from the ignition and looked through the ring for a likely candidate to open the front door. That she and Micah would wind up selling the place was already a foregone conclusion. But she had come this far; she might as well go in and look around.

She put a hand on the door handle, then paused. Her eyes scanned the forest surrounding her, and her breathing quickened. The idea of a bear bursting out of the brush didn't seem nearly so outrageous as it had while she was in Anchorage. Still, people lived here, didn't they? People who, almost certainly, did not allow themselves to be paralyzed with fear every time they walked between their houses and their cars.

She got a grip on herself, took another quick look as far as she could see into the rain, and sprinted to the door.

Made it. Ha!

She clicked open the lock with the first key she tried, pushed open the door to let herself in, then shut it tight behind her.

Oh, my.

Her nose wrinkled. She was in a kitchen, of sorts. It had a sink, a stove, and a refrigerator, the latter of which was making a comforting humming noise, assuring her that the house at least had electricity. Unfortunately, the amenities appeared to stop there. She could tell by looking at the blue plastic barrel just inside the door that her uncle did not have city water. The holding tank was connected to a pump, with one pipe branching out to supply the sink and another heading through the wall. The kitchen counters were cluttered and grimy, and the vinyl flooring was brown with mud.

Warily, she stepped around to her left through an open doorway to the main room. A filthy square of burnt orange carpeting, its edges unevenly sawed off, lay uninstalled over a plank floor. A wood-framed couch and loveseat lined the far walls, their misshapen cushions upholstered with a montage of guns and moose antlers. Real antlers, definitely not from a moose, hung on the near wall beside a wood-burning stove. The entire room was littered with stereotypical "man junk" including empty beer bottles and cigarette packs, dirty dishes, dirtier magazines, discarded clothing, and what she guessed to be a spittoon.

Choosing her steps carefully, she moved just far enough around the corner to see into the front room. The equally cluttered space proved to be a small bedroom, with a slumping, unmade double bed conveniently placed on the other side of the stove. A shotgun hung over the small front window. On the far wall, a closet with broken doors spewed forth clothing like a cornucopia. On the near wall adjoining the kitchen, a tiny alcove roughly three feet square had been carved out and lined with fiberglass panels. A pipe and shower head stuck out near its ceiling. There was no toilet.

Haley stepped back out into the main room and noted the narrow wooden backdoor tucked into its corner. She crossed the room to the rear window, leaned over the nearly waist-high stack of pornography piled up between the couch and the wall, and looked outside.

Yep. An outhouse.

She had seen all she needed to see. She turned, walked back out the front door, and locked it behind her. The rain had slowed to a sticky mist, and she walked back toward the car more slowly this time, her eyes scanning over the rest of the yard. The house sat in the middle of a clearing about twice the size of its own footprint. Besides the outhouse, there were two other buildings in the back that looked like sheds. Her uncle's nearly new truck, emblazoned with a door decal for Taku Lake Boat Sales, sat hauntingly idle not far from the side of the house. The rest of the clearing, if it could indeed be called that, was littered with pieces of rusted metal, gas cans, water barrels, chicken wire, the corroded base of a onetime pop-up camper, broken boat trailers, a set of box springs, chains, tools, and a crudely made target of a moose torso with two-by-fours for legs.

The mere thought of sorting through the mess made Haley mildly nauseous, and she was profoundly grateful that her uncle hadn't chosen to make his nieces his executors. All she and Micah had to do was say "sell it," and Ed and an estate company would handle the rest. Whatever the company's fee might be, she was confident they would earn it.

Her eyes rested on the area outside the back door, and a chill slid up her damp neck. Her uncle's body had been found there. Had he been working in the yard, then suddenly felt ill? Or was he simply on his way back from the outhouse? She pushed thoughts of marauding bears firmly from her mind. Perhaps he had seen a bear, and was running because he was afraid. From what she could recall, he had been overweight just like her father. With the family's genetic predisposition for heart disease, the combination of exertion and fright could certainly be lethal.

They said the body had been mauled by something.

Ed's words rang in Haley's ears as she moved back towards her car. She was only a few feet from it when a sign nailed to a nearby tree caught her eye. She hadn't noticed it before — no doubt because she'd dashed so quickly through the rain.

Her pulse quickened. The sign was red, with the black silhouette of a bear at the top. Large letters underneath read, "DANGER." She stepped closer. The bottom of the plastic sign had a laminated piece of paper attached. "Please read," a typed portion stated. "A bear or bears sighted in this area have been determined to represent a higher than normal threat to human safety. This area may or may not be closed to the public. Extreme caution should be taken in this area until further notice. Incident details and further instructions follow." Below the type, an uneven hand had scrawled two more lines in blue ink. "Man found deceased on June 16 after reporting that a large black bear near home was exhibiting predatory behavior."

Haley scrambled back to her car, swung open the door, lost her footing in the mud, caught herself, fell onto the seat, and slammed the door behind her. She turned her keys in the ignition and shifted into drive. Her breath came in heaves.

Predatory behavior. What the hell did that mean? She had a pretty good idea what it meant, actually, but she didn't want to think about it.

Predators kill prey. They kill it to eat it.

"Oo-kay!" she cried aloud, attempting to calm herself. "This was fun and all, but we are *out of here!*" She turned the car around quickly in the muddy drive, spinning her wheels several times in the process. Once back on the rutted lane through the trees, she drove away from the house in earnest. "How about we get back to that nice scenic, paved Seward Highway now?" she chattered to herself. She flinched again as a back wheel bumped roughly in and out of a rain-filled hole. "The wilderness is definitely overrated. Asphalt is where it's at, people! Lots and lots of wildlife-deterring asphalt..."

She spied another suspiciously deep-looking pothole and swerved to the side. To her horror, the car tipped slightly, then slowed. She stepped on the gas and her wheels spun. "Oh, no," she murmured, still talking out loud. "No, no, no..." She shifted into reverse and pushed the accelerator again. The car jerked briefly, but went nowhere. She tried to steer the tires back up onto the road, but they continued to spin.

Haley planted her face on the steering wheel. This could *not* be happening. Swearing under her breath, she cracked opened the car door and looked down. The muddy shoulder of the road had collapsed, dropping both of her left-side tires into a shallow, rain-filled ditch. A good two inches of water swelled over the tires, and the whole body of the car was slanted to the side.

She closed the door and pulled out her cell phone. No service. *Duh.*

She swore some more. Then she did another faceplant. *Fabulous. Now what?*

If she weren't so blasted nervous, she would probably be laughing. Just a few short hours ago she had been back in ordinary civilization filling out paperwork at the car rental agency, assuring her sister and mother that their fears for her safety bordered on the pathological. What could happen, after all? Please.

And yet, here she was. Stuck in the mud with no cell phone and no way to call for help in the middle of a forest inhabited by a potentially homicidal bear.

It really was too ironic.

Haley allowed herself a good three minutes of self-pity. Then she got a grip. She could either stay in the car all night and possibly any number of days waiting for a good Samaritan to happen along. Or she could suck it up and head back to the cabins on foot. They couldn't be more than a couple hundred yards ahead. At least one of them was occupied, according to Ed. And the cabins had landlines.

Her teeth gritted. She didn't have a choice. The rain had stopped, at least temporarily, and it was still light outside. She glanced at her watch and was amazed to see that it was after ten o'clock. *Freaky.*

She dropped her keys and her phone into her purse and threw it over her shoulder. Her worthless jacket was wet again, but it would have to do. She scooted over to the passenger door, took a deep breath, and hopped out onto the road.

She pointed her feet toward the cabins and ran like hell.

Chapter 5

Haley drew deep gulps of breath and leaned against the back wall of the nearest cabin. Her hand went instinctively to her abdomen. The physical exertion, she wasn't worried about. She had continued to run and do aerobics throughout the pregnancy, so the sprint itself was hardly noteworthy. Running while panicked, however, required a good deal more oxygen.

She rested until her breathing slowed, then got her bearings and tried to think. Though she had nearly twisted her ankle a few times, she had seen no bear, thank God, and had reached her destination unscathed. Now all she needed was a phone.

She walked around to the front of the cabin and compared it to the one on the other side of the drive. The porch of the near cabin was empty, with the exception of a plastic Adirondack chair. The other cabin, however, had several inexpensive lawn chairs on the porch, as well as a grill and a dirty pair of hiking boots.

Haley headed toward the boots. The cabin was clearly occupied, although there was no vehicle parked beside it. She walked up onto the front porch and knocked. After a suitable period of silence, she crept to the window beside the door and peeked in.

She was looking at a kitchen. It was tiny, but serviceable, being equipped with full-sized appliances. The counters were a bit cluttered, but like the wood-laminate floor below them, they were not unclean. The kitchen wasn't a separate room, but was merely an alcove off the larger main room, which had just enough space for a queen-sized bed on the back wall and a couch at its foot that faced the large stone fireplace in front. Haley smiled to herself. To say that the cabin was "tidy" would be pushing it. But compared to her uncle's place, the assortment of clothes, shoes, and camping equipment scattered about it looked pleasantly civilized.

Unfortunately, whatever civilized human being lived there was currently not at home. Haley studied the keys on her ring with indecision. She probably *could* get in. But she was fairly sure that would be illegal. And as unnerving as the past half hour had been for her, she doubted her predicament would rate a true emergency. Particularly when she had keys to the other cabin, too.

She walked back across the drive, still obsessively scanning the tree line at every step. *Keep it together, Haley. It's all good.* She stepped up onto the porch, selected two likely keys from the ring, and inserted one into the door lock. The first didn't fit. But the second one did.

She opened the door, stepped inside, and turned the slide bolt behind her with satisfaction. The floor plan of this cabin, not surprisingly, was the mirror image of its twin. She walked up to the sink to turn on the tap and was relieved when a thin stream of water poured into the basin. She moved quickly out of the kitchen and around the corner by the bed to where she expected to find a bathroom.

A sink, a shower, and a toilet. *Thank you, God.*

She made use of the facilities, which mercifully worked just fine. When she reemerged, she noticed a retro-looking landline phone attached to the wall beside the front door. She rushed to pick it up, but her hope dissolved quickly. There was no dial tone. Could she really expect her uncle to continue paying a monthly bill for an unrented unit? She was lucky he had kept the water and power on.

She studied the rest of the cabin. Besides the bed, side table, dresser, and couch, it was empty. It was reasonably clean, however, and the mattress looked fairly new and was protected by a zipped plastic cover. So why hadn't her uncle rented this one?

Haley sank down on the edge of the bed and realized she didn't care. Now that she was out of the rain, away from marauding bears, and had access to indoor plumbing, she felt safe again. She also felt suddenly, horribly sleepy. Despite the deceptive Alaskan sun, it was past her bedtime. And bedtime was a ritual she practiced religiously, even before she got pregnant.

"I can't do anything until he gets home, anyway," she muttered to herself, taking off her shoes and rolling her damp jacket into a pillow. "I might as well relax until I hear a car or something, right?"

She stretched out on the thick mattress and closed her eyes. Within minutes, she was asleep.

The annoying rapping sound disturbed Ben Parker's slumber not a bit. His brain simply wrote it into the script of his dream. He was out on his own boat in the Au'au Channel between Lana'i and Maui. The water was calm, the sky was blue, and spinner dolphins were leaping in the air off the port side. The rapping was coming from inside the boat's bathroom, otherwise known as "the head." His nephew Brandon had gotten himself locked in again. Ben chuckled to himself, left the wheel long enough to jiggle the stubborn door open, then returned. "It stinks in there!" the eight-year-old complained with a grimace as he joined his uncle at the bridge. "Hey, do you think those dolphins will bow-ride with us?"

Ben smiled and turned the wheel. "Let's see!"

The rapping started up again, but this time it must be his sister trapped, because the voice he heard was clearly a woman's. What was Maggie doing on his boat? She might let her son go with him, but she hated the ocean. He wondered briefly if it might be his sister Lara, but surely she was smart enough to get herself out. Jenna would be more likely to screech at him, but why would she be yelling at him to wake up? He was driving the boat!

Ben's curiosity got the better of him. He was tugging at the stuck door of the head, admonishing whichever sister it was to calm down and knock it off, when gradually he came to the bizarre realization that he was, in fact, lying in bed.

Say what, now?

He sat up and blinked the sleep from his eyes. The rapping was real. But it was coming from the door of his cabin. And the woman yelling demands at him didn't sound like any of his sisters.

"Hello? Please, wake up! I need your help!"

Ben rolled out of bed so fast he nearly fell on the floor. A woman? Out here? In the middle of the night? He groped around for something decent to put on, but quickly bagged the effort. It wasn't like he owned a bathrobe. His flannel sleep pants and pathetically worn tee shirt would have to do. He stumbled into the kitchen, flipped on the porch light, and swung the door open, still blinking to clear his vision.

It was a woman, all right. A woman about his own age, and apparently alone. A quick glance behind her showed no sign of a vehicle. Where the hell had she come from?

"I'm sorry," she apologized quickly, her sharp eyes looking him over warily. She took a step back.

He almost grinned. What woman shows up in the middle of the night, raps on a strange man's door, yells at him to wake up, and *then* gets cautious?

He studied her as his vision cleared. She was tall for a woman. Her clothes were rumpled, she had a red indentation across one cheek that looked like she'd been lying on a zipper, and her bangs were sticking straight up on one side.

"What the..." he began uncertainly, his voice raspy with sleep. He cleared his throat, dropped his hands to his sides, and made an effort to seem less threatening. "I mean, it's no problem. Is something wrong?"

Her green eyes flashed with indecision, but only for a moment. He could tell she was still assessing him, weighing her options. Evidently, she deemed him trustworthy. Relatively speaking.

He considered informing her with a straight face that he had not murdered any trespassers for weeks now.

He decided against it.

"I..." she began uncertainly. "I wondered if I could use your phone."

Her voice was nice, he thought. At least when she wasn't screeching at him. Low and mellow, with an almost musical quality to it. Her long brown hair accentuated her striking eyes and high cheekbones, not to mention forming the perfect complement to her lean, athletic figure. Zipper imprint or no, he could look at her all day.

What was he doing, again?

He gave himself a shake. "My phone? Sure. What's the problem exactly? Are you okay?"

"I'm fine," she said quickly, looking suddenly embarrassed. "I just need to call triple A to get my car out of the mud so I can get to a hotel."

Ben blinked with confusion again. He cast a glance behind him at the clock on his microwave. The car in the mud he understood — he might have gotten bogged down himself if his boss hadn't lent him the truck for tomorrow. The rest of it was a mystery.

"Um..." he said carefully. "You do realize it's four-thirty in the morning?"

Her large eyes stared back at him like a doe in headlights. "It is?"

Ben couldn't help but chuckle. The poor thing sounded mortified.

"But I just lay down for a minute!" she protested. "I couldn't possibly have slept that long!"

He grinned at her. "And yet, here we are."

The ghost of a smile turned up the corners of her lips. She had a beautiful mouth. She had a beautiful face, period.

"In that case," she said sheepishly. "I'm really sorry to bother you. I should have checked the time before I ran over here. But when I saw your truck out the window, I assumed you'd just gotten home. I thought that's what woke me up."

He looked out behind her in confusion. "Your car window? Where did you get stuck?"

"Oh, no," she said quickly. "I've been in the other cabin." Her face flushed. "I'm sorry. I'm not explaining myself well at all. I'm Haley Olson. Theoretically, I'm your new landlord."

Ben straightened. "You're related to Randy?"

She nodded. "He was my uncle."

Now he felt sheepish. "I'm sorry."

She shook her head self-consciously. "Thanks, but I didn't know him."

"Then I'm sorry about that, too," he replied honestly. Randy Olson had been one weird dude, but he did have a few redeeming features. It was a shame that the man had never gotten to know his niece. Nieces, in Ben's experience, were rather delightful creatures.

"Look," he said soberly, fighting a yawn. "Unless you have someplace else you have to be, why don't you just go back to sleep for now and we'll work this out in the morning? I can probably pull your car out with the truck. Where is it?"

She drew in a frustrated breath, drawing his attention to the rise and fall of her chest. *Landlord*, he reminded himself soberly.

"About halfway to my uncle's house," she answered, her tone weary.

She looked as tired as he felt. He considered her predicament. "Hang on," he instructed, then he went inside to his closet, raided the top shelf, and returned to the door. "Here," he offered, handing her a set of clean sheets, a blanket, and a towel. "This should make it a little more comfortable over there. Is there anything else you need?" Another look at the mark on her cheek made him turn around. He pulled a pillow off his bed and added it to her pile. "Okay?"

She smiled at him. Appreciation, as well as surprise, shone in her eyes. "Thanks."

"No problem." He couldn't fight it anymore. He yawned.

She chuckled. "Go back to bed, um... I guess I didn't get your name."

"It's Ben," he replied, still yawning. "Ben Parker."

"Go back to sleep, Ben," she repeated. "And thanks again. Really."

She started off his porch, and he nodded and began to close the door. On impulse, he called out after her. "We'll take half off my rent for the linens then, okay?"

To his surprise, she did not turn around. She merely laughed and kept moving.

"In your dreams, Mr. Parker," she quipped.

He smiled out after her, watching in the first glow of twilight as her long, athletic legs jogged up the stairs onto the porch of her own cabin. Her shiny hair bounced behind her, then swung across her shoulders as she turned to wave at him, then slipped inside.

In his dreams indeed, he thought regretfully.

Chapter 6

Haley awoke to bright sun streaming through a curtainless window in a wall of logs. It took several seconds for her brain to sort through the chaos of her memories and make sense of what she was seeing.

"Oh, no," she groaned aloud. How much had she overslept this time? She grabbed at her cell phone on the bedside table. It was just after seven o'clock in Alaska. Eight o'clock to her California brain.

She looked back at the rumpled bed with a smirk. Who would have guessed she could sleep so soundly? She checked her list of text messages, as she did first thing every morning, and was surprised to see none since yesterday. Her mother and sister were both night owls, and texts usually streamed in long after she'd gone to sleep. It took another few seconds for her to realize that she'd been out of cellular range since sometime yesterday evening. Most likely, as soon as she drove back into it, her inbox would explode.

She set the phone back down. Perhaps her exhaustion wasn't so difficult to understand after all.

They would be worried about her. She would have to send another message as soon as she got in range. Never mind that they *shouldn't* worry. They had no idea what a mess she'd made of last night. The last thing she'd told them was that she was very likely to be out of communication for a while, and not to freak out if she didn't respond. She had promised to contact them sometime today, and that was all she'd promised.

They would be frantic by noon.

Haley exhaled and fell back upon the mattress. If only her car was usable and the landline was working, she could happily lie on this comfy mattress all day. Maybe even all week. A couple trips to the grocery store, and she'd be good.

She lay still a few more minutes, then reluctantly got up. She walked into the tiny kitchen and looked out the window, cringing slightly as she remembered her blunder of the night before. She had still been half asleep when she'd glimpsed the truck outside and gone tearing across to the other cabin to demand a phone. Only when the door had been opened by a towering figure with rumpled clothes, a dazed expression, and wild, ginger-colored hair had she paused to consider the wisdom of her actions. He could have been a total fruitcake, and she was alone.

Thank goodness she'd been lucky. She might have cause to question her uncle's judgment as of late, but at least he'd found somebody nice to rent to.

Her eyes left the window. She would not wake up Mr. Ben Parker twice. She would simply have to cool her heels and wait for signs of life. Which would be no hardship if only she could wash up, brush her teeth, and change into some clean clothes while she was waiting. But of course, her suitcase was still in the trunk of her car.

She rummaged through the cabinets and was delighted to find disposable cups and plates, a roll of paper towels, and an old jar of instant coffee. She'd given up caffeine before the pregnancy, but even a sip of hot water would hit the spot. She filled a Styrofoam cup at the sink, microwaved it, and decided to hold her pretend tea party on the porch.

She pushed opened the door and blinked down with amazement. Her suitcase sat right in front of her.

Did I say nice? She thought to herself with a grin. *The man is a friggin' saint.*

Imagining that he might be watching her through his windows, she quickly grabbed the handle and rolled the bag inside. Before she had to beg another favor, she would at least run a brush through her hair.

She washed up quickly, pulled on some clean clothes, raided her stash of herbal tea bags, and went back outside. She would have loved a shower and shampoo, but she had no idea how much time Ben would have to help her before he needed to leave for work — or wherever. For all she knew, he'd been waiting for her to wake up for hours. He'd obviously been to her car and back already. Under the circumstances, she was glad she had forgotten to lock it up. But he would need her keys to haul it out.

She settled into her Adirondack chair, took a sip of lukewarm tea, and looked around.

Yesterday's clouds were no more than a memory. The morning sky was azure blue. Forests of hemlock and spruce soaked up the sun beneath it, bathing the landscape in a sea of freshest green. From the gentle rise on which the cabin was perched, she could see lofty gray peaks of mountains in the distance, some capped with glistening snow. Birds twittered in the trees around her. She breathed in deeply of the cool, clear air.

Yes, she murmured softly. *This is what I need.*

"Good morning!" a cheerful voice boomed.

Haley jumped a little. She turned to see her tenant standing by the side of his truck, grinning at her reaction. To her relief, he bore little resemblance to the wild-haired, hulking figure she remembered from last night. He was quite tall, yes, but built lean, rather like a basketball player. His red-gold hair was wavy and longish, curling slightly around his ears, but at least this morning it looked comparatively tame. And as the sunshine shed new light on apple cheeks, an ever-so-slightly cleft chin, prominent dimples, and a devilish grin, she threw all caution to the wind.

"Good morning," she returned with equal cheer. She set down her tea and rose. "Thanks for bringing up my suitcase. I wasn't expecting that."

"All part of the service, Ma'am," he said playfully. "Now, how about we get that rental car out of the mud?"

"I suppose the agency would appreciate that," she replied, stepping down off the porch to join him. "Although I think I could stay here and look out at this view indefinitely. It's beautiful."

He glanced in the direction she'd been looking. "How long have you been here?" he asked curiously.

"I just flew into Anchorage yesterday."

He smiled. "Well, that explains it. If you think this view is something, you must not have driven down on a clear day." He opened the driver's door of his truck and gestured her around to the other side. "Hop in."

Haley opened the passenger door and stepped up into the truck, noting the business decal on its side. "You work for Kenai Marine Tours?"

"Yep," he said proudly, starting up the truck. "I'm a boat captain. And a naturalist."

She stared at him a moment. Why the idea should strike her as so preposterous, she wasn't sure. "Seriously?"

"What?" he asked good-naturedly. "Do I look like a lawyer or something?"

She frowned. She did not want to think about lawyers. "God, no," she replied bitterly.

He turned. "You have a problem with lawyers?"

"I am a lawyer," she said dryly. "And yes, I do. Can we talk about something else? What's a naturalist?"

Now he was the one to look startled. "You're a lawyer?"

She sighed. "Well, I was the last time I checked. But I haven't been able to get email since yesterday. What's a naturalist?"

He paused a beat, then answered. "Anybody with some expertise in natural history. There's no real certification. In the tourist industry, it just means whoever's getting paid to lecture on whatever the tour's about. A lot of times it's just some college kid who's done a crash course with the guidebooks."

Haley considered. "And in your case?"

He shrugged. "I have a degree in oceanography, but most of what I tell people on the tours, I picked up myself."

They reached her pathetic-looking, tilted rental car, but he drove the truck on past it.

Haley studied his deeply tanned face and forearms. His skin was lightly freckled, but unlike most redheads, not at all fair. She supposed she could picture him as a boat captain. But the concept of his being paid to take tourists out on the ocean to lecture them about seagulls and glaciers seemed highly surreal. Her gaze moved down to her own hands. Images of herself sitting in meetings in over-air-conditioned conference rooms, typing away at her laptop while others argued across her, rose unbidden in her mind. What was happening at the firm, now? She would be desperately behind when she returned.

Her body tensed.

Ben switched to a different topic. "So, I'm assuming you flew up to check out your uncle's property? Maybe see about selling it?"

"That's right," she answered, attempting to refocus. "It was left equally to my sister and me, so we'll have to decide together. She's ready to sell, but I thought I'd take a look at it first."

He studied her a moment. "And take a look at some of the rest of Alaska while you're at it, I hope?"

She remembered the view from her porch with a smile. "Absolutely."

He pulled the truck into her uncle's drive. This time, Haley's eyes flew immediately to the red danger sign. How could she possibly have missed it last night? She glanced over at Ben to find him looking at the same thing. He frowned. Then he turned the truck around and shifted it into park. "I assume you don't mind if I borrow a few of you and your sister's supplies for the occasion?" he asked.

It took her a second to realize he wanted something of her uncle's. "Sure. Borrow whatever you need," she answered, watching nervously as he hopped out. The morning's sunshine might have temporarily dimmed her memory of last night's terror, but the darkness of the woods surrounding her uncle's house — even in broad daylight — brought it flooding back.

Her eyes scanned the tree line. Ben had gotten out of the car without so much as a glance around. He disappeared around the back corner of the house, and her uneasiness increased. Did he know what he was doing? She was certain he had seen the sign. And he did live here. But, still...

It seemed an eternity before he reappeared, dropped an armload of equipment in the bed of the truck, and hopped back in.

Haley felt a sudden surge of guilt. Was she putting the man in danger, just by asking him to help her? What did "extreme caution" mean, after all? She wanted to broach the subject, but couldn't find the words. Men got testy when their skills of self-protection were questioned, and although dealing with testy men was one of her specialties, she had no desire to do it while on vacation.

Ben drove the truck back around in front of her car, parked it, and again leapt out without a care. He grabbed the equipment he'd borrowed, hooked up the rental to his hitch, then asked her to get behind her wheel. She moved to her car in a flash, then tried hard to focus on his directions rather than whatever might be lurking in the trees. In a few short minutes, her car was parked back up on the roadbed. Ben removed the tow strap and dropped down to examine the rental's front end.

"Not a scratch," he said proudly. Then he stood up with the equipment in hand. "I'll just run this back to your uncle's. It's easier than turning the truck around."

Haley looked through her windshield at the truck in front of her and tensed. She understood his point. The larger vehicle had barely made it around her car when it was half in the ditch. He couldn't turn the truck around to return to her uncle's unless both cars drove to the cabins first.

"But..." she protested, unable to stay silent any longer. "You *can't* just walk there!"

Ben stared at her blankly.

She exhaled with frustration. "I mean," she tried to clarify. "I really don't want you to take any risks on my account."

He raised one ginger eyebrow. "Risks? Like what? Slipping and falling in the mud?"

"No, of course not!" she returned. "Like..." She really couldn't say the words. "Like whatever happened to my uncle."

Ben's expression sobered. He studied her a moment, then dumped the equipment back in the bed of his truck and returned to the side of her car. "What exactly did they tell you?" he asked.

She swallowed with discomfort, trying to look behind where he stood to scan the dense brush. Could they not talk about this someplace else? "The medical examiner's office said he died of a heart attack," she explained. "And that's all they said. But according to my uncle's partner in the dealership, the state patrol thought he'd been mauled by a bear. And clearly, the Department of Fish and Game agreed. Surely you can't think it's safe to be wandering around back here?" More of Ed Miller's words came back to her. Wasn't it her uncle's tenant who had been sent to look for him?

She paled. "You're the one who found his body, aren't you?"

Ben looked at her with sympathy a moment, then heaved out a sigh.

"Listen, Haley," he began. "Yes, I was the one who found your uncle. And I get why you think what you think. But no, I'm not the slightest bit worried about wandering around out here. That sign should have been taken down weeks ago." He frowned, then looked at his watch. "I'm afraid it's kind of a long story, and I've got to get to work..."

His forehead creased for a moment. Then his face brightened. "Hey, if you're not doing anything else this morning, why don't you ride along with me? I've got to drive up to Moose Pass to pick up a boat part from this buddy of my boss's. It's only about a forty minute drive up there, and you'll love the scenery now that you can actually see it. I promise I'll tell you everything you want to know about your uncle. Everything I know, anyway. What do you say?"

Haley smiled. She could already tell that Ben Parker was a far cry from the men she was used to spending twelve hours a day with. For one thing, he wore jeans to work. For another, she strongly suspected he wouldn't be the least bit impressed by her tally of billable hours.

But he could answer her questions about her uncle. And he seemed genuinely eager to show her more of Alaska.

She was genuinely eager to let him.

Chapter 7

Haley jumped into Ben's truck a few minutes later with a drawstring backpack, a fresh cup of tea, and a handful of oatmeal and flax bars.

He looked down at the snack bars with a guilty expression. "Sorry. I didn't even think about your getting stuck out here without any breakfast. I should have offered you a frozen waffle or something."

Haley laughed. "You're not responsible for feeding your landlord. Hauling her suitcase out of the woods and getting her car out of a ditch is plenty sufficient."

"Don't forget the linen service," he said seriously.

"I haven't," she returned. "You're almost up to a five percent rent discount for the month."

"Five percent?" he exclaimed with a mock scowl. "Man, you're cold."

She shrugged dismissively. "I told you already. I'm a lawyer."

He cracked a grin. "Noted."

The truck started down the gravel road toward the highway, and Haley's smile faded as she pulled out her phone. "I really need to get into my email soon," she informed him. "Will I be able to get a signal at Moose Pass?"

His lips twisted. "Probably. But if it's important, I wouldn't risk it. I'll stop out by the highway; you should be able to get a signal from Seward. If not, we'll drive closer until you can."

"Thanks," Haley replied, feeling uncomfortable. She owed the man enough favors already. She made a mental note to have Ed surprise him later with a free month's rent.

Ben parked the truck on the shoulder as they reached the open valley by the highway, and Haley's cell phone sprang immediately to life. "This is good," she said brightly. "Just give me a second here to respond, okay? I'll be quick."

Her relief turned rapidly to dismay. *Downloading... message 64 of 128.*

"No," she murmured miserably, not realizing she was talking aloud. "No!"

As her eyes scanned the incoming list, her stomach went into free-fall. The auto-responder message she'd left at work had accomplished nothing. Updates, questions, meeting requests, and demands for action merely poured in in duplicate, the second ones beginning with perfunctory well-wishes for her trip, then repeating the original request. "What part of *vacation* don't—" Haley cut herself off.

The text messages were worse. As she scrolled through screen after screen of innocently passive-aggressive questions from her mother and nonsensical, panicked babble from her sister, Haley felt like her body was being sucked into an abyss. On impulse, she dropped the phone on her lap, closed her eyes, and breathed deeply.

She could *not* sit here and type out responses to all of this nonsense. She couldn't, and she wouldn't.

She opened her eyes, grabbed the phone back up, and tapped on her mother's phone number instead.

"Haley!" Michelle's voice answered with a quaver. "Well, thank God! Where have you been?"

"I've been exactly where I told you I would be, Mom," Haley said brusquely. "Listen, I can't talk long. But I need you to listen to me. I am perfectly 100% fine. F-I-N-E. I am safe, I am well, and I am whole." *At least for now,* she added silently. In truth, her sanity was growing more precarious by the minute. "But I'm staying at Uncle Randy's cabin and you're not going to be able to text me out there. So here's what I need you to do. Tell Micah to send me one email every day, and I will send one back. I don't know what time of day it will be, but I will send one. And only one. If she doesn't expect anything else, she'll be better off. Okay?"

The line went quiet. Haley had no trouble picturing her mother's drawn, concerned face as Michelle contemplated her next question/criticism. "We almost had to take your sister to the hospital last night," she said finally, her voice heavy.

Haley's throat constricted. "Why?"

"Well, you know how difficult things have been between her and Tim. And you couldn't expect that she would take your leaving very well, did you? It wasn't a full-blown panic attack, but it was close to it. Don't you think your sister is dealing with a little more than she can handle right now?"

Haley felt an unfamiliar pressure around her nose and eyes, and her breathing turned ragged. *Good God... don't cry!*

She was not a crier. She hadn't hauled off and sobbed since that horrible day in college when her Aunt Janie had died. Why now? One more harangue from her mother was nothing new. Neither was a near "panic attack" from Micah. Haley was all too familiar with the phenomenon, but she called it what it was: a hissy fit.

She drew in a great gulp of air. "Mom!" she said firmly. "Micah is a grown woman with plenty of other support around her. If she really cares about the—"

Haley remembered that Ben was sitting two feet to her left.

"This whole adventure is about stress reduction," she amended. "Peace and quiet. Solitude. And that includes a break from my phone and all things digital. I am seeing green mountains and listening to birds and watching blue sky and probably for the first time in my life breathing clean air—" her voice nearly cracked again. *Dammit!* What was wrong with her? "I will *not* back off on this, Mom," she declared, gathering steam. "It's too important to me. We'll email once a day or I swear I'll chuck this phone in the ocean and you'll not hear another word till my plane lands. Do we understand each other?"

The silence on the other end of the line was interminable. Haley could feel Ben squirming in his seat, but she was too mortified to look at him.

When her mother's voice at last returned, it was no longer quavering. "If you think that's the best thing," Michelle said flatly. "For Micah and the baby?"

"Yes, I do," Haley proclaimed. "Absolutely."

Michelle cleared her throat. "And I suppose you want me to tell her, rather than your taking the time to explain this to her yourself?"

"Yep! Thanks for offering. I really have to go now, Mom. I'll email you sometime tomorrow."

"Don't you think—"

"Tomorrow, Mom. Take care. Bye!"

Haley ended the call and tossed the phone into her bag. She stared straight ahead for several seconds, her heart thudding in her chest. The heavy sensation in her facial bones had turned into a hot, moist pounding.

No, no, no, she begged herself. *Not here, not now.* Maybe she shouldn't keep fighting it. Maybe she was overdue for a long hard cry, and maybe it would do her good. But it was not going to happen in front of a virtual stranger. The poor man could be traumatized for life. She would keep it together, and she would go on with her day. She was going to have a good day. She was going to have a *great* one.

Haley rolled down her window, cast a look out at the sweeping snow-tipped mountains that rose out of the landscape beyond Seward, and breathed in deeply.

The air was so crisp. So cool. So *pure*.

She exhaled slowly, then turned back to Ben. "All done," she said with a smile. "Moose Pass, here we come."

Ben drove up the Seward Highway at a leisurely pace, keeping one eye on the road and the other on Haley. To say that his new landlord intrigued him would be an understatement. That she was attractive, witty, and intelligent, he'd picked up in the first five minutes of knowing her, despite his being half asleep. But this morning's interaction, rather than helping him get a clearer picture of her, had only complicated it.

Her nervousness in the woods earlier had seemed flaky at the time, but given that she had been told by the authorities to look out for a dangerous bear — the very one she thought had killed her uncle — it was understandable. In fact, for an attorney who was so obviously out of her element, she showed a good bit of moxie. He could only wonder what she was like *in* her element. He grinned to himself at the thought of her intimidating a roomful of stuffed suits. God help the fool who made a sexist comment!

And yet... there was the phone call. She had obviously been excited about seeing more of Alaska, but all signs of cheer had drained from her face at the first sight of those incoming messages. And as she continued to browse, she had transformed before his eyes from a confident, enthusiastic adventurer to a beaten-down and suffering... what? His mind searched for the appropriate word. The closest thing he could come up with was martyr.

Why? He knew he had no business asking the question. He had tried to give her at least the illusion of privacy, but that was difficult when she was sitting right beside him. And since he was neither deaf nor stupid, he was aware that whatever her problem was, family drama was making it worse.

Unfortunately for him, he could relate to that phenomenon all too well. Perhaps at some point, he would share that fact. But not now. Right now, sheer humanity dictated that he pretend he'd heard nothing at all. It also dictated that he give her a dose of his own favorite medicine.

Nature therapy. It had never failed him yet.

He was anxious to point out the highlights as they drove, but decided to wait until she asked him a question. As long as she faced away from him, he figured she wasn't ready to talk. But as she stared out the passenger window at the scenery, her slumped shoulders began gradually to straighten, and he could tell she was feeling better.

"What are those flowers?" she asked finally, speaking for the first time since they'd left Seward. "I don't think I've ever seen them before."

Ben smiled at the sea of pinkish-purple blossoms that swayed on tall green stems along the roadside. "Fireweed," he answered. "It's everywhere in Alaska. My mother keeps trying to grow it down in Seattle, but she never has any luck. For whatever reason, the flower just likes it here."

Haley's eyes at last turned toward him, and he was delighted to see that their sparkle of good humor had returned. "I'm with the fireweed," she declared. She sat forward and watched out the front window, twisting around occasionally to take in every aspect of the passing vistas. Ben knew how she felt. He had grown up in the shadow of Mount Rainier and boated all over the Washington and Oregon coasts, but his first trip to Alaska had blown him away. It was like any other national park times infinity. The mountains, valleys, forests, rivers, lakes, beaches, and glaciers seemed to go on forever. And for the most part, they were still as wild and untamed as they had ever been.

This stretch of road was particularly stunning, with tall gray peaks standing on either side of rolling green meadows filled with wildflowers. Haley sat forward intently as they passed the edge of a lake, its calm surface reflecting the snowy crags of the Chugach Mountains set against the blue sky above.

"The water is so many different colors," she commented. "This lake is turquoise, but that last one was more of an aqua. Almost chalky looking."

Ben could barely restrain himself. "That's caused by the glaciers. They churn up the bedrock into silt, and that silt gets carried down with the meltwater into the lakes and streams. It's so fine and powdery that it sits suspended in the water, and the sunlight shining on it gives off the different colors."

Haley grinned at him. "I forgot I was riding with a 'naturalist.'"

He shrugged. "Just trying to earn a decent tip."

"Okay," she said playfully, pointing out over his left shoulder. "What kind of bird is that?"

He turned to look at the very large bird winging its way parallel to the truck, then blinked back at her. "Oh, come on. You have to know that one!"

She looked again, and her green eyes lit up. "It's a bald eagle!"

"Ding, ding, ding!" he praised facetiously. "They're like pigeons up here."

Haley watched the eagle until it was out of sight, twisting herself backward as far as her seatbelt would stretch. "That was so cool!" she enthused. "Are they really that common here?"

"You'll see for yourself if you stay awhile," he replied, gratified beyond words by the glow in her eyes. He always got a rush from watching the wonder on people's faces when they experienced a part of nature that was new to them. It was his full-time job, but he never got tired of it.

He waited anxiously for her next question, but to his dismay, it was not what he'd hoped for.

"You were going to tell me about my uncle," she reminded him, her face suddenly serious again. "If you don't mind talking about it, that is."

"I don't mind," he lied. He would, in fact, rather talk about almost anything else. The last thing he wanted to do was bring her down again. But she was Randy's next of kin. She had a right to know.

He cleared his throat. "I hadn't heard what the medical examiner found, but it doesn't surprise me. Your uncle wasn't in the best of health. He was overweight, he smoked, he drank, and he used to complain about how much it cost him to stay on his medication. I got the impression he didn't always take it, and I know he didn't stick to whatever diet he was supposed to. At least not while he was at Seward. All I ever saw him eat was grilled meat and potato chips."

Haley said nothing. Her face had gone blank again.

Ben fought a sigh and moved on. "A couple weeks before he died, he drove up to the cabin and asked me if I'd seen a black bear around. I told him no, I hadn't, but I wasn't home much, especially during the day. He said he'd seen the same bear twice, rummaging around the stuff behind his house. The night before he came over, he'd nearly run into it when he was coming out of the outhouse. He turned and ran back in and then got stuck there waiting for the bear to go away."

Haley's eyes widened. Still, she didn't comment.

"I told him that he shouldn't be surprised a bear was attracted to his yard, the way he left his trash lying around. It wasn't the first time I'd warned him that he was pretty much inviting a visitor. He cleaned it up a little after that, I think. But your uncle wasn't the most... energetic guy."

Ben paused a moment, remembering her uncle's colorful, yet tedious retelling of the outhouse incident. Randy was the kind of guy who would talk constantly to anyone, regardless of whether or not they were actually listening. He'd once invited Ben over to grill some steaks, and after Ben left the bonfire to use the outhouse, he'd come back to find Randy still talking to the place he'd been sitting.

"The bear he ran into wasn't acting aggressive," Ben continued. "I suspect it was just after the bad ground meat Randy admitted he'd thrown out in a trash bag earlier in the day. But seeing the animal so close to the house freaked the man out. He called Fish and Game to complain about it, and they told him the same thing I did — take care of your trash. That made him mad. He wanted them to come out and shoot the bear because it was bothering him."

Ben blew out a breath. He hardly relished the rest of the tale. It would be hard for Haley to hear, even if she and her uncle weren't close. But there was no way to sugarcoat it. "He was complaining to me about their response the morning of the day he died. I explained to him that Fish and Game would only remove a bear if it was a clear threat — if it was acting aggressively or if it kept trying to break into his buildings even after he'd stored his trash right. He listened to what I said, drove straight into town, and called them back to report an aggressive bear. He told them it had charged him."

Haley's eyebrows perked. "He made it up, then?"

Ben nodded. "I think it was probably later that same day that he had the heart attack. He might have seen the bear again and was running from it. He could have been running from a moose. He might have just been walking back from the outhouse in no hurry whatsoever. However it happened, I didn't find his body until the next evening, after his partner called me. By then it had obviously been..." he struggled for appropriate words. "Molested by some animal or other. I'm no pathologist, but nothing about it looked like a bear mauling to me. There was no blood. He was obviously dead before whatever it was got to him."

He paused to see how Haley was handling the gore factor. She looked okay. He pressed on.

"It looked to me like a combination of ravens and some small mammal. A coyote or a fox, maybe even a wolverine. I couldn't find any tracks because of the rain. But it wasn't a bear."

Haley's face remained stony. "Then why the danger sign?"

"Because I wasn't there when Fish and Game came out," he explained. "All they knew was that they had a suspicious death right on the heels of that same person reporting an aggressive bear — a case they hadn't investigated yet, most likely because they'd dealt with him before and didn't believe him. So they erred on the side of caution and posted signs all around the property. When I came back and found one on my own cabin door, I went down to talk to them and told them about my conversations with Randy. It was obvious to all of us then what had and hadn't happened. They took down the other signs pretty quick, but I guess they missed the one up by his house. I'm sorry you had to see it."

Haley sat quietly for a moment. "So..." she said finally. "There is no bear prowling around my uncle's place?"

Ben hedged. "Well, I do believe he saw *a* bear. It's always safe to assume that bears are out there, whether you see them or not. But an aggressive, predatory bear? No. I really don't think so." He stole a look at her, but her reaction was hard to read. "Does that make you feel any better?"

She looked at him as though it were an odd question. "I feel bad that my uncle died so young, and that I never got to know him. I'm glad he didn't die in a violent way. But if you think I'm *ever* going to wander around that creepy place without looking over my shoulder every second, you overestimate my mettle."

Ben chuckled softly. The woman was a trip. Eminently practical, refreshingly down to earth. She was probably not afraid of much.

"Where do you live, Haley?" he asked.

"Newport Beach, California."

He nodded with understanding. Tourists who lived in built-up areas were often irrationally phobic of wild animals.

"You can't enjoy everything Alaska has to offer if you're afraid of bears," he insisted. "Be 'bear aware,' as they say, and you'll be fine."

"I'll be fine because I'm not getting more than six feet from my car," she retorted.

The sign for their destination rose up on the right, and Ben slowed the truck.

"Are there mooses in Moose Pass?" Haley asked.

"No more or less than anywhere else around here, but yes, probably. Are you afraid of moose, too?"

"Of course not!" she said defensively. "They're herbivores."

Ben started to inform her that moose could also weigh up to 1600 pounds, stand over six feet tall at the shoulder, and get belligerent if annoyed, but he decided to keep his mouth shut. The fewer animals she was nervous about, the easier it would be to convince her to go hiking with him.

Hiking? Where had that come from?

"Chuck's place is right on Trail Lake," he explained as they drove through the tiny, picturesque town. "I won't be long, but you might as well get out and enjoy the view while we're here."

"I'll do that," she agreed happily.

Ben pulled up to the cluttered garage, and a stooped older man with wild white hair looked up from his workbench with a wave. Ben's task for the morning was to pick up an outboard motor that had been rebuilt by the semi-retired mechanic. Kenai Marine had its own mechanic in Seward, of course, but whenever an obscure replacement part was needed, it was Chuck who always came through.

Ben waved back and parked the truck. "Just head around the side of the house and you'll see the dock out front," he instructed Haley. "I'll come get you when the motor's loaded."

Haley said nothing. She merely bobbed her head in thanks, scooted out of the truck, and headed for the water. Ben couldn't resist watching her lithe movements as she strode away, her ponytail swishing around her confidently squared shoulders.

He walked on into the garage, where he listened with less patience than usual to Chuck's recounting of every detail of the rebuild, his last fishing trip, and the state of his lumbago. Although Ben knew he would miss seeing Haley's first reaction to the lake, he hoped to join her later and share her admiration for a while before they had to turn around. But by the time he managed to run through the necessary script with Chuck and get the motor securely stashed in the truck bed, it was already too late to tarry.

He hurried around the side of Chuck's ancient house. Haley could have swum to the other side of the lake and back by now, he thought ruefully. But then he grinned to himself. Come to think of it, that was something else he would like to see. He emerged around the corner to find her sitting on the dock, her feet swinging idly over the water. Her hands were behind her, and she hung her head back as if happily relaxed. He wished he had his camera handy. With the calm blue lake spread out before her, bordered with straight green trees and nestled in the shadows of the towering white-peaked mountains, she looked just like a postcard.

He walked toward her and was about to call out when she jerked suddenly, then cast a disparaging glance at the bag that lay on the dock beside her.

No, Ben pleaded silently. *Don't answer it.*

For a long moment, he thought she might not. But finally, with a look of pure torture on her face, she grabbed up the phone and put it to her ear. "Is this an emergency, Mom?"

Ben backed up again. Haley didn't realize he was there, and he didn't want to eavesdrop. But he couldn't retreat fast enough to avoid hearing more than he wanted to. "No!" Haley said heavily. "I will *not* call Tim and I will not tell him anything! And if you really want to save Micah's marriage, you will *stop* letting her complain to you all the time and encourage her to talk to her husband instead!"

He winced as whatever response Haley was hearing caused her body to contract into a knot. She pulled her feet up and wrapped her arms around her knees. "The baby *will* have a happy home," she said fiercely, even as her voice sounded suddenly less assured. "No matter what happens."

Ben moved out of earshot. He sighed to himself as he staked out a spot near the corner of the house where he could watch for her to hang up. Clearly, the sister she mentioned earlier was having problems. Why Haley was so obviously affected by them, despite repeated attempts to disengage, was harder to figure.

He did not have to wait long. Haley rose a few seconds later and stuffed her phone back into her bag. She saw him as soon as she turned and began to walk toward him. She smiled at him, but her eyes were too bright; a child could see that she was fighting tears.

"Captain Parker," she said crisply, avoiding looking directly into his face. "I've decided that I want to know everything there is to know about everything we'll be seeing on the drive back. Natural history, animals, plants, funny local anecdotes. A continuous, running commentary, preferably delivered with a few laugh-out-loud jokes. Know where I can hire a good naturalist?"

Ben's answering smile was guarded. She was obviously just looking for a distraction. She had no way of knowing, after meeting him less than twenty-four hours ago, that with the singular exception of "take me now" she had just said the most exciting words she could possibly say to him.

Chapter 8

Haley's first sight of Resurrection Bay nearly made her heart stop. She considered herself a connoisseur of beautiful views, forking over a significant portion of her salary to rent an upscale one-bedroom apartment from which she could look out over Balboa Island and Newport Bay to a sliver of the Pacific beyond. But the vistas she had seen this morning were beyond compare, and the feast of nonstop beauty that surrounded her on the drive to Moose Pass and back left her feeling surprisingly buoyant. Her mother's last, ridiculous outburst had almost precipitated the crying jag for which she was so overdue, but thankfully, Ben's performance as a naturalist had made her laugh out loud instead. She'd been expecting him to drop her off at the cabins and go on to Seward, but when it became clear that he was worried about getting their cargo back to the marina on time, she had agreed to ride along for the delivery as well. Spending a little more time with her amusing new neighbor was no hardship.

"Welcome to my workplace," Ben said proudly, sweeping a hand before the windshield as they reached the marina. Ocean vessels ranging from tiny fishing craft all the way up to a giant cruise ship sat moored on the edge of a glistening blue body of water. Gentle chop stirred up the bay's surface as seagulls swooped and dived before a backdrop of endless, snow-painted mountains.

"Mine has free bagels," she said tonelessly.

He chuckled. "Yeah, well, I get cookies sometimes. If there are any left after the passengers get done with them."

Haley turned toward him. "What sort of tours do you do, exactly?"

His eyes sparkled with pleasure, and she marveled at the sight. Never in her life had she met anyone who enjoyed his job so much. Certainly no one at her firm. The attorneys all liked the money, of course, and many got a charge out of confrontation and the gamesmanship involved. But in reflecting on the average, hour-by-hour tasks of a typical workday, none of her coworkers would express such glee. She sure as hell wouldn't.

"All kinds," he answered gaily. "Today I've got two short tours of just the bay. A mid-afternoon and an evening. But most days, I do the full-day runs down to Holgate Glacier. Occasionally I'll do a fishing charter, but my boss really loves those, so he does most of them himself. Me, I like handling the first-time tourists. People who've never seen a whale before. That's the greatest."

His face beamed, and Haley couldn't help but chuckle. "Well, I've seen whales before, plenty of times, but it still sounds like fun. I'll have to check it out."

"Our tours get booked up way in advance, I'm afraid," he warned. "But I can keep an eye out for a cancellation if you like."

"I like," Haley replied, smiling.

When they reached the tour company's office, Ben delivered his cargo quickly to the waiting mechanic, then returned to the truck. "I don't have to be back at the marina for another two hours," he said thoughtfully. "I can take you to your cabin now, or we can grab some lunch first. What's your pleasure?"

Haley's stomach growled. Her oatmeal- and flax-bar breakfast seemed like a very long time ago, and she was enjoying Ben's company immensely. "You have someplace particular in mind?"

Within minutes, she was seated at a window-side table with a view of the bay. "Is that another bald eagle?" she asked, staring at the top of a pole rising out of the water just beyond the docks.

He followed her eyes and nodded. "Yep! Told you they were everywhere. Everywhere there's fish, anyway."

"Well, hey, Ben!" effused a waitress who appeared with menus and ice water. She looked young, in her early twenties maybe, and as she flipped her blond hair casually over her shoulder she made her interest in the redheaded boat captain painfully obvious. "Decided to eat up top with the tourists today, huh?" She cast a guarded look at Haley. "What's the occasion? Is this another one of your sisters?"

Ben made no immediate response, so Haley shook her head.

"What have you got today, Alexa?" he asked in a voice that was perfectly friendly, even as he ignored both of her questions. "Is the sockeye fresh?"

Alexa threw out her chest. "Just came in this morning!" she said brightly. "What'll you have to drink?"

The waitress took their requests and departed, and Haley studied the menu. Fish did sound good. She had a choice of cod, halibut, or salmon. She wanted to try the salmon because it was an Alaskan thing, but she couldn't remember which species were taboo. Her hand reached automatically for her cell phone. She was used to texting all such questions to Micah, who had read every major pregnancy guide from cover to cover and could probably quote the mercury content of every fish on the menu from memory.

Haley pulled her hand back. No, she would not consult Micah. She wasn't going to look it up online, either, since she'd be vulnerable to interruption the second she turned her phone back on. There had to be a less stressful way.

"How long do salmon live?" she asked lightly, looking at Ben. For all she knew, he might be able to quote mercury levels from memory, too. But the last thing she wanted to do was explain why she was asking.

He shrugged. "Four or five years, usually."

"Do they get very big?"

"Depends on the species. The king — or Chinook — salmon can get to five feet. But the sockeye, like they serve here, are smaller. Maybe two and a half."

Haley considered. She knew she was supposed to avoid large, long-lived, carnivorous fish. But what was large and long-lived for a fish? "What do they eat?" she pressed.

"Plankton," he answered. "Little invertebrates. Some of the bigger salmon can eat smaller fish."

Haley caught a flicker of something strange in his eyes, and her heart skipped a beat. But she quickly calmed herself. He couldn't possibly suspect her motives. Besides, it would be easy enough to cover her tracks. "And how many species of salmon might one find in Alaska?" she asked seriously. "Be careful. I can verify all this later."

He grinned, and Haley put her concern to rest. They placed their orders (she went with the sockeye), and passed a pleasant few minutes discussing fish and fishing. As she listened with fascination to him expound on yet another subject about which she had no previous interest, it occurred to her how alert he must be to the cues of his audience. The second her attention even came close to flagging, he magically either stopped talking or switched to another topic. If only she could teach her co-workers that trick, she might be home for dinner once in a while.

"So, you have sisters?" she inquired during a rare pause in the conversation, remembering what the waitress had asked. "How many?"

"Four," he said heavily, feigning agony. "All older. I'm the only boy. And no, I am not 'more sensitive' because of their influence, only more traumatized. You're afraid of bears? Well, I'm afraid of dress-up clothes."

Haley laughed out loud. "They didn't!"

"On a regular basis," he said grimly. "With pictures. What about you? Any other siblings besides the sister you mentioned?"

Haley's mirth dampened. She would give anything to keep talking about dress-up clothes. "No," she answered. "It's just me and Micah. We're fraternal twins. And no, we don't look alike. We're nothing alike at all."

The change in tone from the beginning of her answer to the end was so pronounced that Haley could hear it herself. Her last words sounded like a funeral oration.

Ben heard it, too. As usual, his response was spot-on.

"So," he said merrily, clapping his large hands together over the table. "What do you plan to do with yourself the rest of the day?"

Haley smiled with relief. She was really, *really* liking this man. "Well, I hadn't thought about it," she admitted. "But I suppose I'll drive my car back to the marina and walk around a bit, enjoy the bay. I was going to check out the hotels, but now that I know our resident bear is only 10% likely to kill me, I may just stay at the cabin. They really are cozy little places, aren't they? It's a mystery to me how my uncle could build such nice rentals while living in such a dump."

Ben shook his head. "He didn't build them. He didn't build the house, either, or accumulate all that junk. He told me that whoever built the original house sold it "as is" to a speculator about four years ago. That owner built the cabins, but he never lived on the property and he went bankrupt before they could be rented. Your uncle picked up the property on a short sale, just before last summer. He rented to me and another guy who managed one of the hotels in town. He didn't mind the house being a wreck because he spent most of his time on his boat."

"Well, that explains that," Haley said. "But why isn't the cabin I'm staying in rented out this summer?"

Ben's eyes widened. "Oh," he said with sudden remorse. "Crap. I forgot about that. Your shower doesn't work."

Haley's high hopes took a nosedive. "It doesn't?"

He shook his head. "Pipe burst last winter. Randy capped it off underneath until he could get a plumber out, but as far as I know, he never got around to it."

"I see," Haley said miserably. She'd had visions of stockpiling some groceries and basic supplies and spending the rest of the day alternating between staring at the mountains and napping. But she needed a shower. Desperately. She hadn't had one since the day before yesterday. "Well, that's a problem."

She could always move to a hotel in Seward, of course, but the idea didn't excite her. For one thing, she really did like her cabin. It was cozy and quaintly rustic, but still airy and clean, and it came with a beautiful porch view and extremely pleasant company next door. A hotel room would come with fresh linens every day. But it would also come with cellular service. Probably even Wi-Fi.

She sighed.

"You're welcome to use my shower," Ben offered.

Haley raised an eyebrow.

He chuckled. "I wasn't planning on being in it at the time," he clarified. "Although I'd happily consider an invitation." He reached into a pocket, pulled out a key ring, and slipped off one of his keys. "Seriously," he continued, setting it down on the table in front of her. "Feel free. I won't be back until after nine tonight. It's not what you'd call spotless, but it's decent. Just drop the key in one of my boots on the porch when you're done."

Haley hesitated. Neighbors or not, it seemed weird to be using the man's shower. Then again, it was technically *her* shower, wasn't it? And he wouldn't even be there.

"All right," she said finally. "Thank you. I think I already have a key, though."

He shrugged. "Take it, just in case. I have an extra at the tour office."

"Sockeyes!" the waitress called cheerfully as she approached their table with two heaping plates on a tray. She set the food down in front of them and tossed her hair again. "So, Ben," she said pointedly. "Are you going to introduce me to your friend?"

Haley reached for her lemonade and took a sip. This was awkward.

Alexa cast an appraising look sideways at Haley. "Is she your girlfriend?"

"No," Ben said offhandedly, picking up his fork. "We're just shower buddies."

Haley spewed lemonade across the table.

"Ben Parker!" the waitress chastised, grabbing extra napkins off the next table and handing them to Haley, who was attempting to sop up the mess with her own. "You are *so* bad!" She whirled around with a huff and departed.

Ben dug into his salmon.

"You *are* bad," Haley agreed, willing the flame in her cheeks to subside.

He swallowed a forkful of fish and grinned.

"Blame my sisters," he replied.

Chapter 9

Haley awoke the next morning to an insistent rapping on the door of her cabin. "Haley!" Ben called cheerfully. "Wake up!"

Ordinarily, the sound of a chipper voice first thing in the morning would make her blindly grope for something to throw. But not today. Thanks to a hot shower, the quiet cabin, and a blissful lack of cellular service, she had gone to bed early and slept more soundly than she had in months. When her eyes opened to an already bright morning sky, she found herself instantly alert.

She hopped out of bed and glanced down at her entirely decent sleep pants but not so decent cami. "Just a second!" she called. She threw on a tee shirt, ran a brush through her hair, and stepped over to answer the door. If her eyes were still puffy, too bad. This wasn't the office. It was vacation.

"Sorry to wake you up," he said, not sounding the least bit apologetic. If her rumpled appearance disappointed him, he didn't show it. The result of his quick head-to-toe appraisal — which he made a polite but ineffective effort to disguise — was a smirk of approval. "But you said you wanted to do a tour, and I found out last night that we've had two cancellations for today's full-day. You up for some adventure?"

Haley smiled. She could hardly respond otherwise when his face glowed with such enthusiasm. His dimples were showing, his cheeks were rosy, and although she had thought his twinkling eyes were brown, she realized now that they were actually a shade of hazel. In the morning light, the wavy shocks of ginger hair that framed his face set off the green. *Damn, he's cute.*

She wondered briefly what history he might with the inquisitive Alexa, but she shook off the thought. What did it matter?

"I'm always up for adventure," she answered, somewhat insincerely. "What does a 'full-day' entail, exactly?"

His smile broadened. "About nine hours on the water. Be prepared to get wet — and cold. The wind can get pretty wicked out there, and the forecast is calling for rain. That's why we had the cancellations. But personally, I'm betting it'll hold off. Even if it doesn't, we'll still have a good time. Believe it or not, the whales don't mind getting wet."

"Sounds great!" she replied, surprising herself. Nine hours on a boat in the rain? What the hell was so appealing about that?

"Awesome!" He jogged back down the steps and off her porch, then turned around again. "Can you be ready in twenty minutes?"

Haley could. And she was. Fifteen minutes later she walked out of her cabin and looked for his truck, only to see a dilapidated black Jetta with duct tape on a cracked rear window parked in its place. She leaned against the hood and waited. "Nice wheels," she teased as he emerged.

"Beggars can't be choosers," he replied. "It's not mine. It's a loaner. The boss keeps a few junkers around for the seasonal staff. He knows we can't afford to rent anything for four months."

Haley stood up. "You don't live in the cabin year round?" She knew that the whale tours must only run in the summer, when the weather was decent enough. But she never thought about what an Alaskan boat captain might do over the winter.

He shook his head. "Just May to September. Your uncle would have rented to somebody else for the whole year if he could, but it's hard to find people who want to stay the winter." His voice turned distracted. He studied her with a frown.

"No good?" she guessed, looking down at the outfit she had cobbled together from her uninformed packing attempt. The ski parka was overkill, she knew, but her only other coat was the worthless jacket she'd gotten soaked in the day she arrived.

He shook his head. He looked like he was trying not to laugh.

She sighed and shrugged out of the parka. "Well, you said it would be cold! What am I supposed to wear?"

"Layers," he said finally, giving in to a smile. "First layer, something that wicks moisture. No cotton — if it gets wet, it stays wet. Then you layer some tees, long-sleeve shirts, and at least one heavy fleece or sweatshirt. Once you're warm enough, you top it all off with a lightweight jacket, something waterproof and windproof." He considered a moment. "I've got one of those I can loan you. You bring any pants besides jeans?"

She almost said no, then remembered her visions of a four-star hotel with a fitness center. "I've got some yoga pants."

He nodded approvingly. "Anything synthetic is better. If they do get wet, they'll dry out faster."

Haley looked over his nicely fitting cargo pants and slick white jacket emblazoned with the Kenai Marine logo. She had never thought of "boat captain" as being a particularly sexy occupation. She reassessed.

"I don't intend to go *in* the water, you know," she teased, heading back to her cabin to change.

"Hey!" he protested. "I haven't capsized in over three weeks now. And then it was the passengers' own fault. I told them they couldn't all lean off the same side at once."

Haley stopped, then shook her head and pressed on. He was only kidding.

At least she hoped he was.

"You pack any gloves?" he called after her. "Or a warm hat?"

"Sorry."

He looked at his watch. "If you hurry, you'll have time to buy some while I'm checking in the other passengers."

Haley hurried. When she emerged the second time, he seemed more satisfied. The dark purple jacket he loaned her was so large she felt like she'd been swallowed by a giant grape, but she wasn't inclined to complain. It smelled like a brisk ocean breeze, a familiar scent she had always found invigorating.

As the ancient Jetta sputtered toward Seward, she became steadily more excited. She couldn't remember the last time she had been out on a boat. Her childhood and youth had been full of such trips, of course, both on commercial craft and on friends' yachts. But since law school, her record of actually getting out on the ocean she paid so much to see was abysmal. She never seemed to have the time.

Haley's mind skipped back to her family. So far, she had done a pretty good job of not thinking about the guilt trip her mother had laid on her yesterday. But sometimes she couldn't help it.

I know you have a right to take a vacation, Michelle had whined. *But sometimes rights have to be sacrificed, don't you think?*

Micah's own email from yesterday had been terse and to the point — evidence that she was sulking. *I hope you're having a good time. I know it's important to you. Don't worry about me. Whatever happens with Tim is going to happen anyway. It's not your fault.*

Ironically, despite the reverse psychology so obviously at play, Haley knew that in her heart, Micah really did mean exactly what she said, even as she hoped Haley wouldn't believe her. It was complicated. But they understood each other.

Their mother was another story. Michelle genuinely believed that taking care of Micah was Haley's job. *I just don't know what your father would think. You know how much he counted on you, don't you?*

Haley's jaws clenched.

"You're not nervous, are you?" Ben asked suddenly. "I was kidding about the capsizing. The boat wasn't tipped over that far. They probably jumped off on purpose."

Haley looked at him blankly for a moment, then grinned. She had to quit doing that — letting her mind be hijacked, her spirits dragged down. It didn't help anything.

"I'm not nervous... not at all," she teased back, trying to sound nervous. "You *do* have a competent co-pilot, right?"

He narrowed his eyes at her with mock annoyance. "Co-pilot? Please. Remind me to get you a pocket guide to nautical terms. If it makes you feel any better, my *first mate* has had her captain's license longer than you or I have been alive. Carol is the boss's wife. She likes going out, but she prefers leaving the driving to me. More time for her to bird watch."

"I see," Haley responded, feeling her spirits lift again. She didn't know whether Ben was watching her facial expressions or if it was pure coincidence, but his ability to reverse her occasional backslides into misery was uncanny. "In that case, I'll—"

She broke off as her phone rang. She had turned it on when they left the cabin, assuming it would pick up a signal as they neared Seward and that she could send her mandatory emails from the road before turning it off again. She should have left it off until she was ready.

Ben made a sharp intake of breath as if he were about to say something. But he didn't. When she cast a glance toward him, his gaze was fixed on the road.

"Sorry," she explained, looking at the screen. "It's the partner I work with." Her body tensed as she touched the screen to answer. She had been ignoring all her business-related email. She should have known she couldn't get away with it forever. "Hi, Bob," she said brusquely.

She was greeted with a loud, exasperated exhale. "Well, it's about damn time, Haley."

"Cellular service is really spotty out here," she explained, even as she knew the effort was futile. "I'm staying at my uncle's place, tying up his affairs, and it's pretty remote."

"Well, I've got you now. So let's talk. How much are you going to be able to get done this week?"

Haley felt a physical pain in her middle. They had already had this discussion. "I am not going to do anything this week," she said firmly. "Everything is under control until Monday. It'll be fine."

Robert Hardin was not convinced. Haley held the phone off her ear while he barked at her for several minutes, freaking out about actions to be filed and rulings to be issued, repeating the same ground they had covered multiple times before she left Newport Beach.

"Bob," she interrupted finally, using her best negotiation voice. "We have 28 days to respond to discovery. I'm on top of it. The ruling isn't likely to come down this week, no matter what Harrison is telling you. And if it does, I can be on a plane in a matter of hours."

"Harrison told me this morning that—"

Heat flared in Haley's cheeks. Harrison was a second-year associate who got off on impressing the partners at his fellow associates' expense. No doubt he'd been fanning the flames of impending disaster ever since she'd left the office. Hell, he'd probably been dousing them with gasoline.

"Harrison needs to do his own damn work and stop obsessing about mine," Haley shot back. "Listen to me, Bob. You know me. You know what I can do. You know that if I thought the case would go to hell in seven days, I wouldn't be here. And I'm telling you, it's *under control.*"

Haley could feel Ben squirming in his seat again. She was sorry about that; she would prefer not to expose him to the vitriol of her everyday life. But she really had no choice.

As expected, Bob eventually backed off. She wouldn't have dared to push back so hard when she first came on board, but now, in her fourth year as an associate, her success spoke strongly enough that she could afford to be bold. Audacity in general was respected; God help the meek. After a few more civil, if not entirely friendly, exchanges, Bob begrudgingly acknowledged that Haley should in fact know what the hell she was doing and whether she could afford to take a few days off. The conversation then ended abruptly.

Haley put her phone down. Snow glistened off the peaks that towered before her, but she saw them as if they were on a TV screen. Her mind was back at Merriweather, Falstaff, and Tynes. Her senses were on full alert and her heart beat swiftly. Encased in her layers of clothing, she broke out into an uncomfortable sweat. Sad to say, Harrison could very well be right. She didn't know for sure that the ruling they were waiting on wouldn't be issued this week, nor was she fully on top of it. Half of the assurances she'd given Bob were total BS.

Maybe he had believed her, and maybe he hadn't. It was a game they played with each other — the same game they played with everyone else. Absolute truth had little to do with it.

She sat without speaking, running over in her mind everything she would have to do if the ruling proved unfavorable, realizing that if it did get issued while she was in Alaska, she would indeed have to fly back and respond immediately. The rest of the team could pitch in, but there were tasks Bob would insist she handle personally, and Harrison wasn't the only associate she didn't trust not to take advantage. There was a reason she hadn't taken off more than 72 consecutive hours in the last four years. Jump off a treadmill at top speed, and you're asking to break something.

"Do you like your job, Haley?" Ben asked quietly.

She startled in her seat. She looked back across the car at him and felt suddenly disoriented. So sharp was the contrast between the focused ravings of her mind and the sight of him — his tall frame wedged awkwardly in the driver seat of the too-small car, his ginger hair hanging loose about the collar of his jacket and bouncing in the breeze that blew through his cracked-open window — she almost felt dizzy. "What?" she said vaguely.

"I asked if you like your job," he repeated.

"Sure," she said automatically.

He did not appear convinced. "What do you like about it?"

Haley felt a flicker of annoyance. It seemed like everyone was questioning her, lately. "I'm good at it," she said defensively. "I make a lot of money."

He smiled at that, but he wasn't sincere. His real smile made his eyes twinkle; it lit up his whole face. His expression now was subdued. "What do you like to spend your money on?" he asked, his voice still friendly, despite the edge to her own.

Haley started to give an answer, but realized she didn't have one. Her family had always been well off, even before her father's unexpected death had left his wife and daughters with a hefty insurance settlement. Michelle was set for life and Haley and Micah's educations had been covered, leaving trust-fund money to spare. Since starting at the firm Haley had paid off her car and had few major expenses beyond her rent. Theoretically she was looking to buy a condo, but in truth she preferred renting because she liked to move around. She already had her eye on an apartment in the next building with an even better view.

What else *did* she spend her money on? She supposed the truth was "not much." Shopping for clothes and jewelry bored her. She had no time to travel anywhere. She had no boyfriend or pets to spoil. She rarely even went out in the evenings, preferring to curl up in the quiet of her apartment with a movie or a good book. She needed her introvert time, and solitude wasn't expensive.

"I have a great apartment with a view of the ocean. Other than that, I invest." The answer sounded stupid to her, even though it was the truth. It presumed she had a plan for spending her money later, which she did not. "I like the security," she added, improvising.

"Ah, I see," Ben replied.

Haley frowned. He wasn't lying, but he didn't mean it the way he said it, did he? What exactly was he getting at?

"What kind of whales have you seen before?"

She blinked. He was doing it again. Switching topics just in time. He *was* reading her, and he was good at it. Most men were not, but in her profession, the talent was common in both genders. She'd met many an attorney who could read faces like a card shark, spotting a bluff a mile away. It was a big part of what made them so effective. But what Ben was doing was different. He wasn't using the information against her. He was merely trying to keep the peace.

Haley looked away from him a moment, out into the trees. She had been so happy a few minutes ago. Worrying about her family problems was one thing, but the phone call from work had transported her so thoroughly that she had literally forgotten where she was. How could she let that happen? God knew she didn't *want* to be in the Irvine offices of Merriweather, Falstaff, and Tynes, flying on an adrenaline high. She wanted to be right here in Seward, Alaska, feeling the wind on her face.

She rolled down her window, leaned out, and drew in a soothing lungful of the crisp, cool air. Then she drew another. When she turned back to Ben, her smile was genuine. "I'm not sure what kind of whales," she answered. "Humpbacks, I guess? We see spouts from the shore all the time, and I've seen flukes from a distance, but I've never seen a whale up close from a boat. At least not that I can remember."

He grinned back at her, and as she watched the sparkle return to his eyes, she felt a surge of giddy pleasure. "You will today," he announced. "In fact, one will wave at you."

Haley laughed. "You can order that up, huh?"

He shrugged. "It's a gift."

Haley's eyes met his, and as she took in his kindness, his utter lack of guile, she felt a sudden, queer sensation in her chest that caused her pulse to race again.

Ben Parker was everything that she herself was not. Genuine. Uncomplicated. Serene. Down-to-earth. Joyful.

Content.

Hot pressure surged up behind her eyes. Her breathing turned ragged.

Oh, for God's sake, not again!

She swung her face quickly away from him and back out the window. What was wrong with her? Why did she feel like crying now? It made no sense!

Hormones, she told herself firmly. Pregnant women did crap like this. It wasn't her; there was nothing wrong. If she could just get hold of herself, the feeling would pass...

She stared out the window with determination. She forcefully stuffed Haley Olson, Attorney at Law, into the basement of her brain. Likewise with the daughter of Michelle and the twin of Micah. Today, she would just be plain old Haley.

Playmate of Ben the boat captain.

She laughed out loud.

"What's so funny?" Ben asked, seeming startled. They had reached the marina. He was parking.

He must think I'm nuts, she thought with chagrin. Crying one minute and laughing the next. Was there a better definition of hysteria?

It had to be hormones. But she couldn't explain. Her pregnancy was not a secret, guilty or otherwise, but without divulging the whole complicated, ethically divisive story behind it, the topic was impossible to bring up.

And today she was just plain Haley.

"Nothing's funny," she answered. "I'm just happy to be here." Her eyes held his a moment. "I'm sorry about... being so touchy. It's just that my work is very consuming. Sometimes it's hard to switch off that part of my brain."

"You want help?" he offered, almost too quickly.

Haley raised an eyebrow. "Such as?"

He reached forward and plucked her cell phone out of the cup holder into which she had dropped it. "Leave this in the car," he said beseechingly. "You won't be able to get a signal most of the day anyway."

Haley hesitated. She hadn't emailed Micah yet. And Bob had wanted her to take a look at one particular memo...

Ben's hazel eyes saddened, and Haley felt an annoying tug at her insides. The man was worse than a puppy.

"All right, all right!" she acquiesced.

Ben's face brightened immediately. He opened up the glove compartment and tossed her phone inside. Then he opened his door, stuck one foot out, and looked back at her with a grin.

"Let's go see the whales."

Chapter 10

The sky was overcast, and as the boat chugged out into the open bay, the wind that rushed past Haley's cheeks was frigid.

It was the most amazing feeling ever.

The second the boat had been unmoored from the dock and the rhythm of the ocean began to rock beneath her feet, Haley felt as if her soul had been unleashed. A warm, bubbly wave of happiness crept up from her toes and put an uncontrollable smile on her face.

She was *free*.

Free from what, she wasn't sure. She would think it was freedom from her phone, except that she had already spent the better part of her time in Alaska with no reception. Perhaps it was the physical separation of her body from its tether? Or maybe it was the sheer ecstasy of being surrounded — in every possible dimension including straight down — by sights and sounds that were uniformly peaceful, natural, and beautiful.

Whatever it was, it felt amazingly, wonderfully *good*.

"Bald eagle at three o'clock!" Carol called out merrily to the passengers gathered in the front of the boat. Haley watched as another of the giant birds soared high across the water. Binoculars rose and cameras clicked. Everyone aboard seemed to be in a jubilant mood.

Haley cast a glance through the boat's windshield into the bridge. Ben smiled and nodded back at her. The tour company for which he worked was a mom-and-pop shop specializing in small-group tours, a fact for which Haley quickly found herself grateful. The larger companies, whose passengers were just loading up as Ben's boat headed out, operated multi-level vessels carrying a hundred passengers or more. Kenai Marine's 43-foot-long craft was catering to fourteen.

Haley pulled down her newly purchased knit hat more snugly over her ears. Ben was right; she did need it. And her new water-resistant black gloves as well. Yet as cold as her cheeks were, she felt surprisingly snug inside her many layers... and the giant grape.

She put a hand subconsciously to her abdomen, as she had developed a habit of doing ever since her waistline began to swell. As much as she welcomed the separation of her person from everything else she'd been able to leave in the car, she did not begrudge the company of her unborn niece or nephew. None of her problems were the baby's fault.

"You liking this, Fred?" she murmured in a whisper, using the pet name Micah didn't know about and wouldn't appreciate. "I wish you could see it with me. Maybe later... when you're older."

Haley had been warned during the counseling stage of surrogacy that her feelings about the pregnancy could be confusing — that she might begin to fantasize that the baby was her own. But that hadn't happened. From the beginning she had thought of herself as only a babysitter for her unborn niece or nephew. She looked forward to a lifetime of Christmases, birthdays, and trips to the zoo with herself as Fred's indulgent auntie. But Haley could always go back to her own home at night.

Thank goodness.

"Everybody look over at around the two o'clock position," Ben's voice announced over the loudspeaker, "and you'll see your first marine mammals of the day. Sea otters!"

The passengers, including Haley, all flocked to the railing on their right. She grinned to herself as she thought of Ben's earlier jest. If the boat capsized every time this happened, Kenai Marine would not be in business very long. She looked out to see several brown furry creatures frolicking in the gentle chop of the bay. Two seemed to be playing with each other; one head would pop out of the water, followed by another head attached to the first otter's tail, the two turning over and over in tandem like a wheel. The passengers cooed and exclaimed with delight, and Haley wished that she'd brought a camera. A camera *not* attached to a phone.

Ben slowed down the boat as they drove around the otters, maintaining a steady distance from them that Haley presumed was a predetermined safe berth. She had no doubt that if it came to pleasing passengers versus protecting the wildlife, Ben would come down firmly on the side of the animals. She listened as he began a running commentary on sea otters that made his audience laugh out loud. If the whale business ever dried up, she thought fondly, the man could always go into stand-up comedy.

All too soon, the boat left the sea otters to their amusement and began cruising south down the bay. Ben continued his narration with stories of the abandoned army dock at North Beach, which he lauded as a fabulous hike, despite the fact that if you didn't time the tides right, you could easily get stuck there. Haley made a mental note not to get herself conned into that one, even as she smiled to think that with Ben along, she would doubtless have nothing to worry about.

They passed Caines Point, and the waters of the bay grew wider. Ben took a break from narrating and sped the boat up a bit, and Haley decided to explore the rest of the deck. The front section was by far the windiest, while the larger back section was calmer. The center of the boat was enclosed and heated, featuring comfortable seating, a tiny galley area, and an even tinier bathroom. The galley was stocked with supplies for coffee, tea, and cocoa as well as a plate of cookies, and Haley shamelessly helped herself to a cup of hot water and two vanilla creams.

"This, Fred my dear," she said out loud as she returned to the rail with her booty. "*This* is living."

She gazed out in awe at the ragged coastline, where towering peaks plunged steeply into the deep blue water while rock islands like castle spires jutted up from below. Seabirds soared overhead, swooping and diving for fish and calling to their comrades nesting in the rocky crags of the cliffs. Higher up on the steep slopes, tall evergreens clung, and Carol pointed out the nest of a bald eagle to her cadre of dedicated bird watchers.

All the while, the boat skipped nimbly across the waves, and Haley thrilled to the feel of the movement beneath her.

She was *free*.

The boat slowed down again, and Haley almost felt sorry. She glanced at her watch, then on impulse removed it from her wrist and dropped it into her pocket. She would not worry about time today. Today, she wouldn't worry about anything.

"Having fun?"

Haley jumped as Ben appeared at the railing by her side, leaning in just close enough to speak to her without yelling. Their arms and shoulders brushed, causing a tingle of heat beneath Haley's multiple layers of clothing.

Seriously? She thought with embarrassment, inching away from him slightly. What was she, thirteen?

"I am," she answered warmly. "I'm having a fabulous time. At least I was, until I realized no one was driving the boat."

He chuckled. "Carol's spelling me. She knows when a man needs a cookie break. You didn't eat all the vanilla creams, did you?"

She smiled guiltily. "Not *all* of them. Not yet anyway."

"Is that a whale?" an older man called excitedly.

"Whale?" Ben jolted upright and hurried off toward where the man stood, looking out over the open sea. Haley followed.

"Not a whale," Ben announced. "But you've spotted something else for us!" He dashed up to the bridge and exchanged some words with Carol, who immediately steered the boat in the animals' direction as the passengers gathered to watch. "They're Dall's porpoises," Ben shouted gaily to the clustering passengers. "They're black and white, and sometimes get mistaken for orcas, but they're smaller. Only about six feet long, on average. And very fast swimmers."

Haley watched with fascination as the animals came into view, perhaps a half dozen of them, leaping out of the water to display sleek black bodies with white-tipped fins and a broad band of white on their bellies and sides. She was disappointed when, before they reached the same comfortable viewing distance they'd had with the otters, Carol turned the boat to the side and sped up again. "Can't we get any closer?" Haley asked.

"No need," Ben replied, his eyes dancing mischievously. "They know we're here, now." He gave a tug on her sleeve. "Follow me."

As the other passengers moved to watch the porpoises from the side railing, Ben steered her toward the bow.

"They're coming this way!" a woman called joyfully. Cameras and binoculars flew up again as the animals indeed moved steadily closer, despite the ship's speed. For a long moment, the porpoises disappeared. Then, to Haley's delight, a striking black and white form leapt out of the water mere feet from where she stood.

The passengers moved quickly to the front of the boat, pointing and laughing as porpoise after porpoise zipped up through the boat's wake, then sped in front of the bow as if running a race. The animals first swam underneath the boat, darting from side to side, then they would speed ahead of it, leaping out of the water and dropping back, only to catch up and repeat the game all over again.

Haley laughed out loud with the rest of them. She had seen dolphins jumping along beside boats before, but she had forgotten until now just how much she had always enjoyed watching them. "They're bow riding," Ben called from his position farther back, where he had moved when the other passengers came forward. "Nobody knows exactly why they do it, but they sure seem like they're having fun!"

Haley agreed. The porpoises had, after all, come swimming after the moving boat of their own free will. And it did look like fun.

Tremendous fun.

Oh, to be a porpoise...

The animals kept up the game for nearly five minutes before peeling off to less energetic pursuits. As the passengers drifted away from the bow, Ben appeared at Haley's side again. "Did you like that?" he asked, his hazel eyes twinkling at her. His arm brushed hers again, making her acutely aware of his broad shoulders and solid biceps.

"It was amazing!" she replied happily, realizing from the answering glow on his face how much her enjoyment meant to him.

Kiss me.

Haley took a reflexive step back. Where had that come from? Had she been thinking the words herself... or reading them in his eyes?

It felt like both.

"I'm glad," he said, straightening. Was it her imagination, or was his tone a little stiffer, suddenly? "Gotta get back to the bridge. Enjoy!"

In a blink, he was gone again.

Haley gave her head a shake. *Hormones.* Libido was supposed to pick up in the second trimester, wasn't it? Never mind that she welcomed it no more than would a nun. Her body was out on temporary loan, and even if it wasn't, her luck in the romance department was abysmal. She hadn't managed even a semi-serious relationship since college, back in the wild and carefree days before every flippin' man she encountered was another attorney.

When I grow up, Micah had announced from their father's knee, *I'm going to marry a lawyer just like you, Daddy!*

And what about you, Haley, babe? He had teased, bouncing her on the opposite knee at the same time.

I'm going to BE a lawyer just like you! Haley had proclaimed. *And... I'm going to marry one, too!*

She closed her eyes at the memory, its bitter-sweetness reviving the familiar ache in her middle. "Sorry, Dad," she whispered to herself. "We're good on the first part, but the second ain't happening."

Fighting a shudder, she opened her eyes again. Why any two people in the same profession would marry each other was beyond her. She might as well go to bed with a file box of case law.

Ben's voice came over the loudspeaker. "Who knows what's hanging out on the island at ten o'clock?"

"A turkey!" yelled a grade-school aged boy, his voice ringing with mischief.

Ben made a sound like a buzzer. "Sorry! Try again."

"Sea lions!" shouted his excited younger brother.

Ben imitated the ding of a bell. "A hundred points and an extra bag of chips to the man in the red jacket!"

The younger brother punched his older sibling playfully on the arm, and the two laughed as they clambered forward to nab prime spots along the railing. Ben drove the boat closer and everyone gathered to watch the small colony of Steller sea lions hauled out on a rocky shelf of the small island.

Haley smiled as she watched the giant bulls raise their heads and bawl at the much smaller females around them, many of whom barked right back. Sea lions were nothing new to her; their California cousins were viewed as little better than rats in Newport Harbor, where they hauled out on boats in the marina and often caused considerable damage. But watching these creatures felt different. The animals she saw at home were trying to survive in human territory; but to these creatures, she was the interloper. In fact, from where she stood, no other signs of human existence were even visible. These animals were wholly wild — part of a vast, non-human wilderness she felt lucky to be granted even a glimpse of.

Ben continued a lively narration about sea lion biology until, all too soon, he seemed to judge that the people's presence had affected the animals enough, and the boat moved on. It was not long, however, before they came upon another "hauling out place," this one occupied by a very contented looking group of harbor seals. Haley drank in the sight of the cute, speckled gray animals with delight. Ben launched into an amusing description of seal life, and once again he had everyone on board chuckling, until he began to talk about the effects of a devastating oil spill twenty-five years before.

Haley suffered a sudden sick feeling. *The Exxon Valdez.* She knew more about it than she cared to. One could hardly go into environmental law without at least a passing familiarity. Yet she had conveniently forgotten that *this* part of Alaska, this beautiful bay and these islands and cliffs with all their engaging wildlife, had once been blackened and deadly.

As Ben sobered up the crowd with a description of the devastation, Haley's sick feeling turned into a gnawing pain. He obviously cared deeply about threats to the environment. Thank God she hadn't told him any more about her job. Nothing would wipe that gorgeous smile off his face faster than finding out that in the distinguished environmental division of Merriweather, Falstaff, and Tynes, attorney

Haley Olson represented the polluters.

The boat sped away from the seals and headed northwest up into Aialik Bay, where Ben announced that they would stop for lunch near a glacier. Haley forcefully pushed down her grim thoughts, taking in deep breaths of the brisk ocean air and bathing her eyes in the unending beauty of her surroundings. Another group of Dall's porpoises showed up to bow ride, and Carol and her group of bird watchers went practically giddy over huge flocks of puffins. The two boys kept watch along the beaches for wandering bears, and the rest of the passengers mingled and socialized as they cycled in and out of the cabin area to stay warm.

Haley herself spent every second out on deck. Ben hadn't left the wheel for hours now, and she chastised herself for feeling abandoned. The man was *working*, after all. He wasn't intentionally avoiding her.

At least she hoped he wasn't. He *had* left her rather abruptly after... After what? Nothing had happened. It was all in her hormonally challenged mind.

The passengers' stomachs were grumbling — and the cookies were long gone — by the time the boat pulled off into the narrower waters of the Holgate Arm. Rocky cliffs rose up steeply to either side, and Haley felt a spooky sense of unease as the water gradually turned grayer and colder and floaters of ice began drifting down the current to meet them. As they drew nearer to the giant wall of frozen blue water that formed a dead end ahead of them, Ben slowed down the boat to weave around large chunks of ice sticking up above the surface. The water became increasingly clogged with a lacy soup of floaters, and Haley could hear and feel large pieces of ice scraping along the hull of the boat beneath her.

She moved up the side railing toward the bridge, where Ben sat on the other side of an open window. "By any chance have you seen the movie *Titanic?*" she inquired nervously.

Ben's gaze stayed fixed on the water, but his mouth twisted into a grin. "Don't worry," he replied. "I got this."

Haley returned to the back of the boat, not daring to distract him any further. Just when she had decided to ask for a passenger vote affirming that they were *close enough now, thank you very much,* Ben steered the boat sideways to the glacier and turned off the engine. As the rumble of the boat's motor stopped, a new sound reached everyone's ears, and all talking ceased.

Haley held her breath in awe. All around them the floating ice popped and crackled in the water like a very loud bowl of Rice Krispies. A few seconds later, the massive wall of frozen blue water that cascaded down the mountains and into the ocean before them began to make noise of its own.

"Is that thunder?" asked one of the boys.

Ben had materialized on deck. "No, it's coming from the glacier. Watch."

Haley's muscles tensed as the cracking, rumbling sound continued, seeming to vibrate the air around her, almost like an earthquake.

"There!" Ben pointed out. "It's calving!"

The passengers watched silently as a huge section of ice suddenly stirred itself into motion, dropping into freefall along the icy highway of the wall behind it, collecting an avalanche of smaller streams of ice along its path and crashing finally, in a cloud of white, onto the horizontal floes of ice below and into the darker waters beyond.

For several seconds, no one said anything.

"*That* was totally cool," the older boy announced solemnly.

"Lunchtime!" Carol sang out, emerging from the galley with a basket of wraps. "Who ordered the vegetarian?"

Haley remained at the railing, staring out at the gigantic wall of ice. Another low rumble met her ears, and she strained to see another section of ice make its escape toward the sea. But this time, only a thin trickle of white poured down from the glacier's midsection like a waterfall.

She felt suddenly warmer. Ben was standing beside her again. He was holding two sandwiches and two bags of chips.

She looked up at him with a smile. "This is fantastic," she answered before he could ask. "Thanks for telling me about the cancellation."

"My pleasure," he answered, handing her her portion of the food and settling himself against the railing. "The drinks are in the cooler, there."

Most of the passengers went into the warmer cabin to eat, but several, including Ben and Carol, ate their sandwiches at the railing, enjoying the gentle motion of the boat as it drifted slowly away from the glacier along the current created by the melting ice.

Haley had no further chance to speak privately with Ben, as he was soon surrounded by other passengers.

"So," the older man asked. "Did you grow up in Alaska?"

"No," Ben answered, popping open a cola. "Seattle. I went to the University of Washington."

"How long have you lived up here?" a younger woman asked.

Haley smiled at the obvious admiration in which the passengers held their handsome and amusing captain. She made a mental note to see what kind of reviews the tours got online, and if he was personally mentioned in any of them.

"I'm only up here from May to September," Ben answered. "The rest of the year I do tours in Maui."

Haley nearly spit out a mouthful of bottled water. *Hawaii?* What the hell?

Ben shot her a quick, sideways glance, then returned his attention to the other woman. "I follow the humpbacks. The Alaskan coast is their summer playground, but they prefer warmer waters for mating and calving. Peak season in Hawaii is February and March. I do tours there in the Au'au Channel between Lana'i, Maui, and Molokai. It's one of the best whale-watching spots in the world because the water is warm, shallow, and protected — almost like a big bathtub. And the humpbacks don't have to worry about predators so much either, because the orcas prefer colder water..."

The listening passengers remained transfixed, asking so many questions that Ben barely got a chance to eat. Haley finished her sandwich in silence, studying him with ever-increasing fascination. Summers in Alaska and winters in Hawaii? Who did that? Did he even have a permanent residence? Did he own any more belongings than what was stuffed in the tiny cabin? Did he have a significant other in Hawaii? If so, how did she handle such long separations?

The perks of such a lifestyle fascinated her, even as she marveled at the difficulties. It was like living permanently on vacation. But he couldn't possibly make any real money. He must be living from hand to mouth, with no long-term security whatsoever. How could he stand that?

And wouldn't he have mentioned it if he had a girlfriend in Hawaii?

The boat drifted idly near the glacier for some time while the passengers enjoyed their sandwiches and chatted quietly, alert for any signs of another calving. Twice Ben returned to the bridge and drove the boat back up closer to the glacier, then allowed it to drift again. They hadn't passed another boat in some time, making them feel as if they were all alone on the planet. Except, of course, for the half-dozen harbor seals that lounged on the ice flats near the rocky shore and the myriad seagulls and puffins that splashed in the frigid water and bummed rides on the floating chunks.

As Ben entertained the crowd, Haley kept mostly to herself, soaking up as much of the atmosphere as she felt her brain could hold. Why had it taken so long for her to manage a week away? She needed days like this. She needed them more than she had realized.

She had the sensation of being watched and turned to see Ben looking at her. There was a question in his eyes, but she couldn't read it clearly. Before she had a chance to try, another passenger claimed his attention.

If he only knew.

Haley allowed herself a sigh. It wasn't like she had headed off to law school saying, "I want to help businesses that are polluting the planet clean up their act as inexpensively as possible!" She had never had any such intention. In fact, when she had written the Law Review article that ultimately sealed her fate, she had yet to decide on an area of specialization. But the idea of citizen's groups taking on major corporations interested her, and her creative take on patterns in cancer-cluster case law had caught the eye of Robert Hardin, one of the top environmental attorneys on the West Coast. The fact that her article was less-than-subtly sympathetic to the aggrieved little people seemed not to register with Bob or with anyone else. And when she was invited to work with him at one of the most prestigious firms in the region, saying "no" was not an option. She was offered the highest starting salary of anyone in her law school class.

"Are you worried?" Ben asked.

Haley didn't jump this time. She was getting used to his surprise appearances. "Worried about what?" she asked, keeping her tone light. He might be skilled at interpreting facial expressions, but he wasn't a mind reader.

"That we won't see any whales, of course!" he replied.

Haley grinned. "You know, we've seen so many other amazing things today, I pretty much forgot about the whales."

He drew back with feigned horror. "*Forget* about the whales? That's blasphemy. Never. We're going to find one right now." He straightened and adjusted his cap.

"Do you know where they are?" she asked.

He smirked. "I have my ways."

"Like talking on the radio to the other boat captains?"

He pretended a scowl. "A magician never reveals his secrets."

He whirled away toward the bridge, and Haley grinned after his departing form. Her drive to Moose Pass with Ben had certainly been entertaining. But out here, watching him in his element, not only delighting the passengers with his witty banter but skillfully piloting the boat through potentially treacherous waters, he was beyond charming. He was...

Nope! Not gonna think about that!

Haley's teeth gritted. Blasted hormones. How many months would she feel like this?

Let her get back to work at the firm. That would stop it.

She pictured Ben with his hair cut short wearing a stuffy-looking suit with a briefcase under his arm.

Her stomach soured.

Perfect.

Chapter 11

Ben cast a watchful eye out over the horizon. It had started to sprinkle a little, but the heavier rain that was predicted was holding off, just as he'd hoped. He had no desire to bring this group back early.

Haley was standing out along the bow again, braving the cold wind to enjoy the forward view. She looked adorably dorky. Her hastily purchased knit cap kept riding up to give her a cone head, while his jacket hung down to her thighs. Her unfettered hair flung out beneath the cap in a mass of tangles and her cheeks were red with cold.

Damn, she's beautiful.

All morning he'd been imagining what she would look like wearing various other items from his closet. All day he'd been struggling to cut it the hell out.

No women in Alaska.

He repeated the silent mantra for the forty-eighth time. He'd been doing pretty well this year. He'd kept himself busy, minimized his time at the local bar scene. There were always girls like Alexa, who seemed to cross his path more frequently than random chance would predict, no matter how scarce he made himself. But women like her no longer tempted him. At least, not much. All things considered, they were more trouble than they were worth, and after this last, disastrous year, he was officially done with trouble.

Yeah. How's that working out for you?

He growled under his breath and steered the boat toward Chat Island. His buddy Rod had just reported that a boatload of happy passengers was watching a humpback put on a show southwest of there. The larger boat should be moving on just about the time Ben's arrived.

Rod was married. He lived in Anchorage with a pretty wife and two cute kids. He spent his winters sitting in front of a computer working for an insurance agent.

No thanks.

Ben loved his job. He loved his lifestyle. It required certain sacrifices. But it was all good.

Liar.

One of the women pointed something out to Haley. Ben craned to see what had caught their attention and saw more porpoises in the distance. *Sorry ladies, no time.* They had to keep on track to catch up with the whale. This particular male was a favorite with the captains. He was bold, breached often, and almost seemed to enjoy having an audience.

Ben watched Haley's face as she grinned with delight at the frolicking porpoises. She was loving this, and he was loving that she was loving it. God knew she needed it. He'd never seen anyone carry such a weight on her shoulders without seeming to realize it was there. On the surface Haley seemed so strong, so self-sufficient. But there was more going on with her. Something heavy was dragging her down. He saw flashes of it in her eyes at the oddest moments.

What was it?

No women in Alaska.

He frowned. He was perfectly capable of taking an interest in the welfare of a female without the relationship turning sexual. Haley would only be in town for a week, for God's sake.

No problem.

"Excuse me," a man in his mid-twenties said politely, standing just outside the bridge. "I'm Steve. I called earlier and talked to Sam about... the plan?"

Ben smiled. His boss had explained to him and Carol yesterday that a passenger on today's cruise was planning a surprise marriage proposal. The couple had taken a similar tour on their first date exactly one year ago, and the future groom wanted the moment to be perfect. He had also asked for special permission to bring a bottle of champagne, which the boss had granted, as long as the event occurred near the end of the tour and any invitation to toast the couple would be restricted to adult passengers.

"Yep!" Ben answered.

"Well, I was just wondering when would be a good time," the man asked. "Maybe you could give me a cue of some sort?"

Ben took another look at the sky. "Anytime we're not actively watching wildlife is fine with me," he answered. "But the weather could be a problem. I'd say any stretch we get without rain, you should be ready to take advantage. You might not get many opportunities."

"Gotcha," Steve replied, his eyes twinkling with anticipation despite the grim forecast. "Thanks!"

Ben gave an answering nod, and the man returned to his companion on the stern. Ben watched the couple a moment, particularly the woman. They were obviously in love. He'd seen that same look on the faces of his sisters when they had gotten engaged. All four were now happily married, but each had suffered disastrous relationships beforehand, about which he knew far more than he wanted to. Every time some guy somewhere did one of them wrong, the compulsion to properly train their baby brother — or more accurately, demand vicarious retribution from the nearest male of the species — had been irresistible.

Men are scum, Benjamin! Don't you ever treat a girl like this, you hear me?

Never mind that he was only fifteen. Or twelve. Or nine.

If you ever do this to somebody, so help me, I'll...

Sheesh. He was nearly twenty-eight years old now, and they were still hassling him.

You can't possibly expect that any intelligent woman is going to give up her life and career just to follow you around! His oldest sister, Maggie, had lectured not three months ago. *You're not being realistic. The only women who'd do that are brainless leeches looking to suck the life out of you.*

Thanks for the ego boost, Mags.

She had looked contrite then. *Oh, Ben! I'm not saying you're not worth a sacrifice. I'm just saying it's not fair of you to expect it. Not unless you're willing to give up just as much, yourself.*

Rod's boat appeared over the horizon, and Ben welcomed the interruption. He could do without that particular memory anytime, but at the moment, it was especially irritating. Every hour that passed in Haley's presence had only made the chemistry between them crackle louder, and the futility of the situation was maddening. Had she not looked horrified when he mentioned his yearly migration? Of course she had. They all did. And she was leaving in a matter of days, regardless. What could he possibly offer a woman with a lucrative full-time job in California besides a meaningless fling?

He groaned beneath his breath. Thanks to his damned brainwashing sisters, he couldn't even enjoy that.

He was watching Haley again, seemingly unable to do otherwise, when she jerked upright from the railing, turned to get his attention, then pointed out over the water.

A spout. He nodded at her with a smile. She had been the first one of the passengers to see it. She was a natural.

Rod's much larger boat slowly peeled off to the north while Ben continued forward. The passengers gathered near the bow, pointing and chatting with enthusiasm as plumes of water exploded upwards in the distance. Ben judged the whale's speed and direction, moved in a safe distance, then put the engine in neutral and waited for the animal to resurface.

The friendly whale did not disappoint. A spout fired barely 100 yards off the rail this time, and the massive animal surfaced, then lobtailed, raising its giant fluke completely out of the water and then slapping it down hard on the surface. The passengers cried out with delight — as they always did — and then together they watched and waited with bated breath for the animal to come back up. Ben performed his usual routine over the loudspeaker, his mind half on what he was saying and half on Haley's reaction. She was entranced.

"There's no earthly way of knowing, which direction he is going..." Ben sang in a spooky voice, reminiscent of the boat scene in *Willy Wonka and the Chocolate Factory*. A lot of younger people didn't get the reference, but it amused him anyway. Particularly when the whale cooperated by moving even closer to the boat.

Bingo!

Just forty yards away now, the magnificent animal burst out of the water in a spectacular breach, flashing over half its black-and-white streaked mountain of a body to the speechless onlookers before arching back and crashing into the water with a tremendous splash.

The passengers went nuts. Haley in particular looked as happy as he had ever seen her.

Ben smiled to himself. *I love this job.*

He continued his spiel while the bull played its part to perfection, including the particular move Ben was hoping for. Rolling on its back, the whale stuck first one pectoral fin out of the water, then the other, wiggling each around before slapping it gently against the surface.

"See there, Haley," Ben said into the loudspeaker. "I told you a whale would wave at you."

His heart skipped a beat as she turned, her ridiculous-looking hat creeping up over her ears again, and flashed him a smile that could melt glaciers.

Thank you.

He smiled and nodded back.

No problem.

Actually, it was a problem. She was a problem. As gratifying as it was to watch her face light up with such childlike glee, the sight only compounded his frustration. Everyone enjoyed seeing whales. But no woman he'd ever cared about had shown anywhere near the depth of awe that he still felt, every time. The only woman who'd even come close to understanding his passion was Bella, another naturalist he worked with in Maui. Bella loved the whales, the birds, the sea... all of it. Unfortunately, Bella also loved alcohol and made one belligerent drunk.

Why, oh why, did such an attractive, intelligent, and whale-loving woman have to show up now, here, when he couldn't do a damn thing about it?

No women in Alaska. He'd sworn it to himself, and he'd meant it. God knew it was hard enough finding women in Hawaii who would tolerate his absence four months a year. There was no way in hell any woman in Alaska would go for eight.

And Haley lived in California.

Her hat had popped up completely over her ears now. She had cute ears. He could imagine—

Orcas! The word leapt out of the chatter on his radio to penetrate his wayward brain. One of the resident pods had just been spotted off Ragged Island. Ben waited until the humpback had moved away from the boat, then he put the engine back in gear and set course for the orcas. Haley was lucky. They saw the other sea mammals almost every day, but orcas were more elusive, showing themselves in the area only once a week or so.

"The rain's stopped," Steve whispered through the cabin window a few moments later. "I'm going for it."

Ben grinned at him. "Godspeed, man."

He wasn't able to watch the actual proposal, as it occurred in the stern of the ship directly behind him. Carol the incurable romantic was busy filming the whole thing on Steve's phone and clearly had no intention of spelling Ben for the event. But he could tell from the assorted "oohs," "aws" and cheers of the other passengers that the woman in question had said yes.

Lucky guy, Ben thought to himself, turning to look briefly at the future bride and noting the happy tears on her face. Steve had surprised her. Good for him.

"That was *so* sweet!" Carol effused a moment later, popping into the seat beside him. "Damn shame we can't join in on the toast. Where're we headed?"

"Orcas off Ragged Island."

"Perfect!" Carol declared. "Now how about you let me take over a minute while you charm the hellions? Mom and Dad haven't been worth much up to now, and something tells me they aren't going to get any better after a glass of champagne."

Ben looked over his shoulder at the two boys. Ignored by their parents, they were roughhousing near the side rail. As he watched, one of them climbed up on the first level of railing.

"Holy—" he jumped up.

"Uh huh," Carol agreed matter-of-factly, slipping behind the wheel in his place. "Off you go, Uncle Ben."

Ben hastened outside. Carol wasn't fond of children. If she had her way, the minimum age on the tours would be twenty-three. It was theoretically the first mate's job to keep an eye out for child safety problems, but Ben had noticed that any time kids were on the passenger list, Carol either avoided that tour or made sure he was assigned to it with her.

"Hey there, Horace! Bubba!" he called out, just as the younger of the two boys progressed to the second rung on the railing. "Have you taken the quiz yet?"

The older boy frowned at him. "What quiz? My name's not Horace!"

"Oh, you're Bubba? Then this must be Horace," Ben corrected.

"I'm not Horace!" the younger brother insisted, stepping down.

"Okay, Ernest," Ben agreed, dropping to a squat beside them. "Here's your first question. Let's say a little five-year-old girl accidentally falls over the side of the boat and into the ocean. How do you save her?"

The boys straightened importantly and looked at each other. "Jump in after her?" the older one proposed uncertainly.

Ben smiled sadly. The boys really had no idea how dangerous the cold waters of the bay could be. He cast a look at their parents, who were gathered in the stern with all the other passengers, accepting small paper cups full of celebratory champagne. Haley took her cup as he watched, and their eyes met briefly. There was a strange look in hers. Sadness? Regret? He found it odd, in the middle of a toast, but he had no time to dwell on it.

"Well, actually," he explained to the boys. "The first thing that would happen is that the girl would be so horribly cold, she would have trouble catching her breath..."

A few minutes later, the greatly subdued boys were sitting on the bench seats in the bow, assisting their captain in a lookout for the characteristic dorsal fins of orcas. Ben glanced back toward the stern to see a very relaxed and happy passenger group chatting sociably. Haley was smiling and laughing with the rest now, leaning back against the railing with no trace of her earlier angst. But as he watched, she surreptitiously moved the hand that held her cup behind her back and dumped the liquid overboard. Then she pretended to sip.

Ben's forehead wrinkled with puzzlement. Perhaps she wasn't a drinker, but felt it would be awkward to refuse under the circumstances. Or maybe it was lousy champagne.

The boys in front of him jumped up excitedly and began banging on the windshield and pointing. Well ahead in the distance, near another small boat, a dark, angled fin moved swiftly above the water.

Orcas.

He grinned broadly, then reached over to turn on the loudspeaker. This was indeed a banner day. The passengers had seen all the regular marine mammals and birds, plus a nice display of glacier calving, and it had only rained a little. He made his announcement, then looked over his shoulder to see Haley, along with the others, flocking towards the bow with excited smiles.

The wind whipped his too-large jacket around her, and she crossed her arms to hold it steady, inadvertently hiking it up.

Her yoga pants fit nicely.

No women in Alaska!

Haley collapsed on the bed in her cabin, her head still spinning from such a wonderful, fabulous, too-good-to-be-true day. Dear God, how she had needed it. The wind, the water, the animals... the images swirled in her brain in a delicious, numbing wave that pushed the cares of Newport Beach, California firmly away. She had gotten back into her phone just long enough to fire off two quick, happy-sounding emails to her mother and Micah, and then she'd shut it off again. She hadn't read a thing.

And the day wasn't even over yet. Ben had offered to throw a couple burgers on his grill, and she had readily accepted. How could she not? He was an amazing guy, he was cute as hell, and he made her laugh. It was just a couple of burgers.

Right?

A tentacle of anxiety crept into Haley's otherwise perfect mood. Was he hoping for more?

She frowned. She had never intended to flirt with him, but if she were honest with herself, she knew that she had not been discouraging him, either. So far they had only been friendly, and nothing had crossed the line. They hadn't even engaged in the typical game of innocent-sounding questions designed to scope out significant others. She hadn't asked him if he had a girlfriend elsewhere because, being unavailable herself, she didn't figure it was her business to know. Perhaps he was doing the same?

She pictured Steve and Gina on the boat, their faces glowing as the future groom slipped the engagement ring onto his bride's finger. Seeing that kind of love in the midst of such an amazing day... it was almost too much.

Haley's mind drifted to an image of Ben at the bridge, the ginger curls on his neck lifting in the breeze that whipped through the cabin windows. *See there, Haley? I told you a whale would wave at you.* Her heart warmed anew at the sweetness of the gesture.

Dammit. Who was she kidding?

Of course they were attracted to each other. Hot flames had practically been leaping between them all day. In a perfect world, she would have jumped the man's bones the second they reached the privacy of his car. But unfortunately they lived in the real world, where her home was a thousand miles away from either of his homes, and where she was leaving in a matter of days never to see him again. Besides which, oh yeah, she was *pregnant.*

Haley groaned into her pillow. Ben had been acting like a perfect gentleman, but that only meant he was a gentleman. It didn't mean he wasn't harboring hopes. And she had no business encouraging them, no matter how much she enjoyed his company and no matter how much she could use the distraction he provided. It wasn't fair to him.

Particularly when, if he knew what she did for a living, he would probably never speak to her again.

She pulled herself up from the mattress and wondered if she had time for a shower, since her skin was sticky with salt spray and her hair was a disaster. Then she remembered she didn't have a shower.

Well, this is awkward.

It was one thing to slip into Ben's empty house when she was just getting to know him — it would be quite another for her to march around his cabin in a towel after a day like today. So what was she going to do?

A knock sounded on her door. She got up and swung it open.

"Hey, shower buddy," Ben said wickedly, his hazel eyes dancing.

His hair was wet and he was wearing jeans and a hoodie; he had obviously just finished taking a shower himself.

Haley growled at him playfully. "I really wish you would stop saying that."

He laughed. "Just wanted to let you know the facilities are available. I'm going out to fire up the grill, so the cabin's all yours."

Haley hesitated. He looked even better in the soft hoodie and jeans than he'd looked in his captain's outfit. She wondered what it would feel like to bury her face in the curve of his shoulder.

"I'll stay outside, I promise," he insisted, misreading her hesitation.

"Okay," she said impulsively. "I'll take you up on that. Thanks." To heck with it, she snapped at herself as she closed the door behind him. She really did need that shower.

An hour later, as they sat on her porch admiring the view and finishing off the last of their chargrilled burgers, Haley couldn't help but feel as if the day had indeed been perfect. They had hardly talked at all over dinner, but had been enjoying the evening sun — which was nowhere close to setting — in comfortable, companionable silence.

"You look better, Haley," he said finally, watching her as she drank in, once again, the sweeping vista of the snow-covered mountains.

"I feel better," she answered, understanding exactly what he meant. "Thank you."

He looked surprised. "I didn't do anything. It's Alaska you should be thanking. It's a great place to gain perspective, isn't it?"

She nodded. She was sitting in her Adirondack chair; he was sitting in a similar one he'd dragged over from his own porch. The food was gone. Any second now, he would get up to leave.

Then what would happen?

If they were friends, she would give him a grateful hug, probably a kiss on the cheek. He'd been wonderful to her today, and yesterday too, for that matter. She would express her affection, and it would be heartfelt. A return hug would feel fabulous.

But they weren't friends, were they? The boundaries weren't clear. They were still wandering blindly in "maybe" land. And as long as their situation remained ambiguous, he would have expectations and she would feel guilty for letting him.

But how could she say anything? He had quite pointedly *not* made a move. Perhaps he never would.

She wrested her gaze from the landscape and stole a look at him, only to find him watching her. In the fraction of a second before he looked away, the smoky cast in his eyes was unmistakable.

"Listen, Ben," she said, rising abruptly, anxious to do the right thing before losing her nerve. "I know it's too early to say this, and maybe it doesn't need to be said at all. But I happen to like you, a lot, and I want to be straight with you. It's probably obvious that I'm attracted to you, even though I've been trying not to show it. But the fact is, I'm not on the market. I'm single, but... there are things going on in my life right now that would make a relationship — any kind of relationship — impossible. And as much as I enjoy spending time with you, and as much as I'd like to spend *more* time with you while I'm here, I can't keep on like this until we're clear about that. I don't want to be unfair to you."

She paused for breath, surprised to feel her heart thudding wildly in her chest. She really wasn't thirteen. Did she not throw herself into tense confrontations with far more intimidating men every day at the firm? She was famous for keeping her cool!

She'd been maintaining eye contact as she spoke, but his face gave little away. For a long moment, he surveyed her with an odd, blank expression. Then he rose from his chair and moved to stand beside her at the porch railing. Just when she was sure she would explode if he didn't say something in the next two seconds, he folded his arms over his chest, leaned back onto the railing, and crossed his legs comfortably in front of him.

"That," he said with the hint of a smile, "was exceptionally well done."

Haley smiled back, even as her heart thudded louder.

"You think?"

He nodded thoughtfully. "I'd say that was hands down the best 'just friends' speech I've ever heard."

His eyes flashed a friendly twinkle, and her cheeks flushed with relief. "I can't believe you've heard very many," she said honestly.

He made no response to that, but stood up, gathered the trash from their meal, and headed down her porch steps.

She was about to say something, although she didn't know what, when he suddenly turned around.

"There's a high wind advisory out for tomorrow," he said matter-of-factly. "Odds are we'll have to cancel the tours, at least through the morning. If I get the time off, how you would like to hike up and touch a glacier?"

Haley felt her palms break into a sweat.

"I'd love that," she answered.

"I'll let you know sometime tomorrow morning, then," he said, stepping backwards toward his cabin.

"I'll be here," she replied. Did he really have to leave now? "Ben?" she called after him.

He stopped again.

She sucked in a breath. "I'm sorry if... I mean..." *Spit it out, Haley.* "I know the speech was premature."

He stared at her a moment. Then his lips twisted slowly into a smirk.

"No. It wasn't."

Chapter 12

The next morning Haley pulled her rental car off onto the shoulder of the road by the Seward Highway and shifted into park. She could not put off the unpleasantness any longer. She had to at least scan through her work email and make sure she wasn't missing something important. And she had to check in with her mother and Micah. They could have sent her anything yesterday; she hadn't read a word of it. She would catch up on the essentials now, respond in as minimal a manner as possible, then shut off her phone for the day.

And another great day it's going to be, too, she thought with a smile.

She picked up her phone, and her smile faded. The messages were already pouring in. She steeled herself to be ruthless, to compartmentalize. To keep work as work and not let it intrude on her mood and emotions. But work was only half the problem.

Call me NOW! The subject header proclaimed. There were six emails from her mother and two from Micah, all in the last twenty-four hours. Her mother had also left three voice mails.

Foreboding crept over Haley like a heavy, wet blanket. She had no choice. She dialed her mother's number.

"Haley?"

It was not her mother's voice that answered. It was her sister's.

"Hi, Micah," Haley replied tonelessly. "I just saw all the messages but haven't read them. What's happening?"

There was a long pause. A sniffle. Then a sigh. "I moved out of the apartment last night."

"You *what?*" Haley tried hard to rein in her knee-jerk flash of anger. She didn't know all the circumstances. She shouldn't judge. But so help her, if Micah was just acting out for attention again...

"We had another fight," Micah explained.

Haley listened carefully to her sister's voice cues. Micah was trying to sound determined, but every word was laced with regret.

"It's been really hard, waiting for the final results. I know the baby's *probably* fine. But, Haley, I just can't stop worrying. The thought that Tim might not love the baby as much if—"

"He *never* said that, Micah. You know he didn't!"

"But it's how he feels!" Micah insisted. "It must be, or he could never have even suggested... you know!"

Termination.

Haley closed her eyes and breathed deeply. What Tim would give to take those words back, she couldn't imagine. Maybe he meant them at the time, and maybe he didn't. But there wasn't a doubt in Haley's mind that her brother-in-law would love this baby, no matter what. He had said as much a hundred times since he'd sputtered those first hasty, ill-considered words. But Micah couldn't forget. Nor, evidently, could she forgive.

Haley struggled to find the right words. She was no marriage counselor. She was a firm believer in staying out of other people's marriages altogether and her twin's in particular. But this was getting ridiculous.

"I know that what he said hurt your feelings, Micah," Haley replied finally. "But did you ever think that maybe your feelings aren't the most important thing here? What he *intends to do* is love and care for this baby for the rest of his life. And he's willing to do that even though the baby's mother is an overreacting emotional nutcase. Because he loves them both. How can you not swoon over a man like that?"

There was a pause. Haley could tell that she was getting through. Micah always did respond to "tough love" — something she'd never gotten from either of their parents. Haley pressed on. "But if you don't want him, I can always give it a go myself..."

"Don't even think about it!" Micah threatened playfully, her voice choked with tears. "I do love him, Haley. You know I do."

"Then act like it," Haley continued. "Go home and hug it out."

"It's not that easy."

"I didn't say it would be. It doesn't matter. You still have to do it."

Sniffles. "I know."

Haley could hear her mother's voice in the background. Then Micah's again, both muffled.

"Mom wants to talk to you," Micah said after a moment.

"Tell her I—"

"Haley!"

Crap. "Yes, Mom?"

"Where have you been? Have you even been reading my emails?"

"I've been having the time of my life. And no." Haley's muscles tensed. She didn't want to hurt her mother's feelings. Michelle was painfully susceptible to it, and she had a long memory.

"Don't you think you could pay a little more attention to your sister when she's in the middle of such a crisis?"

Micah mumbled something in the background.

Haley considered the question rhetorical.

"I understand you're telling Micah she should go back to Tim? Do you have any idea how much it hurts her that he's rejected this baby?"

Oh, God. Haley held the phone away from her a moment, breathed deeply, then pulled it back. "Tim has *not* rejected his baby," she countered. "And you need to stop interfering. Your taking Micah's side in everything is *not* helping!"

Michelle's voice quavered. "Well, who's going to take her side if you and I don't?"

Haley really, *really* wanted to scream. "Her *husband*. Who loves her to distraction, if you would just open your eyes and see that!"

Calm down, Haley ordered herself. *She really is trying to help. I think. I hope.*

"Mom, please listen to me. Tim and Micah will get through this. They have to get through this, for the baby's sake. Tim wants this baby as much as she does and he is going to love it just as much as she does."

"He will if it's normal," Michelle replied heavily. "Otherwise we just don't know, do we?"

Haley gave up. Neither her mother nor Micah would be satisfied with anything else Tim said, much less anything else Haley said. They wouldn't be satisfied until he *showed* them. Which he couldn't possibly do until the baby was born. And if the baby was born normal and healthy, how could he ever prove to them that he would have loved it even if it hadn't been?

"Micah needs to move back home," Haley said tiredly. "And I have to go."

"Are you still feeling okay? No problems?"

"No problems." Haley's free hand went to her waistline. If there was nothing else she could do to help the situation back home, she could at least insulate the baby from it. Heaven only knew what stress hormones Fred would be tripping on now if she was hooked up to Micah's bloodstream.

"Goodbye, Mom."

"Goodbye, Haley," Michelle said dejectedly.

Haley sat still a moment. She rubbed her hand in circles around her abdomen, thinking. Stress really was bad for the baby. Brooding, holding in her emotions — none of it was good.

She looked around outside the car. There was no one visible. The closest house was down the road and out of sight. She checked to make sure the windows were rolled up tight. Then she buried her face in her jacket and screamed.

Three minutes later, she felt better. "Sorry about that, Fred," she said as she drove back toward the cabins. "But it was necessary."

She pulled into the drive to see Ben lounging on his front porch, and her spirits rose instantly. She hadn't spoken with him yet this morning, but since his Jetta hadn't moved, she was hoping he had the morning off and would be able to spend it with her. A storm had moved in last night, and though the clouds appeared to be lifting now, a wicked wind persisted.

She took the fact that he was dressed in jeans and hiking boots as a good sign.

"So, what's the verdict?" she called as she hopped out of the car.

"I'm off all day," he said evenly, hiding a smile behind his coffee cup. "They're probably still going to run the late afternoon bay tour, but the boss has it covered."

Haley's own smile was plain to see. "I'm glad to hear it."

Clearing the air last night had given her powerful peace of mind — a peace she sorely needed. She couldn't wait to spend more time with Ben, to have him as a friend. Knowing that he wanted the same, or at least was willing to settle for it, melted her.

"I hope you haven't been waiting on me long," she apologized. "I drove up the road to get a signal before we left. I didn't want to subject you to any more of my cringe-worthy phone conversations."

Haley frowned as it occurred to her that she still hadn't checked her work email. It had downloaded, but she'd gotten distracted before she could look at it. She really couldn't turn her phone off for the day — again — without at least scanning it first.

"Go ahead and do whatever you need to do," Ben said mildly, making no move to move. He had brought his deck chair back to his own porch and was sitting comfortably with his feet up on the railing. "No rush."

Haley leaned against the hood of her car and began to scroll. Most of her work emails were meaningless; the rest she prioritized with a pitiless zeal, moving them into various folders she would not crack open until she was back in Newport Beach. But one particular subject line made her jaws clench.

Conference call TODAY, Haley!

The email was from Bob, of course.

Stirjon Chemical's got something going on. They want you. I told them 2:00 PDT for a conference. CONFIRM ASAP.

Haley's happy mojo evaporated. "No! Dammit!"

"Everything okay?" Ben asked with concern, pulling his feet down. Was her angst really so obvious? Or had she sworn out loud?

She had. *Double dammit.*

"Just work stuff," she mumbled, typing her reply. It wouldn't send now, but it should when they got back out to the highway.

Confirmed.

"Must be a tough job," Ben said tentatively. "You look like you lost your best friend."

Haley blinked up at him. Stirjon Chemicals was a client in Washington State. They were known for their innovative R&D in everything from textiles to biofuel. They were also known for improperly dumping toxic waste into a river upstream from Puget Sound, eliciting a nasty legal battle that had lasted over a decade. Theoretically they had cleaned up their act. Bob's email suggested otherwise.

Puget Sound. Where Ben grew up. Where he had learned to drive a boat. Where he had probably seen his very first orca.

"Not yet," she murmured miserably.

"What's that?" he asked, sounding even more concerned.

Haley sighed and took a step toward him. "I'm afraid I have a conference call I can't get out of. At one o'clock. Do we still have time for that hike?"

Ben looked at his watch. "A shorter one, sure. We'll skip the Harding Ice Field and just prowl around the base of the glacier a bit. No problem."

Hot tears sprang immediately to Haley's eyes, and she turned quickly to hide them. How mortifying. Why on earth would she feel like crying now?

Perhaps because she'd been fighting the impulse for too long and was now perilously overdue. The screaming had helped, but anger and frustration were only part of the perfect storm inside her. She had felt it building for weeks now, and it wasn't going away. The leaping porpoises and snow-capped mountains had only been holding it off awhile.

"Just give me five more minutes," she called out as she walked toward her cabin. "What should I bring?"

"Some decent shoes," he advised. "And a water bottle. Lose the phone."

I wish, she thought silently.

"The last part was personal opinion," he added.

Haley hastened into her cabin. She could not cry now. Maybe later, after the conference call. She should be sufficiently miserable then.

She pulled out her running shoes. Thankfully, it didn't look like rain, so the rest of the outfit she was already wearing, including the not-so-waterproof jacket, would do. Her newly purchased elastic-waisted jeans were hardly the height of fashion, but they were comfortable and should keep her out of actual maternity clothes for a while still. She frowned. She was not looking forward to the final chapter of this adventure. It would be awkward at work, to say the least. But she would put off thinking about *that* as long as she could. Right now, no one could tell she was pregnant. People who knew her well might remember her previously slender waist and not-so-bountiful chest, but she was no thicker in the middle than many non-pregnant women, and as long as she was careful about what she wore, she could probably hide the bump for at least another month.

The only mirror in the cabin was high over the bathroom sink, so she couldn't check her profile. But looking down, she was satisfied. The shirttails of her plaid button-down would hide the ugly waistband, even if she took her jacket off. She grabbed up her lightweight backpack, threw in a full water bottle, a couple more breakfast bars, and the damned phone, and headed back out.

"My car or yours?" she asked cheerfully, seeing Ben leaning against the hood of his Jetta, an even lighter pack on his own back. He wore no jacket, but was dressed in layers again, the topmost being an insulated plaid button-down with long sleeves rolled up to his elbows. His ginger hair curled around the brim of a Seattle Mariners hat and a pair of sunglasses stuck out of his shirt pocket. He looked sexy as hell.

Haley tried not to notice.

He shrugged. "You can drive if you want. Doesn't matter to me."

Haley smiled. It bugged her when men considered it beneath their dignity to let a woman drive. Many times she had insisted just to irritate them. But she didn't want to drive today. She wanted to enjoy looking out the windows. "Let's take your car," she decided. "Remind me to reimburse you for the gas, though."

Ben shrugged again and opened the door of the Jetta. They were off.

They drove toward Seward a bit, then turned off to wind down a pleasant road with woods on one side and a rippling river on the other. She purposefully asked questions to keep Ben talking, but as much as his clever commentary always amused her, she struggled to keep her mind off Stirjon Chemicals. What had the idiots done now? Their last atrocities had occurred long before she joined the firm — her involvement had been limited to the final stages of remediation. But she knew the executives all too well. Their corporate culture was as toxic as their effluent, and if they had been cutting corners again—

"What kind of law do you practice, Haley?"

She looked over at Ben with surprise. He usually avoided the topic.

He smiled sadly. "You're thinking about work anyway. Might as well share. You can't say I haven't bored you enough with mine."

Haley shook her head. "You've never bored me. I'm sorry. I am distracted this morning."

"What kind of law do you practice?"

To hell with it.

"Environmental."

"Oh," he said pleasantly. "Who do you work for? The EPA?"

Her stomach ached. "No, Ben," she said softly. "I work for the bad guys."

She could have said "corporate interests," but she wasn't in the mood to play word games. He would interpret her words the same regardless. Environmentalists always did. She watched his face. He gave nothing away overtly, but she could see a tiny muscle clenching in his jaw. "I see."

She fought back another urge to cry, this one almost overwhelming. The explosion she feared was clearly nearing. She forced her back to straighten and her chin to lift. She cleared her throat.

"It's not what you think," she began, her voice not nearly as steady as she would like. "Most of the time, I'm working with clients to negotiate terms for remediation — figuring out how to clean things up in a way both parties can agree to. It's not exciting stuff, but somebody has to do it."

He said nothing.

"I didn't set out to work in this particular area when I went to law school. I just sort of fell into it. But I do have a personal code of ethics where the environment is concerned, and so far, I've never had to violate it."

So far. If the worst was true with Stirjon, how much longer could she make that claim?

"What I do on a daily basis is more tedious than anything," she continued.

He still said nothing.

Haley swallowed. "So, do you want to pull over and beat me up, or what?"

The corners of his mouth drew up slightly. "You're too much, Haley."

She blew out a breath with relief. "I mean it. You can yell at me if you want to. It might make us both feel better."

"I doubt that." He turned for a second to look at her. "I can't say I'm not disappointed. It's a shame your talents aren't being put to use for something... Well, let's just say for something else."

Haley had no response to that.

"How much longer are you staying in Seward?" he asked.

She perked an eyebrow at the non sequitur. Was he ready to get rid of her? "My flight leaves Saturday night. Why?"

He shrugged. "Just wondering how long I've got. To turn you from the dark side."

The mischievous glint in his eyes nearly made her cry again. He didn't hate her. It was going to be all right. She blinked back the telling moisture and smiled.

"Good luck with that, Captain Parker."

A few minutes later, Ben parked the Jetta in the lot of the Exit Glacier Nature Center. "Come look around inside first," he said, opening the door of the building for her. Haley slipped in and perused the exhibits. She was studying a map on the wall that showed how much smaller the glacier was now than it had been in various points in history when she heard a woman's voice call out.

"Ben!"

"Hey, Carrie!"

Haley looked over to see an attractive brunette in a ranger outfit enfold herself in Ben's outstretched arms. "Haven't seen you in a while!" the woman enthused over his shoulder. "Too windy for the boats today, huh?"

Haley's face felt warm.

"You got it," Ben answered, releasing her in no particular hurry. "How's Andy?"

Carrie withdrew her arms from around his neck, bringing the wedding band on her left hand into view. Haley's face began to cool again.

"He's great. Too busy, though. You two going to make that camping trip happen this year?"

"You bet!" Ben replied with enthusiasm. "As soon as the weather turns and my schedule eases up." He looked for Haley. "Carrie," he introduced, this is my new landlord Haley, visiting for the week. Haley, this is Carrie, one of the rangers here. Her husband and I are going moose hunting someday."

Carrie laughed. "Like either one of you would shoot anything. Hi, Haley," she greeted warmly.

Haley answered in kind.

"You hiking up to the ice field?" Carrie asked.

Ben shook his head. "No time. We'll just go up to the edge. What have you been seeing, lately?"

"Well, we've got a moose cow and calf hanging around," Carrie answered, obviously knowing him well enough to interpret the vague question. "We've had some trouble with people getting too close to her, but so far she hasn't charged anybody. And we've got a male black up around the ice field, but he's no problem."

"Any wolves?" Ben asked.

Carrie shook her head. "I saw some tracks back in the spring, but nothing since. Not near the trails anyway." She turned to Haley with a wink. "Make him stay on the trails this time. He's a trouble maker."

Haley felt mildly uncomfortable. Despite Ben's introducing her as his landlord, Carrie clearly had other ideas.

"Thanks for the intel," Ben said, ushering Haley toward the side exit. "We're off. Tell Andy I said hi."

"Will do."

They stepped out of the building and onto a wide, paved trail, where Haley, still puzzling over Carrie's reaction, promptly stepped in a massive pile of animal droppings.

"Lovely," Haley said, scraping her shoe on the grass. "Who left that calling card?"

"A moose," Ben answered with amusement.

Her eyes widened. "Right here?" she protested. They were standing barely six feet from the door.

He grinned at her. "Well, I don't think the rangers bussed it in."

"Are moose that tame?"

"Tame, no," he answered. "Bold, yes. Occasionally. But if it makes you feel any better, I'm sure this particular pile materialized before the building opened."

Haley continued walking down the paved trail. It seemed civilized enough. "That 'male black' Carrie mentioned," she asked nervously. "We're not going wherever he is, right?"

Ben let out a good-natured sigh, then stopped and put his hands on her shoulders.

Wow, that feels good.

For a half-second Ben seemed off-kilter himself, but he recovered quickly. "You have got to get over this bear phobia of yours," he lectured. "You can't experience Alaska from the inside of a car. You've got to get out *where the wild things are.*"

Haley tensed. "Are you trying to make me *more* nervous?"

Ben released her with a chuckle, then started walking again. "Knowledge is power, my friend. So, here's *Bear Awareness 101: Safety Tips for the Environmental Attorney.* Take notes. There will be a quiz later. You ready?"

Haley laughed out loud, stepping up her pace to match his eager, long-legged stride.

"Ready."

They headed off down the trail through the trees, soon leaving the paved path and stepping off onto a more narrow gravel one. Haley learned more than she could possibly process about black bears, brown bears, aggressive versus non-aggressive behavior, and how not to react if suddenly faced with a six-hundred-pound shaggy monster with claws.

"So, wait," she questioned, frustrated. "If the bear does attack you, are you or are you not supposed to play dead?"

"It depends on whether the bear is acting defensively," he answered.

Haley groaned. "I am so going to fail this quiz."

"If it's a brown bear you caught off guard or a female bear defending cubs, then playing dead shows you're not a threat," he explained. "But if it's attacking for any other reason — which is really, *really* unusual — then you're better off fighting back."

Haley stopped in her tracks and glared at him. "Oh, I'm sure that would go just *splendidly.*"

"You're missing the point," he protested. "If you learn what to do and how to respond appropriately, you're more likely to get struck by lightning than you are to wind up in that situation. It's a one-in-a-million thing. You have to put it in perspective."

Haley didn't move.

"Or," he revised, cracking a grin. "You can make sure to always travel with a professional naturalist."

She grinned back at him. "I choose option B."

They started moving again. The trail had begun heading uphill, and the woods surrounding them grew denser. "Ben?" Haley asked a few moments later as she peered warily through the trees.

"Yeah?"

"You have bear spray, right?"

"Sure."

She watched his tall, lean body climb up the trail in front of her. His pack barely looked big enough for a water bottle, and there was nothing attached to his waist. "Where?" she asked.

"Back in the cabin."

Haley groaned again. "All right, fine. How about if I play dead and you fist-fight the bear? That way we can cover both situations."

He turned to look at her, his hazel eyes twinkling. "Deal."

They walked in silence a few moments more. The wind was whipping loudly overhead, but the woods absorbed much of the impact, and the temperature was pleasant. "Aren't we supposed to keep making noise?" Haley asked, still mulling over her bear lesson.

"Yes, we should," Ben agreed. "This trail is usually so busy it doesn't matter much, but I'm surprised how few people are out this morning."

"Tell me more about your sisters," Haley suggested.

He made a face. "Are you trying to upset me?"

Haley laughed. Despite his protestations, his affection for his family was plain to see. "Who's the oldest?" she prompted.

"Maggie," he said, feigning a sigh. "She's the bossy one. Works as a nurse anesthetist in Seattle. Nine years older than me. Born when my parents were both still medical residents. You'd think they'd know better, wouldn't you?"

"Both your parents are doctors?" Haley interrupted, intrigued. No wonder the guy was smart.

"Yep," he replied. "Jenna followed two years later. She's the drama queen, works in sales and marketing for a different company every six months."

Haley tried to commit the names to memory. Why she found his family so interesting, she wasn't sure. But she enjoyed hearing him talk about them.

"Lara's next,' he continued. "She's five years older than me, but you could say we're the closest. She's a chemical engineer, and one of the smartest women I know. Emma is the youngest of the girls, three years older than me. She has a degree in English literature, but she works with her husband in his electrical business. She's the only one besides me to leave Seattle and she only got as far as Yakima." He glanced back at Haley. "Every one of them is over thirty and married with kids, but they still enjoy plotting together to torture me. Is that an acceptable rundown?"

Haley considered. They were still walking through some pretty dense brush. Plenty of hiding places for easily startled bears. "Not quite," she answered. "What kind of doctors are your parents?"

"OB/GYNs."

Haley's eyebrows perked. "Both of them?"

"Unfortunately," he continued. "They're both still working, too. My mom's been delivering babies for three decades now. My dad has more of a lab job — he does gynecological research."

Haley wasn't sure how to respond to that. "Wow."

"Yeah," he said grimly. "Add four much-older sisters into the mix, and you can imagine what I went through growing up."

Haley chuckled. "Must have made for some interesting dinner conversations."

He turned and looked at her. "You have no idea."

She laughed louder. "A well-educated little boy, were you?"

He started moving again. "This conversation is over. Tell me about your family."

Haley felt an unpleasant clenching in her chest. "There's not much to tell."

"Are those bear tracks I see?" Ben joked, looking idly off into the trees.

"All right!" Haley caved. "It's just Micah and me, and my mother. My father died when we were fourteen."

Ben turned. "I'm sorry."

"Thanks," Haley said, ducking her head and continuing to walk. She really, *really* needed to schedule that cry. "It was a tough time, but we got through it. He was an attorney, too. A very successful one. My mother has a teaching degree, but she's never worked. Micah married her boyfriend Tim right out of college, and I went to law school. We all still live in Newport Beach. My mother's parents lived there for decades too, but now they're in assisted living in Phoenix, near my other uncle. My father's parents passed away a long time ago. My uncle Randy was the last relative on that side of the family, as far as I know."

"Does your sister have any children?"

A beat passed. "Not yet. But they're expecting."

Haley stopped talking. Her stomach was beginning to ache again. When Ben talked about his family, he left her laughing. When she talked about hers, it was like the sun slipped behind a cloud.

"Almost there now," Ben said cheerfully. "You ready for a beautiful view?"

"Absolutely." *Please.*

The woods opened up around them, revealing a plateau made up of large, irregular boulders. Farther up the cliff, more mounds of rock were visible, as well as a tantalizing glimpse of another cascading fall of blue ice. "Race you," Ben teased, leaving the trail and heading for the top of the nearest boulder.

Haley scrambled up after him. When they reached the crest the wind picked up considerably, but the sun was shining. "Well," Ben said proudly, gesturing around them. "What do you think?"

Haley rotated slowly, absorbing a full three-hundred-sixty degrees of raw, amazing beauty. The rocks beneath her feet were gray, laced with yellow-green moss and scrub, while darker green trees graced the hillsides, sweeping out, up, and over to blanket the lower hills. A valley below her sported a ripple of fast-moving water that spread out over a mysterious plain of gray-brown mud, while far away in the distance, much higher peaks of rock pushed their snowy tips toward the now-blue sky.

"You can't see the glacier from right here," Ben explained. "but its melt is feeding that stream below. The stream empties into the Resurrection River, which we drove along on the way up."

Haley stood still and let the wind whip her jacket around her. Looking out over the sweeping vista, it seemed as if she could see forever. The enormity of it all made her feel quite small, but at the same time, strangely invigorated. She breathed in giant lungfuls of the brisk air. "Oh, yeah. That's the stuff," she mused. "Better than chocolate."

Ben chuckled at her. He shrugged off his pack, sat down on the rock, and took out his water bottle. "We can rest here a while if you want."

Haley wasn't in the least tired, but knew she should not get dehydrated. The climb uphill had warmed her up nicely, despite the wind. She sat down beside him, took off her pack and her jacket, and pulled out her own water bottle. "Do you really spend the rest of the year in Maui?" she asked, not entirely sure where the question had come from.

"I really do," he answered, stretching out on the rock with his hands behind his head. "Except for a couple weeks in May, and most of October. Then I stop over in Seattle and spend some time with the family."

Haley smirked. "The family who tortures you?"

He smirked back. "Just my sisters. My nieces and nephews are great, and my brothers-in-law are all right, too."

"And your parents?" Haley knew she was being nosey, but she couldn't help herself. She was fascinated. She wanted to know everything about him.

"My mother is an absolute powerhouse of energy. No one can keep up with her. She runs her residents ragged and will probably never retire. My dad is as laid back as they come. We get along fine, except for the whole career thing."

Haley sensed a note of frustration. "They don't approve of yours?"

"It's not that they don't approve, exactly," he answered. "Just that they consider it temporary. Like it's something I need to get out of my system. My dad's favorite line, which he delivers at least monthly, is 'you could be making a lot more money with that brain of yours, son.'"

Haley smiled at the imitation. Ben made his father sound like James Earl Jones. "Well, he is right about that," she said lightly.

Ben squinted at her from under the brim of his cap. "And what exactly do I need more money for, when I already have happiness?"

Haley's eyes darted away. No snappy response came to mind. After a moment, the silence turned awkward.

"Are you really happy, Ben?" she asked finally, not looking at him. "Do you not worry about the future? Your financial security down the road?"

He propped himself up on an elbow. "No, Haley. I don't. I've been supporting myself just fine ever since college. I can live on less because I choose to need less. I also happen to have a family who wouldn't let me starve if I got hurt or sick and couldn't work; and believe me, I don't take that for granted. But for the foreseeable future, I'm good. And yes, I am happy." He swept an arm across the vista before them. "How many other people get to wake up every morning to views like this... and a job they love?"

Haley made no response. She felt like he was trying to catch her eye, but she wouldn't look at him. He had asked her before if she liked her job. *Sure*, she had said, *I'm good at it. I make a lot of money.*

What the hell kind of answer was that?

She stuffed her jacket and water bottle back into her backpack. Ben's philosophy might be well and good for him, but he couldn't possibly understand her own situation. Unlike him, she had responsibilities. Other people who depended on her. The fantasy of living every day like it was vacation was just that — *fantasy*.

All the more reason to enjoy the four short days she had left.

She stood up tall on the rock and marveled again at the amazing display before her. On impulse, she clasped her hands together and stretched her arms high above her head, breathing in a complete chestful of the perfect mountain air.

So nice.

She breathed out again with a feeling of resignation. Only four more days. She had to make the most of them.

"Come on," she said playfully, nudging the still-recumbent Ben with her toe. "Let's go touch that glacier."

Chapter 13

Haley stepped onto the wooden walkway that spanned a deep fissure in the rock and looked back over her shoulder. Ben was lagging for some reason. The trail was out in the open now, so she had dared to take the lead. She couldn't believe that her doing so would bother him. But *something* was bothering him. "Tiring out already, Captain?" she called. "Maybe I need to get you running with me in the mornings. Assuming I can ever get myself out of bed early enough to do it again."

He attempted a smile, but couldn't quite fake it. "At the risk of worsening your phobia, I wouldn't advise running around the cabins. If you're going to run in bear country, you should stick to open areas like the main roads."

Haley paled. "Maybe I'll take up swimming. Unless the orcas would eat me."

"The residents *usually* prefer fish," he said offhandedly, catching up to her. "A transient orca might mistake you for a seal, but since you'd be dead of hypothermia in minutes, they'd probably pass. They prefer live food."

"Thanks," Haley said sarcastically, studying him. He pulled out his sunglasses and put them on, but not before she caught a look of near panic in his eyes.

What the heck?

She looked back over his shoulder at the trail. If he had seen something dangerous, surely he would tell her. "Is something wrong?"

"Of course not," he said unconvincingly, passing her on the platform and beckoning her forward. "Come on and check out this view. You'll love it."

Haley followed him to the edge of a rocky precipice, where a rope hanging off wooden posts was all that separated them from a steep drop and a gorge filled with shining blue ice. The massive column of long-frozen water began far above their heads and stretched down as far as they could see toward the riverbed below.

"It's magnificent," Haley whispered. "I can feel the cold coming off of it from here. But it's too far away to touch."

"It didn't used to be," Ben explained. "It's shrinking fast, like all the glaciers. But you can still touch it at its toe section. We'll hike down there next. Whenever you're ready."

With that, he retreated to another mound of rock and leaned against it, his arms folded over his chest.

Haley wasn't fooled. He *was* upset about something. But what? She thought back over their conversation, but came up with no clues. She hadn't exactly gushed over the wisdom of his choosing to live his life on a shoestring. But he obviously knew what he wanted and what he was about — he didn't need her affirmation or anybody else's. The fact that he didn't easily take offense was one of his more agreeable attributes.

Besides which, the vibe she was picking up from him wasn't annoyance, or resentment, or disappointment. It was more like shock... and confusion.

At some point in the last twenty minutes, something had happened that had totally freaked the man out. And whatever it was, he didn't want her to know about it.

A group of three other hikers started across the platform toward them. Haley looked out at the sculpted wall of ice for another long moment, admiring the interplay of colors within its many textures and depths, then turned away towards Ben. If he kept acting strange, she would call him out on it. Their time together was too precious to waste on a misunderstanding.

She had not quite reached him when a ringtone sounded from her backpack. She stopped abruptly. "No way!" she protested, shrugging off the pack and digging out her phone with annoyance. "I thought there was no reception out here!"

Ben shrugged. His sunglasses still hid his face. "There usually isn't. But you never know."

Haley swore under her breath and looked at her screen. *One bar.* One flippin' little bar. If she answered it, she probably wouldn't get three words in before the line cut out again. She should ignore it.

It was Micah.

Dammit.

Micah wasn't likely to call for just anything. Had the test results come back early?

Haley punched the button. "Micah? I only have one bar; we're going to get cut off. Is everything okay?"

Ben looked disappointed. Haley whirled away from him, only to find herself being glared at by the other hikers. *Fabulous.*

Her sister was sobbing and hiccupping into the phone. "Micah, what *is* it?" Haley demanded.

"Can I move into your place for a while?" Micah stammered. "I can't stay with Mom anymore. You know how she is! All we've done since I got here is argue."

Something rumbled and bubbled in Haley's middle. It was hot, it was heavy, and it was threatening implosion. The arm holding her phone began to tremble. "No, Micah," she ordered, her voice low. "No, you may *not* move into my apartment. Go home."

"But, I—"

"I said no!" Haley barked. She squeezed her eyes shut tight, unable to stand the looks of annoyance she was certain were being directed at her from all sides. She refused to enable Micah's avoidance of the problems in her marriage — problems Micah was creating for herself by acting like a spoiled child. Besides which, if Haley said yes, Micah wouldn't just be there for the night, she would still be there when Haley got back. And Haley's home was her one oasis from the insanity. She *needed* that oasis. For her own sanity.

"I can't believe you're being so unreasonable about this!" Micah screeched. "I'm asking you for help, Haley. I need some more time before I face Tim again. *Please.*"

"Then check into a motel!" Haley hissed.

"But you're not even using it!" Micah pressed. "How can you be so selfish? All I'm—"

The line went dead.

Haley was pulling back her arm to vault her phone into the gorge when she felt Ben gently grab hold of her wrist.

"Mind if I take this a minute?" he asked, his other hand closing over the phone.

Haley's whole body was shaking. She couldn't seem to control it. She released her hold.

"Not that I don't like the concept," Ben said quietly, shutting the phone off and stuffing it back into her pack. "But littering offends me." He began to head back the way they had come and gestured for her to follow.

Haley cast a glance around, unsure if she could move. Her pent-up emotions were preparing to detonate. Right here, right now. Deep inside her ribcage, molten lava was bubbling. Any second a stream of saltwater was going to shoot up out of her eyes.

The other hikers stared daggers at her.

"Haley!" Ben called more insistently. She looked at him. He tossed his head and gestured with his hand again.

She moved. He led her back across the wooden platform, then took a turn downhill and into another stretch of woods. She stumbled after his fuzzy form, getting herself repeatedly whacked with low-hanging branches as she struggled to see through a film of still-restrained tears. She had to get to someplace private. *Now*. But where could she go?

Ben stopped suddenly and turned to face her. At some point they must have left the trail. They were standing next to a large rock in the middle of a thick stand of trees. He beckoned her forward and held out his arms. "Come here."

Haley stiffened. She couldn't. Surely, he didn't mean it. He didn't understand.

She tried to read his expression, but he was still wearing the damned shades and her vision was so blurry she could barely tell his nose from his Mariners hat. Besides which, her face was exploding.

"Yeah, I know," he said gruffly, but with a trace of humor. "You shouldn't impose. I might get the wrong idea, yada yada yada. You gave me the speech already, remember? I heard you. Now, *come here.*"

Haley went.

She buried her face in her hands and pressed both against the soft flannel jacket that covered his chest. His long arms enveloped her and crushed her close.

The volcano erupted. Huge, wracking sobs pulsed up from the soles of her feet, convulsing her like a ragdoll. Her legs might not have held her up, but thankfully they didn't have to. What little strength she had was focused on keeping the stream of fluid flowing out of her face on the cuffs of her own sleeves and off of his shirt. She cried. And she cried.

She cried some more.

And then she was done.

Haley drew in a deep, ragged breath and withdrew a little. Ben released his hold, but kept his hands on her arms as he stepped back to take a look at her.

"Better?"

Haley swallowed. "Much. Thanks." She couldn't breathe without gulping.

"You want to talk about it?"

She shook her head briskly. "No. Yes. I don't know."

He paused a moment. "Well, as long as you're sure," he said lightly.

"Let's keep moving. I'd hate for the rest of the glacier to melt before you get to touch it."

Haley nodded eagerly. Ben turned away from her and led on.

He didn't turn around again for a long time, for which she was grateful. She was less grateful that, true to Carrie's warning, they were obviously way off the trail.

"Listen up, bears," he called out as the underbrush thickened. "We are human. Do not eat us."

Haley stepped high over giant ferns and other strange plants with large fronds shaped like maple leaves. Every last square inch of dirt seemed determined to grow something green while the warm weather lasted. Sunlight sifted through the trees to merely dapple the ground below, but the profusion of plants thrived nevertheless. Though their walking progress was slow, Haley found she didn't mind. It was as if she were drifting through a fantasy world.

"We are human," Ben repeated. "Do not eat us."

"Do you have to say those particular words?" she protested.

"Only to English-speaking bears," he answered. "I don't know what they say in Europe."

Haley laughed. Her breathing had steadied now and her eyes were dry. Puffy and red, still, but dry. The crying jag really had made her feel better. Her problems hadn't changed. But she at least felt calmer about them.

Eventually they merged back onto the trail, which led them down to the rocky outwash plain in the valley below. They stepped out of the woods onto a jumbled field of small, smooth rocks, through the middle of which ran a swift-moving, shallow stream. Cold air blew off the chilly water, and Haley stared at it with wonder, knowing that some of it had only just melted from the glacier above.

She breathed in deeply again, relieved to know that her phone was turned completely off. Micah would be calling back frantically now, trying her best to apologize. It was what she always did. Freak out and say things she didn't mean, then apologize profusely.

Haley didn't want to hear it. They both knew that Micah's calling Haley selfish was laughable. The specific words Micah had blurted didn't bother Haley nearly so much as her sister's seeming instability. Six months ago, it hadn't been like this. Six months ago, Haley had been confident that Micah and Tim would make wonderful parents. Now, thanks to the nightmare known as prenatal testing, Micah was falling apart before Haley's eyes.

It scared the hell out of her.

"The footwork will get a little trickier, here," Ben announced. The rock field ahead of them had met an end, cut off by a large outcropping of cliff that jutted out to meet the stream. "It's not mountain climbing, exactly, but we'll have to skirt around a narrow ledge over the water. You up to it?"

His voice sounded strange again. Haley reached up boldly and removed the annoying shades. "If anyone needs to hide their eyes," she declared, "it's me." She put the glasses on top of her own head and studied him. He looked slightly nervous. Nothing more.

"Of course I'm up to it," she answered. "Lead on."

Ben forged up and across the ledge, looking back frequently to make sure she grabbed the appropriate handholds. Haley had no trouble with her balance, but she could not help thinking — with sudden gloom — that her ability to undertake such stunts would soon be limited. When they reached the other side of the outcropping, the rocky plain opened up once again, and the toe of the glacier appeared before them. After a few more minutes of scrambling over an uneven bed of larger rocks, they at last stood within feet of the triangular chunk of ice that was the glacier's lowest point.

"So," Ben said with a cheerfulness that was clearly forced. "What do you think?"

Haley hesitated. Although the higher part of the glacier, with its frothy cake-frosting edges and milky blue depths, was beyond gorgeous, the "toe" left something to be desired.

"It looks like what you see piled up in the corners of parking lots in Chicago in the winter," she said honestly.

Ben laughed. "Yeah, I guess it does. Step up and touch it."

Haley did. "It feels like ice."

"Really?" Ben said with feigned surprise.

Haley rolled her eyes good-naturedly. Despite the toe's unimpressive appearance, it was indeed fascinating to put her hand on its surface and look upward, knowing how massive the frozen waterfall was and how far back into the mountains it extended. "I should take a picture of this," she murmured, shrugging off her pack again.

"Oh, no you don't!" Ben objected, pushing the straps back up over her shoulders. "I'll get a picture for you." He pulled off his own pack and extracted a tiny, ancient-looking phone.

"Seriously?" Haley asked with a grin. "I didn't even know you owned a phone."

"It's never on," he commented, even as he pushed a button to bring it to life. It was not a smartphone; from the looks of it Haley was surprised it even had a camera.

"But how can you get important texts from your sisters?" she teased.

He made a face. "First of all, sisters don't send important texts. And second, they used to send me a bunch of crap, but I never answered, so eventually they cut it out."

"But what if there's an emergency?" Haley pressed. As much as she resented being chained to her own phone, she had little patience for technophobes.

"When I'm home they can call the landline and when I'm on a tour they can call the office and have somebody radio the boat," he explained unapologetically. "For anything less than dire, they can send an email or leave a voicemail and I'll get it that day or the next."

Haley frowned. She had no good response to that. She only knew that she could never get away with it. Bob would pop arteries on a daily basis.

"Smile," Ben suggested, holding up the Paleolithic phone.

Haley curved her lips, wondering what time it was and how much longer she could relax before the dreaded conference call. As soon as she got back into Seward and turned her phone on, Micah would be calling her, too.

Ben lowered the camera without clicking it. He moved to a nearby boulder and sat down with a sigh.

"Look," he began, watching her with a resigned expression. "Can we get real a minute? I know we just met three days ago and I'm probably not your first choice of confidant. But all this pretending is..." He looked away from her. He pulled off his cap and ran a hand through his hair. "You're dealing with a guy who grew up with four sisters, okay? I breathed in estrogen like second-hand smoke."

Haley's heart beat faster. What was he getting at?

"What I'm trying to say is," he continued, catching her eye. "You're not fooling me, here. I know you've got some serious stuff going on, and no, the waterworks were not my first clue."

Haley made no response. Had she been that obvious? Yes, probably. But he couldn't know about her pregnancy. Not unless he had overheard something...

"I'm not asking you to explain," he said quickly, no doubt perceiving her sudden panic. "You don't owe me anything. I just want you to know you don't have to pretend with me. And if you ever do want to talk... well, I'm here."

Haley smiled at him. Her blasted eyes grew moist again. Of course he didn't know anything. He was only trying to be kind. "Thank you," she choked out.

He said nothing else. Haley turned back around, stepped to the glacier, and laid her palm flat on the ice. The cold crept slowly up through her wrist, and as she concentrated on the feel of it and on the steady rhythm of her breathing, her emotions gradually calmed.

She heard a click, then turned to see Ben staring down at his camera.

"Now, there's a nice shot for you," he said proudly, turning the tiny phone around.

Haley gazed at the picture of herself touching the glacier. She was smiling slightly, her expression serene. She looked almost... *happy*.

It was too much. Without thought she stepped forward, threw her arms around his neck, and hugged him tight. "You are the best shower buddy ever, Ben Parker," she said with a croak.

She held him as long as she dared. The feel of his arms around her, the firmness of his shoulder under her cheek, his warmth... It was all entirely too enticing. Reluctantly, she stepped back and looked at him.

His face was smiling, but his hazel eyes swam with conflict. Haley could understand why. The attraction between them was turning painful.

"Yeah," he said dryly. "I get that a lot."

Chapter 14

Ben shoved a dollar bill in the slot, then pushed the start button. The machine whirred to life with a splash and a swoosh.

Laundry.

Was this any way to spend his twenty-eighth birthday?

Hell, no. He was supposed to be spending it out on the ocean. Preferably, with cake.

He walked out of the laundromat and onto the sidewalk. No way was he sitting in the dim, noisy room for half an hour. He had time for a stroll. Perhaps down to the Sea Life Center.

He started walking. With the bay on one side and towering mountains on the other, he should have been enjoying the view. Instead, his gaze was riveted on the pavement.

The day hadn't been all bad. The first part of his hike with Haley had been amazing. She had made him laugh, she had kept up with him on the trail, and she hadn't whined once. Being witness to her awe was, as always, pure joy for him. And if he hadn't been able to keep his eyes off that adorable body of hers, he had at least managed to keep his mind off what he could do with it. Most of the time.

It was the fact that he'd had so much fun in the first half of the hike that made the second half totally suck.

I'm not on the market. I'm single, but... there are things going on in my life that would make a relationship — any kind of relationship — impossible right now.

She could say that again.

He kicked at an empty water bottle on the sidewalk. Then he caught up with it and picked it up. There was a recyclables bin at the Sea Life Center.

He hated plastic water bottles.

He hated pollution in general.

How could somebody as intelligent and sensible as Haley do what she did for a living? How could she even sleep at night?

Knock it off, Ben.

He realized his jaws were clenched. Who was he kidding? He had no chance with Haley and he never would, no matter what she did for a living. Never mind that she was all he could think about. Never mind that she'd kept him awake two nights in a row now — actually, three — with no relief in sight. Never mind the connection he *thought* he felt with her, the way the slightest touch of her hand could make him shiver like a teenager. Never mind that every feature of her face had become emblazoned in his mind, and that every second he wasn't with her, he was thinking about when he could see her again. Never mind that he couldn't remember ever feeling this way about any other woman... ever.

There was no hope. None. The fact that she lived and worked across the ocean was a problem he had no answer for. Her choice of vocation bothered him more than he would admit. But even without those two extraordinarily difficult obstacles standing in their way, he could not ignore the grim truth his gut kept screaming at him, a truth that cut him to the bone.

Haley was pregnant.

Pregnant!

Ben picked up his pace and started to jog.

He didn't know for sure. He *shouldn't* even suspect it. His crazy upbringing was the problem. It had stuffed his brain with knowledge he didn't need and never cared to use, and now he was stuck with it.

Was it so odd for a woman to ask how long a salmon lived, while contemplating ordering the sockeye? Not really. He had believed that Haley was genuinely curious. And why should he think twice about the ditched champagne? There were plenty of good reasons to avoid alcohol on a boat. Who cared that he'd never seen her drink a cola or a cup of coffee? Only a nutcase would put those things together and come up with pregnant. Only a nutcase with two OB/GYNs for parents who had listened to four sisters spend a total of nine pregnancies going apecrap over mercury, ethanol, caffeine, and every other possible threat to pregnancy, real or imagined.

He could ignore all that. He *had* ignored it.

The baby bump, not so much.

He reached the parking lot of the Sea Life Center, dropped the plastic bottle in a recycling bin, and kept on jogging. When he got to the gravel road on the other side, he started to run.

Pregnant.

He shouldn't have noticed. It wasn't that obvious. He never would have noticed if she hadn't stretched. Stretched her arms straight up in the air, hiking her shirttails above her waistband. She'd been standing within inches of him, for God's sake. Of course he was going to look.

Her waist should have been thin, like the rest of her. Slender and smooth, with an adorable belly button peeking out.

Her belly button *had* been adorable. But her shape was not the shape he expected to see.

Now, it was all he could see.

Pregnant.

Yet with all her talk of family and sisters and husbands, she hadn't said word one about a guy. Why not?

I'm single, but...

Ben frowned and slowed his steps. He'd been running so hard he had a pain in his side. The cool air he'd been gulping burned his lungs.

It made no sense.

Why was Haley acting as if there was no man in her life? If she wanted to keep Ben at bay, she could have dropped "my boyfriend" into the conversation two minutes after they'd met. Why bother with the elaborate "just friends" speech, in which she had specifically said that she was single... and even admitted that she was attracted to him?

Was she hiding the pregnancy just to keep her options open with him?

Ben scoffed out loud. That made even less sense. If she wanted to deceive him and use him for... *whatever*... why bother with the "just friends" speech at all? She could have him any time she wanted him.

He looked around and breathed deeply. He had run a long way. If he kept going at this rate, he'd be crawling back.

He turned around and began to walk. The road ran along a ledge beside the bay, sandwiched between the water on his right and towering cliffs to his left. His eyes drank in the soothing blue color of the water, and he watched the other boats as they moved to and from the marina, the smaller ones buffeted by the strong wind. A day like today was doable within the protected bay; it was the boisterous chop of the gulf beyond that would have been dangerous for the tour boat.

He should be out on the bay with them. What had he been thinking? He always went out on his birthday.

His breathing steadied, but the dull ache in his chest persisted. He hadn't been thinking straight, that was for sure. Whether Haley was pregnant or not, she had told him *no, not interested.* That really should be the end of it.

His mood remained in the doldrums as he slogged slowly back to town, picking up three more recyclable cans and bottles on the way. He dumped them off at the Sea Life Center and arrived back at the laundromat just in time to grab the last two dryers.

Happy birthday.

Thinking wistfully of celebrations past — in those giddy, innocent days before he had realized just how weird his family was — he walked outside again and headed in the opposite direction. His steps took him to the currently empty tour office, where he unlocked the back door, entered the tiny staff area, and extracted his laptop from his locker. He was behind on his email. Perhaps someone had sent him something.

He had not yet finished booting up when his cell phone rang. He had left it on in case Haley called. She had taken his advice and decided to conduct her conference call sitting in her car near the marina, where she could be reasonably assured of a steady signal. He could have told her that she would be better off sitting in the lobby of a motel or even in the tour office, where she would also have access to Wi-Fi. But he was not without an ulterior motive. If all environmental attorneys were forced to conduct their meetings while looking out over Resurrection Bay and the Chugach Mountains, the glaciers might not be melting so fast.

The call was not from Haley.

"Happy birthday, little brother!" came the exuberantly kind, but inevitably bossy voice.

"Hi, Maggie," he said with a smile. "Thanks."

"I can't believe you actually answered!" she teased. "What are you up to?"

Feeling sorry for myself. "Just taking it easy. My full-day got cancelled because of the wind. I'm treating myself to a fun-filled afternoon at the laundromat instead."

Maggie clucked at him. "That is just *sad*, Ben. I wish we were up there. The kids would show you how to party!"

Ben grinned. At the moment, he would give anything to have his nieces and nephews piling all over him. "I keep telling you to come up!"

"I know, I know, but if I have to choose between Alaska and Hawaii, you know what I'm going to pick. And for a family of five, by the way, you're pretty damned expensive to visit."

"I know," he said regretfully. Jenna and her family had made it up in June, which was a total blast. And his parents came up every August. But Maggie and Lara saved their vacation dollars for Hawaii, and Emma couldn't afford to travel at all. Which was why he made a point of spending time in Seattle twice a year, never mind the hit to his own bank account.

"Well, I'm sorry you have no one to party with besides your laundry," she quipped. "How's the soulmate search going?"

Ben closed his eyes with a groan. He had made the colossal mistake, several years ago, of using the S word to explain to a persistent five-year-old niece why he wasn't married yet. The little rat had then promptly quoted his response to the entire assembled extended family — over Christmas dinner, no less. If he never heard the term again, it would be too soon.

"How's the marriage?" he returned.

Subtle sarcasm was lost on Maggie. The woman had no shame. "Oh, we're good. Jim's home today. The vasectomy was totally painless. I didn't feel a thing."

Ben sighed.

Maggie chortled. "Seriously, I hope you manage to have some fun today. I assume you didn't get the package yet?"

"Package?"

"I was afraid of that. Well, maybe it will come later this afternoon. We sent you a big one. All the kids threw something in, even Emma's when they were here last. I hope it gets there today. They said it should."

Ben's smile was genuine. Childish or not, the thought of a giant mystery package lovingly constructed by his nieces and nephews warmed his heart. The birthday might be salvageable after all.

He thanked his sister heartily, and they said their goodbyes. Then he dug into his mountain of email. He deleted huge chunks of garbage, answered one question from his supervisor at the tour company in Maui, then settled down to the real mail. His inbox, as it turned out, was flooded with happy birthday notes. His smile became fixed as he read through and replied to each one. As much as he loved Alaska, almost all of his close friends lived in either Seattle or Maui. It felt good to reconnect, and by the time he had finished and packed up to leave, his mood was much improved.

He collected his laundry and drove back to the cabin, fighting the urge to look for Haley's car on the way. He was no masochist. He knew he needed to back off a bit, stop initiating things. If she initiated, that was different. He had offered her friendship and a sympathetic ear, no strings attached, and he would honor that promise if it killed him. She had done nothing to deserve otherwise.

As much as it irked him to be left guessing, he knew that Haley was under no obligation to tell him her deepest and darkest secrets. She was under no obligation to tell him anything. The fact that she had been so forthright and so quick in saying that she didn't want a relationship had been — ironically enough — the beginning of his downfall. What woman does that? She could have jerked him around all week, enjoyed guided sightseeing, mooched meals, and anything else she wanted from him, and then just disappeared. Instead she'd shown a genuine concern for his feelings.

She had even resisted crying on his shoulder. There she was, falling apart in the middle of the woods, and she would rather have cried alone on bare rock than risk sending him the wrong message. Even that beautiful, spontaneous hug had made her feel guilty, because Haley Olson was nobody's fool. She knew damn well how much he wanted her.

But she was *pregnant*. And he had no shot. And while she might not trust him enough to share her life story, she did at least respect him enough not to lie to him. She had been honest, and direct, and compassionate.

Dear God, she was killing him.

He pulled up to the cabins fervently hoping that her car would not be there.

It was. And so was she. On his porch, with her hair up in a towel, which meant that she had just stepped out of his shower.

The mental image was brutal.

He parked and got out of his car. Haley skipped down the steps and smiled at him. She had released her hair and was casually toweling it off. Ben looked away.

"You got a package!" she said excitedly. "Is today your actual birthday?"

He surveyed the giant box on his porch. It was covered with the words "Happy Birthday" in any number of different colors of ink, including neon green with glitter. He smiled warmly. The green glitter would be from Zora. "It actually is."

"Why didn't you tell me?" Haley protested. "Happy birthday!"

He braved a direct look at her. Her face was particularly beautiful without makeup. But she bore the telltale signs of another crying jag around her eyes. "Thanks," he replied. "How was the conference call?"

"Dreadful," she said tonelessly, passing him on her way back to her cabin. "Besides which, you set me up."

He turned. "Excuse me?"

She kept walking. "Don't play innocent, Captain. You knew it would mess with my mind to talk business with that gorgeous view staring me in the face the whole time."

His heart pounded. Damn, she was smart. And she understood him, too. "Did it work?"

She turned around. For a second she stared right through him, displaying that just-under-the-surface misery he had come to know so well. But in the next second, it was gone again. "Of course not," she said lightly. "You have big plans for tonight?"

He would give anything to say yes. "Nope," he answered. "Just opening up that package."

Her face brightened. "Let me take you out to dinner, then. It's the least I can do. For all your naturalist and bear-protection services, I mean."

No, no, no...

"Sure. That'd be great."

"What's your favorite place? Sky's the limit. Assuming there are no five-star restaurants in Seward, of course."

"That would be a safe assumption. But I do know a nice place close by, with a view of the Resurrection River. I've never been there before, but people say it's good. I've been meaning to try it."

"Sold," Haley called cheerfully. She jogged up to her door and turned around again. "So when do you plan on opening that package? I have to admit, I'm dying of curiosity. It says, 'Warning: May contain marmalade,' on the far side."

Ben smirked. "Well, at least they warned me. They know I hate marmalade."

Haley smiled, but her expression was tinged with sadness. "I'm guessing some kids somewhere are pretty crazy about their Uncle Ben."

"I guess so," he replied, touched.

"I'm not surprised," she murmured.

He dared to look up at her and regretted it immediately. Her eyes were welling with tears again.

Chapter 15

Ben studied the drink menu the waiter had just handed him.

"By the way, how old are you?" Haley asked.

He looked up. "You think I'm not legal?"

She chuckled. "Seriously, how old are you?"

"Twenty-eight."

Her eyes widened dramatically. "You're a baby!"

He frowned. "And how old are you?"

"Twenty-nine."

"Ancient!" he teased.

Haley's laughter warmed his soul like sunlight. She was deeply troubled; she had been all afternoon. The conference call, as near as he could guess, had been a complete disaster. But she was refusing to give in to her misery. She had thrown herself into his birthday celebration like it was some kind of lifeline, delighting in every crayon drawing and sticky home-baked treat they had discovered in the giant box. She had asked him a million questions about his nieces and nephews, his sisters, his parents, and what it was like growing up in Seattle. The more remote the time and anecdotes being recounted, the more relaxed she seemed to feel.

"Would you like some wine?" she asked.

He hesitated. "Would you?"

"I'm not much of a drinker," she replied easily. "But don't let that stop you. Order whatever you like."

He put the menu down. "I'll pass. But thanks."

They studied the regular menus, and after making his decision quickly — the salmon, of course — he found himself staring out the large picture windows at the wildflowers growing on the other side. What would Haley do with herself tomorrow? He was scheduled for two short cruises, morning and early afternoon. Both were already overbooked because of the cancelled tours today. He knew he should be glad that her coming along was not an option. Limiting his time with her over the next few days would be vital to his sanity. But he couldn't make himself like it. Not when he knew that after Saturday, he would almost certainly never see her again.

The waiter returned, and they both ordered the salmon. Ben requested draft root beer, a specialty of the house. Haley sipped ice water.

"Ben?" she asked quietly, interrupting another of his reveries as he gazed across the road at the river. He hoped he wasn't being rude. But he was having a tough time looking her in the face. Her innate attractiveness was bad enough — she was wearing her hair down, and her cobalt blue shirt set off her eyes like emeralds. But the look *in* her eyes was punishing. She was looking at him like he was a dessert she couldn't eat.

"Yes?" he replied, fighting a strong urge to run out across the road and jump in the frigid water.

"I'm sorry if it seems like our conversations are one-sided," she began awkwardly. "You've shared so much about your family and your job, and I haven't shared much of anything. But it's not that I don't feel comfortable with you or that I enjoy being secretive. Frankly, I hate it. It's just that the whole idea behind this week was that I wouldn't think about my problems."

"I get that," Ben said quickly, taking pity on her.

She shook her head. "It's not working. I realized today that it's pointless. My worlds have collided and the fantasy's over. I'm probably going to have to fly back early."

A bolt of fear shot through his chest. "Earlier than Saturday?"

She caught his tone. Smiled at him. Looked miserable again.

"I haven't given up completely yet," she explained. "My plan is to hit one of the internet cafes in town tomorrow and see what progress I can make. Maybe it will be enough. But honestly, I doubt it."

Her eyes glistened with sorrow. "I really love it here, Ben. I don't want to leave. In fact, I don't want to sell. I'm going to try to talk Micah into keeping our uncle's property."

Ben felt a flicker of hope. But just as quickly, it fizzled again. She wasn't talking about moving here. Just visiting once in a while. Maybe.

It wasn't enough.

"I'm glad to hear it," he said, feigning cheer. "Just don't jack up my rent."

Her grin was genuine. "We'll see."

He looked back out the window again.

He heard Haley exhale, then clear her throat. "The way I see it," she began, sounding every bit the lawyer, "we have two choices for the rest of your celebratory meal. One, we both keep pretending. We keep the mood light and the conversation fun and hope to avoid any more 'waterworks,' as you put it."

Ben turned toward her. This sounded promising. "And number two?"

"I completely ruin your birthday by unleashing a horrific torrent of personal angst, going on and on about what my family is putting me through and how incredibly burned out I am trying to manage other people's hysteria while working a never-ending job that's slowly sucking the life out of—"

She stopped suddenly, surprised. She blinked and stared out the window herself. "Did I really just say that?"

Ben's heart pounded. The hope was back, damn it all. He couldn't help himself. "You did," he replied. "And by the way, I choose option two. How do you really feel about your job, Haley?"

She looked at him, seeming genuinely confused. "My job is fine."

He leaned toward her. "You hate it and you know it. Why? Tell me."

She looked conflicted.

"Tell me," he pressed, holding her gaze. *Trust me. Just a little. Please?*

Moisture swamped her eyes again. "Crap! This is so embarrassing!" She wiped her eyes with her napkin. "I swear to you, I'm not normally like this. It's just the damn horm—" Her voice broke off. She looked horrified.

Hormones, Ben finished glumly. He knew he was right.

Haley straightened up again. She looked directly at him and her eyes flashed with a sudden fire. "I do *not* hate my job, Ben. I'm a damn good attorney and I do *not* consider what I do to be unethical. It's just..." Her jaw muscles clenched.

Pain was etched across her face, the pain of an anger long suppressed. He said nothing more, just willed her to get it out.

"I got into law because I promised my father I would when I just a freakin' *child*, and then he died and I could never take it back," she gushed at last. "Everyone expected me to do it and I never even considered doing otherwise. From the day I started law school I've felt like nothing but a stick floating down a river just spinning around in the current. I've got my mother and sister to take care of, and I can handle that, but it never gets better, it only keeps getting worse, and somehow without me ever seeing it coming, I've completely and totally lost control of my own damn life!"

Her voice had risen to a shout. People at other tables turned to look at them.

Ben beamed at her. "Good job, Haley," he said quietly.

The waiter brought their salmon. Haley collected herself. Then she dug in.

"You have a strange effect on me, you know that?" she said mildly, stabbing at a sprig of asparagus.

"Ditto," he replied, admiring her quick cool-down. She undoubtedly *was* an excellent attorney.

"I can't believe you want me to yell at you for a birthday present," she said dryly.

He shrugged. "I wouldn't have thought so either, but hey — it's working for me." He took a bite of salmon. It was perfect. He grew bolder. "Now keep going. Tell me why you feel like you have to take care of your mother and your grown-up sister. Why their phone calls upset you so much."

Haley kept stabbing. "I'm afraid that's a long and messy story. With a disturbingly high 'girl stuff' factor."

"Try me," he begged. "Honesty is cathartic, and you're on a roll."

She stopped her fork and looked at him skeptically. But at least she did not refuse. "My sister is driving me crazy," she said flatly. "My mother, too."

He smiled. "Tell me something I don't know."

She sighed. "Okay, fine. You asked for it. The bottom line is, I've always taken care of Micah. My mother was never reliable, and although my father was very attentive, he was almost never home. My Aunt Janie took good care of us, but she—" Haley paused. "Let's just say we lacked guidance, of a sort. As a result, I grew up super independent — some would say an overachiever."

"You think?" Ben teased.

Haley glared at him.

"Sorry," he said with a chuckle. "Proceed."

"You do realize I don't normally talk about this stuff, don't you? I mean, I really don't. Not with anybody."

Ben stopped a forkful of fish midway to his mouth. "Don't you think that's part of the problem?"

She considered a moment. "Touché."

He smiled and ate the salmon.

"Anyway," Haley continued, "whether it was my fault or not, I don't know, but Micah grew up dependent. On me. And so did my mother, after my father died. We were hoping she would remarry, but now I don't think she ever will. She has a nice condo, plenty of money, and a seemingly endless pool of love interests she can kick out whenever they start to make a mess. But whenever anything goes wrong for either Mom or Micah, it's me they rely on to take care of it. I don't mind, really. I owe that much to my dad. It's just..."

Words failed her.

Ben waited.

"I guess I'm just burned out," she speculated. "I'm starting to wonder if it will ever end. When Micah got married, I thought she would... you know... *need* me less. And she did, for a long time. But as I'm sure you've picked up on by now, her marriage is in trouble." Haley paused a moment, seemingly lost in thought. "Tim is a really great guy, actually. He's smart and sweet and loving. If he has one flaw, it's that he lets my sister walk all over him." Her eyes flashed again. "Honestly, if the man would just grow a pair—"

She broke off. "Whoops. Sorry. Forgot I was talking to a guy."

Ben laughed. Her newfound comfort level exhilarated him. "Go on," he encouraged.

"If he would just stand up to her a little more," Haley corrected, "I believe Micah would respond better. The more he acts like a doormat, the less she respects him. But as much as I'd like to shove the man into a chair and tell him how to fix his marriage, it's really not my place, you know?"

Ben cocked his head at her, impressed. "The concept of minding one's own business does not compute with a single member of the Parker family. I am awestruck."

"Thanks," Haley replied. "I know I should stay out of it. I *want* to stay out of it. But the problem is that Micah won't let me. I hear every detail. Last night she moved out of their apartment, never mind that they have a baby on the way. And my mother is all over it, hyping up the drama under the guise of 'defending' Micah and making everything ten times worse."

Haley gave her head and shoulders a shake. "There. You've gotten me to admit that my job is tumbling me down a river and that my family is dragging my head under the water. Satisfied?"

Not even close. Ben understood better now why Haley felt such a deep sense of obligation to both her family and her career. It was obviously all wrapped up with a sense of loyalty to her father. But she was omitting her most pressing issue.

"Last question," he replied evenly, determined to get it all out —

and now. "I can't help but wonder, Haley. Why isn't there a man in your life?" His gaze held hers, braced for the coming firestorm. Would she look panicked? Guilty? Angry?

She scoffed and rolled her eyes. "Don't even go there. There's no man in my life because the only men I ever interact with are lawyers, corporate shills, and the guy who parks my car. Of the three, I like Desmond best, because at least he has a sense of humor. Unfortunately, he's also married with three kids."

"Bummer," Ben answered mechanically, his mind frantically processing her answer. How could she be so flippant? "If you're trying to convince me that you've been boyfriend-free since law school, I've got to tell you, I'm not buying it," he said, trying hard to sound like he was joking.

Haley made a face. "Law school? Please. I haven't had three dates in a row since college. I have no social life. Nada. And if you tell anyone else that, I swear I'll deny it."

Ben's breath caught in his throat. The room seemed devoid of oxygen. Her tone, her expression — he had never seen her sound or look more genuine, or less guarded. She was sharing with him as she would a close friend. She was showing him every bit of the trust and familiarity he'd been longing for.

Yet she was lying through her teeth.

"Married to the law, eh?" he replied as soon as he could breathe.

She scowled playfully. "Oh, please. Don't say that. How depressing." She took a sip of her water, then looked at him speculatively. "How about you? Leave any girlfriends behind in Hawaii?"

"Nice try," he returned, his voice thin. "But it's my birthday, and I want to talk about you."

She sighed dramatically. "Fine. What else do you want to know?"

Why are you lying to me? "I'll think of something," he replied absently.

Ben felt sick inside. It was as if the honest, down-to-earth Haley he thought he knew had suddenly ceased to exist. He wanted to believe he was wrong about the pregnancy, but he knew he wasn't. The word "hormones" had been half out of her mouth before she'd caught herself. If she'd gotten pregnant through a drunken one-night stand — or worse yet, against her will — there was no way she could fake such a nonchalant response to his question about a man.

No way.

Her denial of any recent relationship had to be a cool, calculated lie.

A lie from an expert. Like, say, an attorney.

I'm good at it.

His head spun.

They ate in silence for a while. "Ben?" Haley asked finally, her tone concerned. "What's wrong?"

He had no idea how to answer her. Mercifully, he didn't have to.

"Will we be having dessert tonight?" the waiter interrupted cheerfully, extending them each a menu.

Haley's eyes remained on Ben. She looked upset. He marshaled every ounce of his willpower and bucked up. "None for me, thanks," he replied, waving off the proffered menu. "I've got an entire orca pinata's worth of candy at home."

The waiter produced their check instead, and Haley paid the bill. Ben struggled to make small talk as they walked out of the restaurant and returned to his car. Haley seemed subdued. The awkwardness between them only mounted during the short drive home, and as they stood between their cabins preparing to part for the night, the tension became unbearable.

"Ben," Haley said finally, her tone pleading. "Please tell me what's wrong."

He couldn't bring himself to look at her. He tried. But he couldn't. If she could lie to him so blithely, they had nothing.

Nothing.

He took a step toward his cabin. "I just wish you'd be a little more honest with me, that's all," he answered, explaining as best he could. She wouldn't understand. But at least he had the satisfaction of knowing that *he* hadn't lied to her. "But I do thank you for the hike this morning. It was wonderful. And thanks again for the birthday dinner." He walked up the steps to his door. "It meant a lot to me that you were willing to listen to me yap about my nieces and nephews for an hour. Not to mention your being brave enough to try Zora's neon green Rice Krispie treats."

"Ben?"

He unlocked his door and opened it, his head down. Her voice was so ridiculously soft. And tender. And sexy. And *genuine*. "Yes?"

"I enjoyed it all, too. Very much. Happy Birthday again."

"Thanks," he stepped inside. "Good night."

He shut the door. He leaned his back against it with a thump and closed his eyes.

God, he was miserable.

Five seconds later, the door vibrated.

"Ben?"

Haley was right behind him. She was knocking. He groaned out loud.

"Open the door!" she ordered.

Ben turned around and jerked it open. Haley stood before him practically trembling, her face set with determination even as her green eyes swam with angst.

"I'm four months' pregnant."

Chapter 16

Haley watched Ben's face with no small amount of terror. He had known she was hiding something from him. She didn't understand why her incomplete unburdening would be so hurtful to him, but the pain she'd glimpsed in his eyes was so raw it cut her own heart like a dagger. She couldn't leave things like that; she couldn't stand another moment of his distance. Nor could she think of another way to make things right.

She knew the cost would be high. He would look at her differently. He sure as hell wouldn't be attracted to her anymore. She knew it was the height of selfishness for her to enjoy their aimless flirting, but the fact was, she did. Now the lightness and fun between them would be gone. Now it would be all seriousness, all the time. And that would be *if* her insane predicament didn't scare him off altogether, even as a friend. For all she knew, he could have ethical problems with surrogacy. He could be repulsed by the whole idea.

But all of that would come later. First — she realized with a new shot of horror — *first* he would think she'd gotten pregnant the regular way. When she had only just assured him there was no guy.

Haley rocked back on her heels with dread. She hadn't thought before she'd spoken; she had merely reacted to his pain. But she should have considered the consequences. He could be even more hurt, now. He could be furious with her for lying to him. He could be disgusted by the sight of her.

As her words hung in the air between them, reverberating in the stillness of the woods, Ben's face underwent a transformation. A transformation that totally baffled her.

"Haley," he said tenderly, his eyes flashing with relief — and something else indescribable. Before she could get the crucial second part of her explanation out of her mouth, he stepped out, wrapped his long arms around her and pulled her to his chest.

Her mouth fell open with shock.

He gave her a squeeze. "I know," he whispered.

Haley's mind reeled, even as her body savored the feel of him. She could stay right here, reveling in his embrace, forever.

Wait. He *what*, now?

She blinked into his shoulder and stiffened. "Excuse me?"

He released her and stepped back again. He didn't say anything. He just looked at her.

"You couldn't possibly know!" she protested.

His grin was lopsided. "Sorry. But I did warn you. I have unnatural knowledge in this area."

"But—" she still couldn't think straight. She was forgetting something major. Still, her gaze flew to her abdomen. "I'm not showing yet," she argued. "Not that much!"

"Okay, I didn't know," he lied half-heartedly. "But I'm glad you told me. Thanks for that."

He smiled at her another moment before his eyes grew stormy. When he spoke again, his voice had a ragged edge. "You want to talk about it?"

The pain was back.

Haley's insides ached anew. *Now* what had she done to the man?

The swirling mess in her brain refused to settle for several long, torturous seconds. When the last piece of the puzzle finally fell into place, she stepped forward with a gasp and put her hands on his arms.

"Oh, God, Ben!" she apologized. "No... It's not what you think. I didn't lie to you!"

His eyebrows rose. He didn't believe her. And why should he?

Haley dropped his arms, but kept hold of one hand. She dragged him to his porch steps and sat down with him. "I told you I'm single, and I am," she explained quickly. "I told you there hasn't been a guy in a long time, and that's true, too." She took a breath. Her heart was pounding. "This baby isn't mine. It's the biological child of my sister and her husband. I'm acting as their surrogate."

Now, she realized with sympathy, was when his brain did the swirling. She could see the succession of thoughts that overtook him, as plain as if he'd been writing them on a white board. First was confusion. Then disbelief. Slowly, the digestion: a rewiring of what he thought he knew, and how it all fit together. Then finally, the acceptance. As she watched the last traces of hurt recede, replaced slowly but surely with relief, respect, and — could that be just a tiny spark of joy? — she felt like breaking down all over again.

"I had no idea you suspected I was pregnant," she said softly. "If I had, I would have told you the truth then. I'm sorry you thought I was lying about being involved with someone else."

He shook his head. "It's not your fault. None of it was my business to begin with. You made that perfectly clear from day one."

"It was day two," she corrected with a smile. "And I wouldn't have had to say anything if we weren't so obviously attracted to each other."

He looked at her with surprise. Another dose of respect.

Haley's insides warmed. "Well, hell, Ben, we might as well get it all out there, don't you think? I adore you. I think you're wonderful. I can barely keep my hands off you. I wish I'd met you some other time and some other place but I didn't and we're here now and it is what it is. We have four days left together at the max. And despite everything I just said, I have nothing to offer you but friendship, for obvious reasons." She paused and took a breath. "The floor is now open to suggestions."

He flashed a grin. "You really can't keep your hands off me?"

Haley rolled her eyes playfully. "Is that all you heard?"

"Pretty much."

Haley smiled and stood up. "Don't taunt me, Captain."

Ben got up also. "Sorry," he said unconvincingly. His hazel eyes sparkled at her, and her knees weakened. So much for his being ethically offended by her pregnancy. Or offended, period. The way he was looking at her, she had to wonder if he had gotten the message at all.

A phone rang inside his cabin. It was the landline. Ben didn't move.

"In the interest of fairness," he said mischievously, "I'm rather fond of you, too. As for keeping my hands off you—"

"Hugs are okay. They're good," Haley said tightly as thoughts of less platonic alternatives tortured her mind. "Are you going to answer the phone?"

"No," he said, showing no response to the insistent ring. "It's the family, calling to wish me a happy birthday. I'll call them back."

Haley's breath caught. She might talk a good game, but if Ben chose to push her boundaries now she wasn't at all sure she could resist him. She was both emotionally exhausted and starved for affection, and his gentle warmth beckoned her like safe harbor in a storm.

You would be using him, she reminded herself firmly.

With a burst of determination she sprinted down his porch steps and back toward her own cabin. "I've monopolized enough of your time already today," she called back. "We can talk more tomorrow if you want. Or not. If you think it's better we don't hang out so much, I totally understand, under the circumstances."

The phone continued to ring. Haley turned to see that Ben hadn't moved. His mind seemed deep in thought. Even standing still doing nothing, his tall, strong figure looked so inviting that her teeth clenched, and she struggled to turn herself around and proceed to her own cabin. If he *did* want to keep spending time together, she could only hope for his sake that he had a strong sense of self-preservation.

Because she was a friggin' mess. A pregnant, dangerous mess.

Run away, Ben. Save yourself.

"A suggestion from the floor," he said finally, his tone amiable. "I'll be at work until late afternoon tomorrow. If you're free by then, I move that we go search for a grizzly."

Haley's pulse pounded. So much for his running away. And so much for her having the strength to push him. "Would this grizzly be behind reinforced Plexiglas? Or better yet, steel bars?"

He grinned at her. "I hope not. It's tough for them to catch salmon that way. But you can stay in the car, safe and sound. I promise."

The phone stopped ringing. Finally.

Trust me, Haley, his eyes pleaded.

"Motion seconded and passed," she said quickly, turning and jogging up onto her porch. "Now call your family. Tell Zora that your landlord said her treats were divine. Ditto to Josh and Mylah for the homemade chocolates. I especially liked the ones with marmalade in the middle, even if you didn't."

"I will not encourage Josh about the marmalade," he returned. "Otherwise, okay."

His phone rang again. He was a popular guy.

He never had answered her question about a girlfriend, had he?

"Goodnight, Ben," she said with finality, unlocking her cabin door. "Happy Birthday."

"Goodnight," he called back, starting towards his phone. He went inside and the ringing stopped.

She would ask him about the girlfriend again tomorrow. He had admitted being attracted to her, but he had never said he *wasn't* involved with someone else. It would make the friend thing a hell of a lot easier if he were.

She closed her door with a sigh. He didn't have a girlfriend. Not at the moment, anyway. If he did, he wouldn't be looking at Haley the way he looked at her. He was too honest to play those games. She might only have met Ben Parker three days ago, but she knew already that he was a one-in-a-million, bonafide gem. Every female twenty-something in the state of Hawaii had to be a complete and total idiot to let him get away.

Her teeth clenched harder.

What was she?

Ben finished his conversation with his youngest nephew, which had been a little one-sided because Aiden wasn't talking in complete sentences yet, and got back on the phone with the tot's mother. Lara's call had been the last of three Ben had received from his various family members, one right after the other. Since his first call with Maggie this afternoon, his spirits had risen considerably, and evidently, the change had been noted.

"You sure everything's okay out there?" Lara asked with her typical take-charge, no-nonsense tone. "Mags said you were upset about something, but to me you sound more on the hyper side. What's up?"

Ben hesitated. He would rather go down with his ship than talk to any of his other three sisters about his love life. But Lara was different. Lara had good sense about people, she didn't overdramatize, and most importantly — she knew how to keep her mouth shut. "Promise this will go no further?"

"You know you don't have to ask me that," she said shortly.

"I know," Ben appeased. "Sorry. But it's important. I don't think I can handle any extra grief right now."

Lara waited.

"When you met Dan," he asked finally, "how long did it take before you started to sense a real connection?" He fidgeted as he awaited her answer. He expected her to be shocked. As many awkward family conversations about love and sex as Ben had been an unwilling party to over the years, he had never, *ever* talked about himself.

Perhaps because of that, Lara's answering tone — much to his relief — was intentionally matter-of-fact. "Well, it wasn't instantaneous, if that's what you're asking. He was working for a supplier, and we were both in the same boring meeting, and there were no sparks whatsoever. But then we met again about a month later, and that time we had to work together on a problem. It's tough to explain, but... just the way he answered things, the way he approached the problem, the little jokes he made. We knew really quickly that we were on the same wavelength, and the attraction grew from there. We decided to try a date, and the rest is history. Married eighteen months later — no muss, no fuss, no drama. Just two happy people enjoying each other. Does that answer your question?"

"Sort of," Ben replied, not entirely sure what he was asking. He only knew that where Haley was concerned, no matter what course he took, he would be playing with fire. "Listen, Lara," he said, running his hand nervously through his hair. He hated standing up in the kitchen to talk, but the ultra-cheap landline was attached to the wall with a cord. "I've met someone, but she's only here for a week. There are about twelve thousand reasons why nothing is ever likely to come of it, but I can't help wondering if there's a way to keep her in my life. In fact, I can't seem to think about anything else."

Lara was quiet a moment. But when she did finally speak, he could tell she was smiling. "Well, damn, Ben! I was about to think you'd never get bit!"

"Yeah, yeah," he said impatiently, beginning to regret the conversation. "Well, I've been lucky before. This time I'm screwed, okay?"

"And you're telling me this why?" she asked perceptively.

"Because I don't know what to do," he responded. "I don't know whether I should go for it and risk a major fall, or run screaming while I still have the chance."

"Too late for that, little brother," she said confidently. "Sounds like you're looking at a major fall either way."

Ben groaned. "Why did I call you?"

"You didn't," Lara pointed out. "I called you. But you did solicit my advice. Which touches me, by the way. Does this woman feel the same way you do?"

"I don't know how to answer that."

She clucked her tongue. "Not good, bro. Just remember this: Actions speak louder than words. You said she's there for a week. Is she on vacation?"

"Sort of."

Lara went quiet.

"What?" Ben prompted.

She sighed. "Do you remember when Jenna did her semester abroad and came back totally gaga in love with that guy Preston that she met in London?"

"Of course not," Ben said shortly. "I was what — thirteen? I blocked out all that crap as it happened."

"Well," Lara continued, unperturbed. "She met him near the end of her stay, and they had a fabulous couple of weeks together seeing the sights. He took her everywhere, even up into Scotland. She came back raving about how she wanted Mom and Dad to ditch the mower and start raising sheep."

Ben sighed. "You know, I think I do remember that."

"What you probably don't remember is how it ended. Jenna saved up to pay for half his plane fare so he could come visit her over Christmas break. But when he arrived in Seattle, she hardly recognized him. She said he was paler than she remembered, he smelled weird, and he had a bad attitude about the weather. A guy from England, complaining about the rain. After four days she put him on a bus to LA and they never saw each other again."

Ben was feeling increasingly uncomfortable. "And your point is?"

Lara exhaled slowly. "You've got to watch out for 'vacation love,' Ben. You more than anyone else I know. You *live* in vacation world. People go to Alaska or Hawaii and they're not their normal selves — they're in vacation mode. Everything looks different. Everything is romantic and exciting. It's hard for a tourist to separate the people she meets, and how she feels about them, from how she feels about the location and the good times. You're a romantic figure to begin with — the sexy boat captain with the killer dimples. You're a charmer; it's part of your job. But to vacation women, you're all wrapped up with the ocean and the whales and the fun and the beautiful scenery. You're part of a whole package they can't help loving. Am I making any sense here?"

Too much. "Yeah. I get it."

"No, you don't," Lara said quickly. "I'm not saying that a woman couldn't fall for you for *you*. Many have already, as we both know — and don't go getting a swell head over it. I'm just saying that if you're trying to decide how much trouble this woman is worth, and part of that is figuring out if she feels the same way... well, I'm not sure either of you can answer that question while she's still on vacation."

Ben wrapped the phone cord idly around his wrist. Lara was right, dammit. He and Haley had known each other for only three days. His feelings for her were strong, despite his getting to know her at a time when she was in crisis, with her emotions in tatters and her dirty laundry hanging out to dry. But her perspective was different. She wasn't seeing him at his weakest. She was seeing him as a lifeline, a rescuer, even as an entertainer... at a time when she was already emotionally vulnerable. He couldn't possibly be sure that what she felt for him was real, and neither could she.

"Ben? You still there? Jeez, I didn't mean to drag you down," Lara said remorsefully. "I'm not saying you shouldn't go for it! I think you should. Look, I know you don't want to hear this, but you don't *need* one more 'meh' girlfriend you're struggling to keep things going with when deep down, you know it's no good anyway. Life's too short and you're too old. You get to be thirty and it's time to go for the real thing. Even if it costs you."

"I'm twenty-eight!" he protested.

"Whatever," she said dismissively. "You want to know when it's real? I'll tell you. When you meet a woman you're willing to give up the whales for."

Ben went silent. It was an old criticism. One which never failed to sting. His entire family thought his lifestyle was nothing but a lark of youth, a wanderlust he would grow out of. Someday he would get tired of never having any money, and then he would settle down. He'd fall in love with a woman and his perspective would change; they'd have kids and settle down.

Settle *down*.

Why didn't anyone ever settle *up?*

"Thanks for the advice, Lar," he said flatly.

"Don't give up on her, Ben," Lara said quickly, no doubt sensing his dwindling patience. "Please don't give up. Just be smart about it. Go slow. Get to know everything you can about her. Don't rush things even if she begs you — and you *know* what I mean. If she leaves and you can't live without her, go visit her wherever she lives. Then you'll know."

Ben unwound the phone cord. "I hear what you're saying. Thanks. Goodnight, Lara."

"Goodnight, Ben," she returned uneasily. "And happy birthday."

They hung up. Ben blew out a breath and crossed to a kitchen stool. It was getting late, but the sun was still shining outside his windows, clinging to the night sky with the same tenacity that defined everything about the short, glorious Alaskan summer. *Grow now. Feast now. Enjoy now.* Soon enough, the cold and the darkness would return.

He looked out toward Haley's cabin. He had no idea what the future held for the two of them. But running away from her was no longer an option.

Chapter 17

Haley walked to the railing of her porch and looked down the gravel road. She saw nothing stirring.

Ben had said "late afternoon." It was nearly 4:30 PM. Did that qualify?

She returned to the middle of her porch and jogged in place. She was itching to run, but had no intention of doing so when she could turn a corner and run smack into a bear. Especially not when she had already forgotten which kind you were supposed to play dead with.

Where was he?

She had been looking forward to their adventure all day. And all last night. Never mind how wretched the rest of her day had gone, she still had her time with Ben. Precious little of it left now, but what she was given, she intended to make the most of.

She smiled as she pictured him out on his boat with another group of excited tourists. It had been overcast and cool for much of the week, but today the sky was blue and the air was practically balmy. He would have a good time out on the water. He deserved to have some fun.

She still could not believe, no matter how often she pinched herself, that he knew about her pregnancy and still wanted to spend time with her. Even when he thought she was pregnant by some mystery man, he had been friendly and kind. If he was some weirdo with three eyes who was grateful for *anyone's* company that would be one thing — but a man who looked like Ben could hang out with a girl who looked like Alexa the waitress anytime. Instead, he was hanging with Haley Olson. Pregnant, emotionally fried Haley Olson.

He was taking her out to find a grizzly.

Her smile broadened at the thought. It was a credit to Ben that she could smile at all. Considering that at this very moment, pretty much every problem in her life was coalescing into one giant, raging inferno.

Micah had further punished Tim by staying away a second night. And instead of going to find her and asking her to come back, he was throwing himself into his work and doing exactly what Micah had told him to do, which was refrain from trying to contact her at all. Micah, of course, wanted desperately for him to come after her and got more depressed each hour he did not. Michelle couldn't believe that Tim was "so ready to let Micah go," and in her last conversation with Haley had inquired about the legalities of child custody. In the meantime, every day took them all closer to receiving the final results of the amniocentesis, which at this point could only make things worse.

Enter Stirjon Chemicals. A fishermen's group had brought a civil action against the company, claiming damage in the form of a fish kill that began soon after "renovations" to the outdated plant upstream. The group was asking for discovery, which meant that Stirjon would be scrambling to hide any damning internal documents penned by their scientific group. Haley's job would be to make sure those documents stayed hidden.

Whether Stirjon's effluent was actually causing the problem, Haley didn't know. At least not yet. But more than likely, she eventually *would* know that every day she skillfully stalled the discovery process and buried the fishermen's group in an avalanche of legal challenges and maneuvers, a little more toxin was creeping toward the orcas of Puget Sound.

Some days she did hate her job. Not that she would condone the company's polluting — she would, in fact, bust her butt to make them stop it. It was in their own stupid interest, besides being the right thing to do.

Still, Ben's suspicions were at least partly right. If she had the choice, she would much rather work for the fishermen's group. She smirked as she imagined herself cobbling together an irrefutable case, soaking the reckless, irresponsible jerks at Stirjon for such a fortune that no other company would risk making the same mistake.

But she didn't have that choice. There was no way she could jump ship now and work as a plaintiff's attorney. She had her hands too deep in the field; she would run into constant conflicts of interest. And if she bailed on environmental law altogether she would lose four hard-fought years of expertise and professional clout. She hadn't been named lead associate on the Stirjon case for nothing. Her acumen was widely respected. She couldn't just give that up.

She looked down the road again, but saw only a raven fluttering in the weeds. "Come on, Ben," she muttered out loud. "I need to see your smile."

The Stirjon situation, irritating as it was, was not even her biggest concern. Bob had been flipping out all day over rumors that a discovery ruling was about to be issued on the Consolidated case. And although that particular minefield risked no new damage to the environment, it risked something of major importance to Haley: her time in Alaska. If the rumors were true and the ruling proved unfavorable, she would have no choice but to hop on the next plane out.

But she refused to think about that. Right now, for the rest of the afternoon and hopefully the bulk of the evening, she wanted to think about only one thing.

Having a fabulous time with Ben Parker.

To her joy, she at last heard the distant crunch of tires on gravel. She stared down the road anxiously until Kenai Marine's dilapidated Jetta came into view. Her heart soared as she watched Ben drive up to the cabins, park, unfurl his long legs from the too-small car, and stand.

His dimples were showing. "You ready?"

"Do I need anything besides what I brought along yesterday?" she asked brightly.

"Nope."

"Then I'm ready."

Ben closed the car door and headed towards his cabin. "Give me two minutes."

Haley went back into her own cabin to collect her pack, debating over whether to bring her phone. With a sigh of resignation, she decided she would have to. She couldn't afford to miss another late-day email from Bob, and it would be easier to check again on the way home than have to fetch the phone at the cabin and then drive herself back out to the highway. She double-checked to make sure the phone was off, then threw it in her bag.

She walked back outside and waited by the Jetta. Ben arrived seconds later, dressed in jeans and another of those soft, plaid button-down shirts that made him look like the world's sexiest lumberjack. His hair was windblown and his eyes twinkled with anticipation as he approached her.

Haley sprang up from the car hood against which she was leaning. Without any critical thought whatsoever she stepped forward, threw her arms around his neck, and hugged him. The gesture was brief, friendly, and surprised her as much as it probably did him. But she didn't regret it.

As she pulled back, he looked at her with amusement, and perhaps a trace of skepticism. "What was that for?" he asked mildly.

"You got me," she said candidly. "Couldn't seem to resist." She started to apologize, but reconsidered. To hell with that. She was done hiding her feelings.

Ben said nothing as they got in the car and drove out through the woods to the main road. He didn't seem upset. Just thoughtful.

"How were the whales today?" she asked cheerfully.

He smiled. "Frolicking. Saw one on the first tour and two on the second. No orcas today, but the porpoises were in fine form. Good day for tips, too."

"Any kids on board? Did the otters do that somersault thing?"

Haley relaxed into her seat as he recounted the day's adventures in colorful detail and with plenty of laughs. She loved hearing him talk about his job and about nature in general. His enthusiasm was always contagious.

"And should I ask how your day went?" he asked much later. "Or are we not thinking about that right now?"

"We are not," she answered matter-of-factly. "But can I reserve the right to start babbling incoherently about it at some random moment in the future?"

He grinned at her. "You may."

An unfamiliar warm and bubbly feeling welled up within Haley's chest. It took her a moment to realize it was happiness.

"You were so right. You know that?" she blurted.

"Of course I was. About what?"

"About the cause of my... you know, the waterworks. When I left Newport Beach, I felt like I was suffocating. Like if I didn't get away from it all, and *soon*, something inside me was going to break. I did need to get away, physically, but the real problem was that I was bottling everything up. Pretending it wasn't getting to me. Pretending I didn't need or want to talk about it."

She let out a contented breath. "It sounds so cliché, doesn't it? Needing to talk about something. But the evidence speaks for itself. It's such a relief to know that *you* know about the baby and Micah's flipping out and that you understand how much it weighs on me. There's no reason I should feel as relieved as I do. Everything still sucks. In fact it's getting worse, and there's absolutely nothing you can do about it. And yet, at this very moment, I am in a ridiculously good mood."

She looked at him with a grin. "Go figure."

His answering smile was broad. "Go figure."

They drove along the Seward Highway beyond Moose Pass, chatting easily about everything and nothing. She learned that he had once been bitten by a mongoose (he insisted it was his own fault), and he learned that for a girl who grew up wealthy, she was woefully under-traveled, having been to both Canada and Mexico but spending no significant time anywhere east of the Mississippi besides Orlando. After a while Ben turned off onto a succession of more and more rural roads, ending their journey on a narrow gravel lane in the middle of dense woods.

"We're here," he announced importantly.

Haley looked around. "Here" was in the middle of nowhere. He had parked the car on a narrow bridge over a stream, as far to the side of the road as he could get, which was not very far, considering the bridge had no shoulder and no guard rail. The trees and brush were thick all around, and the stream that ran beneath them was shallow, but swift. She saw an official-looking sign posted on a tree down by the water and craned her neck to read it. *Area behind this sign closed.*

"Where is here, exactly?" she asked.

His smile was furtive. "A little-known hotspot for grizzlies on the Kenai Peninsula. Right about now, every year, the salmon run through here. It's not a sure thing, but if we hang out for a while, we've got a good shot at seeing a coastal brown bear fishing for his dinner. You game?"

Haley looked around again. Her window was cracked open, and outside the glass she could already see a half dozen mosquitos bobbing around, surveying a likely path to entry. She slipped a hand to the armrest and rolled up the window. There was something spooky about the place. She wasn't scared exactly, but the idea of grizzly bears hiding in the dark depths of the forest mere feet from the car did creep her out.

Still, in the right company, spooky could be fun.

"We're staying in the car, right?" she confirmed, looking again at the ominous warning on the tree. It was a permanent metal sign. It was doubtless there for a reason.

"I said we would, didn't I?" Ben reminded her. "I always keep my promises."

Haley met his eyes. "I know you do. And yes, I'm game. So what do we do now?"

He adjusted his seat back and stretched out his legs. "We wait. And watch."

Haley settled more comfortably in her own seat. "Sounds good." She studied the edges of the stream as far as she could see — which was not very far, because the stream meandered and the brush was heavy to either side.

Ben reached into the back seat and produced a pair of binoculars. "You can use these if you want."

Haley thanked him and gave it a shot. But rather than searching for bears, she studied the clear, rushing stream. "Oh, wow!" she exclaimed after a moment. "There's two gigantic fish swimming down there. Red ones."

"Sockeye, probably," he commented. "They get the bright colors when they're spawning."

Haley lowered the binoculars. She didn't care to equate the scaly free-swimming things below her with last night's entree. Nor could her mind safely dwell on the word "spawning."

"I like fish, but we never ate much of it growing up," she reminisced instead. "At least not at home. My Aunt Janie thought it smelled bad. Even when we had a cat and fed it canned food, she made us give it to him outside." Haley smiled at the memory. She and Micah had broken that rule once, and Janie had had a full-out, foot-stomping fit.

Ben turned to her, his expression curious. "Tell me more about your aunt. You haven't mentioned her much."

Haley's smile turned bittersweet. She had avoided talking about Janie for the sake of her own composure. It would feel good, now, to talk about her whole family.

"Janie was my mother's younger sister," she began. "Much younger. She was a late-in-life surprise to my grandparents, and she was born with Down Syndrome. The doctors said she would have a low IQ and not to expect much from her, and when she surpassed their expectations they called her 'high functioning' and told my grandparents they were lucky. The school put her in special ed, and after years of no one even trying to teach her to read, my grandmother decided to try herself. Janie did learn to read and to do simple mathematics. If she'd had better support earlier and been pushed harder, we all suspect she could have learned a whole lot more. Janie was smart in so many ways. She was bright and energetic and hilariously funny."

Haley paused a moment, her eyes misting. She would not cry again. After yesterday, she was officially cried out for at least a year. But thinking about Janie always made her emotional. "Janie's brainpower was never a problem," she explained. "Her problem was her heart. She was born with multiple defects, and even though she was operated on several times as a child, she never was quite right. She was limited physically, in terms of stamina, and she frequently got sick."

Haley cast a glance at Ben. She hoped she wasn't boring him. He hadn't said a word. But his expression showed no boredom. Only sympathetic interest.

She took a breath. She wanted to tell him about Janie. She would have to, in order to explain what was happening with Micah and the baby. She cast another glance into the eerily dark forest surrounding them.

No bears.

"When my mother found out she was pregnant with Micah and me, she totally flipped," Haley began. "She was terrified at the prospect of twins and wanted to hire a live-in baby nurse. My dad would have agreed, but Janie wouldn't hear of it. She loved babies and wanted to help take care of us herself. So my grandparents moved her out of their house and into ours, and she lived with us until Micah and I were sixteen. Nobody wanted her to leave then, but my grandmother broke her hip and Janie felt they needed her more."

Haley's peripheral vision caught a blur of black to her right. She startled in her seat.

"It's just a raven," Ben said calmly. "Go on."

She tried to slow her heartbeat. "A grizzly wouldn't just attack the car, would it?" she asked, feeling stupid. "Could it break the windows?"

Ben gave her a sardonic look. "I'm not answering that question. Keep talking."

Haley's nerves calmed. "Aunt Janie was like a second mother to us. She rocked us and fed us and sang us songs. She stayed home with us when my parents were out — which was a lot. She did most of the laundry and all of the cooking. She cleaned the house, put bandages on booboos, and listened to all the usual complaints about mean girls and gross boys and crabby teachers. What seems crazy now is how much she loved it. My mother never *made* Janie do any of those things; she never even asked. Janie just liked taking care of people. If my mother got to the laundry before her or tried to mop the kitchen, Janie would sulk and do it over again. Eventually Mom just gave up and let her do whatever she wanted. Janie was nervous in crowds and never wanted to go out, so our home was her kingdom."

"She sounds amazingly industrious, for someone with a heart problem," Ben offered.

Haley nodded. "She was. She hardly ever sat down, unless she was sick or having trouble breathing. Even if she was just wandering slowly around the house wiping random things with a dust rag, she was always in motion. But we didn't love her because of her work ethic, we loved her because she was *good*. She was so incredibly giving. So sympathetic. So kind. She was a perpetually cheerful person who always looked on the bright side, and she expected everyone else to do the same. And we did, if only to humor her. She made our home feel safe and happy, because if there was nothing else to laugh at, she would laugh at herself. One time she accidentally put salt in a pie instead of sugar, and when we all grimaced and spit it out, instead of being embarrassed or feeling guilty she literally laughed herself under the table."

Ben chuckled, and Haley looked at him. "You're easy to talk to, you know that? Stop me if I'm boring you."

"You, boring me?" he asked with surprise. "You could talk for another hour straight and I'd still be ahead in the family stories department."

Haley smiled her thanks. "There's a reason I'm telling you all this now. Janie isn't with us anymore. She died the year Micah and I went off to college. She went under anesthesia for a minor surgical procedure, and her heart just stopped. They couldn't bring her back. We didn't even know she was having surgery that day. We were stunned. And devastated. And completely heartbroken."

"I can imagine," Ben said softly. "I'm sorry."

Haley nodded. "So you can see why... well, let's just say that everyone in my family has rather strong feelings when it comes to Down Syndrome."

She paused and looked away, her eyes sweeping the trees again. She saw some small birds. Nothing else. A pickup truck approached, crept by them on the narrow bridge, then sped up again. The sky was still blue and sunny, but the sun's rays seemed not to penetrate the gloom of the dense woods.

"You're worried about the baby you're carrying, aren't you?" he asked quietly.

Haley's eyes returned to his face. "You know, for a guy, you are scary perceptive about women."

He pretended to frown. "Don't remind me."

Haley couldn't help but chuckle. "Well, you're right," she acknowledged. "With in vitro fertilization, prenatal testing is a part of the bargain. Everything looked fine with this baby in the beginning. The blood tests were inconclusive, but nothing to be concerned about, and the ultrasounds all looked fine. It was the chorionic villus sampling that turned our worlds upside down. It came back with a diagnosis of Down Syndrome."

Ben's expression remained sympathetic, but he said nothing. Haley took another deep breath and pressed on. "The doctors weren't convinced, though. They gave Micah and Tim every reason to hope that the test was a false positive, because it didn't seem to fit with the rest of the data. They suggested confirmation with amniocentesis. But as I have a feeling you already know"—she glanced at him sideways— "we couldn't do that immediately. We had to wait until I was almost a month farther along."

"That couldn't have been easy," he said. "On any of you."

"It was not," Haley agreed. "I honestly thought Micah would lose her mind. In fact, I'm still not entirely sure she hasn't. Because as miserable and heartbreaking as the whole thing was, the worst part of it was Tim's reaction. When the doctor told them the test was positive for DS, the first words out of the man's mouth were 'Is it too late to terminate?'"

Ben winced slightly.

"He didn't mean it, though," Haley clarified. "I know he didn't. Those were the words that came out of his mouth, but I suspect that what he was really thinking was more like, 'Wait, I can't handle this. Can I get off the bus now?'"

Ben smiled at her. "I'd say you're equally perceptive about men, counselor."

"Thank you," she replied, her cheeks feeling suddenly warm. "Unfortunately, Tim said the words that he said. And when Micah heard them, she translated them to mean something entirely different. What she heard was, 'Your Aunt Janie's life wasn't worth living.'"

Ben blew out a breath. "I see the problem."

Haley forged on. "Those four weeks of waiting were a nightmare. Tim reversed his statement almost immediately and told Micah that he didn't want to terminate, that he wanted their baby very much whether it had special needs or not. But he could only appease her so much, because the damage was done. She doubted his dedication to the baby. She tried to make herself believe him, and they eventually came to a sort of truce. But ever since that day, I've watched Micah's mental state deteriorate before my eyes. She's been tortured, not only with worrying about Tim and how he feels about having a baby with DS, but how *she* feels about it."

Haley checked to see if Ben was still with her. He was. "I know how she feels," Haley continued, "because I've been feeling all the same things myself. We loved Janie so much. In a lot of ways, she was more of a parent to us than either our mother or our father. Either of us would be proud, *thrilled*, to have a baby just like her. But Janie's personality and her spirit were one thing, and the physical suffering she endured was another."

Haley's eyes grew misty again. "She died when she was only thirty-six, Ben. I know that children born with DS today have much better odds of living longer, fuller lives than when Janie was born. But still. Micah is torn apart inside because as much as she loved Janie and wants to honor her life, she will be devastated if this baby has DS. She wants her child to be healthy. Everyone does. But whenever she finds herself wishing so strongly for a baby *without* DS, she feels guilty."

Haley saw the tops of some tall weeds moving on the far bank of the stream across the road. She stared for a moment, and so did Ben. But the brush was too dense to see through. And the movement stopped.

"I went in for the amnio a little over a week ago," she continued. "We got the preliminary results the next evening. It was negative. There's still a three to four percent chance the baby could have a rare version of DS, and we can't rule that out until the full results come in. But for now, there's a 96 to 97 percent chance the baby is perfectly fine."

Ben smiled at her. "Congratulations."

"We were all overjoyed," Haley said, smiling. But as she remembered the rest of that evening, she frowned again. "Unfortunately, what should have been a celebration didn't turn out that way. We were all pleased and relieved, and Tim was over the moon, but Micah—"

Haley closed her eyes and gave her head a shake. Not for the first time, she wondered how she and Micah could share as much DNA as they did, even as fraternal twins. "Instead of sharing in his relief, Micah somehow managed to be offended by it. As if the degree of happiness he was showing was in direct proportion to how horrified he *would have been* if the result had been positive. I'm no shrink, but I have a strong hunch that what Micah was really feeling was guilt over her *own* relief. But she couldn't deal with that. So she took it out on him. And she still is. Two nights ago she moved out of their apartment. She's been staying at our mother's condo."

Ben blew out a breath and ran a hand through his hair. "Wow," he said finally. His eyes met hers. "I had no idea. I mean... No wonder you were falling apart, Haley."

She smiled sadly. "I'm afraid I still am, my friend. When I agreed to be a surrogate, the marriage in question was rock solid, and so was the baby's mother. Micah's always been emotional and impulsive, but I've never seen her behave as irrationally as this. I've tried to reason with her, to help her see Tim's side, to understand where all her guilt and anger is coming from. But she won't listen to me. And I can't get her to see a therapist, either. When I made the decision to bail on her and come to Alaska, I really was at the end of my rope. I was afraid that my own angst might be harming the baby."

"It was a good decision," Ben said quickly. "You do feel better now, don't you?"

"I do," Haley said softly, her hand moving involuntarily to her abdomen. "But I still have to think about Fred."

"Fred?" Ben said dubiously. "The baby's name is Fred?"

Haley chuckled. "No. Unofficially it's Sophia or Liam. At least those were the leading contenders the last time I heard. Micah and Tim asked not to know the gender until the baby's born. I've always thought of the baby as a girl, for whatever reason, so I balance that out by calling her Fred. Weird, I know. But it works for me. It also helps to keep that 'safe distance' the counselor advised."

Ben smiled at her. "Fred it is, then."

Haley smiled back. "Fred deserves the best. And as much as I want to shake my sister sometimes, I've always believed she would make a wonderful mother. And I know Tim will be a great father. It's what both of them have always wanted, even before they met each other. I keep telling myself that all this craziness will pass soon, that Micah will get back to her normal, only slightly nutty self and that Fred will have a happy, stable home."

Haley's voice broke. "And then other times..."

She couldn't finish.

"You wonder if you've made a mistake," Ben supplied, his voice barely above a whisper.

Fresh moisture swelled behind Haley's eyes, but she was able to control it. Despite the toll this conversation was taking on her, she did feel stronger today. Much stronger.

"Yes," she admitted. "I do wonder. And then I feel guilty for wondering."

Ben shifted in his seat. Haley could sense that he was itching to hold her, and she wanted that, too. But the bucket seats of the Jetta were hardly conducive. And no way was she getting out of the car.

"You have nothing to feel guilty about," he said gently, instead. "You know that. You've gone above and beyond — *way* beyond — for your sister already, and you're taking good care of Fred now. To second-guess is to be human. Don't beat yourself up over it."

"I don't usually," Haley defended. "Irrational guilt is so terribly *Micah*. I know that sounds awful of — *oh, my God, look!*" She jumped in her seat and pointed frantically out the front windshield.

A giant brown creature trundled out of the tall weeds and onto the road just twenty feet ahead. The bear padded on heavy paws to the midline of the road, stopped dead, and stared right at them.

"It's a *grizzly!*" Haley exclaimed with a squeak.

"No, it's not," Ben whispered back, a catch of humor in his voice. "It's a black bear."

Haley wanted to glare at him, but could not take her gaze off the roughly three-hundred pound mammal that remained still as a statue, its dark eyes locked on her own. "It's *brown!*" she protested.

"Well, obviously it's brown," Ben said with amusement. "But it's a brown *black* bear."

"Of course it is," Haley said wryly.

Ben chuckled. "Look at the shape of its head and the slope of its back. Grizzlies' faces are more dished in and they have shoulder humps. This bear is smaller, too."

"That's *small?*" Haley said with disbelief. Even with the car between them, her every muscle was taut. "Why is it staring at us?"

"He's just checking us out," Ben explained. "Deciding if we're a threat. Whether he wants to risk messing with us or not."

"*Not!*" Haley suggested in a whisper.

As if on cue, the bear broke eye contact, lowered its head, and moved quickly the rest of the way across the road. It plunged into the weeds ahead of them and disappeared.

"Awesome," Ben murmured.

They watched silently for a few more seconds as the tops of the weeds on the stream's far bank jostled, betraying movement beneath. They saw a flash of brown as the animal moved from the bank into the trees. Then the bear disappeared again into the ferns and heavy brush of the forest floor.

Haley stared after it, speechless.

"See there?" Ben crowed. "That's what happens 99% of the time. Bear sees human, bear goes the other way. They're not stupid. They have better things to do with their time than tangle with the likes of you or me."

Haley flashed him a skeptical look. "Or a three-thousand pound car," she quipped.

Ben laughed. "Did you enjoy that?" he asked eagerly.

She grinned at him. "You know I did."

He grinned back.

Haley's heart skipped a beat. She cursed the wide plastic console that separated them. She was also profoundly grateful for it.

The things I do for you, Micah...

Haley shook herself. She couldn't think like that. She *could not.*

"Well, I *was* promised a grizzly," she teased, breaking the spell. "But I suppose a brown black bear will be acceptable."

Ben shook his head. "No way. At Parker Naturalist Services, we guarantee 100% satisfaction or your money back. We can try again another time. Or we can refund your money, in the form of my buying you a barbecue sandwich at this little dive I know of not far from here. You hungry?"

At the mention of food, Haley's stomach growled. "Starving. I accept your offer, Captain Parker."

"Which one, counselor?"

Haley considered. "Well, I'm hungry now. But it would be fun to try again another day, too. Can I have both?"

Ben's eyes twinkled at her, and within their depths Haley read the same emotions she knew were written plainly in her own. Fondness. Longing. And frustration.

"You can have anything you want," he replied.

Chapter 18

Haley picked up her suitcase — very slowly and carefully — and slid it into the trunk of her rental car. She could have waited and asked Ben to lift it for her. But she had asked him for more than enough already. Besides, the bag wasn't that heavy. Not nearly as heavy as her heart.

She closed the trunk and walked back to the front porch of her cabin. Her eyes drifted out over the distant snow-laced mountains, and she drank in every inch of the view, attempting to memorize it. *I'll be back*. She promised herself. *I will*.

She had it all worked out in her mind already. If Micah was willing, Haley would make arrangements to buy out her sister's interest with some kind of payment plan. If not, Haley could sell off the back acres around her uncle's house as payment to Micah and keep the cabins for herself. She would find a property management company to handle the rentals — with the understanding that Ben had first dibs, of course. The other cabin would have to be rented by the week. That way, whenever she visited, she could stay here. And enjoy this very view.

Her mind had been frantically plotting such scenarios for hours now. Ever since the internet cafe in which she had parked herself this morning was invaded by the ring of her cell phone and ominous words from Bob. *The discovery ruling was issued this morning. It's just what we were afraid of. In fact, it's worse. We need to move fast, Haley. You've got to get back here ASAP.*

He had no idea that, just as he was speaking those dreaded words, Haley had been looking out the cafe's front windows to see a bald eagle swoop down over the water of Resurrection Bay and dive for a fish. Nor, she suspected, would he have cared.

I'll be back.

Haley repeated the mantra which, ever since, had been the only thing keeping her from crumpling. She had thought that she was finished with the crying. But she'd also thought she had more time with Ben.

Their first real outing together since her full disclosure had been as close to a perfect evening as Haley could remember. It certainly exceeded any date she had ever been on, despite the fact that nothing physical had happened between them. In fact, if not for that aggravating omission, the evening would have *been* perfect.

She breathed in another lungful of the crisp air, then let it out with a sigh. The weather was beautiful again today. Ben was out on a full-day tour, which meant he would take his passengers all the way to the glacier again. The longer trek was his favorite, and Haley smiled to think of him enjoying his day. She tried not to think about how little time they would have together when he returned. She had offered to cook spaghetti tonight, and he had offered her another shot at seeing a wild grizzly. The spaghetti sauce was ready and waiting. But she would have to eat and run.

Was it crazy to think that she could return to Seward before Ben left for the season? It had taken her years to manage even six days off. But now she was more motivated. Even three days in Alaska would be worth the flights. What was the money, to her? She had nothing better to spend it on.

I'll be back. I will.

Even as she repeated the words to herself, Haley's heart felt like lead. The six days she had just taken had not come without a price. She would return to her office significantly behind, and would immediately be hit with both the Consolidated crisis and the looming disaster at Stirjon. It could take months to dig herself out again.

A rumble sounded down the gravel road, and Haley's heart began to pound. Ben was back. And early, too. He must have tidied up the boat — or whatever it was a captain did — in record time. She crossed the driveway from her porch to his, then went inside to start the pasta boiling. It felt a little too intimate, cooking in his kitchen, but hers had no cookware and it seemed silly to drag everything over and back. Besides, she was already using his shower.

Except for last night.

Haley's cheeks flamed at the thought. She had been taking her showers when Ben was out, but yesterday she'd had no time. When they returned last night he had extended the offer as always, but the moment had been an awkward one. As well-behaved as they had both managed to be throughout a friendly evening of barbecue, bear watching, and the sharing of embarrassing family stories, the undercurrent of attraction between them was impossible to ignore. Their increasing emotional closeness had, of course, only made things worse. And with those embers already glowing, the idea of her unclothed self showering within a ten-foot radius of his bed was the equivalent of lighter fluid.

Ben's footsteps pounded up onto his porch. He opened his front door to see her standing in his kitchen, stirring a pot over his stove.

Hi, Honey. I'm home!

Haley's cheeks flared further. She'd had no intention of setting up such a pat scene of domesticity. The idea was too funny. She was a working maniac — she was never home at dinnertime and hadn't regularly cooked for herself, much less anyone else, since law school. She lived on energy bars, protein shakes, take-out, and anything that could be eaten straight from the fridge. The spaghetti sauce, her signature contribution to any family gathering, was a favorite of her Aunt Janie's. It was also the one and only dish she could actually make.

She didn't have to tell him any of that. She had admitted the same last night, and more. But she could tell from the startled, yet distinctly delighted, twinkle in his eyes that his coming home to find her in his kitchen was less than objectionable.

Too bad she was about to ruin his fun.

She said nothing. But as she looked back at him and he took in her expression, it was clear she didn't have to.

"You're leaving early," he stated.

She nodded miserably.

"When?"

"Tonight." She averted her face, presumably to stir the pot. "There's been a major development with one of our biggest clients. Bob wants me in the office tomorrow, so I'm booked on an overnight flight. I have to meet with the executor of my uncle's estate again, too, to give him back the keys and discuss what happens next."

She turned her head slightly to brave a glance at Ben. His face looked every bit as wretched as she felt.

"What does happen next?" he asked, his voice strangely gruff.

She knew what he meant. She bucked herself up and lifted her chin. "I'm going to keep the property," she announced. "I'll buy Micah out if I have to, but I'm not going to let it go." She attempted to smile at him. "So you can live here as many summers as you want. I won't even jack up the rent... *that* much."

He attempted to smile back at her. "In that case, I'll be forwarding a list of requested improvements."

Haley chuckled, despite herself. "Knock yourself out, Captain." She swiped a drop of moisture away from one eye. Steam from the stove, no doubt. She wanted to answer his other question. The larger, implied one. But she didn't have an answer. "This will be ready in fifteen minutes. Shall we eat on your porch or mine? I don't want to miss out on that gorgeous view a second longer than strictly necessary."

He stepped up and took the spoon from her hand. "Let me finish this, then. You go back outside and indulge yourself."

Haley smiled her thanks. And then she obliged.

They enjoyed a pleasant-enough meal of the world's simplest spaghetti (Janie was never a fussy cook) and kept their banter light-hearted, despite the gnawing pain that had settled in Haley's middle. A part of her wanted to talk about it, to cry on his shoulder again, to explain how much the past few days had meant to her and how much she hated for them to end. But the feelings that alternately uplifted and pummeled her were too complicated to explain. Alaska had been awe-inspiring, and that awe had rejuvenated and soothed her. Having someone to talk to, a compassionate third party to whom she could unburden her soul, had been more helpful than she could ever imagine. But there was more.

She had feelings for Ben, and those feelings were no accident. They weren't gratitude for his help, rubbed-off romance from the spectacular scenery, or even a healthy, lustful response to the fact that he was freakin' gorgeous. She was falling in love with the man.

And now she had to leave him.

What else could she do? Despite the attraction between them, their relationship had yet to cross the line, and for that she was grateful. As things stood, they were friends. She could remain his friend even if they saw each other rarely. They could be friends who talked and joked and laughed, and maybe even sent bizarre packages to each other. They could be friends even when she was waddling around eight months' pregnant with ankles like an elephant. They could stay friends even if he went back to Hawaii and shacked up with some suntanned blonde who surfed in a bikini.

"What are you thinking about, Haley?" he asked.

Her face flushed again. "All sorts of unpleasant things," she replied.

He gathered up their dishes and opened the door.

"I can wash those," Haley said quickly, getting up. "I feel bad enough about returning your linens dirty. I hoped to get to the laundromat before I left. Sorry about that."

Ben frowned at her. "Would you stop? The dishes can wait and I don't need the sheets. None of it matters. How much longer can you stay?"

Haley looked at her watch, and her spirits sank. It was later than she thought. Before he drove up the road, the day had seemed endless. Whenever they were together, time flew. She swallowed a lump in her throat. "I only have a few minutes," she croaked.

Ben leaned into his cabin just far enough to dump the dishes on the counter, then closed the door and turned around. "Are you packed?"

Haley nodded. She had put everything in the car before he got home.

They stood silently a moment, just a few feet apart. Haley's eyes roved over the landscape. If she looked in his eyes again, she knew she would cry.

"Oh, to hell with it," Ben said roughly. He stepped forward and wrapped his arms around her, hugging her close. "You're killing me, Haley. You know that?"

She collapsed against his chest, her own arms circling his waist. This time, she didn't cry. He was wearing the same shirt he'd worn all day, and he smelled like the ocean. He was warm and strong and tender, and she was, for the moment, completely happy. In fact, she might never move again. "Likewise, Captain Parker," she murmured.

"I don't suppose," he said tentatively, "you have any idea what we can do about it?"

She shook her head into his shoulder. No matter what other circumstances stood in their way, she was only going to get more pregnant. Her body was not her own. And it wouldn't be for five long months.

As much as she was tempted, she couldn't ask him to wait for her. She wasn't even sure what he would be waiting *for*. Her job — her entire life — was in Newport Beach. And she couldn't imagine him doing anything other than what he was doing right now. Being out on the water, migrating with the humpbacks, living every day in the most beautiful places in the world... it was all too much a part of him. It fed his soul. The vibrant, gentle, mirthful soul that had attracted her so much in the first place.

She could never take that away from him. She had no right to ask.

With a valiant effort, she straightened herself and pulled away a little. Then she made the mistake of meeting his eyes.

He felt the same way she did. And he wasn't bothering to hide it.

"I guess my 'just friends' speech didn't work so well, huh?" she cracked, taking another half step back.

His hazel eyes glimmered. "If it hadn't, you think we'd still be standing out here?"

Haley laughed out loud. "Good point."

The urge to kiss him was almost unbearable. If he leaned toward her so much as a millimeter, she would cave. But she knew it wouldn't help anything. She could kiss him once or drag him back into the cabin for an hour, and the end result would be the same. They would wind up right back where they were now. Only then, the pain would be greater.

"I'm going to try to come back," she said weakly. "I'm just not sure I'll be able to get away from work."

He nodded.

"How long will you be here?" she croaked.

"Until the end of September, give or take," he answered. "It depends how long the weather holds."

"I can't make you any promises," she whispered roughly.

"I understand," Ben said flatly.

"Do you?" Haley asked, her eyes welling up with moisture again. She looked fully into his face, hoping to memorize every detail of it. Involuntarily, she lifted her hand, then brushed her fingers gently across his cheek.

Ben caught her hand in his and pulled it away. Haley started a little in surprise.

"Don't, Haley," he said softly, his eyes nearly as moist as her own. "Not if we're never going to see each other again."

Haley stepped away from him, embarrassed. She wiped her eyes and grabbed her jacket from where she'd left it on his porch railing. "I agree to your terms, Captain," she announced, clearing her throat. "But I'm afraid that never seeing each other again is not acceptable. We'll have to renegotiate that point."

She braved another look at him.

He smiled sadly back at her. "You know where I live."

Haley could look at him no more. She stepped off the porch and down the stairs and walked to the door of her car. She opened it, drew her keys from her jacket pocket, and paused.

"Thank you, Ben," she called without raising her head. "For everything. As much of a wreck as I seem right now, I feel a hundred times better than I did, and I owe it all to you. I hope you and the whales have a wonderful rest of the season here in Alaska, and a frolicking fine time in Hawaii." Her voice threatened to crack again. "And for what it's worth, I'm glad you're able to live your dream. You deserve to do what makes you happy."

She could tell that he had moved to the edge of his porch. "So do you, Haley," he said softly. "So do you."

She got into her car and turned the key in the ignition. She waved at him, once, as she pulled out of the drive and onto the road. Her vision was blurry, but she could see that he waved back.

She cried all the way to Anchorage.

NOT ALASKA

Chapter 19

Haley hung up her office phone for what seemed like the fortieth time since she had crawled into her desk chair early this morning. She had no idea what time it was. Her plan to sleep on the plane had been a dismal failure, and she had been operating on pure adrenaline ever since. If she had experienced a more impossibly demanding day in her entire professional life, she could not remember it. Of course, she could also not remember what she ate for breakfast this morning. Or for lunch.

A knock sounded on her closed door, and she responded to it mechanically, knowing from whom it came by its crisp timbre and relatively lower position in space. "Come on in, Ty."

A petite African-American woman in her early forties slipped around the heavy oak door and approached Haley's desk with her hands empty. Haley looked up at her with a quizzical expression. Tyrene always had something in her hands. A phone message, a memo, a padfolio. Too often, an entire banker's box of documents. Indisputably the sharpest paralegal at the firm, Tyrene's services were highly sought after, and it was a credit to Haley's clout that she was able to enlist the woman's services as often as she did. There was no doubt in the mind of anyone who worked with Tyrene that she should have been an attorney. Lack of finances and a disastrous early marriage had removed that possibility, but Tyrene was not one to bemoan the fact nearly as much as her coworkers. She simply did damn good work, demanded exorbitant compensation, and got it.

"What's up?" Haley asked nervously. She didn't care for the look in Tyrene's eyes, which was distinctly sympathetic.

"I need to tell you something," the paralegal said in her usual frank manner. She sat down in the chair beside Haley's desk, rather than either of the ones across from it, and Haley swiveled to face her.

"Shoot," Haley agreed. How much worse could the day get, after all?

"You know I don't do gossip," Tyrene began.

Haley nodded. When it came to matters of business, Tyrene had eyes and ears everywhere. Including — mysteriously enough — other law firms. But not once could Haley remember a word of personal gossip passing the other woman's lips. They both considered such triviality to be not only unprofessional, but a bore.

"In this particular case, I've decided you need to know," Tyrene continued. "Harrison has been flapping his jaws all day about how you took the week off to get a boob job."

Disbelief came first. Then Haley's entire body ignited with heat. She resisted the urge to look down at her jacket, whose buttons she already knew to be straining. They had been for weeks now. She had gained nearly two cup sizes. "I see," she said steadily. Only Bob and the relevant personnel in HR knew about her pregnancy. She had no desire to advertise the situation any earlier than necessary. Evidently, she had waited too long.

Tyrene rose. "That's all I've got to say about it."

"Thank you," Haley offered to her departing back. But as Tyrene put her hand on the doorknob, Haley spoke again. "I'm four months into a surrogate pregnancy for my sister and her husband. That's all the information anyone in this office needs."

Tyrene turned, her eyes showing more surprise than Haley expected. Whether she was surprised by the pregnancy itself, or by the bizarre nature of it, Haley wasn't sure. Nor did she want to know.

Tyrene nodded once, sharply. Then she walked out and closed the door behind her.

Haley's heart pounded as she fired off a stiffly polite email to Harrison, asking him to drop by her office whenever he got a minute. She had known from the beginning that she would eventually have to make her situation public. But did it have to happen *today?*

Her cell phone rang. She glanced at it with disinterest, then quickly focused her thoughts. Tim? Her brother-in-law almost never called her. Certainly not in the middle of a work day.

She answered. "What's up, Tim? Is something wrong?"

He made no response for a beat. "No, Haley. I mean, nothing like you think. I'm sorry to bother you on vacation. But—"

"I'm not on vacation," she interrupted. She cringed at the obvious impatience in her voice, but lacked the energy to control it.

"Oh," he replied, pausing again. "I thought—"

"I haven't told anyone yet. They think I'm still in Alaska. What's up?" She should be more forbearing, she chastised. Her abysmal mood was hardly Tim's fault. But with images filling her brain of herself turning the spit while Harrison's snarky, well-dressed carcass roasted slowly over an open flame with an apple jammed in his mouth, she had difficulty sounding pleasant.

More silence ensued. Haley stifled a scream.

"You know I hate having to involve you in this," he began finally. "But I don't know what else to do. I've been trying my best to give Micah whatever she says she needs, but nothing I do is helping. She's gone off the deep end this time and I don't know how to reach her. I thought I understood her as well as anybody, but obviously I don't." His faltered a little. "So I'm asking you, Haley. She keeps telling me she needs space. But my gut is telling me that's not really what she wants. I think she wants me to go after her."

"Yes, Tim," Haley said with relief.

He paused another beat. His tone hardened. "Does she expect me to *guess* that?"

"Yes, Tim."

He swore, and Haley smiled to herself. She knew the man had a backbone buried in there somewhere.

Another knock sounded on her door. Not Tyrene this time. Someone brash and demanding. She ended the conversation with Tim as politely as possible, hung up the phone, and called for the person outside to enter.

Harrison.

"You wanted to see me?" he asked, his voice a little too loud for the venue, as usual. He stepped into her office with his typical cocky swagger, even as his beady little eyes betrayed apprehension. Haley was not his boss, but she had seniority, and as she rose and moved confidently to the front of her desk to face him, her every movement was designed to make sure he remembered that.

She leaned back against her desk and folded her hands loosely in front of her, making no effort to hide any part of her body. She looked straight into his eyes, satisfied to note that despite her slouching posture she was still taller than he was.

"I understand you've been showing an inordinate amount of interest in the size of my breasts," she said coolly.

Harrison's face flamed. For a man who aspired to be a shark, she had always found him embarrassingly easy to intimidate. He should work on that.

His mouth moved as if to say something, but no words came out. Haley felt a sudden wave of pity for him. The emotion surprised her.

"I'm four months into a surrogate pregnancy for my sister and her husband," she explained, using the exact words she'd just spoken to Tyrene. "And I have nothing else to say on the topic, to you or anyone else." She straightened and stood. "Thanks for dropping by."

She turned her back to him and took a leisurely stroll around her desk to her chair. By the time she sat down, he had disappeared. The door clicked softly closed behind him.

Haley allowed herself a smile. *Ben would have enjoyed that*, she thought. She could picture his face in her mind, chuckling along with her. Her spirits buoyed.

Then they crashed all over again.

Ben was thousands of miles away. She would not see him tonight, or any night even remotely soon. Besides, she had work to do.

A mountain of it.

Suppressing a sharp pang of bitterness, Haley buried her head behind her laptop and applied herself to her work. After an untold number of hours, the steady stream of incoming phone calls and emails as well as the ambient office noise abated somewhat, and Haley cast a glance toward her clock. The dinnertime hours were often when she got into her best groove. But that would not be happening today. She could feel the last of her adrenaline-fueled energy draining away and realized, with foolish surprise, that she was exhausted.

It was time to go home.

When she finished climbing the steps up to the door of her apartment one torturous commute later, her limbs felt so heavy she was nearly numb. She would take a shower and fall straight into bed.

Shower buddies.

Haley cursed the refusal of her brain to shut down along with the rest of her. Surely she had exhausted its capacity to torture her; her neurons had far more reason to feel limp than did her long unused muscles. But even as her hands fumbled to unlock her door, images of Ben swam before her eyes. His long legs jogging up her porch steps. His broad back climbing the trail ahead of her. His arms, holding her tight against his chest...

"Haley!" Micah's soprano voice echoed from the drive behind her. "Wait!"

She turned to see Micah leaning out the open passenger window of her husband's car. Tim was driving.

Thank God, Haley thought tiredly. *They're together.*

She waited as Tim found a visitor's spot and her sister came hurrying up toward her. Amazingly, Micah was smiling. When she reached Haley she threw her arms around her and hugged her with enthusiasm. "We have news," Micah announced, her blue eyes sparkling as she drew back. "We were going to surprise you at work, but the receptionist said you'd just left. Can we come in?"

Haley nodded mutely. Micah said nothing else until all three of them were settled in the living room of Haley's apartment. Haley had collapsed into her recliner while Micah and Tim sat close together on the sectional couch, their faces beaming.

"The results came in," Micah announced. Her cheeks were rosy and her skin glowed. "The baby is fine, Haley. Absolutely fine. There is no evidence of Down Syndrome or any other chromosomal abnormality whatsoever."

Haley smiled as a welcome dose of happiness bubbled up within her. She rallied her exhausted limbs and rose to put one arm around Micah and the other around Tim, soliciting a group hug. "I'm so very happy to hear that," she said sincerely, even as she dropped quickly back into the comfort of the recliner. "Congratulations all around."

Micah and Tim exchanged a knowing glance, complete with smiles, and Haley's spirits rose further. The cool distance that had come between the couple, the wall of doubt and disappointment that had seemed so impenetrable when she left for Alaska, had evaporated. She tried to place how many hours had passed since Tim's desperate call, but she had no idea. She decided that it didn't matter.

"There's something else, Haley," Micah said with barely suppressed excitement, her eyes sparkling again. "Tim came by Mom's earlier and we talked — this was before the doctor called. He told me—" she cast an admiring glance her husband's way, then continued. "He told me that if our baby had special needs of any kind, we should probably have just the one child, because he or she would need every bit of our attention. And I agreed."

A twinge of uneasiness stirred in Haley's gut. Where was Micah going with this? They had discussed the issue when Haley had agreed to be a surrogate. She had committed to one pregnancy, acknowledging the possibility of twins, but secretly praying that no multiples would occur. Whatever the couple chose to do with the remaining embryos was their business. Never had Micah even suggested that Haley carry a second pregnancy.

Haley felt a spurt of fury deep within her psyche. *Once is enough, Micah,* something inside her threatened to scream as an image of Ben loomed front and center in her mind. *Don't you dare even ask!*

She barely managed to squelch the impulse when Micah spoke again.

"But then Tim said—" she looked at her husband adoringly again. "That if our baby is normal and healthy, then maybe a few years down the road, after we get our feet wet and learn how to be good parents, we could think about adopting a little sibling." Micah's blue eyes swelled with tears. "A special needs baby, he said. A child like Janie, maybe, who needs just as loving and supportive a family as she had. With a mother and father who understand what it's like to feel different, and will love her for who she is."

Haley felt her own eyes begin to moisten. She looked at Tim, and as her gaze met his she reaffirmed that her sister had done very well indeed. "I think that's wonderful," she said sincerely. "Really, truly wonderful."

"And we *will* be good parents," Micah said with sudden defensiveness, drawing Haley's attention back to her. Micah's face blazed with a determination Haley hadn't seen in a very long time. "I've been frightened out of my wits and acting like a fool, and I'm sorry. I have no excuse for myself except temporary insanity, and I hope you can both forgive me for what I've put you through." She turned pleading eyes on Haley. "I'm so glad you had the sense to take some time away. I'm sure it had to be helpful. Why did you come back early?"

Haley's newfound joy dimmed a little. "Something blew up at work. I had no choice."

"Oh, Haley," Micah said, discouraged. "You work too damn hard, you know that? How much sleep did you get last night? You look exhausted!"

Despite herself, Haley had to grin at the sudden role reversal. Was Micah seriously mothering *her?*

"Well?" Micah demanded, her mouth set fiercely.

"Not much," Haley replied. "I took the red-eye from Anchorage."

"Oh, my God," Micah said with exasperation, rising. "Come on, Tim. Let's go. Haley is going straight to bed."

Micah rose, and Tim rose with her. Haley thought about getting up to see them out, but when nothing happened, Micah clucked her tongue impatiently, took hold of Haley's arms, and pulled her up from the recliner. "To bed!" she ordered, giving Haley a gentle push in the direction of her bedroom. "What time do you plan to leave for the office in the morning?"

Haley yawned. "I don't know. Seven, probably."

"I'll be here with a healthy breakfast by 6:45," Micah announced.

Behind her, Haley could hear her front door opening. Ahead of her, she could see her bed. Forget the shower. She would be lucky if she made it to the mattress.

"Goodnight, Haley," Micah and Tim both called. "I love you," Micah added.

"Love you, too," Haley answered in a murmur, stumbling forward. She heard the front door close just as she collapsed onto her bed.

Her last thoughts were of ginger hair curling around the brim of a Mariners cap, bouncing with the motion of the waves, shining in the Alaskan sun.

Chapter 20

"I'm really not all that hungry," Haley insisted, staring at the kale salad with more apathy than distaste. She remembered liking kale, as well as all the carefully chosen toppings Micah had added to it. But the memory seemed too distant to be relevant. All of her memories did. She had been back from Alaska for over two weeks now — time which had seemed to stretch into eternity.

"Eat it," Micah ordered, her eyes flashing. "It's barely six bites' worth. And I made a special trip out just to get those dried cranberry fixings you like."

Haley picked up her fork. She doubted that Micah had really made a special trip, but guilt had proven an effective tool before and Micah wouldn't hesitate to use it again. She would do almost anything to get Haley to eat.

"That's better," Micah praised when the tiny bowl was at last consumed. "Now, how about an after-dinner protein chaser? I've got the strawberry kiwi and the mango pomegranate."

Haley resisted the urge to make a face. She felt like a child, which was easy to do with Micah mothering her like she had never been mothered before. Aunt Janie had been practical and kind, but never overindulgent, and Michelle's attentive periods had always been unpredictable, frequently ending without warning. Micah's ministrations, in contrast, were dogged, steady, and lavish.

Micah frowned, and Haley suspected she had accidentally made a face after all.

"Well how about an ice cream float, then?" Micah offered. "I could run to the convenience store and get some orange soda or root beer. Full sugar and everything. A special treat."

Haley looked into her sister's so obviously worried face and felt horrible again. "Micah, please," she begged. "I can eat a snack later tonight, but I'm really full right now. I ate all the turkey, didn't I?"

Micah blinked back at her, unassuaged. "Have you weighed yourself since Friday?"

Haley groaned. Ever since her return, the newly reformed and nearly unrecognizable Micah had made it her mission in life to keep

Haley happy and healthy in spite of the unprecedented onslaught of work that plagued her. With both the Consolidated and Stirjon accounts imploding simultaneously, Haley had been living in her office, returning to her apartment only to shower and sleep. Micah had been making sure that Haley always had something to eat, stocking the apartment fridge and even bringing lunch to the office, but Haley's OB appointment the previous Monday had raised Micah's game to a whole new level.

"Do not groan at me," Micah fired back. "Haley, I'm worried about you. *You* should be worried about you. Even if you weren't pregnant, you couldn't possibly keep up this pace. But as of yesterday you are *twenty weeks* pregnant, and you are *losing weight*. And for your blood pressure to be creeping up, too—" her voice broke off. Micah's brow was deeply furrowed, but no tears filled her eyes. Only consternation. "I *know* you're busy at work. You're always busy at work. But something else is going on with you." Her voice gentled. "You seem so sad all the time, Haley. It's not like you at all. And frankly, it's starting to scare me."

Hot tears threatened Haley's own eyes. She was so very tired. At some point day and night, weekday and weekend, had all begun to coalesce into one endless stretch of obligation and misery. She was able to function at work. It was during her relatively rare hours at home that her brain and body both seemed to shut down, fatigued beyond endurance. And Micah was right. She had been busy and sleep deprived before. But she had never felt so wretched.

"The baby is fine, Micah," Haley reminded, attempting to calm her sister's angst. "The doctor said so."

Micah's jaw muscles clenched. If steam really did come out of people's ears, her head would look like a teapot. "Dammit, Haley!" she fumed. "I am not just worried about the baby! I'm worried about *you!*"

Haley wiped her eyes. "I know that," she whispered. "I'm sorry."

Micah rose from the table, took Haley's hands, and led to her to her couch, where they sat together. Ever since the ominous OB appointment, Micah had been coming to Haley's apartment every morning and every evening delivering food, doing laundry, tidying up, and generally making herself useful in any way she could. Haley found her sister's babying nearly intolerable at first, but as time went on she had become too exhausted to resist. What Micah didn't realize was that her wrap-around services were actually encouraging Haley to spend more time working, when she would otherwise be knocking off early to do those same tasks herself. Most of them, anyway.

"Talk to me," Micah pleaded. "Something happened to you in Alaska, didn't it? You keep insisting that it was wonderful, that everything was beautiful, that it 'restored your soul.' You do not seem 'restored' to me. You seem depressed. What am I missing, Haley?"

Ben.

A stray tear spilled onto Haley's cheek. *I miss Ben.* She swiped at the tear, avoiding Micah's eyes. She'd had no communication with him at all since she'd left. And she still wasn't sure why not. She thought of him almost constantly. His face was always in her mind — the twinkle in his hazel eyes, the way his dimples popped when he grinned, the merry rumbling of his laughter. But when the wood-paneled walls of Merriweather, Falstaff, and Tynes closed in around her, he seemed to belong to another world. Alaska, the mountains, the cabins... none of it seemed real anymore.

She had tried to bring it back, and to some extent, she had succeeded. Whenever she felt herself teetering on the edge — when she was about to lose her temper over someone else's incompetence, or to despair at being blamed for things she couldn't control — she would close her eyes, breathe deeply, and watch the porpoises bow-riding. Or the humpback breaching. Or the glacier calving or the panoramic view from the hike or the brown black bear crossing the road. She felt better then. For those precious seconds, she was transported and she was soothed, and for a while thereafter she felt able to cope better. But missing Alaska was one thing. Missing the feel of Ben Parker's arms around her was another.

"Alaska *was* wonderful," she attempted to explain. "My memories of it are about the only thing keeping me sane right now. I just wish they were more than memories. I needed more time there, Micah, and I got cheated. That's all."

Liar. Haley chastised herself, not for the first time, for the omission. She had told Micah nothing about Ben. Why she felt so compelled to keep the secret, she could not explain even to herself. She clutched her memories of him tightly to her heart, as if she feared that by sharing, she could lose them. Or perhaps she feared Micah would trivialize her feelings — making cracks about "summer loving" and deriding him as no more than a vacation fling. Whatever the psychology behind it, Haley's mouth stayed shut.

"Well, we'll just have to make sure you get back there sometime," Micah insisted. "I told you I'm perfectly fine with keeping Uncle

Randy's property. It's not like either one of us was looking for a
windfall. We didn't even know we were in the will! In fact, Tim and I
talked about it, and we want you to have the title outright. He's going
to contact the executor and see how to go about signing my share
over."

Haley was startled. "Micah, I don't know the specifics yet, but
property values in Seward can run pretty high. I can't just let you—"

"You can and you will," Micah ordered. "You obviously love the
place. Do you think we can put a price on what it means to *us* for you
to sacrifice your body for nine months? Now shut up already!"

Haley managed a grin. "You just begged me to talk to you."

Micah grinned back. "So I did. It's good to see you smile, Haley."

Haley did feel a bit better, suddenly. She would own all her uncle's
property, including the back acres. Ben would be happy about that. He
could trek around back there all he wanted, now. As long as he carried
his bear spray. She would extract a promise about that.

Micah leaned forward suddenly and hugged her. "I like to see you
happy," she said as she released her. "Now, if you'll excuse me, I'm
going to go lavish some attention on my wonderful husband. You need
anything else before I leave?"

Haley shook her head, still smiling. The irrational, frantic, childlike
Micah that had taken over her sister's identity during what they now
referred to as "the prenatal testing hell" had disappeared. The woman
before her wasn't the old Micah, either. She was a new, more confident
and more capable version. Her maternal instincts had most definitely
kicked in.

"I'm fine," Haley insisted. "Maybe I'll even have that protein shake
later."

Micah smiled. "And then straight to bed, okay? You've skipped the
last two weekends entirely, and the next one is five days away still.
Don't forget that Tim and I are kidnapping you for a mystery outing
on Sunday. And we mean *all day*. No excuses. If I have to, I'll call your
boss and tell him you have chicken pox or whooping cough or
something even more embarrassing. Understood?"

Haley gave her sister a salute, and Micah gathered up her things and
departed. For a long time afterwards Haley remained motionless on the
couch, staring at the cell phone on her end table.

You could call him.

A stab of pain assaulted her middle, and her hand went to her
abdomen. The baby bump was bigger now, but the pain hadn't come

from Fred. It was missing Ben that made her stomach ache.

Why hadn't she called him? Or texted? Or emailed? Her brain made another attempt to separate the endless stretch of time into days. She had left Alaska on a Thursday night. Today was a Monday. It had been almost three weeks now.

Three weeks! How many times had she stared at her computer, opened a new email, blinked at the bare screen, and closed it again? How many times had she clicked on his name in her contact list, looked at the graphic icon of a faceless, generic head and declined to hit 'call?' How could she miss him so terribly much and yet feel so far away from him?

Phones, keyboards, computers... she knew that he was reachable through them all. Catching him on either of his phones at any given time would be a long shot, but he did check voicemail and email. There was no reason she couldn't send him *something*. She could even hear his voice again. It would not take that much effort.

Still, Haley didn't move. What could she even say to him? What promise could she make? There was no way in hell she could take enough time off from work to get back to Alaska before he left. Would he understand that? Or would he think she didn't care? She dreamed of going to see him in Hawaii later in the fall, but in her dreams she was not waddling around heavily pregnant with somebody else's kid. The grim truth was that she had nothing to offer the man. Not now. Not until next year, after the baby was born. And even then, how could they truly be together unless he was willing to give up his whole way of living for her? And why the hell *should* he, when she couldn't imagine herself being willing to do the same?

She fell over sideways on the couch and closed her eyes. He had not contacted her, either, and she was not sure of the significance of that. There would be nothing stopping him, if he was so inclined. God knew that if either of his numbers had popped up on her phone she would have answered immediately, no matter what else she was doing. But the way they had left things, the ball was in her court. She was the one who had done the leaving. She was the one who was supposed to try to come back. She was the one who had thrown the brakes on their relationship in the first place. And while he had been willing to play by her rules, he had never left her in any doubt that he wanted more.

You know where I live.

Haley suffered an even worse pang as she remembered his final — and only — rebuff. *No, Haley,* he had said, pulling her hand away from his face. *Not if we're never going to see each other again.*

What guy does that? He could easily have taken advantage of her feelings for some pleasure in the moment. She would have been out of his hair within the hour, most likely never to be seen again. She was a little bit pregnant, true. But, hey — at least he'd have no fear of a paternity trap.

Haley frowned into her couch cushions. Ben wasn't like that. And she knew exactly why he had pushed her away. Because men had feelings, too. And he didn't want to get his trampled any more than they already had been. By her.

She sat up. For all her wallowing in self-pity, it had never once occurred to her what Ben must be feeling. She had driven off and left him with the assurance that she wanted to see him again. She had then buried herself so deeply in her work that over two weeks had passed, numbing and timeless to her, perhaps, but hardly to him. He had no way of knowing how much he had been on her mind; all he could see was that she hadn't bothered to contact him. For all he knew, she had forgotten him entirely.

Haley grabbed her phone and clenched it tightly. She had to let him know otherwise. She couldn't bear for her silence to hurt him. He had probably wanted to call her, too, but was afraid of the result, particularly if he thought she was trying to forget. Forgetting would be a perfectly reasonable plan, after all, for both of them. But she couldn't bear it. She wanted Ben Parker in her life.

She stared at the phone in her hands. It was time she asked herself the real question. The question which, more than likely, underlay all the rest of her misery and indecision. *Just friends* might very well be all that she and Ben could ever be to each other. If that was the case, did she still want to keep him in her life?

Her face suffused with warmth, and the rest of her body followed.

Yes, she proclaimed to herself. *Hell, yes!*

She raised her phone once more. But then, with sudden clarity, she lowered it. Of course she had felt removed from him all this time. Three thousand miles of land and sea was a formidable barrier. But her damned phone, useful device that it was, was its own form of impediment. Ben didn't like talking on the phone. He didn't like answering emails or checking voicemail and he flatly refused to text. He wasn't a *contact.* He was a real, flesh-and-blood man who liked nature and the outdoors, who thrived on hugs and laughter and the sharing of meals and car rides and adventure. Reducing him to anything less, converting him to her high-tech world of digital and voice like he was any other attorney or business acquaintance, was an abomination. Of course she had been avoiding it; she had been avoiding it because it didn't feel right. As accessible as he *seemed* to be, she had been mourning all this time because deep down, she knew she couldn't reach him by any of those means. Not the real him.

But she had to reach him somehow. Or lose her mind trying.

She set down the phone and considered a moment. Then she rose with a jerk, walked to the small desk in the corner of her living room, and pulled two sheets of paper out of her printer. She collected her lap desk, two pens, and the mango pomegranate protein shake, fluffed up the pillows on her bed, and snuggled in.

Yes, she thought to herself smugly, her mood brightening with an excitement she hadn't felt for weeks.

She clicked her pen and smoothed the blank paper before her. Tonight, she would touch it. In a few days, his hands would touch it also. He would look at her god-awful, squiggled handwriting, squint to figure out what the hell she was trying to say, and trace his fingers lightly over the messy ink. He would hold the paper in his hands and know that it had been held by her own. Maybe he would even smell her avocado moisturizer.

Haley grinned to herself. Then she began to write.

Chapter 21

Ben turned his Jetta off the Seward Highway and started down the gravel road toward his cabin. Now that August was half over, the days were getting shorter rapidly, with the sun setting another five minutes earlier every night. The change suited him, although he didn't care to ponder why. Ordinarily, he mourned every hour of the brief Alaskan autumn that crept in so noiselessly, seeming to eschew attention as it made a perfunctory stop, then fled again before the assault of winter.

The temperature had settled in the fifties now, and the sky was overcast more often than not. By the end of next week, kids across the country would head back to school, and the tourist traffic in Seward would slow to a trickle. He had told his boss he wanted to stay on as far into September as the business could support him. But that was then.

He frowned into the still-light sky. He preferred to come home after dark, but he was getting tired of killing time in town. His few forays back into the bar scene had been distinctly unsatisfying, and it was growing too cold to roam the marina with no particular purpose in mind. He should be out gathering wood instead, so he could spend the evenings catching up on his reading by a blazing fire.

But the evenings were still too bright. Only darkness could obscure the depressing specter of the vacant cabin next door.

Get over it, Ben. Forget about her.

His frown deepened. God knew he had been trying. Every day that passed with no word from Haley was another bar of platinum tipping the scales toward "vacation love." He had dared to hope otherwise, but evidently he'd been wrong, and it was time to face up to that. She might indeed come back some day, but if she did, he knew now that it would not be him she came back for. Only the good times he represented.

Forget about her.

Alexa had been in the bar last night. She had practically fallen all over herself when she'd caught sight of him. He'd been so miserable he'd even agreed to have a drink with her, but had regretted it as soon as her lips started moving. She was a nice enough girl and objectively attractive, but her brainless prattle about reality TV, her hair, and some other girl's shoes buzzed in his ears like the hum of a mosquito. He had been able to filter that sort of thing out once, but he seemed to have lost the ability. How he had managed so long with girlfriends just like her he had no idea.

You don't need one more 'meh' girlfriend you're struggling to keep things going with, Lara had told him. *Not when deep down, you know it's no good anyway. Life's too short and you're too old.*

Ben exhaled with a sigh. His sister had been right, dammit. Even though things with Haley hadn't worked out, he'd had a glimpse of what a solid, mature relationship *could* be like. He'd been seeing it for years in other people's marriages, but he'd never actually felt it himself. Understanding that sweet reality now was a doubled-edged sword. He was more certain of what he wanted, yes. But anything less would never satisfy him again.

He could find another woman as intelligent and beautiful and self-sacrificing as Haley. Somewhere on the Hawaiian Islands there had to be at least one, didn't there? Maybe even one whose day job didn't directly oppose his own life's passion. He would just have to look a bit harder this season. Be more discerning.

A dull ache stabbed at his middle. He thought he *was* discerning. He thought he had discerned that Haley's feelings for him were as strong as his were for her. He had, in fact, been sure of it.

Well, you were wrong, dude! Now get over it.

Ben's jaws clenched. He'd been trying to get over it. He kept his head down every morning when he walked from his porch to his car, forestalling the memories that flooded back with the sight of her cabin. Her porch, her chair. The window of her erstwhile bedroom, where she had slept between his raggedy castoff sheets. He couldn't even go hiking at Exit Glacier any more. Everywhere they had been together he would picture her, smiling and laughing, warming his heart. The images were pure irony, of course — most of the time he was with her, she had been close to tears. But it was the smiles that stayed with him, because he had been the one to put them there. He had made her happy, as she had him.

But some part of that had been illusion. Her feelings might have seemed real at the time, even to her. But they must have been superficial, dependent on time and place and circumstances. Whereas his own feelings, unfortunately for him, were rooted deep.

Now he hurt like hell.

He pulled the Jetta off onto the shoulder by the crossroad and parked the car to check his mail. Many days he didn't get a thing, but he was due for his favorite oceanography magazine, a more exciting find than the usual advertising circular or credit card application. He located his box among the dozen or so belonging to the other residents of the crossroad and opened the metal door. His magazine had arrived. Curled around the outside of it was a large cardboard mailer. He pulled both out, then studied the mailer curiously.

It was an Express Mail folder. The overnight, cost-you-a-fortune kind. His eyes rested on the return address, and his heart froze. It was from Haley.

Your landlord, you mean, he reminded himself quickly. This was no love note covered with hearts and flowers. She had sent him some sort of business document. Probably trying to tie up his lease for next year.

His heart began to beat again, only this time way too fast. He started to open the folder, stopped himself, then started again. What was his problem? Avoiding whatever papers she had sent him would accomplish nothing. At the very least, he would have a firmer idea of exactly where they stood. That she had comped the entirety of his August rent, he already knew. Ed Miller had explained as much in the note accompanying his returned check. But Haley had arranged that little gift before she left Anchorage. He wanted to believe that she meant it as a kindness and a bit of an inside joke. But perhaps she had seen it as a business transaction. A payment for services rendered.

Ben closed the mailbox door and returned to his car. He tossed the magazine on the empty seat beside him and ran his fingers over the ink on the mailer's address label. *Haley Olson.* At least that's what he assumed she had scribbled. Her handwriting was horrific. Like a cross between a mad scientist's diary and one of the puffin paintings from the Sea Life Center.

He tried not to smile. He tried not to hope. But he failed on both counts. When at last he ripped open the cardboard mailer and a single, letter-sized envelope fell out onto his lap, relief overtook him like a warm, Hawaiian wind.

It wasn't official papers. It was a letter.

A letter!

His eyes roved over the addresses, which duplicated those on the mailer. Haley had gotten it ready to mail once, then decided to send it overnight. Whatever it was, she had wanted him to have it in a hurry.

He ripped the thin envelope open. Inside were two sheets of paper, covered nearly completely with the same dreadful scrawl in at least two shades of ink. His pulse pounded in his veins.

She hadn't forgotten him.

With maddening slowness, he began to decipher.

Dear Ben,

I know you think I've forgotten you, and I can't apologize enough for that. Nothing could be further from the truth. I came back to work and was buried in an avalanche, and I'm still buried, but that's not why I haven't called, or texted, or emailed. I've thought about you constantly. I've missed you every moment. But none of the above seemed anywhere near adequate to bring you back. I've been so sad about everything I want that I can't have, getting only a tiny dose of it seemed more painful than satisfying. So I just did nothing. And sulked. And worked till I was exhausted. And was so selfish I didn't realize until today that my silence must surely be leading you to draw the wrong conclusion.

If you've already given up on me, it's no more than I deserve. But if you haven't...

I don't know what to tell you, Ben. You know I have nothing to offer you besides friendship, at least not now, and maybe not ever. I can't promise you anything and I have no right to ask you to wait until I can. I don't want to disrupt your life and I don't want to keep you from living. The women of Hawaii have other plans for you, I'm sure. (Just don't make me think about that, please. It makes me crazy.) I've told myself a thousand times that there's no point in continuing any kind of relationship with you, not when there's nothing in it for you except the thrill of my stellar personality. I've told myself I shouldn't even ask — that I should do the considerate thing and just leave you the hell alone. But as we established above, I'm not a very considerate person.

The bottom line is, I want you in my life. In whatever capacity you're comfortable with. We can be friends; we can be penpals. We can throw messages in bottles into the ocean and make prank calls and trade Halloween candy. I don't care how it happens. I just want to keep you alive in my heart, to feel some connection with you, to know that you're still real. That's all I'm asking. It's

> all I have any right to ask.

Ben's breath caught in his throat. The paper was discolored here, the ink smudged.

> And now, Captain Parker, you have brought on the waterworks again. I blame you entirely. Before we met, I maintained perfect emotional control at all times and only cried when the barista ran out of hazelnut macchiato.

Ben felt his own eyes moistening. Haley's words were warming every part of him; his cheeks were aflame and his smile had become so broad it was painful. Still, she wrote more.

> Now, I will make this easy for you. To indicate YES, I am willing to condescend to communicate with an attorney for the dark side, if only to further educate her on the awesomeness of the natural world, please write back. To indicate NO, thanks anyway, but I need to get on with my life — simply do not reply. There will be no hard feelings, and if your rent increases, it will be entirely unrelated.

> I miss you terribly, Ben.

> Appropriate closing,
> Haley

Ben sat in the Jetta by the mailbox a very long time, staring at the letter, rereading it, willing his overflowing heart to stop racing like he was an adolescent. He had *not* been wrong! Haley's feelings for him were as real as his own. She missed him. Not just Alaska, which she hardly even mentioned, but *him*. It wasn't "vacation love," it hadn't disappeared already, and it wasn't just friendship, either. She hadn't asked him not to date other women, but she was obviously bothered by the thought of it. He liked that. He liked that a lot.

He raised the letter to his face and sniffed, wondering if her apartment — or her office? — had left any lingering aroma. He expected coffee, but remembered that she was laying off the caffeine. Perhaps there was a vague fruity smell? Most likely he was making it up.

No matter. Nothing mattered except that what he and Haley had shared was not over. It might only have just begun.

He laid the letter on the seat next to him and started the car. But after a quick mental inventory, he did not turn toward home, but instead made a U turn. There was no suitable paper in the cabin. He would drive back to town and get some. And some envelopes and stamps. Then he would gather that wood, light that fire in his fireplace, and settle down with a notebook and a brand new pen.

His smile widened further at the thought.

Ben Parker had a date tonight.

Chapter 22

Haley held her breath as she turned the small key in her apartment mailbox. She didn't expect anything. Today was the first day she could possibly receive a response from Ben, and only then if he'd shelled out for next-day mail, which hardly seemed his style. She looked inside to see a curled up cardboard mailer, and her pulse began to pound in her ears. *It could be anything*, she reminded, pulling it out with an unsteady hand.

She glanced anxiously at the return address.

Ben Parker.

"Yes!" she shouted, giving a very unprofessional hop in the middle of the drive. No one was watching, but she wouldn't have cared if anyone had been.

He had answered her! And that meant *yes*.

She headed across the drive and up the steps to her apartment at a near jog. A little exercise would do Fred good. Haley had been getting entirely too lazy, lately.

She reached her door, hustled inside, threw everything else she was holding in a heap on the couch, and plopped down. Her hands ripped open the mailer and a regular-sized white envelope, just like her own, fell out. She picked it up and smiled at the single word written across it. *Haley.* His handwriting was better than hers — a practiced cursive that was competent, yet breezy. Just like him.

Her fingers started ripping. She pulled out two pages of paper, folded together, and something else that looked like a clipping from a magazine. It was folded small and sealed shut with a yellow sticky note. *Environmentalist propaganda,* the label read. *Open at your own risk.*

Haley chuckled merrily and set the article aside. She fell back against her cushions and held the letter in front of her.

Dear Haley,

I plan to Express Mail this, but just so we're clear, don't expect such extravagance every time I write. My life's calling may be fun and virtuous, but the pay is crap.

Yes, I figured you had forgotten me. And yes, I've been miserable about that. Your letter meant more than I can say, Haley. I miss you terribly, too.

She drew in a ragged breath, and her eyes misted over. It was okay. It really was. He *did* feel the same.

I don't know what the answer is either, but I accept your terms, counselor. (With the obvious exception of throwing trash in the ocean, which I choose to believe was some kind of metaphor.) I will be in Seattle over Halloween, trick or treating with the nieces and nephews, so it should be easy to steal some of their candy to trade. As for the penpal thing — bring it on. Just promise me you'll work on the handwriting before I go blind. Seriously. It's terrible.

Haley released a foolish giggle, her heart soaring.

It's colder and cloudier here now, but still just as amazing. As for the grizzly you were hoping to see, he apparently got tired of waiting for you at the fishing spot and came to visit you at home. I was out getting wood earlier and found tracks all over the ground on the far side of your cabin, even right under your window. I hope he wasn't too upset to miss you.

Haley chilled at the thought of a bear rummaging around mere feet from her bed, but she figured Ben was probably kidding. Wasn't he?

And no, I'm not kidding. From the look of the tracks, I'd say it was a large male. Wish I'd been around to see him. If he does ever come back, I'll be sure to pass on your regards.

How is Fred? You should be feeling her moving around about now. (Do not tell anyone I know that.) I hope she passed her tests and that her parents have gotten their act together. You deserve that peace of mind, at least, as you dig your way out from under that avalanche. My own workload will be easing up soon, which means I'll finally get to make that trek through Denali with my buddy Andy. Last year we waited until mid September and got snowed out. This year I'm determined to catch a glimpse of some gray wolves. I'll give them your regards, too.

Haley pictured Ben and his friend trekking deep into the backcountry of Denali National Park, pitching a tent on the cold ground and stringing their food up in a tree to keep the carnivores out. He sounded like he was going to Disneyland. She was certain she'd be scared to death.

> Now, about your leaving Alaska early. I was promised two more days to turn you from the dark side, and I didn't get them. Now that we're penpals, I figure I have another shot. So, please enjoy the enclosed educational materials, which will accompany each installment at no additional charge.
>
> As for my mysteriously reduced August rent, I thank you for the gesture. It was completely unnecessary, since I always invite women who knock on my door at 4:30am to use my shower. But I appreciate the thought.

Haley grinned to herself. She knew that Ben took pride in living within his means, which she respected. But she was glad he hadn't refused her offering, which she considered to be fair compensation for his tour-guiding, car-hauling, linen-loaning, shower-sharing, and chauffeur services. She wondered, briefly, if he were the kind of man who would chafe at having a significant other make more money than he did. Somehow, she doubted it.

> Last but not least on the agenda, here is your quiz for Bear Awareness 101. You didn't really think I would forget, did you?
> 1. You are hiking on a state park trail and come across a moose carcass. What should you do?

Haley laughed out loud. He hadn't said a thing about moose carcasses. At least, she didn't think he had. She read through the other nine questions and couldn't answer a single one of them. But answer them she would. Maybe he'd give points for creativity. She was still chuckling to herself as she came to his signature, which was crammed diagonally in the bottom corner of the otherwise filled up second page.

> Equally appropriate closing,
> Ben

She hugged the papers to her chest a moment, enjoying the thrill of actually feeling *happy* again. He missed her. He wanted to write. Whatever the future held for them, it was better than no connection at all.

She glanced down at the folded magazine clipping and opened it tentatively. It was an article about the lingering effects of PCBs in mother orcas and the high death rates of their calves. She scanned through it quickly, then folded it up again.

Her elation dimmed. Ben had never made any secret of his distaste for her job, but his comments on the topic were always light-hearted and never judgmental of her as a person. How much did it really matter to him? Maintaining a friendship with someone you disagreed with professionally was one thing. But what if she and Ben *were* romantically involved? Could she make him understand she really wasn't the enemy... or would she forever have to walk on eggshells?

A frown crossed her previously glowing face. Sharing her life with a man, if she ever chose to do so, would mean sharing all of herself. Maybe some couples could manage the total separation of their work and personal lives, but she didn't want to live like that. Her work was too consuming; she would be withholding too much. It was no fluke of statistics that nearly all the partners in her firm were divorced. But what was the alternative? Marrying a co-worker?

Haley shuddered. She wadded the article up into a ball and tossed it into her waste can. The last thing she wanted to think about right now was PCBs. There was no reason to get ahead of herself. All that mattered was that Ben wanted her in his life.

I miss you terribly, too.

Haley's smile returned as she opened the letter and began to reread it.

"Knock, knock!" a cheerful voice cried from the hallway. "Haley? Are you there? My hands are full."

Haley stashed the letter in a pocket. "Just a sec!" She rose and opened the door to Micah, who bustled in with a casserole dish in her hands and two shopping bags slung over her wrists.

Haley took the casserole dish from her sister and set it on the table. "What did you bring me?" she asked cheerfully, lifting the lid and taking a sniff.

Micah closed the door and joined her. "Polish bigos and kluski," she answered. "It's a new recipe I found online."

"It smells wonderful," Haley enthused. "Are you going to stay and eat with me?" When her sister didn't answer for a moment, she looked up to see Micah staring at her oddly. "What?" she asked.

Micah continued her appraisal. "Nothing," she said unconvincingly.

"Well, excuse me if I go ahead and dig in," Haley exclaimed, grabbing some utensils and a napkin and taking a seat. "I'm starving!"

Micah put away the groceries she'd brought, then sat down at the table herself.

Haley looked up many mouthfuls later to catch her sister with a knowing smile. "What?!" she repeated.

Micah's blue eyes sparkled. "Something's happened to you," she proclaimed. "Your face is glowing and your appetite is back. You haven't been hungry for weeks, much less starving. What gives?"

Haley felt her face redden. Was she really so obvious? Transparency was a major liability in her business. She never had any trouble keeping her game face on at work, but perhaps that was because work *was* a game. Keeping her personal feelings from people she cared about was trickier.

"Can't a pregnant woman be hungry once in a while? This is really good!" She started to rise. "I think I'll squirt some hot sauce in it."

Micah waved her back down into her chair. "I'll get it. You keep eating." She opened the refrigerator and handed Haley the hot sauce.

Haley seasoned up the casserole and dug back in, keeping her face in her plate. She knew she was still being stared at. But she really was hungry.

Micah rose and began to tidy up the kitchen.

"Would you stop?" Haley protested good-naturedly. "You're going to spoil me rotten, and then where will I be when you're tied up with a newborn? I'll be calling you at six in the morning complaining that I can't find the paper towels!"

"Well, I'll be up anyway, won't I?" Micah tossed back, moving out into the living room. "Besides, I've already enlisted Mom to spoil you then. I hope you don't think we plan on deserting you while you're recovering."

Haley looked up, distressed. "Mom? Seriously?"

Micah chuckled. "She has been in neglect mode for a while now, hasn't she?"

Haley made no response. They had all rejoiced when the amniocentesis results came back normal and Micah and Tim had reunited. But having the family drama wrap up so neatly had left Michelle at loose ends. She had taken off soon afterwards to visit a college friend in Florida, and last the girls had heard the two friends were hanging out in a timeshare in Bermuda.

"She's bound to cycle back around to smothering by then," Micah teased. Her face turned suddenly wistful. "Tim and I don't want any help with the baby. No recovery necessary for me, so no excuses. We're going to dive right in and figure everything out for ourselves." She smiled at Haley. "And we're going to make sure you stay spoiled, too."

Micah bent over to straighten the pillows on Haley's couch. She froze in place a moment, then straightened with a jerk. "Haley Olson!" she exclaimed sharply.

Haley's heartbeat quickened as she observed the mangled Express Mail folder in her sister's hands. "What?"

"You know perfectly well *what?!*" Micah chastised, descending on her in three strides. "How could I have been so stupid? This explains everything!"

Haley pretended ignorance. "Excuse me?"

"Oh, knock it off!" Micah ordered, dropping into a chair beside her and slapping the mailer on the table between them. "No wonder you've been moping around all this time! And I thought you just liked the scenery in Alaska. Why didn't you tell me you met a guy?"

Haley swallowed. She should have known Micah could add two and two. She was an accountant, after all.

"I..." she stammered, suddenly embarrassed. "I didn't want to talk about it. I wasn't sure I'd ever see him again."

"But now he's written you?" Micah pressed. "And that's why you're so happy?"

Haley put down her fork. There was no point in keeping her sister in the dark. She had thought that keeping Ben a secret would protect her heart somehow, but she realized suddenly just how very much she *did* want to talk about him — to describe the color of his hair and the effect of his dimples, even just to say his name out loud. Perhaps if she had shared her experience with Micah from the beginning, it would never have felt so surreal.

"His name is Ben Parker," she began, knowing that it wouldn't be necessary to tell Micah how she felt about him. She could hear the answer to that question quite clearly in her own voice. "He's a boat captain and an oceanographer, and he travels across the Pacific twice a year, following the whales. He's intelligent and sweet and he has a wicked sense of humor just like mine. He's also tall and redheaded and freakin' drop-dead gorgeous." She paused a moment, sliding down in her chair and staring wistfully at the crumpled mailer. "And the reason I'm so happy is because I just found out he misses me as much as I miss him, and he wants to keep on communicating." A furtive smile crossed her face. "We're going to be penpals."

Micah made no response. After a moment, Haley looked up at her. She was shocked to see her sister's face turn ashen. Her eyes were watery and her lower lip trembled.

"Oh, my God, Haley," Micah said miserably, her voice barely a whisper. "I'm so, so sorry."

"Sorry for what?" Haley demanded, sitting up.

Micah leaned forward and put her hand on Haley's arm. "It's all my fault," she explained, her voice quavering. "I've waited so long for you to fall in love. I've wanted it for you so badly. But all those guys... Just, none of them were ever even close to what you deserved!"

Haley was still baffled. "What are you talking about?"

Micah rose. "For God's sake, Haley!" she cried. "He sounds absolutely perfect for you! And now you're *pregnant*, because of me! You're so happy because you have a penpal? You should be sailing off with this man, just like you always dreamed! And because of me, you're in this impossibly awkward—" she began to pace. "Does he know? What did he say about it?"

Haley gave her head a shake. Who was this woman and what had she done with Haley's predictably childish, self-absorbed twin sister? "I don't—" she stammered, not sure which question to answer first. "I mean, we're not at that point yet. I was only with the man for five days. We're still just friends, technically."

"Oh, don't give me that!" Micah scoffed. "You're obviously in love with him!"

"Yes," Haley admitted easily, "but nothing *happened*. I never even kissed him!"

Micah's frown deepened further. "Well, why the hell not?"

"Because—" Haley broke off. *Because it wouldn't have stopped there.* "Because I'm not free at the moment, obviously," she finished. "And he lives thousands of miles away and I didn't want to start something I couldn't finish. And what do you mean 'like *I* always dreamed?'"

Micah looked back at her with disbelief. "What you always used to say, every time Mom took us out to play on the beach! You would stare out over the water with this faraway look on your face, and you'd say how when you grew up, you were going to jump on one of the big boats and see what was on the other side of the water. You wanted to sail all around the world and never come back again." She stared back at Haley accusingly. "Don't you remember that?"

Haley's eyebrows lifted. "No."

Micah rolled her eyes. "Of course you wouldn't. For you, every time was just another day at the beach. For me, it was one of my greatest childhood fears. I couldn't understand why you wanted to go so far away. The whole idea scared me to death. One day I told you that you couldn't go because I refused to go with you, and you laughed and said it didn't matter, that you'd go without me. And I was so upset I cried."

Haley blew out a breath. Had she really said that? The scene did sound hauntingly familiar. And all too plausible.

"I ran to Mom and pitched a fit," Micah continued, "and she told you that you were being mean and that of course I could go along with you wherever you went."

Haley chuckled wryly. "Of course she did."

Micah sighed and sat down again. "Mom was wrong to say that," she conceded, her eyes begging her sister for forgiveness. "You have every right to sail away, Haley. With whoever you want. I'm just really, really sorry about the timing. If you fell in love with this guy in five days without ever even kissing him..." She shook her head in frustration. "My God, don't let him go! Hang onto him."

"I'm trying," Haley admitted, ashamed at the sudden quiver in her own voice.

"Does he know?" Micah repeated.

Haley nodded. "He figured out that I was pregnant before I could tell him, actually. My feelings for him were so obvious... he was totally confused."

"Well, of course he was," Micah said bitterly. "He had to wonder why you weren't with the baby's father." She covered her face with her hands. "I've been so incredibly selfish, Haley. I never even thought about this. You haven't dated anybody seriously in years, and nine months didn't seem that long. But I *should* have thought about it. About how strange it would be to try to get close to a man when—" She cut herself off. "How did he take it?"

Haley smiled a little. "As well as could humanly be expected," she answered. "He really is a wonderful guy."

Micah's blue eyes sparkled through her tears. "I can see that." She grabbed a tissue and wiped her face. "So, how did you leave it with him?"

"Badly, at first," Haley confessed. "I thought it would be kinder to let him go. Turns out I couldn't hack it. I missed him too much. So now, like I said, we're penpals. No promises either way." She tried to smile at Micah, but to her dismay, heard herself sniffle instead. "I can't ask him not to date other women. It wouldn't be fair. All I can do is be the best damn friend he ever had and hope he's still available next February."

Micah's hand closed over Haley's and gave it a squeeze. "I owe you everything," she said quietly. "We'll figure this out somehow, I promise. And I'll do absolutely anything I can to help make it happen."

"Thank you," Haley replied genuinely. "But there really isn't anything you can do."

Micah's blue eyes flashed with fire. A determined, righteous fire that struck a tiny chord of anxiety in the depths of Haley's heart.

"We'll see about that," Micah retorted.

Chapter 23

"Well, will you look at this?" Jenna said suggestively, plucking an envelope from the stack of mail she was carrying and dropping it onto the kitchen table in front of Ben. "It's from that mysterious Harvey Olson person. Again."

Ben kept his eyes on his cereal bowl. *Crap.* He knew this was coming. The worst part of dealing with his sisters was that they were all so damned smart. Ever since he'd returned to the Parker family headquarters he'd tried to be "helpful" and get the mail himself. But it didn't arrive consistently, and he couldn't be walking out to the street every five minutes all day long. "Oh?" he muttered, allowing himself only a brief glance at the letter before returning his attention to his cereal. What he wanted to do was snatch the letter up, haul it back to his room, and rip it open immediately.

"So who's Harvey Olson?" Jenna continued, slipping into a chair opposite and leaning forward toward him, her elbows on the table. She had just put her kids on the bus and was still in her bathrobe.

Ben sighed internally and looked up at her. His second oldest sister, better known in the family as "the drama queen," was also a redhead. They were the only two in the family, and people always said they looked alike. As a child, Ben had resented the comparison, but by adolescence he grew to appreciate it. Even first thing in the morning and without makeup, Jenna was a strikingly beautiful woman.

"Just a friend of mine from Alaska," he answered with a shrug.

"This letter is from California," Jenna pointed out. "A rather ritzy part of California, I might add. Does your friend own a yacht, by any chance?"

Ben shrugged again. "Do you have any more bananas?"

"You ate the last one yesterday," Jenna retorted impatiently. "Does he live in Alaska or California?"

"Why do you care?" Ben replied, only to wince at the defensive tone of his voice. He was blowing this. "I'm sorry I ate all the bananas. I'll buy more this afternoon."

Jenna's eyes rolled. "I don't care about the damn bananas. You know we love having you here — it's your idea to pay for your own food in the first place. You're avoiding the subject."

"What subject?" Ben said lightly. His parents had sold the house they'd all grown up in to Jenna and her husband two years ago. It worked out for everyone because his parents wanted to downsize to a low-maintenance carriage home and Jenna needed a larger spread for her family of five. Jenna was more than happy to carry on the tradition of hosting holiday gatherings and housing visiting relatives, and she insisted that her kids would pitch a fit if Ben stayed anywhere but with them. They had plenty of room, and the tradition of having Uncle Ben take the kids trick-or-treating on his last day in Seattle was — next to the candy, of course — the highlight of their Halloween.

Ben did genuinely appreciate his sister's hospitality. She was a generous soul by nature and she meant well — most of the time. But she was also maddeningly nosy.

Their gazes met, and Jenna's shrewd eyes, the exact same shade of hazel as his own, flickered with a studious intensity. She smiled a small, mischievous smile and inched her hand towards Haley's letter.

Ben slammed his fist down over it and slid it to safety.

Jenna laughed merrily. "I *knew* it! Who is she, Ben?"

Dammit! He'd been tricked. "Who is Harvey, you mean?" he asked stiffly.

She cackled. "This is the second letter I've seen from that address in a week, and the other days, I didn't get the mail. I might buy 'Harvey' if you were gay, but I know you're not, so I'll ask again. Who is she?"

Ben's jaws clenched. "I told you. A *friend*."

Jenna shook her head and clucked her tongue. "Ben, Ben, Ben. You are so out of your league, here. Give it up. You think that when I handed you that first letter I didn't notice how your eyes started to dance? How a little glow of red flared up in those adorable apple cheeks? Right now your entire face looks like a tomato. And if I tried to steal that letter back, I do believe you'd body slam me."

Ben growled low in his throat.

Jenna laughed again. "What is her name, really? Holly? Hermione?"

Ben waited a long moment, his gaze locked on his sister's. Further resistance was futile. "Her name is Haley," he grumbled.

A brilliant smile spread across Jenna's face.

"And we *are* just friends," he qualified.

"How unfortunate," she joked easily, leaning back in her chair. "So what's the problem, little brother? Losing your touch?"

His answering frown affected her. Her smirk disappeared, replaced with a look of concern. "Seriously, Ben. What's wrong? What's keeping the two of you apart? You're obviously crazy about her."

Ben blew out a breath. He had no intention of divulging the whole story. His plan had been to confirm Haley's existence and be done with it. He thought he might talk to Lara while he was in Seattle, or maybe his mother, whom he knew had treated at least one surrogate mother as a patient. The truth was, he really *did* want to talk about it. To somebody.

But Jenna? One word to her and every adult in the family would know. Not the kids; Jenna was always careful what she said around them. But everyone else he cared about would know about his relationship with Haley within days. Maybe hours.

He wondered, suddenly, if that would really be so horrible. He wasn't ashamed of loving Haley. She was a wonderful person, and she was doing a very selfless thing.

"What's keeping us apart," he began slowly, "is that she's serving as a surrogate mother for her twin sister. When I met her in Alaska she was four months' pregnant. Now she's six and a half. The other problem is that she lives and works as an attorney in Newport Beach. She grew up there, and her family is there, and she doesn't want to leave there. Probably ever. Does that explain things?"

Jenna's hazel eyes blinked. "She's carrying a baby for her sister? Is it her first?"

Ben wasn't sure which woman she was talking about, but the answer was the same. "Yes."

"Wow," Jenna said simply. She was quiet for a long time, gazing idly into space. "That's pretty amazing, Ben," she said finally. "I mean, you know I love the Sisters Parker, but I don't know if I would do that. Being pregnant is... challenging, under the best of circumstances. And she's taking a risk in terms of having her own children later. How old is she?"

"Twenty-nine," Ben answered, growing anxious. "What risk are you talking about?"

Jenna looked at him a moment, her eyes sympathetic. "Are you going to stick your fingers in your ears and hum again?"

He frowned at her. "Just tell me."

"It's only a very small risk," Jenna explained. "But you know how many things *can* go wrong, in rare cases. No one could guarantee her *zero* risk of a serious threat to her own health, or a hysterectomy. Even if everything otherwise goes perfectly fine, but she needs a c-section, she'd be putting future babies at slightly higher risk for placental problems. Do you know if she wants kids of her own?"

Ben stiffened. "I don't know. We never talked about it." The conversation had taken a distinctly disturbing turn. One he didn't want to think about.

Jenna leaned forward and put her hand over his. "I'm not trying to scare you. The odds are hugely in favor of both her and the baby being perfectly fine. It's just that I'm impressed that she would do something like that, as a single woman without children of her own. She must be a very giving person."

Ben released a breath. "Yes. She is."

"And smart, too," Jenna said, smiling again. "An attorney in Newport Beach! I knew you'd eventually see the appeal of dating a woman who's your intellectual equal. And might I say it's about damn time."

Ben gave a rueful smirk. The sad truth was, Jenna was right. None of his previous girlfriends had been particularly bright. "Maybe I was looking for someone as different from the four of you as possible," he said jokingly, realizing only as he said it that that was *exactly* what he'd been doing.

Jenna laughed out loud and bounced back in her chair. "Well, if that's the case, we apologize. If we'd all been brainless ditzes you might have been happily married years ago!"

Ben grinned back at her, heartened by his own revelation. Jenna obviously took no offense. His sisters were all well aware of the hell they'd put him through.

"So what happens now?" she asked. "When is she due? Around Christmas?"

"First week in January."

Jenna's lips twisted. "And she's expecting you to wait around all that time, content with a bunch of letters?"

Ben felt another jolt of defensiveness. "No," he explained. "I keep telling you, we're only friends. She said specifically that I shouldn't put my life on hold. That she doesn't want to stop me from seeing other women."

Jenna sat still a moment. Then she leaned slowly forward, her eyes trained on his. "Wait a minute. How often does this woman write you?"

Ben hesitated. "As much as I write her. Almost every day." He was fudging a little. They wrote *every* day. Their letters crossed constantly, but it didn't matter. They had been keeping up a steady stream of family anecdotes, thoughtful musings, silly quizzes, nature-related trivia, and the occasional heartfelt discussion, and they were both enjoying it immensely. His evenings spent by the fire, reading his daily letter from Haley and composing his response, had been the highlight of his autumn in Alaska.

Jenna's mouth dropped open.

"What?" Ben demanded.

Jenna's face flashed a sudden, brilliant smile. She popped out of her chair, moved around the table to where he sat and threw her arms around his neck. "Oh, Ben!" she cooed, planting a kiss on his cheek. "I *like* this one!"

He stared back at her in confusion.

She laughed. "Oh, come on!" she exclaimed, dropping down in the chair next to him. "Can't you see? This woman isn't just dazzled by your dimples! She really does care about you!"

He looked at his sister skeptically. He believed that was true. But how could she possibly know?

Jenna let out a contented sigh. "Listen, little brother. No woman sits down and writes a letter every day if she's not crazy about the guy. But there are all kinds of crazy. An obsessive, infatuated type could do the same thing. But there are only two conceivable situations in which *any* woman would give a man permission to sleep around while she sits at home nursing her hemorrhoids. The first one is if she doesn't give a crap about him in the first place, which the letter writing thing rules out." She smiled at him again. "The second is a woman who loves you enough to set you free — all the while biting her nails till they bleed hoping to God you don't take her up on it."

Ben felt a mysterious warmth creep pleasantly through his chest. "She did hint rather strongly that she'd be jealous."

Jenna beamed. "She adores you." She rose and tousled his hair like he was a four-year-old. He would be offended if he didn't feel so good. Besides, Jenna's own hair looked worse than his.

She moved to pour herself a second cup of coffee. "When will you see her again?"

Ben's pulse sped up a bit. "I don't know. I'm hoping to do a layover in LA on my flight back to Honolulu. I'd only have a day and a half. But I need to see her again. We need to talk."

Jenna studied him. "You're really still 'just friends?'"

"We were only together in Alaska for five days," he answered, somewhat defensively. "Since then, it's been nothing but the letters."

"Then you absolutely have to see her," she confirmed. "You have to tell her how you feel and let her know you're willing to wait for her. She's a keeper, Ben. Don't screw this up."

He looked at his sister reproachfully.

"I'm serious!" she shot back. "Don't you think she deserves a little security at a time like this? No matter what she gave you permission for, if you so much as *look* at another woman before she has that baby, I swear to God, I will personally—"

"Jenna!" he protested hotly.

Her expression softened. "Sorry," she apologized. "Old habits."

Ben growled under his breath. All of his sisters had taken their anger out on him whenever one of their boyfriends cheated, which happened frightfully often. "You would think," he said pointedly, "that now that all four of you are married to great guys, I would finally be off the hook for the collective sins of the male race. Will you give me a little credit, please?"

Jenna smiled sheepishly. She walked over and hugged his shoulders, dropping another kiss on top of his head. "I know you're one of the good guys, Ben," she said softly. "You always have been. That's why I'm so excited. You deserve a woman who loves you like you should be loved."

Ben was grateful his sister couldn't see his face as an unexpected wave of emotion took him aback. He couldn't remember he and Jenna ever having talked like this. They didn't talk much, period. All they ever did was banter or argue.

But she understood about Haley. She understood parts of it better than he did.

"Thanks for that," he managed.

She pulled away, and her expression turned mischievous again. "But for the record, and purely hypothetically, you understand," she began, picking up her coffee cup again. "If you *did* take her generous offer at face value, and started screwing around with other women while she was suffering through her last trimester with no baby daddy to rub her back and massage her cankles, The Sisters Parker *would* tear your limbs off." She flashed a stunning smile. "Just sayin'."

Ben smiled back. He rose from the table, collected his dirty dishes, and put them in the dishwasher. "Knock yourselves out," he quipped, pulling Haley's letter from his pocket and eyeing it with anticipation. He headed for the door.

"You're going to pick the kids up at school for me today and get Wendee to Brownies, right?" Jenna called after him. "I have that job interview at three."

"No problem," he threw back over his shoulder. "It's on my calendar."

"Thanks, Ben," she called after him gratefully. "You're a lifesaver."

He waved back at her and moved out the door. He had been headed to his favorite recliner in the living room, but with Haley's letter practically smoldering in his hand, he only made it as far as the hallway before he began to read.

Dear Ben,

Your appeal regarding your failing grade on the "What Every Boat Captain Should Know About Hot Yoga" quiz is hereby rejected. If you want to pass, you'll have to study harder. And a little less sarcasm on your essays wouldn't hurt either.

He chuckled to himself and leaned against the wall.

"Hey, Mags!" he heard Jenna saying in the kitchen, presumably on the phone. "Guess what? Ben's in lo-ve!"

He shook his head and sighed. But a smile remained on his face.

Chapter 24

Haley pulled her chair away from her desk and rolled it up to the table by her window. The view of Irvine from her third floor office wasn't nearly as refreshing as the view from her apartment, but it was better than staring at the stacks of papers on her desk. She dug into the shrimp salad Micah had packed for her and smiled with satisfaction. Her sister was becoming quite the gourmet. She wondered if Micah would keep it up after Fred was born or revert to mac and cheese and chicken tenders like every other new parent.

Her initial hunger satisfied, she reached into her bag and pulled out Ben's latest letter for rereading. It was an especially interesting one, and she wanted to savor it all over again.

> If you really want to know the grim story of the romantic life and times of Ben Parker, I'll tell you.

She smiled to herself. She had debated forever about whether his dating history was any of her business, given their stated 'just friends' status. She had succumbed to her maddening curiosity just a few days before, by reasoning that if they really *were* just friends, she wouldn't hesitate to ask him because then it wouldn't matter. Of course, they weren't really just friends and it *did* matter, very much, but she wasn't above hiding behind the ploy. After all, she had confessed her own sad, boring history ages ago.

> I dated a fair amount in college and grad school, but nothing that lasted more than a few months. I've had exactly three girlfriends who lasted longer, all of whom I met in Hawaii. The first one I gave up on because she drank too much. The second said she was okay with me spending the summer in Alaska, but after three weeks of being lonely she dumped me via text. The third relationship was the longest, but it was the worst. She also said she would be okay with my leaving for a few months, that it would be tough, but that she wanted to stay together. She did keep in touch while I was gone and we picked things up again when I got back to Maui. Three months after that, I found out

she'd been sleeping with another guy all summer and that she didn't break up with him until a week after my return. I guess I should have been grateful I was her first choice, but somehow I was no longer interested.

Haley's jaw muscles clenched. As relieved as she was to know that Ben wasn't still carrying a torch for some great lost love, the stupidity of his exes enraged her. Could they seriously not refrain from cheating for four freaking months? How could they possibly weigh their options and decide he wasn't worth it? How could the wenches not understand how rare it was to find a guy willing to go all summer without cheating on *them?*

She chewed another bite of salad and considered. Come to think of it, why would a guy as smart as Ben date such idiot women in the first place? Her face twisted into a frown. She would inquire about *that* in her next letter.

She read further, but he had said nothing more about his love life. Just answered her previous questions about what his nieces and nephews planned to be for Halloween.

They voted on what I should dress up as, and the winning suggestion was Olaf the snowman. I was pretty happy about that, since the second place finisher was the Little Mermaid.

Haley finished the letter chuckling, but as she stuffed it back into its envelope, her smile faded. *Oh, right.* He had included more "environmentalist propaganda" with this one, and she had yet to open it. She always opened them, but rarely read them through. They were too damned depressing. She took a breath and unfolded the square of newsprint. It was an article from the local paper in Seattle.

Stirjon Chemicals Factory Linked to Fish Kill, Environmentalists Claim

Haley's stomach soured. It was coincidence, of course. Ben had no idea that Stirjon was a client of hers. But he was in Seattle and he obviously read the local news. She was aware that the story had broken in the media — the fallout had kept her hopping for days. She should have expected him to hear about it.

She crumpled the article into a ball and flung it into her trash can.

She didn't need to read it. She'd read it quite thoroughly already, along with every other news report on the topic. It said that the fishermen's organization had been pushing Stirjon for discovery, but was getting nowhere fast. It did not include the words "thanks to a series of brilliant legal roadblocks placed by Haley Olson, Esquire," but it could have.

Haley blew out a frustrated breath. She didn't honestly know whether Stirjon was causing the problem or not. She had seen no science to back up the environmentalists' assertion that the chemical in question was toxic to fish. She also knew that meant exactly nothing, because the scientific team at Stirjon had a long history of responding to unpleasantly suggestive internal data by killing the offending study.

She threw out the rest of her salad and whirled back around to her desk. What she did know, and what perturbed her immensely, was that the Stirjon facility *was* in fact leaching the chemical in question, and that despite her strongly worded advice, they had yet to stop doing so. She was certain she could make them see reason eventually, but her arguments, ironically enough, were being undercut by her own effectiveness at stalling discovery.

The powers that be at Stirjon saw no reason to sink precious resources into eliminating a theoretical problem. Not with the esteemed Haley Olson as their firewall. With her at the helm, what the hell? They could continue leaching the toxin indefinitely. It *probably* was safe. And if it wasn't, what were a few dead fish, anyway?

Or the mammals that ate them?

Haley fought back a wave of nausea. She hadn't dealt with a situation like this before. It was far more typical for the polluting incident to be over and done with before she ever came on board. In those rare cases when it wasn't, her clients had always been reasonably diligent in addressing the problem. But despite the horrendous publicity Stirjon had received over their last disaster, they had succeeded in fending off any major financial loss, which in their view meant they'd gotten away with it.

And they're going to get away with it again, she thought with consternation. The fishermen's group was so underfunded and their counsel so third rate that applying even the most elementary of her bag of tricks made her feel like she was bludgeoning a baby seal. The newspaper article was grossly misleading, not in fingering Stirjon for the pollution, but in raising reader hopes that something constructive was being done about it. The truth was that this particular legal challenge to Stirjon, legitimate as its basis might be, wasn't scary enough to stir them to action.

She supposed that Bob had knocked on her door before entering. He usually did, at least perfunctorily. But this time she hadn't heard a thing, and by the time she saw his feet on her carpet he was already standing in front of her desk.

She lifted her chin without enthusiasm.

"You sick, Haley?" he asked, not entirely without sympathy. At seven months, she was quite obviously pregnant now, and starting to look a little puffy.

"No," she answered automatically. "I'm fine. What's up?" She didn't care for the look on his face. Over the last four years, she'd learned to read the man like a book. He had come to give her bad news.

He didn't answer immediately, but pulled up a chair and sat.

Very bad news.

"It's the fishermen's group," he said without preamble, drumming his fingers on her desk. Haley braced herself. Drumming fingers signaled more than anxiety. They signaled fear. "They've got new counsel."

Haley felt an odd prickle of elation. *Good for them.* "Who?" she asked. There were a few national nonprofit teams that picked up such cases when they could, but their funding had its limits as well.

"Sylvester," Bob answered.

Haley's heart skipped a beat. "*Donny* Sylvester?!"

He nodded gravely.

"But how?" she demanded, rising from her seat. "They couldn't possibly afford him!"

Bob wiped a handkerchief across his brow, then over the bald part of his head. "He's taking it on pro bono. The clean water people got to him. Convinced him it would be a crowd pleaser."

Haley swore and dropped back in her seat.

She had been content to give her adversaries a sporting chance. But Donny Sylvester was one of the best plaintiff's attorneys in the business. He was a rock star. He was legendary. Worse still, he was teaching at a university now, which meant his services would come complete with every corporate attorney's worst nightmare — an endless source of cheap labor in the form of idealistic, overzealous, tirelessly energetic law students.

"Stirjon's going to have to face facts," she said sharply. "You know what we're working with, Bob. We can hold Sylvester off a while, but he'll get to the crux of it. He won't give up until he does."

Bob nodded. His cool blue eyes studied her intently. "Taking on Sylvester could be the making of you, Haley."

She swallowed. He was right. Her chance of getting the best of Sylvester with a case as lame as Stirjon's was in the single digits, but a good showing on her part could open doors, regardless. It could be a defining point in her career.

"So how carefully are you going to be able to time that maternity leave?" he asked.

The seeming non sequitur stopped Haley cold. She was entitled to three months off with pay, because the policy drew no distinction between women who took home infants and those who did not. But she had assured him that she would be out no longer than strictly necessary — probably no more than a week, unless she had a c-section or other complications. But lately, she'd been thinking differently. Lately, she'd been thinking of Maui.

"You know I can't predict that," she said flatly. "We'll have to play it by ear."

Bob nodded and made no further comment. He rose. "I'm going out of town this weekend," he announced morosely. "Possibly the last chance to save my marriage. Let's meet first thing Monday morning. Sylvester won't be taking over the case for at least a week."

Haley looked up. Everyone knew that Bob's second wife was on a hair trigger. She had burst into his office three days ago screaming like a maniac. It seemed inevitable that he would once again fall casualty to the partner divorce curse, but Bob never gave up easy. "I'm sorry," Haley said simply. He rarely talked about his wife and had never mentioned marital problems before, so she didn't either. "Monday morning is fine. Have a good weekend."

He lifted a hand in farewell and departed.

Haley's mind spun with a barrage of conflicting desires. Her competitive streak was glad that Sylvester was on board, no question. Wrestling a polar bear was a whole lot more sporting than bludgeoning a baby seal, and she was not above dreams of professional grandeur.

But that was the attorney talking. She had certain skills and traits that served her well in her job, and those qualities had been carefully honed, valued, and promoted through intensive years of law school and practice. What she was only now coming to realize, since her near breakdown had sent her screaming to Alaska, was that in the process of becoming a damn good attorney, she had slowly been losing the rest of herself.

There was more to Haley Olson than some robotic legal machine. There was a woman who laughed with delight to watch porpoises bow ride and sea otters romp in the waves. A woman who loved the woods but was deathly afraid of bears. A woman who could sit for hours watching the cool Alaskan sun linger over snow-capped mountains, sick at heart to know that the glaciers were melting. A child who looked out over the ocean, longing to see what was on the other side.

She liked that Haley Olson, dammit. And she didn't want to lose her.

She pulled over a stack of particularly tedious work and put her head down. She would not think about the whole Stirjon / maternity leave / Bob-acting-weird thing now. She had promised Micah she would try her best to take part of Saturday and all of Sunday off this week, and she *needed* to do that. If she didn't lose focus this afternoon, she could make it happen.

She had an ulterior motive as well, one that made her heart speed up whenever she thought about it. For weeks now, Ben had been making cagey references to arranging a layover in LA on his flight back to Maui. He told her he would be in touch with details, but wouldn't allow her to pin him down on date and time, which was suspicious. As best as she could reconstruct, he normally left Seattle right after Halloween, and today was the first of November. All day she had been darting hopeful glances toward her phone.

Hey there, she imagined herself reading. *I'll be at LAX in three hours. Can you meet me?* She had dreamed up a variety of scenarios, and every one of them made her heart flutter and her limbs fidget.

She worked steadily for hours, hearing nothing from Ben, but resolving to stay hopeful. When at last she reached a reasonable stopping point, she didn't hesitate to pack up for home. So what if she was leaving a little earlier than usual? She had already worked a nine-hour day.

The drive from Irvine back to Newport Beach was painfully slow, as it always was when she joined the rest of the world for rush hour. She could cut down her commute by moving to Irvine, but couldn't bear the thought of losing her ocean view. Besides which, in what little time she wasn't working, the last place she wanted to be was close to the office.

After what seemed like an eternity of stopping and starting at smoggy-smelling intersections, she finally turned into her apartment complex and parked. Daylight Saving Time was over, and it was pitch dark already. She got up out of her car — a feat which had lately become more difficult — and looked down at her phone with disappointment. Nothing. Surely Ben wouldn't wait until he was on the ground at LAX to call her? It could take forever to get to him if the traffic was bad. And the traffic would be bad.

She headed for her mailbox, but opened it to see nothing but a grocery store flier. That was odd. Ben always sent her something.

She walked toward the stairs to her apartment, head down and spirits flagging, and noticed in the lamplight a pair of men's feet standing at her bottom step. Her head whipped up.

"Hi, Haley."

Chapter 25

It took several seconds for her to process the sight of him. He was just as tall, and just as redheaded, and just as handsome. It had been three long months since she'd last laid eyes on him, on that dreadful night when she'd left him on the porch of his cabin. He was dressed a little differently now, in cargo shorts and a short-sleeve shirt, ready for Hawaii. But he smiled at her with the same heart-melting smile, and his eyes held the same mischievous but good-natured twinkle.

"Ben," she breathed, unable to move.

He took a step toward her, and her trance broke. With a cry of glee she closed the distance between them and threw herself into his arms.

Surprisingly, she bounced back out. There was a volleyball between them. With a groan of frustration she turned her belly sideways and attached herself to him at a slant, throwing one arm around his neck while the other hugged his waist.

Laughing merrily, he made an equal effort at accommodation. "I see Fred has grown."

"Just a bit," Haley agreed, her voice muffled by his shoulder. He felt so good. She didn't want to move. "I can't believe you just showed up here!" she chastised, even as she continued to hold him. "You're a rat. You misled me."

He laughed again. "Don't you like surprises?"

"Not usually," she said honestly. "But I'll take this one."

"Well, good," he said, attempting to draw back a little. "Because I'd hate to have to drive back through all that mess again tonight."

Reluctantly, Haley let him go. A little. She could tell he wanted to see her face. "You rented a car?"

He nodded. "I just got here a couple minutes ago. I didn't know when you'd come home, but I was prepared to wait you out."

"You're not..." Haley was afraid to ask. "You're not going back tonight, then?"

His hazel eyes sparkled at her as he shook his head. "My flight leaves Sunday morning. We've got all day tomorrow. If you're free, that is."

"I'm free," Haley said immediately. She didn't give a damn what was waiting on her desk. In this instant, she couldn't even remember what it was. "What are your plans?"

He grinned at her again. "Well, I was kind of hoping you'd invite me inside. But if you want to stand out here all night—"

"Shut up!" she laughed, letting go of him at last to lead him up the stairs. "Of course you can come in. You weren't planning on paying for a hotel were you?"

"Not if I can avoid it," he admitted, picking up the duffel bag he'd dropped at his feet.

"You can crash on my couch," she decided, opening her door and stepping back to let him through. "I think you'll like the place. I'll even let you use my shower."

He grinned at her slyly and walked inside. She turned on the lights and shut the door behind them.

As she expected, he gravitated straight to the picture window in her living room. He dropped his bag on the floor by the wall and looked out.

"What do you think?" she asked proudly, stepping up beside him. The sweeping vista before them was a sea of twinkling lights that angled down the hill, over Balboa Island, across the boat-clogged harbor, and then over the peninsula on its other side. Beyond lay the darkness of the open ocean, broken only by the occasional glimmer of a distant ship.

"Impressive," he said softly, all too quickly turning back to her. She fought a stab of disappointment. Her view hadn't seemed to dazzle him. He was more interested in looking at her. "You look good, Haley. Pregnant, but good."

She made a face. "Don't try to humor me," she ordered. "I know I'm puffing up. Micah's all in a tizzy about preeclampsia, but so far I'm in the clear. You want something to drink?"

He didn't answer for a beat. "Yes," he said finally, moving away from her towards the kitchen. "But can I get it? I appreciate the offer of your couch because I'm poor, but no way am I letting you wait on me. I'm a professional houseguest — I know how to keep the invites coming. What can I get *you* to drink?"

Haley's smile broadened. She really couldn't stop smiling. She could hardly believe he was here. "Water's fine," she replied, following him. "Glasses are over the dishwasher. Take whatever you want from the fridge. Micah keeps it thoroughly stocked."

He smiled back as he poured her a glass of water. "I'm glad to see she's taking care of you."

"So am I." Haley took the glass, but swallowed only a sip before setting it down on the counter. She could not take her eyes off him as he moved around her kitchen, his warm-weather clothes showing off skin she'd never seen before. His biceps were strong and his long legs sinuous. Once or twice he caught her staring, and the answering sparkle in his eyes told her she was busted.

The small talk and serving of refreshments seemed grossly inadequate.

"Ben," she said finally, when he had finished pouring his drink and they both walked back out to the living room. "Could you possibly do me a favor?"

He set his glass on her end table. "Anything."

"Would you sit down for a minute?"

He looked at her quizzically, but dropped down onto one end of her sectional couch.

"Perfect," she praised. She studied his position, then sank down sideways onto his lap and nestled her head against his shoulder. She exhaled slowly, reveling in the feel of him as his arms wrapped compliantly around her shoulders. *Heaven.*

"Terribly sorry to take advantage of you in this way, Captain," she murmured unapologetically. "But God, I've missed you."

Ben made no reply. She wondered at his expression, but couldn't bear to lift her head long enough to see it.

"You know," she said dreamily, "I've wanted to do this ever since the day we walked into the nature center at Exit Glacier, and I saw you hug your friend Carrie. I was wicked jealous of her. I could tell you were an exceptional hugger, and I wanted a piece of the pie."

Ben shifted his position slightly. He cleared his throat. "I could do a hell of a lot better than this if we were more than friends, Haley."

A warm fire kindled in her chest, spreading upwards to flame her cheeks. She lifted her chin and looked at him. His eyes were blazing. "I'm sure you could," she whispered. "But..."

"But what?" he challenged.

She sat up a bit to face him. "But the baby isn't due until January," she said softly, reasonably. "And it will be at least February before..."

"I understand that," he insisted, his hazel eyes locked on hers. "I can wait."

Her heart skipped a beat. "I can't ask you to do that."

"You're not," he said earnestly. "I'm telling you it's what I want. I want *you*, Haley. I don't have all the answers, but we can work it out somehow. I want you in my life, and 'just friends' isn't good enough for me. Is it good enough for you?"

Haley's pulse pounded in her ears. Still gazing into his eyes, she raised her hand slowly to his face, just as she had tried to do in Alaska three months before. He had pulled her hand away then. This time, he sat perfectly still. She touched his cheek, then traced her fingers gently along his scratchy, not-shaved-since-this-morning jawbone. There wasn't a doubt in her mind that she loved him.

"No," she whispered. "Not even close."

Their lips met full force, with equal fervor and no pretense of hesitation. They devoured each other hungrily, and Haley felt herself slipping away into the most amazing bliss, the likes of which she'd never known before and of which she wanted infinitely more. He *did* want her. And he was hers now. All of him.

She was sinking lower onto the couch — she could not get him close enough. She squiggled and squirmed, aching for him to close the persistently annoying distance between them, when suddenly, that distance took offense.

Haley blinked. Ben pulled his lips from hers and laughed out loud.

Fred was kicking the hell out of him.

They laughed together as Ben sat upright again and lifted Haley with him. "I don't think she likes me much," he said tenderly.

"She adores you," Haley responded. "She's just feeling a little left out."

He raised his hand to her face and grazed her own cheek softly with his knuckles. Then he breathed out heavily, his eyes sparkling. "Well, I guess we've settled that issue, more-than-friend Haley."

"Yes," she agreed. "We've also just made the next few months a hundred times more difficult for ourselves. For me, anyway. I may be less than desirable at the moment, but you look as delicious as ever, Captain."

His eyebrows perked. "Am I *acting* like you're not desirable?"

She chuckled. "That's desperation talking. I look like a whale!"

He grinned. "And?"

Haley punched him playfully in the chest. "Bad metaphor. I look—"

He put a finger across her lips. "You look like one of the most incredibly self-sacrificing women I've ever known. Next to what you're going through, what's a few more months of deprivation for me?" He shifted her weight from his lap and stood up.

"A lot," Haley replied soberly.

He turned and leveled a grin at her. "Feel sorry for me all you want. You're welcome to make it up to me later."

Haley grinned back.

"And now," he announced suddenly, shaking out his arms in an obvious attempt to regroup, "the main attraction." He picked up his bag, rummaged around inside it, and extracted a brown paper lunch sack with a bulge at the bottom.

"What is that?" Haley asked.

"My contribution to the trade of course," he explained, dumping the contents onto her coffee table. "It's mostly what the nieces and nephews didn't want, but I did manage to steal some mini candy bars off of Mylah. She's only two, so she wasn't watching as closely."

Haley laughed out loud at the assortment of colorful wrappers. In her first letter to him, she had suggested they trade Halloween candy.

"Wait a minute," she said, rising. Once again, she was struck by the difficulty of such a simple action. It would be a very long third trimester. She crossed to her kitchen and located the bag of candy that Micah had supplied in case any trick-or-treaters bothered to scale her steps. As it turned out, Haley had worked too late to know. She ripped open the bag and poured a part of its contents onto her table.

"I'll give you a Kit Kat for two Sprees and an Airhead," he offered.

Haley scoffed. "Please. Who do you think you're dealing with? I want the Kit Kat *and* a dark chocolate Milky Way."

He scowled. "You drive a hard bargain, counselor."

She smirked. "Well, duh."

They haggled their way through their respective stashes, joking, laughing, and consuming so much of their booty in the process that Haley completely forgot she had never eaten dinner. When Ben mentioned that he had skipped dinner also, she quickly offered the entire contents of her fridge and was relieved when he agreed to eat in. She knew that inviting him to stay in her apartment overnight was like fanning an open flame, but she truly couldn't help herself. They had less than thirty-six hours together. She refused to waste a moment of it.

When their dinners had been eaten and the dishes cleared away, Haley contented herself with sitting beside him on the couch and trying to catch up on everything they hadn't put in their letters. He sat with one arm around her shoulders and she cuddled into his side, fighting a constant yearning to kiss him again.

The struggle was not an easy one. She was well aware that from a purely physical standpoint being seven months' pregnant was no impediment to a good time, and her selfish side taunted her endlessly with a string of *well maybe* and *but ifs*. But in her more lucid moments, she knew that no matter what Ben might be willing to overlook or accommodate, she did not want that part of their relationship to begin until her body was her own again. It even occurred to her, with a sudden rush of anxiety, that he'd never even *seen* her natural figure, which was a good deal less curvy than when he'd met her in July.

No. If he was willing to wait, so could she. If they were going to start something, they were going to start it right, with all cards on the table and every possible factor stacked in their favor.

"Haley?" Ben asked, rousing her from yet another tortured reverie.

"Yes?" she asked, embarrassed at having drifted from the conversation.

"You're falling asleep on me."

"No! I'm—" she looked around to find herself lying horizontally across his lap with her head cradled in the crook of his arm. "Oh, wow," she amended, blinking. "I guess I'm more tired than I thought."

"Evidently," he replied, his eyes dancing with amusement.

"What were you saying?" she asked, sitting up again. "I'm sorry."

"I wasn't saying anything. You were telling me about the dog you had when you were twelve. Then you said you were afraid to kiss me again and murmured something about a boob job."

Her eyes widened. "I did not!"

He laughed out loud. "I assure you, you did. Care to share the background on that one?"

She forced herself to stand. "Hell, no. And if I fell asleep in your lap, it's your own darn fault, Captain." She smiled down at him warmly. "I can't remember ever being more comfortable."

He smiled back at her just as warmly. The room temperature rose. "Maybe you should get some sleep," he suggested quietly. "We have a big day tomorrow."

Excitement flickered through Haley's still-drowsy mind. "Oh, we do, do we? And what might you have planned for us here in beautiful Newport Beach?"

He shook his head at her, pretending a sigh. "Really. You have to ask?" His eyes twinkled at her devilishly. "We're going to see the whales."

Chapter 26

Ben awoke to the sound of Haley's front door opening. He sat up quickly, having no trouble shaking off the few cobwebs he had acquired. The couch was comfortable enough, but imagining Haley in bed on the other side of her door was hardly conducive to peaceful slumber.

He watched curiously as the front door was opened by a curvy, petite blond woman carrying a shopping bag over her arm. She entered without hesitation and was halfway to Haley's kitchen before she noticed him on the couch. She jumped a little, then froze in place, staring at him.

Her blue eyes blinked. She was extremely pretty. A little like Haley, perhaps, but softer somehow, and less self-assured.

"Hello," he said amiably, trying his best not to intimidate her. He was dressed in perfectly decent sweatpants and a tee shirt, but he'd been told by more than one woman that bedhead made him look like a serial killer. "You must be Micah."

Her lips curved slowly into a smile. He caught a gleam in her eye that could only be described as catlike. "And you must be Ben."

"That's right," he confirmed, rising. "It's nice to meet you finally." He shook her free hand.

"You too," she agreed, still staring at him. "I'm so glad you're here!"

He smiled back at her. She clearly meant that. "Thanks," he responded.

Micah stared at him for another slightly too long, awkward moment, then carried her bag into the kitchen and began putting things away. "Is Haley still asleep?" she asked, keeping her voice low.

He nodded. There was no need for clumsy explanations; the sheets and blankets on the couch left no doubt that Haley had slept alone. "She seemed exhausted."

Micah frowned. "She's always exhausted, Ben. She works like a demon. She's at the office twelve hours most days, and she usually works weekends, too. I made her swear to me she'd stick to a half-day today and then take Sunday off completely."

Ben's brow furrowed. He knew that Haley worked a heavy schedule.

He had no idea it was that bad, particularly now. "She told me she was free today," he said helplessly.

Micah looked relieved. "That's fabulous. How long can you stay?"

He got the distinct feeling she wanted him to say forever. "Just till tomorrow morning."

Micah frowned again. "Oh, I wish you could stay longer. She must have been so happy to see you!"

Ben had no response to that.

Micah giggled at him. "Don't be modest. I know *exactly* how excited she was to see you." She smiled her feline smile again. "Haley needs you in her life, Ben. Even more than she realizes."

Ben struggled for something to say. He wasn't comfortable sharing confidences about Haley with a person he'd just met, even if Micah was her twin.

"Considerately discreet, too," she said after a moment. "I so totally approve." She moved a step closer to him and put a hand on his arm. "If there's ever anything I can do... to make things easier for the two of you, please let me know." She dropped her hand and stepped away from him towards the door. "I'll leave you alone. The longer Haley sleeps, the better." She opened the door, then turned around again. "Whatever it is you've been doing to make my sister so happy, please just keep it up. Okay?" She winked at him, then disappeared.

Ben stood still a moment, staring after her. Was Haley really that bad a workaholic? It was difficult for him to picture. Granted, she had been chained to her phone the entire time she'd been on vacation in July, and she had left early. But when he remembered their time together, he pictured her reveling in the unhurried pace of Alaska and eager for impromptu adventure. Was he missing something?

Frowning, he moved into the kitchen to make himself a cup of coffee. He noticed her phone charging on the counter and decided that its location was a good sign. At least she didn't text until the wee hours, sleep with the device blinking at her bedside, then reach for it the second she woke. That way lay madness. Even as he looked at it, the phone made a buzzing noise and the screen lit up with an incoming message. He wasn't trying to read it. He didn't care. But one word leapt out at him.

> Invitation: Stirjon group.
> Mon Nov 3. 10am - 11am Room 5B
> from Bob Hardin

A viselike cold clamped around his chest.

Stirjon.

It wasn't possible. It couldn't mean what it seemed to mean. She couldn't possibly—

I work for the bad guys.

"Good morning," a cheerful voice called behind him.

Ben whirled to see Haley standing in the entrance to her kitchen. She was barefoot, wearing a fluffy cream-colored robe that she could only keep closed over her middle by holding the sides together with one hand. She wore no makeup and her eyes were puffy, but her shining hair had been brushed smooth and her face was bright with anticipation.

She looked beautiful.

"Good morning," he returned hoarsely.

"Did I hear Micah out here, or was that a dream?" she asked.

He turned away from her. He fussed with the coffee machine and tried to regroup. "It was her. She dropped off some groceries, I think."

"Well, that must have been... interesting. Sorry about that. I should have warned you, she's used to letting herself in."

"It was fine," Ben said shortly, still looking away from her. He closed his eyes and focused on squelching his rising anger. He knew he had no right to be angry. Haley had told him what she did for a living; she was hardly obliged to provide him with a client list. She had no way of knowing that Stirjon would be such a hot button for him. He had only sent her the article a few days ago.

She moved closer to him. "What's wrong, Ben?" she demanded. "And don't tell me nothing. What is it? Did Micah say something?"

He shook his head and blew out a breath. The last thing he wanted to do today was get into an argument. He wanted their time together to be joyful and carefree — not strained and contentious. But there was no way around it now. All he could do was be honest with her.

"Are you working for Stirjon Chemicals, Haley?"

He watched as her eyes flooded with distress. Still, her tone was calm and measured. "They are a client of the firm's, yes," she answered. "And I am working on the case. In fact, I'm the lead associate. I got the article you sent, but I can't talk about the case with you. I'm sorry."

His anger spiked, and again he struggled to control it. How could she possibly sound so cool about this? "Twelve years ago, Stirjon Chemicals poisoned nearly every living thing in Puget Sound!" he said bitterly. "The effects are still being felt, particularly by the marine mammals!"

Haley shrank back ever so slightly. "I know that," she replied.

Ben focused on breathing deeply, calming his tone of voice. But his passion on the topic ran deep. Despite years of litigation and mountains of evidence, the plaintiffs had bungled the case and Stirjon had gotten off with a slap on the wrist. He had only been a teenager when the first, horrific reports of what was happening hit the media, but the incident had been a prime motivating factor in his choice of college major and profession. He wasn't cut out to be a lawyer, but he could damn well motivate people to care more deeply about marine wildlife.

"I know that none of that was your fault," he said more calmly, trying to remember some of the approaches to the topic he had been practicing in his head. He *did* want to talk about the issue; if they were going to be more than friends she needed to understand how he felt about her job. He just hadn't pictured it happening like this. "I'm not trying to make you responsible for it. I'm not implying that you're responsible for whatever they're doing now, either."

He ran a hand through his hair. "But *why*, Haley?" he asked, Micah's words still ringing painfully in his head. *She works like a demon.* "Why are you giving the greatest part of yourself — your energy, your talent, almost *all* of your time — to work for clients who..." he struggled to find the right words, words that would not insult her.

"Who are evil incarnate?" Haley finished for him, her tone defensive. "It's not a matter of good versus evil, Ben. It's *business.* Corporations hire my firm because in the long run, we save them money. Saving them money and doing what's best for the environment are not mutually exclusive. I happen to believe that being environmentally responsible *does* save corporations money."

Ben's jaws clenched. He had heard that line before. "And what about those times when it doesn't?" he argued.

Haley's eyes flickered with annoyance. He had struck a nerve.

"You think I don't understand how the system works, but I do," he pressed. "I know that much of what you do personally *is* helpful to the environment. Maybe you even do more good than harm, in balance. But answer me this. If I'm getting ready to feed my nieces and nephews a nice meal of fish caught downriver from the Stirjon chemical factory, and I hear that Haley Olson is on the case, which side should I *hope* she's on?"

Haley's eyes flashed fire. She leaned back against the counter, her arms crossed stubbornly on top of Fred. "You haven't been kidding about trying to turn me from the dark side, have you?"

His pulse quickened. "No."

She straightened and faced him squarely. "If I had it to do all over again, I would be a plaintiff's attorney, okay? But I *can't* switch sides now. It's a conflict of interest issue; it just isn't done. I would have to start all over again in another area of specialization, which means I would lose everything!"

Her green eyes flashed again, and this time he was the one who felt like shrinking. She could certainly command a man's respect when she wanted to, even standing barefoot in a bathrobe.

"You mean you've thought about it?" he asked thinly, surprised.

"Of course I've thought about it!" she shot back.

"Before or after I started harassing you?"

"Before," she confirmed. "Although your efforts have been exceptionally annoying."

Ben couldn't help himself. He grinned at her. "I'm glad to hear that," he said softly.

He watched as his response not only snuffed out the fire in Haley's eyes, but replaced it with a liquid look of longing. She set her beautiful mouth firmly and growled beneath her breath. "I cannot debate with you when you look at me like that, Captain."

Ben's grin widened. "So don't." He didn't stop to think, just acted on the ever-present impulse he wasn't used to being able to act on. He reached out, pulled her close, and pressed his lips firmly over hers. She kissed him back fervently, her hands fumbling to pull him closer, drowning him in the satisfaction of knowing she wanted him as much as he wanted her. How much time passed, he didn't know, but it took another ninja jab to the gut before he remembered exactly why he'd been resisting the ever-present impulse in the first place.

He released her and stepped back. "You win, counselor," he said breathlessly. "I'll suspend the campaign, at least for today. But only if I get first dibs on the shower."

Haley smiled at him. She was breathing heavily herself, and her robe had started to gape at the neck. "Flip you for it," she teased.

Ben averted his eyes and ran another hand through his grubby hair, which felt like it was sticking straight up from the top of his head. When Haley unexpectedly giggled, he was sure of it.

"I need it worse," he countered.

In one sudden motion, Haley stepped forward on tiptoe, kissed him gently on the lips, then backed away again. "I concede. You may go first, Captain."

Ben blinked at her dumbly, his body flushing with heat. It was a simple, affectionate gesture. Yet it affected him, in some bizarre way, even more than the steamier session that had preceded it.

"I've always wanted to do that, you know," she told him, her green eyes turning liquid again. "To be able to kiss you, just because." Her robe was still gaping and her voice was like silk. "I'm liking this more-than-friends thing. I'm liking it very much."

Ben said nothing else. He turned away from her and grabbed up his duffel bag.

It was time to take that shower.

Chapter 27

"Not a word about my real identity," Ben ordered, pulling his mirror-lensed sunglasses down over his eyes like a secret agent. "I like to do these things incognito."

Haley chuckled at him. In his light cargo pants and purple windproof jacket, he still looked every inch the boat captain, despite trading his skipper's hat for a U.W. Huskies cap. The whale-watching boat was lightly loaded, carrying only a dozen passengers or so as it backed away from the dock and out into Newport Harbor. The couple sat in the stern on the second level, where Ben not-so-surreptitiously watched the captain through the windows to the bridge.

"Does he pass inspection?" Haley teased.

"That remains to be seen," Ben said critically.

"First mammal! California sea lions," Haley said brightly, pointing to a cluster of the giant animals lounging on the end of the dock. And another swimming in the harbor. And two more stretched out on the hull of a half-sunken sailboat. "Five points for me."

Ben smirked at her. "You really want to take me on? Shall we include seabirds and fish?"

"On second thought," Haley said smoothly, "Let's just say you win." She was so incredibly happy to be here, with him, out on the water on such a beautiful day, she would agree to just about anything. The morning might not have started out well, but even when it came to his issues with her job, she felt more at peace than before they had discussed it. Their differences were not insurmountable. They could work *something* out. God knew they both wanted it badly enough.

More pressing on her mind, as she took him out on a driving tour of the city this morning, was how they were going to be together after Fred was born. She had no conscious strategy cooking in her brain... at least not a coherent one. But she had a strong sense that it was terribly, vitally important he get a good impression of her beloved hometown.

"I have a confession to make," he said lightly.

"Oh?"

"I've brought you here under false pretenses. We might not see a whale today."

Haley threw him a mock glare. "Don't toy with me, man. You know how much I'm counting on getting waved at again."

She felt a prickle of remorse when he actually looked guilty. "I know," he said. "But this is pretty much the worst time of year to take this kind of cruise. The blue whales have left and the grays haven't come in yet. We might see a stray humpback, or even a minke or a fin if we're lucky. But for this short a trip, odds are, we won't."

"Well, that's a shame," Haley said evenly. "Because if we don't see a whale, I can't think of a single other reason why I would want to spend two and half hours out on the ocean on such a beautiful day," she teased. "With you."

"We'll probably see dolphins," he countered, still sounding a tad bit guilty.

Haley groaned and pulled off his sunglasses. "It's hard enough to tell when you're serious without these!" she complained, resolving to buy him a more transparent pair as soon as they returned to the pier. It would be fun to spend some money on him. On *them*. She couldn't think of anything she'd rather spend it on.

It took a full twenty minutes for the boat to chug out of the harbor, dodging myriad other boats and the occasional swimming sea lion. When at last they reached the open ocean, the captain announced that they would be heading toward Catalina Island, and as the boat picked up speed, Haley thrilled again to the movement of the ocean beneath her.

They walked to the rail, and Haley watched Ben's face intently as a sweeping view of the California coastline developed before them. "Look there," she said, pointing toward Mount Baldy, which had just the tiniest dusting of white on its tip. "It must have snowed already! Just to remind us of Alaska, I'm sure."

Ben wrapped his arm loosely around her shoulders and gave her a squeeze, but there was a hint of indulgence in the gesture that troubled her. He was enjoying himself, clearly. He just wasn't enjoying himself quite as much as she wanted him to. She looked out over the stretch of Southern California she had called home for her entire life, and her mind filled with happy memories of days at the beach: both the rare ones when her father had taken time off to spend with his daughters and the more frequent ones when her mother had gone sunbathing while the twins ran around unsupervised. There had been elaborate birthday parties and expensive dresses, dance recitals and dinners on friends' yachts, dates on Catalina Island and wedding receptions in the

Grand Ballroom at the Harborside. She had always counted herself lucky to live here. A place of endless opportunity for both fun and profit, complete with never-ending sunshine and sparkling blue water.

A place which, she refrained from pointing out, hosted whale-watching tours year round.

But as she stood beside Ben now, watching him take in the vista with the wind whipping his ginger hair around the brim of his cap, she couldn't help but wonder if he saw it differently. She tried to imagine the same view through his eyes, and her smile dampened. There were mountains here, true, but compared to the endless, towering peaks of Alaska, these seemed dry and practically stubby. The entire visible coastline stretching in either direction was jam-packed with buildings clear to the sand. Almost everything in sight besides ocean and sky was manmade and artificial, and the little that wasn't was uniformly brown.

"Something wrong?" Ben asked, rubbing his hand gently across her back.

Haley shook her head vehemently, then nestled it against his shoulder. They were together now. What else mattered?

The captain picked up his microphone and began a long and somewhat rambling explanation of how unusual it was to find whales this time of year and how fortunate they would all be if he spotted one today. As the boat skipped off at a good pace toward Catalina, he regaled them with stories of other successful hunts, and as Haley watched the little muscles in Ben's jaw repeatedly pop she finally had to laugh out loud. "You really can't stand it, can you?" she chuckled. "What exactly is he saying wrong?"

Ben's eyes rolled. "The man can handle a boat well enough," he said begrudgingly. "But he doesn't know jack about the rest of it. Minkes are baleen whales, for God's sake. They don't *have* teeth. And if he's really gotten this boat to 'within inches' of a blue then he should be reported to NOAA and flogged with a swim noodle besides."

Maybe you should replace him.

Haley stifled the thought. It was too much to hope for. She needed to cut it out.

"Now, here's what we've been waiting for!" Ben said brightly, looking out over the horizon ahead at... nothing. He took her hand and led her down the stairs toward the bow.

"What?" Haley begged. "What do you see?"

"Dolphins," he said reverently as they settled in along the front rail. "I'm betting quite a few of them. Most likely 'common dolphins,' although that name doesn't do them justice in my opinion."

Haley still saw nothing, but after a few more moments the captain announced the same thing, and the other passengers settled along the rails around them. "I hope they feel like bow riding," Haley said hopefully, at last catching sight of a suspicious splash and glint of fin. The water surface ahead was teeming with seabirds, which, she prided herself on knowing, meant they were following a school of fish. "I've always loved watching the dolphins," she called over the wind to Ben's ear. "Once when I was in high school, a group of us had dinner on somebody's boat before a formal dance. The others stayed inside, but when the dolphins started jumping I just had to step out. My corsage blew off and I totally ruined my hair, but it was the best part of that date, as I recall."

Ben's laughter rumbled in his chest; Haley could feel its pleasant vibration as she leaned into his side. *So nice.* The luxury of having him physically close, being free to touch and hold him, made her practically euphoric. There were limits, of course. There was a point beyond which they would only be torturing themselves. But compared to when they were just friends, that point had shifted in a very gratifying direction.

The boat drew closer to the pod of dolphins, and just as Haley had hoped, the animals were more than happy to bow ride. The passengers all laughed with delight as the large gray and white mammals not only streaked through the current alongside the front of the boat, but also leapt up into the air behind it from the waves created by its wake. Ben enjoyed the spectacle every bit as much as everyone else, explaining to Haley that only rarely did he get to watch the animals from the bow railing. There were so many dolphins in the area — literally hundreds — that as soon as one group tired of the game another would appear, and time passed swiftly as the boat encountered new pods again and again.

As their allotted cruise time dwindled, the captain headed closer into shore, and Ben and Haley returned to the upper deck. From their new position they could see across the water all the way to the Los Angeles basin, and once again Haley found herself studying Ben's expression with a combination of hopefulness and apprehension. When she caught sight of the telltale clench in his jaw again, her heart fell. She followed his gaze to see a red-brown cloud of haze adhering to the LA shoreline. *Smog.*

She cursed internally. Why did it have to look so bad *today?*

"What kind of dolphins do you see in Maui?" she asked. She knew the question would distract him, and it did. In the next five minutes she learned more about dolphin species in the Hawaiian Islands than most people learned in a lifetime — and, as always, enjoyed herself in the process.

"I want to go to Hawaii again so badly," she said wistfully, noting once more how incredibly manmade and built up this part of the coast appeared from the water. She had always thought of Southern California as beautiful, and she still did. But until she spent time in Alaska it had never occurred to her how much differently a place could feel when its landscape was unaltered by development. Alaska had felt wonderfully, fantastically *wild*. Was that part of what drew Ben back every year, despite the toll on his bank account — and his love life?

"When we went to Honolulu before, we were only ten," Haley recounted. "And if we went anywhere besides the beach and the hotel, I can't remember it. All I remember is being babysat by some hotel sitter nearly every evening, and my parents fighting when my dad had to fly back early. My mother had been looking forward to that trip for a long time."

Unpleasant memories stirred. She and Micah had been angry with their father, too. He frequently promised family vacations that never happened. The few that did all too often ended up like Hawaii. In retrospect, she understood exactly what kind of pressure he had been under. But that didn't completely take away the sting of his neglect, even now.

I'm going to be a lawyer, just like you, Daddy!

Haley frowned.

"If you never left Waikiki," Ben said lightly, looking away from her and back out to sea, "You never saw Hawaii. The rest of Oahu is different; most of it's still country. The other islands are, too. Not that I've seen them all yet."

Haley was surprised. She assumed he would have explored every inch of the Aloha State by now. "You haven't? Why not?"

He shrugged. "Island hopping is expensive. My flights connect through Oahu, so I've nosed around there a bit, but I've never made it to the Big Island, or to Kauai. Someday I'll work it out, but for now, it's hard to manage the time off."

Haley stared at him quizzically, a new fear creeping into her heart. "How much time off do you get?"

His gaze remained at sea. "The tours run every day of the week in season, and the outfit I work for only has the two captains. I don't have the flexibility I'd have working for a bigger company, but I like their boats and their attitude and they pay decently, with benefits. I have plenty of free time, just not many whole days off, and never more than two in a row, with the exception of Christmas."

Haley's fear ratcheted up a notch. "Christmas?" she repeated dumbly.

He nodded. "I can only afford the two flights a year, but my parents usually give me a ticket home as their gift." His eyes left the horizon and turned to Haley, and his voice grew more intent. "You think you might be able to come to Maui sometime?"

Her heart thudded in her chest. If it wasn't one impediment, it was another. The day was proving an endless parade of them. "I don't get a lot of time off either, as you know. I'd love to visit you there, but I don't think... I mean, I wasn't planning on traveling again until after the baby's born."

His eyes darted quickly out to sea again. "No," he said evenly. "I didn't think you would."

Haley's euphoria dwindled rapidly. She *had* thought about flying out to see him, maybe around Thanksgiving. But she knew now that wasn't realistic. Even if she did feel good enough for the journey, it wouldn't be medically responsible for her to go. Micah was hauling her into the OB's office every week now over fears she was headed toward preeclampsia, and if Haley ever failed her labs on that score she would be looking at bed rest for the duration. She hadn't told Bob that fun fact and she didn't plan to worry Ben with it either, but the upshot was, she couldn't travel.

She had been hoping, instead, that she could convince Ben to fly back and see her. She realized the plane ticket might be too expensive for him, but money was no obstacle to her. His work schedule was another matter.

"Ben," she cried out suddenly, her tone drawing his gaze back to her immediately. "What the hell are we going to do? How are we going to see each other? I was thinking I could fly you back here for long weekends or something." To her horror, her voice nearly cracked. "I never thought you might not be able to come."

His eyes swam with a melancholy equal to hers, but his voice remained upbeat. "I'm sorry. I should have explained. But I'll be back at Christmas, and I'm sure my family won't mind donating a day of my Seattle time to the cause."

A day? Haley's face felt hot. Her lower jaw began to tremble. She snapped her mouth shut furiously. *Hormones!* Once this endless pregnancy was over with, she swore she would never cry again.

"I'll look awful at Christmas," she murmured, regretting the childish words the second they left her mouth. Like *that* was all that mattered!

Ben hugged her shoulders and dropped a kiss on the top of her head. "It won't be that long, Haley," he said gently, choosing — and wisely so — to address the real issue rather than her idiotic words. "We'll figure something out."

And what exactly would that be? Haley asked herself.

Ben suddenly jerked and straightened. Haley looked up to see his gaze darting between the horizon of the open ocean and the captain in the bridge. "What is it?" she asked.

"Humpback spout," he explained. Then he looked at his watch, sighed, and relaxed against the railing again.

"The captain didn't see it?" she asked.

"No, but it wouldn't have mattered anyway. We're out of time and headed into port."

"Oh," Haley said dumbly. The time had flown by, indeed. It was afternoon already. "Do they have full-day tours?" she asked suddenly, remembering how the longer trips had been his favorite in Alaska.

"May to October, there's a full-day to Catalina," he answered. "That would be fun. Might see an eagle or some harbor seals around the island."

He smiled at her, and Haley's spirits crept up a notch. He had answered that question terribly quickly. And precisely. Had he researched the topic purely to plan their outing today, or had he been checking into it for another reason?

All too soon, the boat returned to the mouth of the harbor, and Ben frowned as the captain pulled the boat so close to the sea lions sunning themselves on the buoy that the people on the lower deck could practically reach out and touch them. Haley felt a strange desire to defend the captain's actions, pointing out that the sea lions themselves had no qualms about jumping up onto boats docked at the marina, whether humans were nearby or not. But she knew that such an argument wouldn't fly with Ben. He would only remind her that the sea lions wouldn't be jumping up on manmade structures in the first place if more of their natural habitat remained.

As the boat made its way back to the slip Haley stuck close to his side, feeling a sudden, intense need to relish every second they were together. Once he left again her mind would want to replay them all, and she was determined to make the rest of the day as perfect as possible.

They spent the afternoon in a heavenly spree of unstructured light-hearted fun, eating ice cream, strolling on the Balboa Pier, window-shopping the tourist traps, critiquing the surfers, taking their shoes off and wading in the Pacific, and — her favorite part — drawing their initials in the sand with their toes. Their joy simply to be in each other's company was mutual and profound, and only when the weak November sun began sliding from the sky did Haley's soaring spirits begin to drop along with it.

She took Ben to the Newport Pier, where they sat by the window in one of her favorite diners eating vegetarian chili and cornbread while watching the sun set over the water. Darkness came all too soon, and as they finished their meal and began a lamplit stroll down the paved boardwalk, Haley's unexpressed worries began to surface.

Ben had not let her buy him a new pair of sunglasses. He had insisted that he didn't need them and that he had several other pairs already. It was a small thing, of course, but it had started her thinking. Whenever they went out together, even in Alaska, they had always paid separately. The only exception she could think of was when he allowed her to buy him dinner on his birthday and when he bought her a barbecue, ostensibly as compensation for not seeing a grizzly. The fact that he didn't automatically pick up her checks didn't bother her in the slightest — not because she was wealthier, but because she viewed the expectation that it was the man's responsibility as sexist in the first place. But now that she was essentially his hostess for the day, his not allowing *her* to buy *him* anything was disconcerting.

A gust of warm wind blew by, rustling the palm trees along the boardwalk. To the couple's right lay a stretch of sand sloping gently downhill to the ocean. To their left, the concrete patios of beach houses came to within inches of the pavement.

They strolled silently for a while, hand in hand. They walked by a house with unscreened windows where a man sat in a recliner a few feet away, watching a football game. Haley tensed as Ben frowned and turned his gaze back toward the ocean.

She debated with herself another moment, then decided she would say something. It would bother her too much otherwise.

"Is it just my imagination," she began, "or do you have a thing about not letting a woman spend money on you?"

His eyes were half hidden in the darkness, but she could see well enough to catch the wary flicker that accompanied his smile. "I like to pay my own way, that's all," he explained. "I didn't think you'd mind. Most women complain if I don't offer to pick up *their* checks."

"So do you?" she asked, wondering suddenly if he acted differently with her. "Pay their checks, I mean?"

"Not usually, no," he answered. "I'm a believer in dating Dutch. You can blame my sisters for that, too. They used to say they didn't want to feel like they owed the guy anything, which made sense to me. Plus, it's a terribly convenient philosophy to have when you're broke."

They stepped on the sand a moment to make room for an oncoming surrey bike.

"So when does dating become something else?" Haley pressed, her pulse rate kicking up a notch. She had a niggling suspicion that he was hiding something — something she needed to know. "Hypothetically speaking, of course," she couched. "Let's say your girlfriend has an apartment and wants you to move in with her. Would you have a problem with that?"

A beat passed. "Not if I could afford to pay half the rent," he answered.

Haley's jaws clenched. He couldn't afford a third of her rent. "So you *do* have a thing about taking a woman's money," she accused.

He slowed his steps and faced her. "No, I don't," he defended. "If I was married and we were mingling all the finances legally, then mine versus hers wouldn't matter. But aside from that, I'm not living off anybody else's money. Period."

Haley looked away from him out towards the water. Twinkling purple lights flew over the beach; she could just see the dim outlines of two boys tossing an LED flying disc.

Ben gave her hand a squeeze. "Maybe I'm over-sensitive on the issue because of the way I live and the way people look at me," he explained. "I may be a nomad, but I'm not a bum."

Haley huffed out a breath and faced him again. "Accepting a gift does not make a person a bum," she insisted. She still suspected there was more. Something he wasn't saying. Something he didn't want to say. She considered how to extract it.

"Let's say, hypothetically," she began again, "that I bought you a plane ticket as a present. You wouldn't have a problem with that, would you?"

Haley waited. If there had been crickets on the beach, she would have heard them chirping. As it was she heard a combination of traffic, ocean, yapping dog, and ESPN. Ben's gaze dropped to his feet. Her heart fell along with it.

"You let me pay your rent," she reminded.

"That was different," he said quietly. "You were my landlord, waiving a charge I owed you. We weren't dating. I didn't know if I'd see you again. Besides, that was before..."

He winced slightly as his voice trailed off. He clearly hadn't meant to say that.

"Before what?" Haley said sharply, even though she knew exactly what. *Before I knew you worked for Stirjon.*

She stopped walking. "This has nothing to do with dating Dutch, does it?" she demanded, her cheeks growing hot with ire. "You won't take anything from me because you see it as dirty money!"

"Don't put words in my mouth, Haley," he said sternly.

"Then choose them yourself," she fired back. "Why won't you let me buy you anything?"

A couple walking two dogs approached them from the opposite direction down the boardwalk, and Haley and Ben stood in awkward silence while the mini-parade passed. The dogs, both boxers, were dressed up in his-and-her coats that made them look like a bride and groom, complete with pearls and a bow tie. If Haley wasn't currently furious, she would have laughed and cracked a joke about how even house pets live better in California.

"Haley," Ben said softly, taking her hand again and trying to catch her eyes. "I don't know how to explain it any way that isn't going to make you angry. And right now, that's the last thing I want to do."

"Well, I'm angry already," she admitted. "So go for it."

He exhaled slowly, then began. "Please try to understand how I feel. I'm not just some guy who's crazy about whales. It's more than that. Protecting the environment is my life's passion. I don't make a huge amount of money, but I probably make more than you think I do. I just donate a fair chunk of it to the causes I believe in."

He took her other hand and held both of them. "Can't you see how hypocritical it would be for me to benefit from the major bucks corporations are paying out to fight environmental regulation — when I'm scraping to give my own paltry change to get those same laws enforced? It's not my place to tell you or anyone else what they should do for a living. Your money isn't 'dirty' and I don't think what you're personally doing is 'evil.' But for me to profit from it would be, to use your own words, a conflict of interest."

His eyes begged her forgiveness, even as his jaw was set firmly with resolve. "And I don't see how that's ever going to change," he said softly.

Haley felt her hands begin to tremble. Whether from grief or rage, she wasn't sure. An image of Bob Hardin popped unbidden into her mind — an image of how he looked whenever he was thwarted by the opposition. *Bullheaded, that's what they are!* He would carp, his pasty face reddened and his voice ruthless. She had heard him say the same words literally hundreds of times. *Damned environmentalists!*

Ben studied her another moment, then pulled her into his arms and held her. "Don't be mad at me, Haley," he said miserably. "I can't stand it. Not tonight. We'll work out something somehow. I promise you."

Actually, Haley thought as she revised the image in her brain, Bob only rarely used the word "damned" in that context. When referring to environmental activists, he preferred a more vulgar adjective. His condescending, adversarial attitude had irritated her at first, but she had quickly grown used to it. Her success, after all, depended on impressing the man, which included pretending to share his philosophies. It was a game she'd had to play, a game she'd become astonishingly good at. And when you played at something for over ninety percent of your waking hours, it was easy to forget you were pretending.

She settled into Ben's embrace, wrapping her arms around his middle and nestling her nose beside his collarbone. There was still a volleyball between them. There were a lot of obstacles between them, but she'd be damned if she'd let her professional life be one of them. She was under no obligation, right this very minute, to argue the world according to Bob. She had never agreed with Bob. She did not even particularly like Bob.

Ben had a right to his feelings about her job, and she had the right to accept them without defending herself. She was tired of defending herself. She wasn't even sure she gave a damn.

After a long, wonderfully restorative moment in Ben's arms, she stepped back. "Have you ever flown an LED slingshot on the beach at night?" she asked casually.

Ben's face lit up with relief. He smiled at her. "No. What is that?"

Haley took his hand, reversed their direction on the boardwalk, and started walking. "Let's go buy one, and I'll show you," she suggested, swinging his arm as they moved. Another gust of breeze rustled the palm trees, and Haley turned her face into the wind, letting her tousled hair blow freely. "But as soon as you're done playing with it," she ordered, "you have to promise to give it back."

She looked up at Ben's face in the lamplight. He was smiling at her again, his hazel eyes sparkling with tenderness.

"You have my word on it, counselor," he replied.

Chapter 28

"It's probably not my place to say this," Tyrene said evenly, tapping her pen on one of the few free inches of space on top of Haley's expansive desk. "But you do realize you look like hell, right?"

Haley growled under her breath. "I am aware."

It had been three weeks since Ben's painfully short visit. Three weeks in which Haley had felt increasingly wretched, not only emotionally, but physically. It was one thing to sprout a basketball from your waist. It was quite another to retain so much fluid you could almost feel yourself squish as you walked.

Tyrene's lips twisted. "You're not going to make it, Haley. If you think cutting back to forty is going to get you to New Year's, you're delusional. My sister was preeclamptic. So was my niece. You want to go on pretending, fine, but I'm telling you — you're going to screw the rest of us over when you just don't show up one morning."

Haley turned her tired, heavy-lidded eyes on her favorite paralegal. "I am *not* preeclamptic. I'm borderline."

Tyrene scoffed. "As of *now*. You've got six weeks to go. You'll get there. May be sooner. May be later. No... actually I'm pretty sure it'll be sooner. You get puffier every time I see you."

"You are so incredibly comforting, Ty," Haley said wearily. "Why do you think I called you in here? I'm trying to delegate! I know I've got to cut back."

"What you've got to do," Tyrene said sharply, "is get the hell out of here. Let somebody else have Stirjon. I'll bring them up to speed."

Haley's teeth gritted. She couldn't believe this was happening to her. She was in excellent health and had done everything right. But her blood pressure was all over the place, she was retaining water like a camel, and the labs she'd just finished couldn't possibly have been closer to the official cutoff for a diagnosis of preeclampsia. When she'd insisted on going back into the office after her appointment this morning, Micah had completely flipped out on her.

"Ty," Haley said heavily. "I don't trust anybody else." She had managed, finally, to convince Stirjon to stop the chemical leach. With Sylvester as her new boogeyman, she had painted such a vivid picture of impending financial apocalypse that the Powers That Be had begrudgingly surrendered. But there was still more to do. "How many extra hours could you pick up?" she asked.

"No more than I already told you!" Tyrene retorted. Then she cast a wary glance at the door and exhaled. "Look, you didn't hear this from me, but we're going to be short-handed soon. You know Ruth?"

Haley nodded nervously. Ruth was the second best paralegal at the firm.

"She's leaving. Got poached."

"Poached?" Haley said incredulously. Nobody hired paralegals away from Merriweather, Falstaff, and Tynes. They paid better than anybody, and they only hired workaholics to begin with. "By whom?"

Tyrene's voice lowered. "You know that national clean water group Bob was complaining about? The one that got Sylvester involved with Stirjon? They're part of some environmental consortium that's got a new project in the works, a database of case law that could be accessed by plaintiffs' attorneys around the country. Rumor has it they just got a crapload of money, and they're recruiting experienced paralegals." She smiled slyly. "They asked me first, but they couldn't afford me."

Haley put up her hands to massage her temples. She could *not* have a headache. She was supposed to report any and all headaches to the clinic ASAP. "Well, that's just peachy." Lovely as it was for the underfunded plaintiffs' attorneys of America to have a slightly more level playing field against the corporate giants, it did not help her figure out how to shift her caseload. "I'm not going to get any extra help in the next couple months, am I?"

Tyrene shook her head firmly. "Pass it off, Haley," she ordered. "For God's sake, just let it go."

Haley's cell phone rang. She looked down at the number. It was the clinic. "This doesn't look good," she said soberly.

Tyrene rose as if to give her privacy, but Haley gestured for her to stay and keep working. She answered the call.

Five minutes later Haley hung up and did a faceplant on a pile of briefs.

"Your doctor?" Tyrene asked.

Haley nodded into the papers.

"Yelled at you, did she?" Tyrene asked with amusement.

Haley groaned. "She just reviewed my chart. After my sister called her and told her exactly how many hours I'd been working."

"Mmm hmmm," Tyrene agreed.

"The doc said — in colorful and no uncertain terms — that I had no business working more than twenty hours a week at most, that they're going to step up my monitoring schedule, and that if my numbers creep up even the slightest bit more, she's going to mandate bed rest."

"Told you," Tyrene said smugly. She rose. "I'll tell Bob you want to see him."

Haley didn't move. She heard her door quietly open and close. Only ten minutes later, when Bob knocked and walked in simultaneously, did she bother to raise her head.

She felt terrible. It was hard enough ticking away the days until she could see Ben again, torturing herself with worry over whether or not he was considering moving to California and whether or not he could be happy if he did. But physically, her body was failing her. She was puffy and sluggish; even her brain seemed to be slowing down. Nothing seemed real anymore; not even Fred's insistent kicking and squirming. It seemed as if she was merely watching while her life happened to somebody else.

"What's up, Haley?" Bob asked, his tone a perfect combination of detached concern and irritation. He didn't bother to sit, but stood on the other side of her desk glaring down at her.

"I have to cut back to twenty hours a week until the baby's born," she said flatly. "Doctor's orders for borderline preeclampsia."

"Preeclampsia!" Bob fired, dropping into the nearest chair like he'd been shot. He rubbed a hand over the bald part of his head and let out a sigh. "Well, that's it for Stirjon," he announced bitterly. "There's no way, Haley, and you know it. Not when you could drop out at any moment. For *weeks!* Consolidated, too. You'll just have to take a support role for a while."

Haley's jaws clenched. He was right, and she knew it. But it was *so* unfair. "I'm sure I can—"

"No you can't," Bob said sharply. "You knew when you took this pregnancy on that it could end like this! Hell, there's always risk!" His voice softened slightly. "You can get back up to speed afterwards. You've got what it takes, Haley. You're the most promising associate I've ever worked with. But I won't let your ego get in the way of this firm's doing the best damn job we can for our clients."

He rose. Haley said nothing else. He walked out the door and closed it, with more force than strictly necessary, behind him.

Haley put her head back down on her desk. She lay there a long while, aware that the tip of a mechanical pencil was digging into her cheek, but lacking the initiative to move it.

It was over. Stirjon. Consolidated. All the work she'd done; the relationships she'd built. Bob would give Stirjon to one of the sixth-year associates and probably move Harrison onto it, too. And Harrison would talk a good game, but ultimately botch the hell out of it.

She realized that her pulse was pounding, and a chord of fear struck through her chest. What was she doing? She had Fred to think about, and she was supposed to be *lowering* her blood pressure. She closed her eyes and imagined Ben on his boat in Hawaii, skipping across the blue waters with the green peaks of Maui behind him. She imagined telling him she'd been bumped off the Stirjon case. He would be appropriately sympathetic to her pain, no doubt. But inside, he would be shouting with glee.

Glee.

Haley raised her head slowly. There *was* one bright spot to this nightmare, wasn't there? Ben would be happy she was no longer working for Stirjon. Despite his honest promises of toleration, the man would be freakin' *ecstatic.* The only thing that would make him happier would be if she stopped working for the corporate side altogether.

Her feeble brain churned at half speed.

Then it churned some more.

Why couldn't she, exactly? She knew there were good reasons why she felt she had to continue in environmental law, but at the moment those reasons didn't seem nearly as convincing as they used to. What was the big deal, anyway? She had learned the field quickly; she could learn another. She was only 29 years old. Who said her career was set in stone? If she was hoping and praying that Ben would be willing to give up his nomadic yearnings for her, could she not make an equal sacrifice for him? *And,* she thought with a sudden, almost feverish excitement, if she switched to another area and married the stubborn mule, he would finally be forced to let her spoil him!

Her slightly numb lips stretched into a smile. Spoil him she would. Thoroughly and completely, in one of California's most wonderful playgrounds. She would get the two of them a bigger place with an even better view. She would get him a hybrid to tool around in. And someday she would really surprise him. She would buy him his very own boat.

With her mind filling with gratifying pictures of a happy Ben enjoying the fruits of her no-longer-objectionable labor, she rose slowly and collected her things. She left her office, sloshed down the hall to the elevator, and pushed the button for the sixth floor.

She was aware that her brain was bleary and that her emotions were at the mercy of her hormones and her blood pressure. She was even aware that, most likely, she wasn't thinking nearly as clearly as she thought she was.

Or maybe, just maybe, she was thinking more clearly than she had in years.

She settled herself in the executive suite of a rather surprised Tom Paris, senior partner in the Merriweather, Falstaff, and Tynes employment law division, and she did not mince words. She faced him squarely and confidently, even though she suspected she still had the indentation of a mechanical pencil on her cheek. "You once said that if I ever considered leaving the environmental group to look into another specialty, I should come and talk to you first."

Tom's bushy gray eyebrows perked. His lips drew into a smile.

"So here I am," Haley announced. "Can we talk?"

Chapter 29

Haley reached a hand out to her bedside table and picked up Ben's latest letter. Like all of them, it made her laugh out loud.

> So just before we got back into Lahaina today, I spotted this big brown animal in the water. Turns out it was a grizzly bear, and it was swimming right up to the boat. I leaned out and asked him what the hell he was doing off the coast of Maui, and he said he was looking for you. I told him you were in Newport Beach, and he swore and swam off to the northeast. But don't worry. I didn't give him your address.

"Haley?" her mother called from her kitchen. "You want some more tea?"

"No thanks," Haley called back. "I'm good."

"Something else to eat?"

"No, Mom." Haley shook her head with a smile. Michelle truly did have only two settings: neglect and smother. Her trip to Bermuda with a college friend had turned into a four-month odyssey involving a new boyfriend with whom, against Haley's strenuously worded objections, she had invested in a fractional share of a condo. After months of infrequent calls and confusing texts, Michelle had returned to Newport Beach unexpectedly just a few days after Ben's visit, weeping and wailing and insisting that Haley sue for fraud. Now she was back in smother mode, taking shifts with Micah to ensure that Haley followed doctor's orders and stayed in bed doing absolutely nothing.

Haley finished rereading Ben's letter and set it back on her bedside table. Her eyes caught sight of the large cardboard box on the floor by the wall, and she grinned. In a few more minutes, Ben should be done for the day. Then she would call him. They had added calls to their repertoire now, but still kept up the letters. Calls were reserved for special occasions, of which today was one, because after three weeks of strategizing and finessing, Haley's new position was secured. She would not return to the environmental group when her maternity leave was over. She would join the employment law division instead.

She hadn't said a word to Ben yet. The news had her practically bursting, but she hadn't wanted to raise his hopes till she was sure.

Michelle's petite form appeared in Haley's doorway. Although well over fifty, Michelle looked far younger and delighted in that fact. "Are you going to call him soon?" she asked, her blue eyes twinkling just like Micah's.

"A couple minutes more," Haley answered.

"You think he'll have an announcement of his own?" Michelle teased.

Haley's answering smile was strained. Both Micah and her mother knew how she felt about Ben and where things currently stood between the couple. It was hard to keep secrets from the two women who had been waiting on her hand and foot the whole last week, particularly when she knew they might have to keep it up a while yet. The first week after Haley cut back her hours, her test results had improved dramatically. But after the second week her numbers had crept up again, and the bed rest order had come down. Now, at the 37-week mark, they were all in a waiting game. Haley was still only borderline preeclamptic, but now that the baby was officially full-term, if things went south even the slightest, she would be looking at an immediate induction.

"I wish you'd quit talking about that, Mom," Haley replied tiredly. She was always tired now, even when she was in a good mood. "He hasn't said anything about moving here. I don't even know if he's thinking about it."

Michelle entered and perched herself on the foot of Haley's bed. "Well, of course he must be!" she insisted. "It's the perfect solution! It's not like you live in the middle of a cornfield somewhere. We're in the whale capital of the world! You said yourself, it's one of the few places on earth that he *could* live year round."

Haley breathed out with a sigh. "I know, Mom. But it's not the same."

"The same as what?"

Haley had no answer. At least not one her mother would understand. Her feelings on the issue were so conflicted, she couldn't possibly put them into words. Not an hour passed that she didn't catch herself fantasizing about the possibility of Ben's moving to California. But every time that fantasy arose, it came with the grim, aching worry that he wouldn't be content.

"I don't know, Mom," Haley replied. "But at least after the baby's born we'll be able to visit each other more often."

Michelle frowned. "You don't really think you'll be satisfied with a long-distance relationship forever, do you? If you want to live in the same place, there's really no other option but for him to move here, is there? Surely there's nothing for you in those little touristy places where he works now?"

Haley tensed. Her mother was right. Even if she were fortunate enough to secure a spot with a law firm in Honolulu or Anchorage, their problems would not be solved. Anchorage was hours from Seward and Honolulu was a plane ride away from Maui. Furthermore, regardless of which place she worked, they could not stay together all year unless Ben gave up half the whale migration.

"No, Mom," she agreed sadly. "It's hard to see what else we could do. Unless I want to take up flipping burgers."

Michelle's eyes widened. "Haley Olson, don't you even think about it! No man worth his salt would ask you to do that. You're a brilliant lawyer. You were born for it. There's no question you have the higher earning power; if anyone should quit work, it should be him. He's not sexist, is he?"

"Mom," Haley said wearily. "Do you seriously think a sexist would last five minutes with me? I was joking about the burgers. He wouldn't want me to do that."

Haley felt her spirits slipping again and struggled to rally them. She did not want to think about the future right now. She wanted to think about the present, and the fact that she was about to make Ben very, very happy.

"I'm going to call him now," Haley announced. "Can you shut the door?"

Michelle smirked. "I could still eavesdrop if I wanted to, you know."

"But you won't, because that would be wrong," Haley retorted.

Michelle smiled unrepentantly, but rose and went to the door. "Actually, Micah should be coming for the switch-off any minute now. If I don't see you before I leave, remember to flip back over to your left side. We want plenty of oxygen going to that baby, don't we?"

"Yes, Mom," Haley agreed, relieved when the door closed. Her mother had been taking good care of her in the last week, but the two women hadn't spent this much time together since Haley was in the womb. And although Micah had frequently been the object of their mother's babying over the years, it was an unaccustomed role for Haley.

She picked up the phone and dialed Ben's number. He answered on the second ring. "Hi there," he said tenderly.

A wave of goosebumps crept up Haley's spine. She loved to hear his voice. She had been tempted to ask him if he would videoconference from his laptop, but since her own face looked like a pile of pudding, she contented herself with a call. "Hi yourself," she replied. "Can you talk a minute?"

"Sure," he said. Haley could hear strange birds squawking in the background, along with the familiar clanking and sloshing of a marina. "I'm just finishing up. Everything okay?"

"Fine," she answered. "No worries." He knew that she was on bed rest, but given his past trauma with 'girl stuff,' she had kept her explanations bare bones.

"Yeah," he said uncertainly, "about that. My mother wants me to ask what you mean by 'borderline' preeclampsia. She seems worried about you." He paused a beat. "Should I be?"

"No, you should not," Haley said firmly. "It means that I don't meet the stated criteria for a diagnosis of preeclampsia, despite them telling me for over a month now that it was only a matter of time. I just keep hanging in there, bouncing around right under the cutoff. Now that Fred's full-term, though, I'm pretty sure they're all secretly hoping my next labs will cross the line. Then they can justify inducing labor and be done with me."

Ben was quiet for a moment.

"Uh oh," Haley said. "Too much information, Captain?"

"No," he said quickly. "I just wish I could be there."

The goosebumps did their thing again. "You will be. In a week," she said brightly. She cast a glance at the cardboard box on her floor. "I got a package today."

"Oh?" he said, sounding surprised. "From who?"

Haley grinned. "The Sisters Parker."

Ben groaned.

Haley chuckled merrily. "Oh, stop! It was very nice. They sent all sorts of lovely things. Spritzes and lotions, interesting pillows, massage oil, aromatherapy, herbal teas, some paperback novels, puzzle books, and chocolate. They seemed to know exactly what a woman on bed rest would want to spoil herself with."

He grumbled. "Well, I guess that's—"

"Including," Haley interrupted, reaching toward her bedside table, "the most unbelievably adorable picture I've ever seen."

A beat passed. "Oh, God," he said miserably. "Which one is it?"

Haley dissolved into laughter. She picked up the photo again and traced her fingers lovingly along the edge. The baby in the picture couldn't be more than a year old. But the wild ginger hair and hazel eyes were unmistakable. "The one with the tiara and the bright pink tutu," she answered.

Ben exhaled gruffly. "Fabulous. Well, at least that's better than the one in the bathtub."

"Which one, now?" Haley teased.

"Never mind," he returned. "I will deal with them later."

"Please don't," Haley said sincerely. "It really was very sweet of them."

"Sweet has nothing to do with it," he insisted. "They're trying to recruit you."

"Recruit me for what?"

"Their side, of course," Ben said heavily. "So you'll gang up with them against me."

Haley smiled to herself thoughtfully. She knew that Ben was joking, but she suspected there was a grain of truth to his words as well. "Ben," she said evenly, "I promise I will never join forces with your sisters against you. I'll always be on your side."

He was quiet for a long time. "Can I have that in writing?" he asked finally.

"Sure," she chuckled. "I'll draw up the papers tomorrow."

"No, you take it easy," he insisted. "I'll get a lawyer here to do it."

Speaking of lawyers...

Haley put the picture back on her bedside table and propped herself up a bit. "Listen, Ben," she said eagerly. "There's something I need to tell you. I think you're going to like it."

"Does it have anything to do with my sisters?"

"No."

"Then go ahead."

Haley took a breath. "It's my job. I told you that I lost the lead role on the cases I was working before I left. But it's more than that. I'm getting out of the environmental group. When I finish my maternity leave, I'll be going to work with the employment law division instead."

Birds chattering. Distant shouts. A car horn.

After several seconds, Haley could hear her own heartbeat. "Ben?" she asked uncertainly.

"I'm here," he answered, his voice strange. "But won't you have to start all over again?"

"Yes," she replied, disappointed. It was hardly the exuberance she had expected. "But that doesn't mean it isn't doable. And before you get too full of yourself, Captain, I should explain that it's not all about you. I've never been overly fond of Bob Hardin and working with him for forever was less than appealing to me. I hear Tom is much more amiable. Some of his associates only work fifty hours a week."

She paused, but Ben said nothing.

"So I hope your place in Maui has a nice shower," she continued, "because I might actually have enough time off to fly out and borrow it once in a while."

"It's a hole," he said mechanically.

"Excuse me?"

She could picture him shaking his head, running his hand through his hair. He was trying to think quickly. She had caught him off guard.

"My place is a dump," he explained. "I'm trying to get out of the lease, actually."

There was another awkward pause. Haley began to worry. "This is not exactly the reaction I expected, Ben," she admitted. "I thought you'd be happy."

"Are you happy, Haley?" he demanded.

Now he caught her off guard. "What do you mean? I just told you why I'm doing it!"

"And you told me before that it would mean starting all over. That you would lose years of experience and expertise, and that you like the environmental area itself — that unlike most people you actually *enjoy* digging into those regs."

"I do, but I—" Haley stammered and lost her train of thought. "Why are you fighting me on this?"

"Because it's just one more sacrifice!" he said intently. He sighed and calmed his tone. "Haley, don't you see? Of course it means a lot to me that you'd even consider changing specializations to make me happy. But I don't want you to do it if it's not right for you."

"It *is* right for me," she argued. Whether she was telling the truth or not, she wasn't entirely sure. But she refused to think about it now. The deed was done.

She decided to make light of it instead. "Employment law will offer plenty of new and exciting regulations to dig into, believe me. Besides, I've always harbored a secret desire to help corporations fire people. I mean, hasn't everyone? I think you're just trying to get out of taking my money, Captain."

"That's not true," he said quietly.

"Excellent. So what gift can I buy you with my nice clean money?"

He considered a moment. "The cabin in Seward could use a new showerhead. Preferably an extra wide with multiple massage options."

Haley sighed. "You really think big, you know that? Don't you need anything for the place you're living now?"

He scoffed. "Nothing short of a bulldozer would make a dent in it."

"Hey, Ben!" a man's voice shouted in the background.

"Just a second!" Ben called back.

"You have to go?" she asked, feeling suddenly empty.

"Yes, for now," he answered. "Listen, Haley. I'm sorry. I *am* glad you're leaving the dark side. When I tell the humpbacks, they'll be leaping out of the water. As long as you're happy, I'm happy. Probably happier."

"I'm glad," she said, feeling slightly more encouraged. "Goodbye, Ben."

"Bye."

Haley hung up the phone. She rolled dutifully onto her left side and put her hand on her bulging abdomen. As wretched as she'd been feeling the last six weeks, the one bright spot was that Fred was doing great. She was big for her age, kicking up a storm, and could safely be born anytime now. The greater threat with preeclampsia, as Micah reminded her daily, was to Haley's own health.

"We're going to be fine," Haley soothed. "Not much longer now, and you'll be out of your cocoon and in your mommy's arms. Then everyone will be happy."

She sank lower on her pillows and closed her eyes. She had only just dozed off when her phone made the sound of a whale song. It was the ringtone she'd picked out for Ben — the one she almost never heard. And it wasn't a phone call. It was a *text*.

She stared at the screen in disbelief.

Thank you, Haley. Sincerely, The Earth

A smile spread across her face, and she lay back and closed her eyes again. He *was* happy. She had surprised him a little, that was all. But the more he thought about it, the happier he would be. She was sure of it.

She started to compose her next letter to him in her head. But before she could finish, she was asleep.

Chapter 30

Ben swiped a sleeve across his forehead, attempting to stem the sweat as he walked hurriedly down the hallway, scanning the confusing room numbers with frustration. Where the hell was she?

It did not feel like the day after Christmas. The last twenty-four hours had been more of a nightmare. He hadn't been all that concerned when he didn't hear from Haley on Christmas Eve. He figured she was busy with her family, or else would assume that he was. But when Christmas Day turned into Christmas afternoon and his calls to her went straight to voicemail, he began to worry. His phone had finally rung at dinner, and he had been relieved to see her number. But when he picked up the call he had found himself speaking not to Haley, but to her mother, who had accosted his ear with such frantic and incoherent babble he thought he would lose his mind. If Haley's brother-in-law hadn't stepped in and wrested the phone from Michelle's hand, Ben would almost certainly be babbling incoherently himself now.

This is Tim, Micah's husband, the calm male voice had said. *Don't worry. Haley's going to be fine. It's just that she needs a c-section. Micah is going in with her now.*

After listening to Michelle's terrifying stream-of-consciousness rant, which included the words "seizures," and "organ failure," Ben had not been easily convinced of the "fine" part, but Tim had done his best to cut to the chase.

Haley woke up with a headache yesterday morning, and her blood pressure was up a little, so they decided to induce. She's been in labor since yesterday afternoon, but it was going slow, and just now her pressure went up again and they made the call to do a section. Haley's been bleary and a bit out of it, but she hasn't had any other complications. The stuff her mother was saying was just what the doctors were worried about if they didn't do the surgery.

After Ben had scraped himself off the floor, relayed the information to his family, and received his mother's assurance that Haley's care sounded perfectly reasonable and appropriate, he got on the phone to the airlines. Unfortunately, screwing around with one's flight schedule on Christmas Day was not the easiest thing to do. He went straight to the airport hoping to make a standby, but not only did he fail at that quest, his original flight was cancelled and the next one out was delayed. He had reached LAX this morning only to encounter ridiculous lines at the car rental counter and traffic on the 405 at a complete standstill.

It had been nearly twenty-four hours since Haley went into surgery, and he still hadn't talked to her. Tim had called back late yesterday to say that everyone was fine and that Haley was sleeping. Micah had texted him this morning to say the same thing.

It wasn't good enough.

Room 3524. Ben stopped short, reeling a little. He hadn't slept a wink last night. He double-checked the number on the paper in his hand, then knocked softly.

The door opened a crack, and Micah peeked out at him. Her blue eyes twinkled as they took him in. She greeted him with a smile that changed quickly to a grin, which he interpreted to mean that she was glad to see him, but that he looked like a serial killer again. She swept out of the room and pulled the door almost closed behind her.

"Oh, I'm so glad you're here," she said sincerely, throwing her arms up to hug him.

Ben hugged her back, but was anxious to get inside. "Is she okay?"

"She's going to be fine," Micah assured. "But she's had a rough time of it, and she's exhausted. She's sleeping right now, but you can come in. I just didn't want to wake her. Let Tim and me put the baby down and we'll leave you alone for a while." She frowned slightly. "They won't let us take the baby out of Haley's room and we can't be in the nursery, so it's been frustrating — I'm afraid Haley hasn't gotten much sleep."

Ben said nothing. Two more seconds, and he was going to bust his way in.

Micah seemed to read his mind. She stepped back and opened the door. Ben entered to find the small room darkened by pulled curtains. A man, presumably Tim, sat in a chair by the window holding a bundle. Ben nodded to him, then zoned in on Haley.

Her face was in shadow, but the gentle rise and fall of the sheets over her chest comforted him immediately. She looked peaceful. He reached for the chair that sat next to the empty bassinet, moved it quietly to her bedside, and sat down.

As his eyes adjusted to the light, his heart began to beat faster again. Haley's arms and face were swollen, and there were wretched dark circles under her eyes. The hair that splayed over her pillow was stringy, and her lips looked chapped.

Ben continued to watch her breathe while in his peripheral vision he saw Tim rise and settle the bundle into the bassinet. After a moment, Micah touched Ben's shoulder. "We'll be in the cafeteria," she whispered. "Call me if the baby wakes up; we'll come right back. You have my number?"

He nodded, and the new parents slipped out.

Ben took the hand Haley had left outside the blanket and cradled it in his. Even her fingers were swollen and puffy. Feeling another rush of angst, he lifted her hand to his mouth and kissed it.

Haley's eyes fluttered open. She looked around in confusion for a moment, but when she saw him, her face lit instantly with a smile. "Ben!" she said hoarsely.

"I didn't mean to wake you up," he apologized. He hadn't meant to, but he couldn't say he was sorry. The sight of her beautiful green eyes looking so bright and alive was entirely too soothing to his soul. "How are you feeling?"

"Fabulous," she answered with no trace of sarcasm. "I'm sorry I didn't call you. I knew the labor could take a while and I didn't want you to worry about me all through Christmas. But when they said I'd need a c-section I told Micah—"

"It's okay," he said quickly. "I didn't expect you to call. They kept me informed."

Haley looked concerned. "Micah called you?"

"No. Your mother."

"Oh," Haley said heavily. "I'm sorry."

For the first time in many hours, Ben allowed himself a chuckle. "Yeah, well. It worked out all right. Tim grabbed the phone and saved me."

Haley smiled. "Tim's a good guy." She attempted to sit up, but winced. Ben quickly helped her raise the head of the bed. Once settled more upright, she became fully alert. "Why is it so dark in here? Can you open the curtains? I want to see you better!"

Ben did as she requested, and Haley grinned at him. "I know I look awful," she said with a laugh. "But what's your excuse? Are you trying to make me feel better?"

Ben grinned back. He couldn't even remember his last shower. "Sorry."

"Did something happen to you?" she asked with sudden distress.

Ben looked at her in disbelief. "The only thing that happened to me is that I spent one sleepless night in an airport. *You* just went through a day-long labor followed by a c-section on top of preeclampsia — the last thing you should worry about is me!"

She shrugged. "I'm fine now. Have you seen the baby?"

Ben didn't know whether to laugh or cry. The magnitude of what she had done for her sister still didn't seem to register.

"Take a peek!" Haley urged, gesturing toward the bassinet.

Ben honestly hadn't given a thought to the baby, but at Haley's insistence, he stepped over and peered down at the sleeping bundle. She was uncommonly beautiful for a newborn, with a delicate bone structure set in a perfectly round face, unblemished pink skin, and thick white-blond hair. "Hello, Fred," he said gently.

Haley chuckled. "Shh! That was our secret, remember? Her name is Sophia Jane."

"She's beautiful," he praised. "I would say she looks like you, but–"

"But you'd be lying, because she looks exactly like Micah." Haley laughed again, and the sound of her low, melodic voice made his heart skip. He loved her voice. He wished he could hear it more. No, he *would* hear it more. He was going to make it happen.

He returned to her bedside, sat down again, and took her hand. "How are you feeling, Haley, really? Don't fake anything for my benefit."

She shrugged again. "The labor wasn't fun, but that's all kind of a blur, now. And when the incision hurts I can take whatever I want, since I'm not nursing." She raised his hand to her face, holding his knuckles against her cheek. "All that matters is that Sophia is healthy and happy... and over *there*." She grinned at him. "I'm singular again. And the next time you see me, I promise I'll look a whole lot better than this."

She moved his hand to her mouth and nibbled on his index finger.

His reaction was strong and immediate. He tried to draw back his hand, but Haley held it, grinning at him. "Don't look so scandalized, Captain," she teased. "I assure you, you're perfectly safe from me. For the moment, anyway."

For a long time, Ben could think of nothing to say. He had expected her to be tired, to be nauseous, to be miserably overwhelmed and cranky. For her to be so ebullient and claim to feel so good was too wonderful a surprise to be believed. She had to be faking it. Either that, or she was a little delirious.

"Talk to me," she said wistfully, sinking back into her pillows a little. She still held tight to his hand. "How was Christmas with your family?"

Ben indulged her curiosity about his holiday, but his mind was hopelessly distracted. There was too much he needed to say to her. When at last she ran out of questions about his sisters and parents and nieces and nephews, he steered the conversation back on his intended course.

"Haley," he began, holding both her hands in his. "I need to ask you something. I need to know how you would feel about my moving to Southern California."

She blinked at him. He tried to read her eyes, but her emotions seemed garbled. She made no response.

"I've been thinking about it a long time," he said quietly. "And it's what I want to do." He pulled her hands to his mouth and kissed them. "I love you, Haley. I'm not going to be happy anywhere unless we're together, and the best place for us to be together is right here. I just need to know if that's what you want, too."

Still, she merely stared at him. Her chest heaved under her thin nightgown. For the life of him, he couldn't tell if she was delighted or horrified. Somehow, it looked like both.

"I love you, too," she said finally, her voice cracking. "But..."

She trailed off. He waited for her to finish, but maddeningly, she did not. "But what?" he prompted.

"But I don't want kids!" she blurted.

Ben was taken aback. Literally. He scooted several inches in his chair. "Haley, what... I mean, where did that come from?"

Her eyes swam with angst. "I don't want children of my own," she said stiffly. "I never have. I should have mentioned it before, but it just never seemed to come up, and I was too afraid that you... Well, you have a right to know."

She squeezed his hands. "It's not that I don't like kids," she continued earnestly. "I'm really looking forward to being an aunt. It's just that... well, ever since I can remember, Micah has always wanted to be a mom. She's wanted to bake cookies and plan birthday parties and start family traditions and host the holidays and mold somebody's little mind. Whatever gene it is that causes that, whatever evolutionary instinct it comes from, I just don't have it. When I think about my future I see a lot of things I want to do, but being a parent isn't one of them. People always told me that when I fell in love I would change my mind, but I love you, and my mind hasn't changed. I'm sorry."

Ben's head spun. He felt like he'd been dropped down into some alternative universe. "Don't apologize to me," he stammered.

"But I am sorry," she insisted. "I shouldn't have waited so long to say anything. I know how much you love your nieces and nephews—"

"Haley!" he interrupted, his spirits lightening. "I don't want kids, either."

"What?" she breathed.

"I don't want kids, either," he repeated, smiling at her. It was almost like some cosmic joke. Then again, the two of them thought so much alike about so many things... "I do love my nieces and nephews," he explained. "But part of the reason I put so much effort into being everybody's favorite uncle is because that's all I ever plan to be. Kids are wonderful creatures, but they need stability, and I'm not a stable guy. I'm a nomad."

Haley regarded him skeptically. "Are you lying to me?"

He leaned down and kissed her lightly on the lips. "I've never lied to you. I swear, I don't want children of my own, either. And I thought about telling you that a couple times, too, but I never got the nerve. So if that's all the ammo you've got to keep me from moving here, you'll have to think of something else."

The baby stirred a little in her bassinet, and they lowered their voices.

"Do you really, honest to God, want to move here, Ben?" Haley asked, her green eyes moistening.

"I really do," he answered. It was, after all, the only solution. He had one caveat, and he would state that now. "There's only one thing I ask: that you be open to moving somewhere else someday. I don't think I'd be happy here forever. But I can be happy here now. As long as I'm with you."

She studied him intently. "I wish I could completely believe you," she said, her voice dropping close to a whisper. "But I know how much you love Alaska. And Hawaii. If you give all that up for me, eventually you're bound to resent it."

Ben looked back into her puffy, blotchy face, and his teeth clenched. "Excuse me, counselor," he said firmly. "But your hypocrisy is showing. You have been sacrificing what *you* want for the people you love your whole damn life. You became a lawyer because it's what your dad wanted. You gave up your youth to take care of a mother who should have been taking care of you and a sister who should have been taking care of herself. You gave up your body, your health, and nine months of your life so that Micah could have a biological child. And you gave up four years of experience in environmental law for *me*."

He pulled her hands close to his face again. "So if I decide to sacrifice one small damn thing for you, the least you can do is shut up and accept it graciously!"

Their gazes locked. He stared her down without mercy. At last, her eyes blinked with tears and her lips curved into a smile.

"Aye, aye, Captain," she replied.

Chapter 31

"Now, just wait," Micah said excitedly, holding Sophia up in her lap. "She'll do it again in a second!"

Haley smiled. She and her sister were sitting on a bench at a playground near the Balboa Pier, taking a rest from Haley's daily beach walk. Ten days after the birth, Sophia was starting to gain weight, and Haley was starting to lose it. They were both getting stronger every day. And so was Micah.

"Here it—Oh, no. That wasn't it." Micah had her feet propped up on the parked stroller, and she leaned the baby back against her thighs. "I swear, she'll do it again. Just keep watching."

"What am I looking for?" Haley asked with amusement.

"You'll know it when you see it," Micah retorted. A moment later, she sucked in a breath. "There, look!"

Haley stared into her niece's adorably perfect little face, which had begun to screw up in consternation. The baby clenched her little fists and squiggled down lower in the soft pink fabric that engulfed her. It was a full-blown baby pout, and as Haley started to giggle at its cuteness, another face popped into her mind.

"Aunt Janie!" she said with a gasp. "Oh, my God. It's her mad face!"

Micah exploded into laughter. "Isn't it? I told Tim you'd see it, too!"

Haley grinned broadly. Janie had always been good-natured, but whenever the girls tracked mud in the house or made noise after nine PM, the "mad face" would warn them that apologies were expected. It was, despite its implications, a warm and happy sight that Haley still missed.

"I can see so much of Aunt Janie in her," Micah said fondly. "Her eyes are the same color. And definitely the shape of her chin." She pulled the baby closer and dropped a kiss on the top of her soft blond head. "What can we say? She's perfect."

"Yes, she is," Haley agreed. She looked out across the beach toward the sound of waves, but from where they sat, she couldn't see the ocean. Sophia was indeed a little miracle. Micah and Tim both appeared to be deliriously happy, despite their claims that the baby howled every hour all night long. If Haley had ever harbored doubts about the wisdom of her decision, seeing the reflection of her aunt's face just now had officially put them to rest.

Micah was a mom. She had a loving husband, a nice place to live, and everything else she'd ever dreamed of. Perhaps now it would be Haley's turn.

"Haley," Micah said softly, "have you set a date yet to go to Maui? You've been recovering so quickly. I'm sure when you go in tomorrow you'll get the all-clear to drive again. You really should just go. Why not spend the rest of your maternity leave there, with Ben?"

Haley shook her head uncertainly. "No. I don't know. I haven't made any plans yet."

Micah was quiet for a moment. When she spoke again, her voice was low and determined. "Listen to me, Haley. You have that look in your eye again, and I don't like it. It's that sad look. I know you're not depressed — you're doing great physically and you have more energy than I do. But you're not happy. And I don't understand why. Ben is coming! It's only a matter of time. He said he thought he could be here by the end of April, right? And if you go to Maui now, you can stay there with him until March. So what's the problem?"

Haley looked back out toward the ocean she couldn't see. She wished she could answer her sister's question. In some ways, she felt wonderful. It felt amazingly good not to be pregnant anymore. The retained fluid was almost all gone and her incision didn't hurt nearly as much as she expected it would. But she had a long way to go to get her real body back, and that bothered her more than she wanted to admit. It seemed incredibly shallow, but she didn't want Ben to see her like this. She didn't want to limp and wince her way to Maui, obligating him to take care of her while she ever-so-slowly got back to normal. If her pregnancy had been his doing, that would be different. But the only thing he had gotten out of her adventure was a free trial at monkhood.

"I'm not ready to go to Maui yet," Haley said evasively. "But soon, maybe. We'll see." She could feel her sister's eyes on her, studying her. Micah wasn't fooled. She was merely planning a new angle of attack.

"Have you talked about what he's going to do when he gets here?" Micah asked. "Has he applied for a job yet?"

Haley nodded. "He's contacted all the whale-watching companies. He was looking into that before Christmas, actually. But he doesn't know anything yet. There aren't that many of them. He says he could take any kind of captain job, though. Charter, sightseeing, fishing."

"Well, that's good!" Micah said brightly. "If he can't get what he wants at first, I'm sure an opening will come up eventually. Will he move in with you?"

Haley's mouth twisted. "Not unless I can get him to marry me."

"Are you serious?" Sophia started to fuss, and Micah stood up with her and bounced slightly. "I mean, by all means, yes — marry the man! But why won't he move into your apartment?"

Haley did her best to explain the chip on Ben's shoulder without making him sound sexist.

"Yikes," Micah said sympathetically, reaching for Sophia's bottle. "So where do you think he'll be until you get that ring on his finger? Somewhere in Santa Ana, maybe? I hope he won't wind up all the way out in Riverside!"

Haley felt herself frowning again. "I don't know."

It wasn't a subject she liked to think about. Her own commute was long enough. Ben would hate commuting. He would hate every second of it.

"Haley," Micah said heavily. "You're doing it again."

"Doing what?"

"That damned sad look!" Micah gave up on the bottle and laid Sophia in her baby seat. She sat down next to Haley again and began to rock the stroller back and forth gently. "We're going to get to the root of this right now. What were you thinking about? Tell me!"

. Haley sighed again. That was at least twice in the last hour; she had to stop. She might as well be honest, too.

"Ben isn't going to like it here, Micah," she lamented. "He isn't going to be happy."

Micah studied her. "Did he say that?"

"Of course not. He's doing it for me. He insists everything will work out fine, that if he can't find work as a captain, he'll go ahead and go back to school and get his doctorate in oceanography. He says he's always planned to do that anyway. Someday."

"That sounds perfect!" Micah agreed. "Haley, if this is something he wants to do, why are you second-guessing him? Is it so wrong for someone else to make a sacrifice for *you* for a change?"

Haley looked at her sister in surprise. "That's what he said."

Micah rolled her eyes. "Well, he's right! Obviously."

Haley's eyes drifted to her shoes. A few feet away from them, a seagull was toying with a plastic wrapper. It lifted the trash in its beak, struggled with it as if trying to determine whether it was edible, then released it. The plastic blew away on the breeze, and the gull turned its attention to another piece of litter.

"It's more than just Ben's not being happy," Haley said slowly, at last voicing the disquiet that had been steadily growing inside her. "It's me. Do you remember my friend Lois, from high school?"

"Loey?" Micah replied, brightening. "Of course! I mean, she was more your friend than mine, but I always liked her. Why?"

"I called her the other day. I wanted to see if we could go out to lunch or something."

"That's nice."

"No, it isn't," Haley retorted, her voice suddenly bitter. "She and her husband moved to Toronto six months ago. All the years I've worked at the firm, she lived within ten minutes of me. But I didn't see her once. We tried to get together a half dozen times, and I always wound up having to cancel. Eventually, she stopped calling. Now, she's gone." Haley's cheeks flared with heat. "Do you realize I honestly can't remember the last time I went out with a friend — to do *anything?* I'm not sure I even have any friends left!" She stood up, fighting another wince. "Did Mom tell you about the paint job?"

Micah looked at her blankly.

"To the side of the picture window in my bedroom," Haley continued, "there's a strip of wall that's still white. It got primed, but never painted. I've lived in that apartment almost a year, and not once did I ever notice until I got stuck on bed rest. And you know why that is? Because I'm never there in the daylight!"

Sophia had stopped squawking. Haley had noticed that her own voice often seemed to calm the baby. But Micah's attention was focused on her sister.

"You work too much, Haley," Micah said softly. "I've always said that."

"So has everyone else!" Haley exclaimed. "But you have to understand. My job just can't be done *well* any other way. It's the nature of the beast. That's why it pays so much. That's why so few people make it to the top. I was on track to be one of those people, Micah, and it got to be like an addiction. I worked hard, I did well, and the rewards just showered down. I could see how single-minded I was becoming; I could see how everything else in my life — even the things I used to enjoy the most — was slipping away. But I couldn't stop it. I couldn't stop because stopping was synonymous with failure. Failure and irresponsibility."

Haley paced a few steps. Micah watched her, but said nothing.

"It's not that I'm unhappy being an attorney. I don't regret going to law school, even if I did do it for Dad. I like the work; it's always been a good fit for me. But having this kind of job, at this level with this firm, is costing me everything else in my life!"

Haley felt suddenly tired. She turned and sat down again.

"What about your new job?" Micah asked.

Haley shook her head. "It won't be any different. This partner is easier to work with on a personal level, but the demands will be the same. If I do it, I'll feel a compulsion to do it well. That will mean getting up to speed on a whole new set of regs, catching up to the other associates, proving I'm sharper and more effective than they are. I know myself. It's what I'll do. I'll get back in that environment and it will become a compulsion again. Maybe some people can stop at 'adequate' or 'good enough' and feel gratified, but I can't do that, Micah. I'm just not made that way."

Haley rubbed her face in her hands. "It's like being tumbled along in a really strong current. When you're in it, it seems like the only way to go, so you just keep going. It's only when you're standing on the bank that you see people flailing around in the water and wonder why the idiots don't just swim to shore."

She blew out a breath. "The last time I let my job consume me, the only person who really suffered was me. But next time, it will be Ben." She turned her eyes to her sister. "I can't do that to him, Micah. I won't."

Micah's blue eyes glistened with moisture. "So what are you saying, exactly?"

"I don't want to go back to Merriweather, Falstaff, and Tynes," Haley announced, saying out loud the words that, up to now, she hardly dared to think. "I want my life back," she finished softly. "A whole, full life."

Micah wrapped a skinny arm around Haley's shoulders and hugged her tight. "And you deserve it," she said firmly. "What do you really want, Haley? If you could throw away every responsibility you've ever had, right now, and just do what *you* really wanted to do, what would it be?"

The images filled Haley's mind like sunlight. Cold, clear blue water. Endless snow-capped mountains. Fields of fireweed, rippling in the wind. Dense forests, filled with bears. Black and white porpoises, leaping into the spray. Ben's broad back climbing up the trail ahead of her.

"Alaska," she proclaimed. "I want to be with Ben, back in Alaska. And not just for a stolen week once a year. I want to live there with him all summer, like he was so happily doing before he met me. And when snow completely blankets the place, I want to run off with him to Maui, and I want to chase the whales and romp in a bikini and dig my toes in the sand and..." her voice broke off. Another wave of melancholy enveloped her. "And I don't know why I'm telling you all this because I don't know how to make it happen."

To her surprise, Micah scoffed. "Well, figure it the hell out!" she ordered. "Don't give me a bunch of bunk about what's not possible. When did that ever stop you in your job? Where's that creative genius and take-no-prisoners bravado when you need it for your own selfish purposes? Freakin' *make it happen*, Haley!"

Haley stared at her sister in amazement. "Do you really mean that?"

Micah smiled sadly. "You think I don't know how much I've held you back? How needy I've always been? I know, and I've always known, and I felt horrible about it, but not guilty enough to get over myself and let you go. Inside there's always been that terrified five-year-old who didn't want to be left behind. But when you were so sick with preeclampsia for no reason other than my own selfishness, I swore I would never ask you to do another thing for me ever again. I don't *need* you anymore, Haley. I love you, but I don't need you. I'll miss you terribly, but you need to go. For you."

Haley still stared at her, disbelieving.

Micah laughed. "You're wondering how long it will be before I change my mind and pitch a fit for you to stay? Well, I can't promise you that won't happen. It probably will. But I'm giving you permission *now* to ignore me *later*, no matter what I say." She grinned mischievously. "You've gotten pretty good at ignoring me lately, anyway."

Haley's heart bubbled over with warmth, and she started to say something sweet. But before she could get the words out, Micah jumped a little, then bent over the stroller.

"Whoa," Micah said, her delicate nose wrinkling. "Diaper blowout!" She looked at Haley. "If you'll excuse us just a minute? I think this might explain the 'mad face.'"

The smell reached Haley's nose, and she stood up and offered her place on the bench. As Micah spread out the changing pad, Haley walked away across the playground and up onto the rise of the beach, from where she could see the ocean.

Being an aunt totally rocked.

The same seagull — or maybe it was a different one? — wrestled with another piece of trash near her feet. A woman walked by with a tiny dog on a leash. Out on the water, she could see a boat much like the one she and Ben had been on, speeding out toward Catalina. Still farther out, several freighters dotted the horizon.

You were going to jump on one of the big boats and see what was on the other side of the water, Micah had told her. *You wanted to sail all around the world and never come back again.*

Haley smiled to herself. Sailing away to adventures unknown had indeed been her childhood dream. It was funny how Micah remembered that, when Haley herself had forgotten. But now, looking out over the calm, blue waters, she was sure she could feel again that very same pull — a tugging at the deepest part of her soul, a longing to move on.

I'm a nomad, Ben had told her. Could she be one, too? Perhaps her psychologically unencumbered five-year-old self had been able to see what the responsible and overachieving adult could not.

When she imagined the perfect life, she need imagine no further than traveling the oceans with Ben. The humpbacks had it right. Alaska in summer and Hawaii in winter was paradise on earth. The way he already lived was the stuff her dreams were made of. All that was missing was a source of income for her — something that provided enough for both of them to live decently and to get back and forth often enough to visit family. She didn't want to miss her little niece's growing up. And she knew how important it was to Ben to stay close to his nieces and nephews, to take them trick-or-treating every Halloween.

How could she do it?

Haley had no answer, but the thought of spending time with Ben's family put a smile on her face. She had teased him about her making a stealth trip to Seattle to introduce herself to the Sisters Parker, but he had refused to sanction a meeting until he had her no-collusion affidavit in hand. He wasn't kidding, either — he had actually printed out and mailed her a document to sign. It wasn't prepared by an attorney, but Ben's attempt to fake it had been highly amusing, even including space for official notarization. She had planned to take it into the office with her; Tyrene was a notary and would get a kick out of applying her stamp. But Haley hadn't been back to the office, and the document had remained on her bedside table for weeks, unsigned.

She smirked. As soon as she could drive, she would meet up with Tyrene and get that notarization. Then she would send the document not to Ben's apartment, but to his place of business... via Express Mail. She chuckled to herself as she envisioned her plan, but somewhere in between imagining Tyrene's laughter and Ben's, her brain hit a full stop.

Tyrene. Something the paralegal had told her weeks ago jumped back into her consciousness with a start.

Yes... Why not?

It was a long shot, of course. A long, *long* shot. It would take research, some very carefully directed networking and schmoozing, a rock-solid proposal, and a whole heck of a lot of negotiation.

Lucky for her, Haley Olson, Esq. was pretty damned good at all of that.

She could do it. She knew she could.

And when she did, she would make Ben the happiest boat captain / naturalist on earth. And she would be the happiest attorney.

Freakin' make it happen, Haley!

"Micah!" she called out, swinging around so suddenly she nearly lost her balance on the shifting sand. "Can you take me home now? I've got work to do!"

Chapter 32

Haley hopped up onto one of the low rock walls that bordered a picturesque series of planters between the street and the edge of the marina. A warm wind blew over her, tousling her long, unfettered hair and ruffling her skirt.

Maui. She was in love with the place already.

It had been a long, exhausting day thus far, but the word exhausted was no longer in her vocabulary. Her flight out of LA at the crack of dawn this morning had gone smooth as a dream, her goodbyes to the family had been far less traumatic than she had feared, and she'd had no trouble whatsoever renting a car, driving to the West Side, and moving into her vacation rental. She'd even managed a quick trip to the grocery store to stock up on food and essentials. Once she had lured her prey into her den, she planned to keep him there a while.

She gazed out over the blue waters of the Lahaina harbor and smiled. Another boat was approaching. Ben should be bringing his last tour of the day back into port any minute now. She stepped back from the edge of the planter and settled herself in the shade of a palm tree. It wouldn't do for him to see her prematurely. She had waited this long; she could manage a few minutes more.

Her smile didn't waver as she watched the boat draw nearer, and when it came close enough for her to overhear the voice on the loudspeaker, her heart began to race. It *was* Ben. She could see him up on the bridge, making his passengers laugh, as always. She remained in the shadows, not moving, as the boat pulled up and docked a few slips away. The passengers cheered their gratitude, and Ben moved out of Haley's sight. He would go down and say goodbye to everyone now, she thought, no doubt collecting a significant amount of well-earned tips in the process. As the first passengers began to file off, their faces clearly showing their enjoyment, Haley glowed with pride. Ben's degree might be in oceanography, but he was a natural born entertainer. His vocation might be unusual and not especially lucrative, but there was no question he was fantastic at it.

And he would continue to be fantastic at it. Unbeknownst to him.

Haley's lips were almost sore from smiling. She'd been smiling ever since she cast her eyes over the bright green peaks of Maui and smelled the fragrant scent of flowers on the warm, moist breeze. Ben didn't know that she was coming. At least not today. For weeks now she had been sidestepping his constant and beguiling pleas for her to visit during her maternity leave with vague excuses about her physical recovery and how busy she was with negotiations for her new position. The vagueness was necessary, since once she had confessed to HR that she wouldn't be returning to Merriweather, Falstaff, and Tynes, her paid maternity leave was no more. And although the negotiations for her new position had indeed taken a significant amount of effort, it wasn't the position Ben thought it was. She knew that her excuses hadn't completely satisfied him, and she hated that he might be worrying, even a little, that she was less than eager to see him. But she had done her best to reassure him on that score. And now, *today*, came the moment she had been waiting for. It was February, she had her body back, and she'd been given a clean bill of health. All her plotting and planning was at last coming to fruition.

Right now.

She watched the last of the passengers unload, then she stood up again, itching with impatience. She knew Ben had things to do on the boat before he could leave for the day, and she wanted to make sure he was completely free before he saw her. But she was so antsy she could hardly stand still.

Ten minutes crawled by before a group of twenty-somethings who looked like the ship's crew stepped off the boat and made their way down the dock. To Haley's relief, Ben was not among them. She wanted to catch him alone. As the group turned away without seeing her, she suffered a moment of indecision. Where should she stand? If she got too close, he might see her before she saw him. But if she waited too far from the dock, he might not see her at all, and chasing him down was not what she had in mind.

After a few more moments of deliberation, she slipped from her hiding spot and settled in front of the bow of the next ship over. He wouldn't be able to see her as he walked out between the boats, but once he reached the wharf, he would be within feet of her.

It was perfect.

Her heart pounded with anticipation as she listened for the sound of his footsteps. Facing away from the water now, she took a moment to admire the quaintness of Lahaina town, with its historic plantation buildings and giant banyan tree nestled before a backdrop of sharp green peaks in an azure sky. No wonder Ben loved it here. He loved things that were beautiful.

She smiled as she looked down at her own flat stomach, intentionally displayed to effect by the drop waist of her figure-hugging tank dress, which also conveniently showed off her newly tanned shoulders. She couldn't hold a candle to either Maui or Alaska, of course, but she had been working her butt off to get her original figure — such as it was — back again. She knew from the 3,465 pictures Micah and Tim had taken after the birth exactly how ghastly she had looked the last time Ben saw her, and every time she thought of him smiling into her bloated, blotchy face as he gallantly offered to uproot his life for her, she felt an almost uncontrollable urge to cry. But she didn't. She just worked harder to make sure he got the surprise he deserved.

Haley heard footsteps. It was him. She was sure of it. She moved herself into position.

Ben did not move into her line of sight until he was about eight feet away. She was not directly in front of him, or in his path, but he couldn't walk by or turn either direction without seeing her. Haley held her breath and stood silently, watching him.

He was gazing ahead and down slightly, as if his mind were elsewhere. He passed within a few feet of her and his eyes drifted up, then lingered over her torso just long enough to indicate a healthy male appreciation. He cast a polite smile and nod in her direction, then returned his gaze to the ground and walked right past her.

He took exactly five more steps. Then he froze and swung around.

He stared at her with an expression of such total and profound shock that the sultry "Hi, there, Captain," Haley had been preparing for weeks never made it out of her mouth. Instead, she burst out laughing.

"Haley," he breathed. In the next instant his arms were around her, her feet were off the ground, and Lahaina was spinning. He swung her around for several seconds before letting her slide, a bit more slowly than necessary, down his chest and back to the ground again. Then, holding her hands in his, he stepped back just far enough to look at her.

"Haley," he said breathlessly, "you look... Wow. Just... *wow.*"

She laughed again. "I thought you'd be surprised. I never thought you wouldn't recognize me!"

"Of course I recognized you," he defended, his cheeks reddening.

"It's just... I mean, you're so..."

"Skinny? Flat-chested?" Haley suggested coyly. "I *was* four months' pregnant when you met me, you know."

His cheeks flared further, but his eyes danced. "I was going to say *hot*, actually." He grinned and took a step closer to her. "Then and now. But especially now."

He let go of her hands and ran his fingertips lightly up her bare arms. Haley suppressed an embarrassing shiver of goosebumps and grinned back at him. The only other time he had seen her arms, they had been puffed up like sausages. He had never seen her shoulders before.

His frank approval was impossible to mistake. "I'm almost afraid to touch you," he said softly, belying his own words as his fingers traveled tentatively around the curve of her shoulders and back down her arms again. "I'm afraid I might wake up."

"I'm real," she assured tenderly. "And I'm really here, too."

He stared at her for another moment, then leaned down and kissed her gently on the lips. "For how long?" he whispered.

A joyous warmth spread up from Haley's toes to flush her already beaming face. "As long as you want, Captain," she answered.

Ben took a half step back. "Don't tease me, Haley," he said soberly. "I need to know what's going on with you. You've been hiding something from me for a while now."

His eyes flashed with hurt, and Haley's heart nearly burst. She threw her arms around his neck and held him tightly. "I'm sorry, Ben. It's just that I've been trying to surprise you."

She pulled back and looked at him again. Her eyes moistened, despite herself. "I'm not teasing you. And I'm not leaving you. Not ever again. Unless you get sick of me, of course."

She collected herself and smiled at him. "Just listen to me, okay? I know you have your heart set on moving to Southern California, but both you and Micah keep telling me I need to do what *I* want for a change, and frankly, that plan doesn't excite me. I own property in Alaska now, and I want to enjoy that property all summer long. And even though I know it means you'll miss the blue whales at Newport Beach, I'd really like it if you could live in the cabins with me, so I'll have somebody to fight the bears off. As for the rest of the year, I know I've only been here a matter of hours, but I'm really liking this island. I've been thinking about investing in a condo for years, and the place I'm renting now is absolutely gorgeous, just fifteen minutes up the road on some beach I can't pronounce that starts with a K and has a dozen vowels after it—"

"Ka'anapali?" Ben breathed.

"If you say so," Haley smiled again. She waited for him to speak, but his expression remained blank. "If you still want to move to California in April, I suppose I can't stop you," she continued gaily. "But I've already given notice on my lease and moved out of the apartment, and my new job starts next Monday, so I'm afraid you'd be living there by yourself."

Ben gave his head a shake. His eyes swam with confusion. "Your new... where?"

"Probably on my lanai," she answered wistfully, enjoying herself. "With an ocean view, if I can afford it. I'll have to move my laptop inside if it rains, though. In Seward, I'm thinking a cozy little office somewhere near the marina. We could get internet at the cabins, I suppose, but I think I'd rather leave my work behind at the end of the day."

Her meaning was starting to penetrate. The corners of Ben's mouth turned up ever so slightly, and although his muscles remained taut with caution, his eyes began to sparkle. Haley stretched up on impulse and kissed him soundly, but he did not respond. He remained standing still as a statue, staring back at her with disbelief.

"What are you saying, Haley?" he asked hoarsely.

"I'm saying that my new job is one I can do remotely. All I need is my laptop, a phone, and an internet connection."

His chest heaved with a sudden intake of breath. "They'll let you do that?"

"Who?" Haley asked, only to realize how poorly she was explaining herself. "Oh," she said dismissively, "screw Merriweather, Falstaff, and Tynes. I quit them. But I did decide to stick with environmental law."

She watched with amusement as the lights in his eyes dimmed ever so slightly again. "My new employer is a non-profit," she announced. "Their mission is conservation, and their goal is to level the playing field by supporting plaintiffs' attorneys across the country. Specifically, they just secured funding for a major database project that they had planned to staff with paralegals. I've spent the last month convincing them that the project would be far more effective with an experienced attorney at the helm — someone with a solid knowledge of the regs and the case law. Ideally, someone who's also familiar with the kind of games corporations play. And as I explained to the board so eloquently, so long as said attorney serves purely as a resource, there will be no conflicts of interest. They decided I was right."

Haley watched as the last remnants of self-preserving caution disappeared from Ben's eyes, replaced by sheer, unmitigated joy. In one motion he pulled her into his arms, crushing her against his chest so tightly she could scarcely draw a full breath. Just when she thought she might cough from lack of oxygen, he released her enough to look at her again.

"You really mean it?" he exclaimed, his hazel eyes misty.

"I really mean it," she whispered back, her own eyes moistening in return. "I'm here to stay, Ben. With you, wherever you go. And yes, this is what *I* want. So deal with it."

He pulled her back into his arms again, but this time his embrace was gentler. For a long time, they simply stood still, holding one another, basking in the pleasure of each other's touch. Haley had missed him with a physical pain, and she knew he felt the same. They had been in love for six months. In all that time, they had been together for only a few, precious days.

It wasn't enough.

Not nearly enough.

"You feel so good," Ben whispered finally.

"Likewise, Captain," Haley murmured into his shoulder.

Ben cleared his throat and straightened a bit. "Um... counselor?"

"Yes?"

"Perhaps you haven't noticed, but we're standing on a wharf in the middle of a rather busy town. And I really don't know how much longer I can keep my hands off you."

Haley lifted her head. She stepped back from him with a smile. "You've kept your hands off me for a very long time, Captain. How close do you live?"

Ben's eyes smoldered, even as a look of distress crossed his face. "Walking distance. But I meant what I said about my place being a dump. If I'd known you were coming, I would have—"

She placed a finger across his lips. "Never mind. I was hoping you might want a tour of my condo, anyway. My rental car is parked right over there." She stepped back and pointed past the banyan tree, grinning with pleasure to see how his eyes followed every movement of her new and improved body. His breathing was ragged and his face was flushed.

"Race you!" she taunted, breaking into a run.

She left him standing on the dock, but when she reached the side of her car half a minute later, he was fully on her heels. Laughing heartily, he grabbed her around the waist and lifted her off the ground, swinging her around for another moment before letting her slide slowly down his chest again. "I love you so much, Haley."

She planned to respond in kind, but didn't get the opportunity. He leaned down and kissed her, deeply and thoroughly, making her quickly forget whatever it was she was about to say. His embrace felt so wonderfully, amazingly good she found herself melting into him, swallowed up by a rising tide of passion that wiped all conscious thought from her brain. She had no idea how long it was before she realized that *she* had pressed *him* up against the side of her car and that his warm, caressing hands had wandered to her hips.

Reluctantly, she drew back. "Ben," she whispered.

"What?" he murmured, his eyes dazed.

"We're still in the parking lot."

"Mhmm," he grumbled, unconcerned. He pulled her back against him, then leaned forward to kiss the nape of her neck.

Haley chuckled. "Um... I'm pretty sure we're still in plain sight of your place of business."

He groaned. But he didn't stop.

"If you'll let me go long enough to get in my car," Haley negotiated, "I'll take you straight to my condo. You'll like it, I promise. You can look for humpback spouts from my lanai."

He lifted his head and smiled at her, his eyes brimming with a message she had no trouble reading. A message that had nothing whatsoever to do with whales. "How's the shower?"

"I have an amazing shower," she answered, grinning back at him. "All ceramic tile, extra-wide showerhead with multiple massage options. Just like the one I'm having installed in your cabin in Seward."

"You don't have to do that," he chuckled softly. "I was only kidding."

"I know," she replied. "But I'm not. Being able to spoil you is an important part of my happiness plan. I won't be making as much money at this job as I was before, but I did manage to negotiate a respectable salary for myself, considering how many fewer hours I'll be working. All I have to do now is figure out how to get you to marry me."

His eyes widened slightly. "I don't think you'll have any trouble with that," he whispered.

She looked into his honest hazel eyes, relished his adorable dimples and strong, tanned jawbone, and impulsively kissed him again.

Some immeasurable amount of time later, when his hands circled her waist and physically lifted her off of him, she realized that not only was she smashing the man up against her car again, but her side-view mirror was poking him in the thigh.

"Oh, I'm sorry!" she said, flustered.

Ben stood up straight, his hands braced on her upper arms as he held her away from him. "Don't apologize," he whispered gruffly. "Just take me home. Now."

"Home?" she asked, her heart beating fast. "You need to stop at your place?"

He growled beneath his breath. "No, I mean—" He shook his head with frustration. "Home is wherever we're together, Haley. Can we just go?"

Her heart leapt. She reached up a hand to touch his cheek, then ran her fingers lightly across his jawbone.

Ben groaned, caught her hand in his, and pulled it away. His eyes swam with smoke and his breath came in heaves. He whirled away from her, moved to the other side of the car, and put his hand on the door handle. "I can only take so much, counselor," he said roughly. "Now are you going to start driving, or am I going to lose my job?"

Haley pushed the button on her remote and unlocked the car doors.

"Come on, shower buddy," she said with a grin. "Let's go home."

ALASKA AGAIN

Epilogue

"Wait!" Ben called from the drive, his voice insistent. "Don't you dare!" He dropped the suitcase he had been pulling out of the trunk and practically vaulted over the railing and up onto the porch of his cabin, where Haley stood.

"You know the drill, counselor," he chastised, swinging her up off her feet. "Really!"

She laughed and reached for the doorknob. It was awkward inserting the key from such an angle, but eventually she managed it. "You've carried me over two thresholds already," she defended.

"So I have a thing about thresholds," he teased. "In our case, the more, the merrier. Besides, this is our honeymoon, remember?"

"Oh, right," Haley laughed as she pushed open the door. "What does this make, our third now?"

"Who's counting?" he replied merrily, setting her on her feet in the kitchen and looking around. "Hey, this place looks pretty good!"

Haley looked around herself, and a wave of emotion threatened to choke her. She hadn't set eyes on the cabin since the day she'd driven off and left Ben standing on his porch, not knowing if she'd ever see him again. To be back here with him now, after all that had happened in her life since, meant more than she could say.

"I like that new management company," Ben enthused, stepping around to check the place out. The belongings he had left behind were neatly stacked, the rest of the cabin having been cleaned around them. "That second year I rented from your uncle, I had to clean it myself. I guess he figured I couldn't complain about my own dirt."

"Told you I would spoil you," Haley reminded. "Both cabins have working showers, too."

He grinned at her. "I was kind of hoping you wouldn't fix yours."

Haley attached herself to his side and nuzzled her head against his chest with affection. They had been together for four months now, and still, she savored every touch. Being able to hold him was a gift she never planned to take for granted.

"We can share them both," she offered. It would be a little bizarre, living together spread out across two cabins with a driveway between them, but neither of them could imagine spending the summer anywhere else. Someday she hoped to build a decent house on the site of her uncle's shack, but right now that was hardly a priority. Right now, they were simply having fun.

"You do realize," he said huskily, dropping a kiss on the top of her head, "That having you here in this cabin with me will be the realization of all my fantasies from last summer?"

"Surely not," Haley protested. "We were only just friends then."

He laughed out loud.

She grinned up at him. "I had a few fantasies of my own, you know. From the very first time I saw you."

He raised an eyebrow. "The very first time?"

She chuckled. "Well, okay. The next morning, anyway."

"Then I have you beat," he said smugly.

Haley laughed and lifted her head to kiss him. She was so happy. Happy to be in Alaska, and happy period. They had married somewhat impulsively in a private, sunset ceremony at sea — a move which Ben still swore was entirely coincidental with the lease running out on the dump he was renting in Lahaina. As much as Haley enjoyed teasing him about that, she truly didn't care what had motivated him to propose so quickly. All she cared about was knowing that he loved her — and on that score, he left no room for doubt. Ever.

She made a point of returning the favor.

"Oh! Let's see the view," she said with enthusiasm, breaking off the kiss to lead him by the hand outside to their porch railing.

"I'm pretty sure it's the same as before," he teased, seeming reluctant to leave the cabin's cozy interior.

"No, it's not!" she insisted, looking out over the trees to the sweeping white mountains beyond. She breathed in a lungful of the clear, still-nippy air and sighed with contentment. "May is different from July. There's a lot more snow than when I left," she insisted. "And everything lower down isn't quite as green yet. But it will be soon. I can't wait." She leaned back against him, and his arms wrapped around her.

He let out his own sigh of contentment. "You know, Haley," he said seriously. "I would have been happy enough, living with you in Newport Beach. But the truth is, I really would have missed Alaska. I would have missed it terribly."

"I know that," she answered.

He kissed her on the cheek. "Thank you. And thanks for setting things straight with the Sisters Parker, too. They never would have believed me, you know."

Haley grinned. Their ceremony at sea might have been private, but their mutual families had thrown them a rockin' wedding reception in Seattle just last week — complete with all the nieces and nephews, including baby Sophia. Both Haley and Micah had gotten along famously with the Sisters Parker, but the latter had indeed given Ben a hard time about Haley's giving up her life to follow him around. What he couldn't see — no doubt due to remnants of childhood trauma — was the obvious irony of their barbs.

"Of course they believed you," she assured. "They know you would never *make* me do anything. Their whole purpose in teasing you was to point out that I wouldn't be doing what I'm doing if I didn't love you so madly. They were happy for you, Ben. That's all."

He was quiet a moment. "That makes no sense."

Haley chuckled. "How long did you live with those women?"

"Too long." He pulled his arms away from her and stepped back. She remained looking out over the railing a moment, hoping he would return, but when she realized he was leaning out over the side rail looking intently at the ground below, she turned.

"What?" she asked, her heart beginning to race. She loved being in Alaska every bit as much as Ben did, but there was one thing she didn't think she'd quite ever get used to.

He made no response. He merely smiled, stepped behind her, and pulled her back into his arms again. "Now," he whispered, kissing her lightly below the ear. "About that third honeymoon..."

Haley stiffened. "You saw grizzly tracks. Didn't you? Right beside the porch!"

Ben continued to nuzzle her neck. "No, I didn't. You want to light a fire in the fireplace? I remember one particular fantasy—"

"Don't lie to me!" Haley protested, shrinking back against him. "I know that look. There was a grizzly right here, wasn't there!"

He raised his head just long enough to look at her. "You know I would never lie to you." He returned his attention to her neck. "It was a black bear."

Haley groaned.

Ben laughed and tightened his embrace. "Don't worry, I'll protect you," he teased. His warm breath tickled her ear. "Not that you need protecting. You're the smartest, most capable woman I know, counselor."

Haley's tense muscles began to relax. He was right. She really did need to get over this bear thing. Eventually. Somehow.

"You're just building up my confidence so I'll go hiking with you," she accused playfully.

Ben chuckled. "I wasn't thinking that far ahead, actually. I'm still just trying to get you back inside. In fact, now that I think of it, maybe those *were* grizzly tracks..."

"Stop it!" Haley squealed, spinning around to face him. She looked up into his laughing hazel eyes and realized with a sudden burst of deja vu that they were standing exactly where they had been standing when she had walked away from him last summer. Forced to leave him, not allowed to touch him, not knowing if she would ever see him again. How had she stood it?

She threw her arms up around his neck and hugged him tightly.

She would never stand it again, that was for sure.

"I don't suppose you could lend me that bear spray of yours, could you, Captain?" she asked suddenly, releasing him.

He blinked at her. "Sure. But why? Where are you going?"

She smiled coyly. "To gather that firewood."

About the Author

USA-Today bestselling novelist and playwright Edie Claire was first published in mystery in 1999 by the New American Library division of Penguin Putnam. In 2002 she began publishing award-winning contemporary romances with Warner Books, and in 2008 two of her comedies for the stage were published by Baker's Plays (now Samuel French). In 2009 she began publishing independently, continuing her original Leigh Koslow Mystery series and adding new works of romantic women's fiction, young adult fiction, and humor.

Under the banner of Stackhouse Press, Edie has now published over 25 titles including digital, print, audio, and foreign translations. Her works are distributed worldwide, with her first contemporary romance, *Long Time Coming*, exceeding two million downloads. She has received multiple "Top Pick" designations from *Romantic Times Magazine* and received both the "Reader's Choice Award" from *Road To Romance* and the "Perfect 10 Award" from *Romance Reviews Today*.

A former veterinarian and childbirth educator, Edie is a happily married mother of three who currently resides in Pennsylvania. She enjoys gardening and wildlife-watching and dreams of becoming a snowbird.

Books & Plays by Edie Claire

Romantic Fiction

Pacific Horizons
Alaskan Dawn
Leaving Lana'i
Maui Winds
Glacier Blooming
Tofino Storm (2020)

Fated Loves
Long Time Coming
Meant To Be
Borrowed Time

Hawaiian Shadows
Wraith
Empath
Lokahi
The Warning

Leigh Koslow Mysteries

Never Buried
Never Sorry
Never Preach Past Noon
Never Kissed Goodnight
Never Tease a Siamese
Never Con a Corgi

Never Haunt a Historian
Never Thwart a Thespian
Never Steal a Cockatiel
Never Mess With Mistletoe
Never Murder a Birder
Never Nag Your Neighbor

Women's Fiction

The Mud Sisters

Humor

Work, Blondes. Work!

Comedic Stage Plays

Scary Drama I
See You in Bells

Made in the USA
Middletown, DE
08 July 2021

43837374R00156